## TENDER HEART

As their kiss deepened and Raven heard soft sighs of desire—his and hers—for the first time the flames within her didn't burn with pain, but with a glowing warmth, a shimmering heat that enveloped her as gently as his arms did, desiring but not imprisoning.

"What do you want, Raven?" he asked softly.

Raven wanted to make love. It was something she had never really wanted before, nor had it ever really been a choice. It had been a compulsion instead, a desperate need to be accepted, to belong to some imaginary circle of love, to escape from her icy loneliness and fiery pain.

Raven pulled away. "You don't have to do this, Nick. Downstairs, in front of all of them, I really appreciated how you pretended—"

Nick stopped her words with a gentle finger on her lips. He needed her and wanted her and had fallen in love with her.

"Tell me what you want, Raven," he repeated quietly.

"You," she whispered. It was a whisper that seemed to echo throughout time, far beyond tonight. "I want you, Nick."

## YOU WON'T WANT TO READ
## JUST ONE — KATHERINE STONE

**ROOMMATES** (3355-9, $4.95)
No one could have prepared Carrie for the monumental changes she would face when she met her new circle of friends at Stanford University. Once their lives intertwined and became woven into the tapestry of the times, they would never be the same.

**TWINS** (3492-X, $4.95)
Brook and Melanie Chandler were so different, it was hard to believe they were sisters. One was a dark, serious, ambitious New York attorney; the other, a golden, glamourous, sophisticated supermodel. But they were more than sisters — they were twins and more alike than even they knew
. . .

**THE CARLTON CLUB** (3614-0, $4.95)
It was the place to see and be seen, the only place to be. And for those who frequented the playground of the very rich, it was a way of life. Mark, Kathleen, Leslie and Janet — they worked together, played together, and loved together, all behind exclusive gates of the *Carlton Club*.

# HAPPY ENDINGS

# KATHERINE STONE

**ZEBRA BOOKS**
**KENSINGTON PUBLISHING CORP.**

# Part One

# ❀ 1 ❀

*Love* you, Raven? Love *you?* Loving you would be like loving ice. No, that's wrong, because given time ice would melt. And you never do . . .

Thankfully, the painful memory of Michael's cruel words was interrupted by the buzz of the intercom on her desk. Thankfully and *appropriately,* Raven thought as the interruption forced her to abandon the memories of the past and focus firmly on the present. She was at work. There was absolutely no excuse for allowing her mind to drift from present to past, from professional to personal.

In this elegantly appointed penthouse office, aptly located high above the Avenue of the Stars, she was Raven Winter, attorney to the stars. And here, she thought grimly, she was expected to be precisely what Michael had so cruelly accused her of being. Pure ice. Cool, unyielding, without a heart.

Before depressing the intercom button, Raven drew a deep breath. Maybe a large gulp of air from this room, in which she negotiated multimillion-dollar deals, would fill her lungs with oxygen that was saturated with professionalism, and thus, perhaps, help banish the ancient, personal pain.

"Yes?" Cringing at the uncertainty she heard in her own voice, Raven drew another deep breath as she listened to her secretary's message.

"Barbara Randall on line one."

The contracts manager from the New York publishing company needed no further identification. Also an attorney, Barbara was the person with whom Raven dealt when one of her clients—Hollywood's top producers, directors, and actors—wanted to buy the movie rights to one of the company's books. Usually it was Raven who initiated the dialogue, but now Barbara was calling, presumably in regard to a yet-to-be-published book.

Raven thanked her secretary, took another breath, and depressed the blinking light on her phone.

"Hello, Barbara." Raven felt a surge of relief as she realized that her voice was back to normal: warm yet cool, friendly yet professional, and, above all, confident.

"Hello, Raven. I'm calling about *Gifts of Love.*"

Raven's voice had recovered, but now she heard in the voice that greeted her from a continent away a note of uncertainty that was as uncharacteristic for Barbara Randall as it was for Raven Winter. Like Raven, Barbara was a masterful negotiator, an expert at playing the calculatedly unhurried games of chess in which each piece was worth millions and the goal was never to checkmate but only to draw.

The negotiations for *Gifts of Love* had been tough and challenging, but finally each side had captured all that it could—and had given all that it would. When the deal was the best it could be, the fully executed contract had been signed and the right to make a motion picture based on the bestselling novel had become the exclusive property of Jason Cole.

"Is there a problem, Barbara?"

"Probably not. I *hope* not. I just got a call from Lauren Sinclair. When her editor initially informed her about the sale, she was very pleased that Jason Cole had optioned the

8

work. Who better? But now she has some concerns. She's worried that he might make changes in the story."

"He has every right to. There's nothing in the contract that prevents him from making any changes he wants. It was my understanding that the publishing company, not Ms. Sinclair, controlled the movie rights."

"That's right, and we sold them without consulting her, which was my mistake. We didn't need to consult with her, of course, and it honestly didn't occur to me to do so." Raven heard Barbara draw a breath, as if hoping to exhale the worry and inhale something more confident. The effort wasn't entirely successful. "I know it's a done deal, Raven, but I guess why I'm really calling is to see if this is a nonissue."

"You want me to ask Jason if he's planning to make changes?"

"Would you? I've tried calling him myself, many times over the past five days, and I'm beginning to think that I may never get beyond what seems to be an immense stone wall."

A slight smile touched Raven's lips. Jason Cole didn't own Gold Star Studios. Indeed, because of a megamillion-dollar four-picture deal negotiated by her, it could be argued that Gold Star actually owned him—at least his extraordinary talent. Still, within about a minute of the Academy Award–winning actor turned Academy Award–winning writer-director's arrival at the studio, everyone who answered a telephone throughout the vast complex somehow understood that they were to rigorously screen all of Jason's calls. Most unsolicited calls, even from Hollywood's top stars, weren't returned; and such calls from total strangers never were.

But calls from Raven Winter to Jason Cole were always put through—promptly.

"I'll be happy to speak to Jason, Barbara. But you need to know that he may not yet have given any thought to his plans for *Gifts of Love*. Right now he's in the midst of post-production on *Ripple Effect,* and in three weeks he'll be in Hong Kong on a two-month location shoot for *The Jade Palace,* and after that there's still another film before *Gifts of Love."*

"So it may be quite a while before we can reassure Lauren Sinclair."

"Yes." Raven didn't embellish, as she might have, that "reassurance" could be a long time coming, like maybe never. Knowing Jason, he *would* want to make changes. "However, I will check. Was there something in particular that worried her, something that she thought it likely he would change?"

"Have you read the book?"

Of course not, Raven thought without a flicker of apology or guilt. She was an attorney, not an agent. By the time she became involved, all the agenting—the pitching of concepts, treatments, storylines, and talent—was over and the involved parties had agreed, in principle, to make a deal. Raven's task was to negotiate the price of that deal and then to legally etch the dollar signs and other fine print onto a contract.

Raven had not read *Gifts of Love,* but she had seen some of the many rave reviews of the bestselling love story set against the backdrop of the Vietnam War. The critics had compared the novel's scope and emotion to other classic sagas of war—*Gone With the Wind, Casablanca,* and *Dr. Zhivago;* and even the literary critics, those with a distinct preference for the angst and anguish that typified "real" literature, had sung its praises, happy ending and all.

Raven had no doubt that *Gifts of Love* was quite wonderful; but that didn't mean that she was the least bit tempted to read it. The book was, in essence, a romance. And Raven Winter did not read romances.

Maybe you should, a voice taunted. It wasn't a professional voice admonishing her that it would make her even better at what she did. Raven Winter, attorney at law, could not be any better than she already was. Both she and

10

the taunting voice knew that. No, the voice was quite personal, an icy reminder of all her failures and all her flaws.

"I haven't read it," she admitted finally. "I do know a bit about the story, however. It takes place in Vietnam and centers on the love between a soldier and a female surgeon."

"Sam and Savannah," Barbara clarified. By identifying the hero and heroine by name she sent the clear message that not only had she read the book but that she, like millions of readers, viewed them as far more than mere characters. Like Rhett and Scarlett, and Yuri and Lara, and Ilsa and Rick, Sam and Savannah were mythic, legendary, unforgettable. "They fall in love, and then are separated, and each has reason to believe that the other is dead. They find each other again just before Savannah gives birth to their daughter. In the book the baby survives, but Lauren is afraid that in the movie she won't, that Jason Cole will want to change her purely happy ending into a more bittersweet one."

"Okay. I'll give Jason a call and see what I can find out." Raven glanced at the gold and diamond watch that encircled her slender wrist. Three forty-five, which meant six forty-five in New York. "You're probably about ready to call it a day." Then, remembering that it was Friday, she added, "In fact, you're probably about ready to call it a week."

"Yes. But I will wait right here until I hear from you."

Lauren Sinclair must be very upset indeed, Raven thought as she felt a ripple of annoyance at the bestselling author's fit of pique that someone might tamper with—make more authentic—the ending to her war-torn romance. Was Lauren Sinclair from another planet? The improbable world of Sam the Soldier and Savannah the Surgeon perhaps? Or was the writer's own life really that wonderful, her own romances that glitteringly untarnished, that flawlessly happy, that blissfully perfect? Had no one ever said to Lauren Sinclair, *Love* you, Lauren? Love *you?*

"It may take me a while to reach Jason, Barbara, so why don't I call Ms. Sinclair?"

"I do have tickets for the Met," Barbara murmured. "You really don't mind?"

"Of course not." I don't mind explaining to Ms. Lauren Sinclair that love doesn't always work out perfectly. "And if I can't reach Jason today, I'll let her know that as well."

"Okay. Thank you. I'll call her now, then, and tell her she'll be hearing from you later no matter what."

After Barbara had given Raven Lauren Sinclair's phone number, and Raven had repeated it back for accuracy, she asked, "Where's Area Code 907?"

"Kodiak, Alaska."

"That's a long way to commute for book parties."

"She never does. She's our top-selling author, but she's never been to New York, much less gone on tour. No one here has ever met her, and we don't even have a photograph of her to put in the books."

Raven frowned at the surprising information. She had formed a very clear image of the romance novelist who had the unabashed nerve to write happy endings, not to mention the extraordinary presumptuousness to dare to tell Jason Cole how to make his movies. It was a dazzling image of glamour combined with an almost compulsive need to be in the spotlight, the limelight, as much as possible. Amid the glitter Raven also imagined in Lauren Sinclair a demanding petulance, an expectation that there would always be—just for her—a plush red carpet, lined with sparkling fountains of champagne, that stretched from Alaska to New York.

Raven had imagined a gifted yet self-absorbed prima donna.

She had not imagined a recluse.

\* \* \*

"Your timing is perfect," Jason's secretary Greta told Raven a few minutes later. "He has just made his first appearance in a week."

"He's been in the editing room."

"And nowhere else—until this minute. Hold on a second and I'll connect you."

As Raven waited to hear the effortlessly seductive voice of one of Hollywood's sexiest men, she thought about what Jason Cole probably looked like at this moment. He would be wearing a black T-shirt, a faded pair of jeans, and battered cowboy boots. The shirt and jeans would both fit loosely; but his innate sensuality, the taut yet graceful power of his lean body, would be eloquently conveyed nonetheless. His thick dark hair would be tousled, and his handsome face would be unshaven, and there would be dark circles beneath his dark blue eyes. There would be no fatigue, however, in the cobalt depths. Instead, they would be quite energized, brilliant with intensity and glittering with deep fires of satisfaction.

In short, Jason Cole would look like a man who was sated—but not spent—from a sleepless night of extraordinary passion. Hollywood was filled with beautiful women who had seen Jason after such a night. But last night, and for every day and night for the past week, Jason's extraordinary passion had been devoted only to his film.

"Raven."

"Hi. How's *Ripple Effect?*"

"Getting there. It takes patience."

And you're not a patient man, Raven thought. At least that was what Jason's many spurned lovers always claimed. He wasn't impatient in bed, of course, they amended swiftly. But he was impatient, restless, with the other aspects of relationships. He was, quite simply, unwilling to put in the time necessary to make them work.

Jason was impatient with relationships, and impatient with incompetence, and impatient with stalled negotiations. But he had infinite patience when it came to making a film meet the vision of what he believed it could be—a vision that was always magnificent, always beyond what most others could even imagine.

Perhaps, Raven mused, Jason simply had no such grand visions of what relationships could be. Smart man.

To the impatient, and gifted, and passionate man at the other end of the phone, Raven explained as succinctly as possible the reason for her call, finishing with, "I guess the heroine—Savannah—gives birth to a daughter at the end? Well, apparently Ms. Sinclair is afraid that you might be planning to kill off the baby."

"The baby does fine," Jason answered with matching succinctness. "It's Savannah who won't survive childbirth."

"We're not going to have a happy camper on our hands."

"Tough. Besides, it's not really our hands. It's between Ms. Sinclair and her publishing company."

"Except that I'm the messenger. I told Barbara Randall I'd call Lauren directly."

"That's perfect, then. It will give you the chance to remind her that although *Gifts of Love* is her book, it's my movie."

"I'll remind her. If need be, I'll even give her the buying movie rights to a book is like buying a house analogy: only the address stays the same. The new owner can do whatever he likes with the structure itself. You just happen to be doing a little remodeling."

"A little necessary remodeling," Jason amended quietly but with an undeniable edge of impatience.


If Raven didn't already hate herself, if Michael's recent cruel rejection hadn't already confirmed anew what she had known all her life—that she was as unlovable as a statue of ice—she might have experienced a twinge of remorse for the whispers of pleasure she felt as she dialed Lauren Sinclair's number in Alaska. The romance writer who had the nerve to tease the hearts and minds of millions of readers with fantasies of perfect love and happy endings was about to get a little taste of reality.

"Hello?"

The voice that answered the phone on the first ring was small, almost terrified. Lauren Sinclair's secretary, no doubt, having endured—and barely survived—an entire day of the author's petulant pique.

"This is Raven Winter calling for Lauren Sinclair."

Lauren Sinclair was her *nom de plume;* but without hesitation Holly replied, "This is she. Barbara Randall told me that you would be calling."

Raven frowned at the revelation that the fragile voice belonged to the writer herself. "I've just finished speaking with Jason Cole."

"Yes?"

The faraway frightened voice held a new note now, fragile still but a little brave, a little hopeful. The rush of pleasure Raven had felt was long gone, and as she shattered the brave hope, her own voice was apologetic and gentle.

"Jason believes that the story will be more compelling, more authentic, if the heroine does not survive childbirth. The baby will survive, of course, but—"

"Oh, no."

It was, Raven realized, a whisper of pure despair, as if she had just informed Lauren Sinclair that a loved one had died. Despair—and perhaps shock, because the anguished whisper was followed by silence. "Ms. Sinclair? Lauren? Are you still there?"

"Yes."

Moments before, that word, that single syllable, had soared with brave hope. Now it was filled with the hopelessness of death. But there hadn't truly been a death, Raven reminded herself. As beloved as Savannah might be in the hearts and minds of millions of readers, she was, after all, just a fictional character.

Raven's mission was accomplished, and Lauren Sinclair had accepted the message with despair but without protest—as if the decision that Savannah would die was irrevocable, as if in fact she had already died.

But she hasn't died, not yet, not really, Raven thought as an idea began to dance in her mind. It was a dangerous idea, and a foolish one; and although it twirled with dazzling hopefulness, it was undoubtedly as hopeless as the hopelessness in the author's faraway voice.

Say goodbye to Lauren Sinclair, a wise voice commanded. Tell her that you're sorry if you must, murmur some platitude like "That's show business," but do *not* speak aloud what you're thinking.

Raven ignored the sage command. "It's obvious that you feel very strongly about this," she began quietly. "You could tell me why and let me explain your reasons to Jason, but I honestly think it would be best if you discussed your concerns directly with him, preferably face to face. Would that be possible? Would you be willing to come to Los Angeles to meet with him?"

Holly's silent answer came with swift confidence: No. *No.* Everything that Raven Winter was suggesting was impossible. For the past fifteen years, Holly Elliott had not ventured out of Alaska. Indeed, only rarely, only when necessary, did she leave the safe seclusion of her cottage.

But you *do* leave, she reminded herself. You walk the four miles into town for groceries, and to go to the post office . . . and to watch again and again the movies of Jason Cole whenever they are playing at the local theater. And in the beginning, during the first five years that you lived in Alaska, you were almost adventurous, remember? You explored the Arctic wonders, and made yearly trips to Barrow, and as recently as 1989 you traveled to Prince William

Sound to help towel the oil off the sea birds and otters after the Exxon *Valdez* mishap.

She *could* go to Los Angeles. It was possible. But the rest of what Raven was suggesting, that she meet with Jason Cole and explain to him why she didn't want him to change the happy ending of her story, was not.

And yet, Holly knew, that was precisely what she *must* do. Seventeen years before, when she had been thirteen, she had failed to save the life of the mother she loved; and now there was another mother who needed to be saved, a fictional character, yes, but still . . .

Her voice was solemn as she finally answered Raven's question. "Yes, I can go to Los Angeles to talk with him." Then, with a little hope, she asked, "Would you be at the meeting too?"

Holly's hopeful question triggered something very deep within Raven: deep, and painful, and searing. The burning came from her heart, from the white-hot fires that smoldered there.

Mostly, when Raven felt pain, it came with a trembling chill: sharp, piercing slivers of ice. Indeed, her heart was so encased with ice, so tightly bound, that sometimes she couldn't even feel her own heartbeat. But Lauren Sinclair's question caused a smoldering ember to burst into flame, igniting an anguished memory. It was brilliantly illuminated now, and achingly clear: the raven-haired little girl she once had been, the child who had wished so desperately for just one person, just *one,* to help her, to defend her, to love her.

Now Lauren Sinclair was asking for Raven's help, and there was something more, something stunning, in the brave yet fragile voice. For some inexplicable reason, Lauren believed that Raven would give that help without betrayal.

"Yes, I'll be there," Raven promised. And I will help you . . . without betrayal.

Of course, she thought wryly, Jason is undoubtedly

going to kill me long before the meeting ever happens. In fact, I'm probably going to get to see exactly how gorgeous he looks at this moment, because as soon as I tell him what I have done, he's going to come over here and strangle me.

## ✿ 2 ✿

"You did what?"

"Don't you think it's worth troubleshooting her concerns before the movie is made?" Raven countered calmly. "There's precedent for authors telling their fans not to see a movie. She has millions of readers and if she decided to make it a *cause célèbre*—"

"Is that what she's threatening to do?" Jason interjected. His voice was filled with contempt for Lauren Sinclair but it held not a trace of worry about the film he planned to make. Adverse publicity drew audiences as much as rave reviews did, and the truth was that no matter what anyone said, the movie-going public was unlikely to stay away from a Jason Cole production—especially one in which he was also the male lead. The role that Lauren Sinclair had written for Sam was already an extraordinary one, but it would be even more compelling when the man who had already endured so much faced the emotional devastation of Savannah's death . . . and then went on, cradling his just-born daughter, love's greatest gift of all, and with tear-glistening eyes, whispered to her all the solemn and joyous promises of love.

"She's not threatening to do anything, Jason," Raven said. Then, sighing softly, she added, "I just thought . . ."

"This face-to-face meeting was your idea?"

Raven answered with a sigh that was slightly heavier than the last, and dazzlingly eloquent: a confession to her crime. After a long moment of tense silence, she heard the soft, deep, sexy laugh for which Jason Cole was so famous.

"You're supposed to be on my side, remember?" he teased. "Okay, Raven, why not? I love meeting with petulant writers. Do you mind if I pick the time, though? I can't really drop everything at the moment."

"I imagine that any time will be fine with her," Raven said, embellishing silently, And I'll make whatever adjustments are necessary in my own schedule.

"All right. Let me look at my calendar." The pause while Jason flipped his calendar ahead was quite short given that in just those few seconds he had swiftly traveled fifteen days into the future. "How about lunch on Monday the twenty-seventh?"

Raven's long tapered fingers advanced her calendar as well, a fluid and graceful process that came to a precipitous halt when they reached the weekend before that Monday. "Chicago," written in her elegant script, spanned across Saturday and Sunday. The word had been traced and retraced, and now it glared back at her, a heavy and indelible symbol of her foolishness—and of her failure. By tracing and retracing, as if etching in stone, she had tried to make memorable that weekend in advance. It *would* have been memorable, of course, walking into the Imperial Ballroom at the Fairmont on the tuxedoed arm of Michael Andrews. He would have been recognized instantly, and they all would have been terribly impressed, and at long last, she would have shown them all.

*Love* you, Raven? Love *you?*

Raven forced her mind and her fingers to leave that shattered weekend and move forward to the next page of the calendar. But there, on Monday, March

20

twenty-seventh, she was confronted with more wonderful memories that were never to be. "Awards," she had written, "Dorothy Chandler Pavilion, 6:00 p.m. (limo—4:45)."

Convincing Michael to accompany her to Chicago on the weekend before Hollywood's most important evening had been a monumental struggle. In return, and with deep gratitude, she had most willingly agreed that they would take the first flight back on Sunday morning, thus forgoing the lavish brunch that was scheduled to begin at eleven.

Michael Andrews, whose latest blockbuster had garnered five Academy Award nominations, had insisted on returning from Chicago early Sunday because of the ceremony that would take place in Hollywood on Monday night; and now Jason Cole, whose *Without Warning* had been nominated for seven awards, was proposing a business luncheon for that afternoon.

"According to my calendar the twenty-seventh is Academy Award day," Raven said.

"Which everyone regards as an unofficial holiday . . . including you?"

Jason was asking if she was planning to spend the day luxuriating at one of Rodeo's posh salons, preparing for the appearance she would make at Hollywood's most glittering gala. Even when she had been scheduled to attend the ceremony with Michael, Raven had not planned such pampering for herself. That Monday would have been a workday, as always.

"No, it's fine with me." Raven hesitated. Jason wouldn't care, of course, but as soon as he emerged from his cocoon of postproduction on *Ripple Effect,* he would hear the gossip and might be mildly annoyed that she hadn't told him. "Just so you'll know, I'm no longer sleeping with the enemy."

Jason ignored the allusion to Michael Andrews as his enemy. Michael was simply a competitor, a most worthy opponent, in the battle for the box office. Jason focused instead on the meaning of what Raven had just told him. "You and Michael aren't together anymore? I had no idea."

"It's a pretty recent development."

"I'm sorry."

Raven frowned at the surprising gentleness in his voice. Her relationship with Jason had always been very cordial, and immensely profitable, but not the least bit personal. You've never had a personal relationship with anyone, an icy voice taunted. Yes, you've had sexual relationships, *oh yes*. There have been many men who have wanted your perfect body, and you have always been so willing to please, to do anything they wanted . . . if only they would love you.

"It happens," she answered finally, flatly. *It always happens.* "Anyway, lunch on that Monday is fine with me. I'll confirm it with Lauren and get back to Greta."

"Good. I really am sorry about you and Michael."

"Thanks, Jason," she said softly. "So am I."


En route from her penthouse office on the Avenue of the Stars to her two-bedroom bungalow in Brentwood, Raven stopped at a bookstore on Wilshire Boulevard and bought a copy of *Gifts of Love*. Ten minutes later she was home.

Home. The small but expensive house in the prestigious neighborhood had been Raven's official residence for the past five years. But for much of those five years, she had unofficially lived elsewhere—in Topanga Canyon with an actor, and in Santa Monica with a tax attorney, and in a beachfront cabin in the Colony at Malibu with one of the city's most powerful agents, and most recently in the Beverly Hills mansion of producer-director Michael Andrews.

For the past five years the bungalow in Brentwood had

been more closet than home, a place where seasonal clothes were stored in their off season—and a place, too, where Raven herself was stored between seasons of desire, after a man who had once wanted her desperately had grown tired of her iciness and before she found someone new.

It looks like the inside of a freezer, Raven thought grimly as she walked into the bungalow's pure white living room. There was no color in her home, no warmth or personality. It was, quite simply, a frigidly sterile place where the ice sculpture dwelled between appearances.

After a shivering moment of pain, Raven drew her sky blue eyes from the white starkness of the room and gazed at the color outside. The lawn was a luxurious carpet of emerald green, meticulously tended by the service she employed, but the flower beds that framed the plush emerald were a disaster, riotously overgrown with weeds and in shameful disarray. She had had a gardener once, but he had long since retired, and she hadn't hired anyone new because of the foolish belief that at any moment she would be moving, permanently, to the mansion in Beverly Hills.

I need to find a gardener, she thought. Before my neighbors start to complain.

The thought felt heavy, as did all thoughts about the future that had been handed to her so cruelly three nights before, literally moments after Michael's return from a seven-week shoot in Madrid. Once again, Raven Winter had to start over. There was no wondrous sense of a new beginning, of course, no pristine hopefulness about a sparkling fresh start. Indeed, each time was harder, heavier, than the last, because each new time carried with it the immense weight of yet another monumental failure, more and ever more proof of how incapable she was of being loved.

Raven wanted to change, to be warm not cold, to be soft not brittle—and oh how she tried. But with each successive rejection she only became more wary, more aloof, more fragile.

Raven lifted her delicate shoulders in a shrug designed to cast off the heaviness of her thoughts. It was a valiant effort, but in moments she was weighted anew, this time by a leaden cloak of exhaustion. Her fatigue was both recent and ancient. For thirty-three years the heart whose smoldering flames were encased in ice had struggled simply to beat. Raven's heart was exhausted, as always, and her bright mind was exhausted too from three nights of tormenting memories and no sleep.

For a tantalizing moment she thought about falling into bed right now. She was so tired that perhaps at last she could sleep, a long dreamless night of rejuvenating rest. But succumbing to the tantalizing prospect of sleep was not the way that disciplined Raven Winter lived her life. It wasn't the way she had survived, and it most certainly wasn't the way she had succeeded, at least professionally, far beyond all expectations.

It was balmy spring twilight, and there was still ample light outside, and because of a predawn conference call to the East Coast she hadn't taken her daily run this morning.

So now she had to run.

No matter how fatigued she was.

No matter how fit her slender body already was.

No matter how dangerous it was to run along San Vicente when your mind was filled with recent echoes of contempt.

No matter that those recent echoes summoned other ones, distant yet still painful, a lifetime of them . . .


Your name is Raven?

*Raven?* But that's the name of a bird, isn't it, an ugly black bird of death?

Like a *buzzard.*

Or a vulture!

What's that slimy stuff on your bare legs, Vulture?

Is it Vaseline? Cooking grease? Come quick, everyone, come see what the buzzard has smeared on her scrawny legs!

Why is it there, scary Crow? Don't you have any stockings? Can't your slut mother afford to buy you any? She could, you know—if only she charged for her *services* she would be rich!

For every punishing inch of her five-mile jogging route, the cruel taunts ran with her. No matter how fast she ran, they kept up the pace. Sometimes they were faster even than she, waiting around the next corner when she arrived, cruel taunts from cruel children . . . until, quite unexpectedly, the long-ago words that greeted her were suddenly her own, the solemn and anguished promise that she had made to herself at age ten when she had read the poem for the first time.

"Quoth the Raven, 'Nevermore,'" Poe had written—and it was as if the tormented writer were reaching to her from beyond the grave, understanding her plight, her pain . . . and giving her permission to end it forever. Someday, when the pain was simply too great to endure any longer, she would take the ultimate control of her life. She would make the somber and irrevocable decision to set herself free.

Some day she would simply say, "Nevermore, nevermore, never . . ."

If Nicholas Gault hadn't slowed considerably in anticipation of making the right-hand turn off San Vicente onto Barrington, and if he hadn't had lightning-quick reflexes, and if he had hesitated even a tiny fraction of a second because of concern that his truck might be hit from behind, he would have struck her.

As it was, Nick managed to screech to a skidding halt just inches before gleaming metal collided with fragile flesh, a drama of noise and motion that startled the black-haired jogger from the near lethal reverie that had permitted her to run from the sidewalk into the street without even the most casual glance for traffic. In her surprise, in her fright, she spun and fell, the bare skin of her palms and knees shredding as it met the concrete's unyielding hardness.

Nick was out of his truck instantly, and he moved with swift, angry strides toward the woman who had nearly killed herself—and who, in so doing, had nearly caused him to become a killer.

Ever since assuming the solemn—and joyous—responsibility of raising his two daughters, Nicholas Gault had vowed never to swear, at least not aloud. It was a pledge that he had kept. Indeed, only occasionally, and invariably because of the girls' "mother" Deandra, did he even swear in silence.

But now, fueled by adrenaline, elaborate oaths and eloquent expletives flooded his mind . . . and as soon as he had the full attention of the woman whose carelessness had almost caused disaster, Nick planned to open the floodgates.

She was on the ground still, on her knees in the middle of the street. Because her head was bent, he couldn't see her face. She was glowering at the pavement, Nick decided. Glowering, as if the pavement were somehow responsible for her unceremonious fall.

She's going to try to shift the blame, Nick thought with disgust as his steel gray gaze drifted from her downcast head to the jogging outfit she wore. It was several hundred dollars' worth of Ellesse, a robin's egg blue and blush pink ensemble of shorts, shirt, headband, and socks.

Nick knew all about rich, self-absorbed women. In fact, it was fair to say that he was an expert on such women: those who cared passionately about designer clothes, even for jogging, and who accepted the blame for nothing, even when they were responsible.

Contempt began to twine itself with his anger, embellishing further the harsh words he would speak to her. He was hovering over her now, willing her to look at him, silently commanding her to shift her glower from the stone-hard pavement to his stone-hard eyes. Nick knew that she knew that he was there, but still her head remained down, trying to deflect his assault, to garner sympathy.

*Look at me.* Have just an ounce of courage, just a trace of integrity . . .

She obeyed his silent command then, lifting her face to his angry and contemptuous gaze—and Nicholas Gault was silent still.

It wasn't her extraordinary beauty that so swiftly relegated the tirade he had planned to the realm of almost-forgotten memory. Nick was quite immune to the bewitching power of such beauty. He knew too well its treachery . . . and its betrayal.

Beauty alone, even as stunning as hers, could not have halted his angry words. He could have completely ignored the lush fullness of her trembling lips, and the sculpted elegance of her high cheekbones, and the sensuality of the silken strands of midnight black that escaped their expensive pastel bondage at her nape to caress, in lustrous swirls, her exquisite face.

What stopped Nick's angry words, what he could not ignore, were her eyes. They were bright blue, that rare, brilliant sapphire that filled the first clear sky following a winter snowstorm. But, despite their brilliance, these eyes had neither the shimmering hopefulness of such a sky, nor its dazzling defiance.

Nick had expected defiance from the beautiful woman dressed in Ellesse. He had imagined a glower that would communicate clearly that she blamed him for what had happened.

But what he saw was something quite different. She

had her own expectations, and they were quite astonishing ones. She expected him to swear at her, to berate her for her carelessness. She seemed resigned to his rage, accepting of it, as if she were accustomed to such contempt, as if, in fact, she even *deserved* it.

There was another message in the dark shadows of her bright blue eyes, and it was the most astonishing—and troubling—message of all. She seemed to be telling him that it would have been all right if he had struck her, *if he had killed her*. All right . . . perhaps even better.

Nick moved then, crouching down to her level, and as he did, she recoiled with fear.

Raven's fear was both instinctive and learned. She had instantly seen the dangerous power of him, the lean strength taut with anger, the jaw that rippled to restrain the words she deserved to hear, the gray eyes that smoldered with banked fires of disdain and rage.

His hair was as black as hers, and as he had hovered over her with the predatory watchfulness of a panther about to strike, Raven had felt both his power and his control. The power belonged to the panther, tightly coiled in his sleekly muscled body; but the control belonged to the man. It came from deep within, from an inner core that was pure steel, the proof of which glinted in his steel-gray eyes.

What does she think I'm going to do to her? Nick wondered with disbelief when he saw her fear. Hit her?

True, he had planned a verbal assault, and in the instants before he had abandoned that plan, she had undoubtedly seen his anger, but . . .

"Hi," he greeted gently. "Are you all right?"

"I'm so sorry," she whispered. "I was . . . distracted."

By what? Nick wanted to know the answer to that question and to the other more troubling ones. Would you really not care if you'd been killed? Does some part of you truly believe that it would have been better if I had not been able to stop?

Nick wanted those answers—later. Now he reached for the delicate white hands that rested motionlessly, their wounded palms facing each other, on her bare and slender thighs.

White and crimson hands, he amended silently as he turned the palms up and saw the badly torn flesh that was awash in a sea of blood. No wonder her head had been bent and her body had been so still. She hadn't been glowering at the pavement, nor planning how she would shift the blame to him. She had been merely using every ounce of energy to block the screams of pain.

Who are you? Nick wondered. Who are you who dresses as if appearances were everything, and who expects rage from men, and who might even welcome death, and who endures even extreme pain in regal silence?

For now she was Snow White, her snowy skin spilling crimson not from the prick of a poisonous thorn but from whatever poisonous—and near lethal—thoughts had been so distracting that she had run blindly into the street.

"I'd better get you to a hospital."

"Oh, no, thank you. I'm—"

"Fine?" Nick's smile was very gentle. "No, you're not."

"But I will be. I really don't need to go to a hospital."

"Okay," Nick agreed easily. Perhaps medical care wasn't necessary. It was impossible to know until the crimson was washed away and the torn flesh beneath was fully exposed. "I'll drive you home then."

Raven had no choice but to accept his offer. She knew, and he would know as soon as she stood, that her knees had also been shredded by the pavement. She probably could walk the mile to her house in Brentwood, but it would be a journey of curious and disdainful stares.

What's that dripping down your scrawny legs, Vulture? *Blood?*

29

"Thank you," she said softly, rising then—and being instantly assisted by hands that were strong and gentle as they cupped her elbow and encircled her waist.

Nick frowned when he saw her badly skinned knees, and when his gaze returned to her face he saw the same look that had first greeted him, the astonishing expectation that he would mock her. Changing his worried—and somehow disapproving?—frown into a worried—and gentle—smile, he asked, "Do you have a huge supply of gauze bandages at your house?"

Tendrils of midnight black silk danced as she shook her head in soft apology.

"It doesn't matter," he assured. "There's a pharmacy nearby. We'll stop there first."

As Nick guided her to the passenger side of his pickup truck, Raven's eyes fell on the cargo in the back. There were bushes of roses, a lush tapestry of color and fragrance, so many roses and so tightly packed that they had tilted slightly with the abrupt stop but none had overturned.

Before flexing her tattered knees in preparation for the large step up into the cab of the truck, she offered quietly, "I'm glad that your flowers weren't damaged."

## ❃ 3 ❃

"Are you just moving in?" Nick asked as he brought the truck to a gentle stop in the driveway of the house in Brentwood.

It was a logical question, one that would explain a number of things: the snow-whiteness of her skin, as if she had just arrived from a place with long sunless winters; and her lack of familiarity with the dangers of jogging in the traffic-laden streets of Los Angeles; and it would most certainly explain the stacks of cardboard boxes that cluttered the front porch.

Raven stared at the boxes that had arrived at the house since she had left for her run. She knew who they were from—Michael; and she knew what they contained—clothes and other belongings left behind at the mansion when she had fled three nights before, unable to endure any longer his cruel words of contempt and disdain.

Arranging to have her possessions retrieved was on the long list of things she needed to do, but she hadn't yet had the energy to face that task. And now, for a relationship that had spanned over two and a half years, it was painfully obvious that a grace period of three days was all that Michael would allow. Maybe he already needed the closet space for someone new. Maybe what the tabloids had been reporting about the steamy

31

romance in Madrid between the celebrated director and the sultry Spanish ingenue were true. Maybe he had found someone warm, hot, a creature made of flesh and blood, not of ice.

But I am made of flesh and blood, Michael! Raven's heart cried silently as she took her gaze from the cardboard boxes that were such painful symbols of her flaws and let it fall onto the upturned palms that were such eloquent proof of just how human—and how fragile—she truly was.

Nick had assumed that his logical question would be met with an easy answer, and he had hoped that it might even lead to an effortless discussion of where she was from and what she thought of L.A. so far. But his question only seemed to cause pain.

Snow White was alone in her new city, he decided. Alone, and lonely, and terribly sad.

"I've lived in Los Angeles all my life," he said finally. "If you have any questions, I'd be happy to help."

The beautiful blue eyes that were lured from her torn and bloodied flesh by the gentleness of his voice were surprised and confused.

"Thank you," she murmured, "but I've lived here, in the Los Angeles area, for fifteen years."

Now it was Raven's words that caused surprise—and such interest, such intensity, in the glittering steel that she hastily looked away. It was a while before she spoke again, but when she did, the coolly precise voice belonged to the attorney for the stars, the woman who spent her professional life dealing in matters of money. "Well, if you don't mind waiting, I'll just go inside and get my purse."

"Why?"

"So I can reimburse you for the bandages."

"No," Nick said. "No to reimbursing me and no to going inside by yourself." When he saw that his quiet yet forceful command had caused apprehension, he continued reasonably, "Until you have some sort of protection on your palms, it's going to be very difficult for you to use your hands. So why don't you let me help you? I want to help, and I also want to be certain that you don't need to be taken to a hospital."

"I thought you were a gardener. Are you a trauma surgeon too?"

Her voice was soft, and neither hopeful nor accusatory, but Nick felt a rush of annoyance nonetheless. Snow White had deduced that he was a gardener. It was a logical deduction, of course, given the denim jeans and workshirt he wore and his truck filled with roses. Would her obvious reluctance to permit him inside her house suddenly vanish if he revealed himself to be someone wealthier—*better?*—than a gardener? Did the beautiful woman who wore Ellesse when she ran, and who had a house in one of Los Angeles' most expensive neighborhoods, and a forest green Jaguar in her driveway, care about money and appearance above all else?

Nick hoped not. Indeed, suddenly and powerfully, he wanted to believe that she would regard a thirty-six-year-old gardener as a man who had made important choices for his life, not a man who had wasted it. And Nick *would* learn her feelings on the subject. But for now, until it was absolutely safe to entrust her with the entire truth about himself, he would let stand her logical deduction regarding his career.

It was true, of course, that he was a gardener. But the job that had once helped pay his way through college had evolved into a few other things . . .

Nicholas Gault had still been in college when he invented the exercise equipment which simulated the aerobic—and body-toning—benefits of gardening. The revolutionary invention made him a millionaire long before his *cum laude* graduation in landscape architecture. But that was merely his first fortune. Eden

Resort Hotels followed, and the recent completion of the Eden-Aspen and Eden-Carmel had brought to fourteen his collection of small luxury hotels located in magnificent gardens designed by him.

What if he told Snow White that he was the owner and CEO of Eden Enterprises? And that the truck filled with roses was for his hilltop estate in Bel Air. Would her beautiful blue eyes shimmer with happiness? With *seduction?* Would he suddenly be joyfully welcomed into her expensive home?

It had been a very long time since Nick had wanted anything as much as he wanted to believe that it would make no difference at all to her what he did, that her reluctance had something to do with her own vulnerability, not contempt for who she believed him to be. Nick wanted to believe, and a surprisingly confident instinct told him that he was right to do so, but it was a risk that he simply could not afford to take—not now, not yet. He had two daughters to protect, two lovely girls whose sensitive young hearts had already been broken once by a selfish woman who cared only about appearances and money.

"I'm not a trauma surgeon," he said. "I'm a gardener."

"A gardener who knows about skinned palms and knees."

Nick smiled. "That's right." *Because I'm also a father.* He forced his smile to hold as his thought continued solemnly: A father whose daughters' happiness is more important than anything else—far, far more important than this remarkable, and remarkably powerful, desire to learn all I can about Snow White.

You already know who she is, a voice warned. Who she is—and what she is. Maybe, Nick conceded. But as he gazed at her and saw still the lovely vulnerability, he amended, And maybe not. "So, may I come in?"

"Yes . . . thank you." She had no choice, of course.

Her raw and bloodied hands made her quite helpless.
Even curling her ravaged palms around the front
doorknob with enough force to turn it might be
impossible. She had to let him help her, and she wanted
to reimburse him for the bandages, and something very
foolish—and so dangerous—made her want to trust his
surprising gentleness.

"Key?" Nick asked when they had woven through the
maze of cardboard boxes and reached the front door.

The key was in the right front pocket of her pink
shorts, a deep pocket from which it could not fly free as
she ran. Nick followed her gaze as it traveled from her
useless and bloodied palms to the pocket where the key
was nestled. He knew, without conceit or arrogance, that
he was as strikingly handsome as she was bewitchingly
beautiful; and he also knew that almost any other
woman, even one as injured as she, would have
acknowledged the awkward yet delicious inevitability of
what was about to happen with at least the suggestion of
a smile.

But Snow White did not smile. She merely accepted
the certainty of his touch with what looked to Nick like
resignation, and in lieu of blushing, her snow-white
cheeks became even more pale.

For a long moment there was silence, she expecting
him to reach for the key without invitation, and he not
making even the slightest move to do so.

"I guess . . . if you don't mind . . . the key is in this
pocket."

"Okay," Nick said softly. *Stop looking me as if I'm
going to hurt you, damn it!*

For the past twenty years, ever since that fateful
summer when she turned thirteen and suddenly became
irresistibly desirable, men had wanted Raven Winter.
Any of the many men who had been her lover during

those twenty years would have leered at her now, lewdly anticipating the contact—and then making it lewd, enjoying immensely her helplessness and his control.

But this man did not leer. His gray eyes remained solemn, and when at last he reached for the key, his touch was so gentle and so careful that Raven felt a trembling rush of gratitude.

If Nick felt her tremble, he kept the realization to himself. After removing the key, he opened the front door and held it for her as she entered the freezer white starkness of her home.

He believes that you're just moving in, Raven reminded herself. He won't imagine that you've lived here for five years without bothering to decorate.

Nick wanted to suggest that she take a long hot shower. He would turn the faucets on for her, of course; and after, when she was bundled in a warm and bulky bathrobe, if she had one, he would help her clean the wounds more deeply, if such additional cleansing was necessary; and then he would carefully wrap her snow-white skin in snow-white bandages. But Nick sensed that the suggestion that she shower while he waited might frighten her. He was a stranger, after all, and even though it bothered him to be lumped with a group of men who would take advantage of a naked and vulnerable woman, he knew that it would be prudent for her to be wary.

They went to the kitchen instead. After Nick had carefully adjusted the temperature and stream of the tap water, Raven exposed her bloodied hands to the liquid warmth. The water flowed gently, and she held her shredded palms beneath it without flinching, but as the blood swirled down the drain, her pale skin stretched tautly over her elegant cheekbones, and her long black lashes, like the tiniest of fans, fluttered closed over her remarkable blue eyes.

"Maybe I should make you a stiff drink," Nick said.

He had thought about it earlier and dismissed it with the same logic with which he had dismissed the suggestion that she take a shower while he waited. He wanted to do nothing to make her feel more vulnerable or wary than she already did. But her pain was obviously immense and needed to be numbed. "I really think it would help."

"No . . . thanks." Her voice was as taut as her skin, and her eyes remained closed, but after a few moments the faintest whisper of a smile touched her lips and she added, "It's actually getting better."


When the gently flowing water was no longer tinged with crimson, Nick turned off the faucet. He had hated watching her pain and dreaded what would come next: the pain he himself would inflict as he cleansed more deeply with dampened gauze.

"Let's see how they look," he said softly.

Her eyes opened slowly, a dread to match his; but as he held her hands and they examined the damage together, both of their expressions relaxed with relief.

Her palms were raw, yes, *raw*. But the skin had scraped off almost surgically, as if she had fallen on the smooth razor-sharpness of a knife, not the rough irregularity of pavement. The deep trenches of damage that both had feared weren't there, nor were there pockets of dirt and sand that needed to be probed.

It would be quite a while before she had the use of her palms, of course, but the delicate fingers that had been covered with blood were miraculously free of injury. She would be able to unzip her shorts, and untie her shoes, and turn on the shower faucets, and cleanse her skinned knees, and even put pristine white bandages on snow white skin by herself.

Nick smiled, and when he looked up from her palms to her face, he was greeted by a smile that was soft, hopeful—and breathtaking.

Nick willingly let his breath be stolen, and while her smile held it captive, he indulged for a moment in tantalizing thoughts. He wanted to see this lovely smile over and over again; and he wanted to see other smiles, more confident ones, happier and more radiant.

You want to see a radiant smile? the taunting voice of reality demanded. You want an invitation to unzip her shorts and join her in the shower? It's so easy. Just tell this woman who wears designer clothes for jogging and has a house filled with stylishly stark but fabulously expensive furniture who you really are.

"Well," Raven murmured finally, taking her hands from his before he sensed that she was trembling. During the endless dark minutes, when her eyes had been closed as the water had cleansed her weeping wounds, she had fought the pain by focusing her thoughts on something else: a bold idea that danced in her mind despite the silent screams of her wounded flesh. By the time she opened her eyes, the idea had become a plan, and when she had seen his gentle smile, she had even bravely imagined that he would be pleased. But just now, quite suddenly, all gentleness had vanished. The planes of his face had hardened, a steel that matched the sudden unyielding darkness of his eyes. He can always say no, Raven reminded herself. Then quietly, she began, "I suppose you noticed my garden, or rather the absence thereof? I wondered if you might be interested in planting a new one for me?"

Nick had long since reclaimed the breath that she had taken from him, and now, even though her voice was as soft and tentative as her smile had been, he greeted her invitation with unsmiling solemnity. It was an invitation to see more smiles, to learn more about Snow White . . . but was it as well an invitation to disaster?

No, he decided, because he would make very certain that she knew him only as Nick the Gardener, not Nick the CEO. He knew that such deceit rivaled quicksand as a foundation for a relationship; but he also knew that such deceit was necessary until he discovered who she truly was, in her heart.

"Sure." He smiled. "I'd be happy to—with one condition."

"Yes?"

"You have to be an active participant in the garden's design. You have to tell me what you want, the kinds of shrubs and flowers that you prefer."

Nick had hoped for a sparkling smile, but instead her beautiful face clouded with worry and her shoulders sagged as if he had just weighted her with another in a long list of unwelcome assignments.

"I don't know anything about flowers."

"But I do. All you have to do is look at photographs in the catalogs I'm going to give you. Pick the flowers you like—for no reason except that you like them—and I'll do the rest." Nick paused to visualize his calendar. Time spent with his daughters was inviolate; time spent managing his vast empire was far more flexible. He and the girls were leaving early tomorrow morning to spend the weekend at the ranch in Santa Barbara; but sometime next week the CEO of Eden Enterprises would find time to be a gardener for Snow White. "Here's what I'll do. Tomorrow morning, long before you're awake, I'll leave a small stack of catalogs on your porch. You can look at them over the weekend and we can meet next week to see what you've decided. When would be a good time for you?"

"Anytime." With a soft shrug and softer smile, she amended, "Well, I do have to go to work."

"So, before or after work?"

"Before, if that's convenient for you. I have more control of my schedule at that end of the day."

"Name the day and time."

"Well . . . Monday? I don't have to be at work until nine-thirty."

"I'll be here at seven forty-five."


Despite a soft protest that was entirely undermined by grateful blue eyes, before leaving Nick moved the cardboard boxes off the porch and into the spacious white living room. Earlier, when they had passed swiftly through the room en route to the kitchen, he had formed the impression that it was devoid of all color. But there was a little color, he realized when he saw the room for a second time. On the floor beside the couch rested a bulging burgundy briefcase. It was engraved in gold with the initials RWW, as was the matching Coach purse that lay beside it. There was that splash of burgundy on the thick ivory carpet, and on the alabaster coffee table lay a book with a striking—and familiar—gold and lilac cover.

*"Gifts of Love,"* he said. "My mother says it's terrific."

"That's what I hear too. I just bought it today." As Raven tilted her head thoughtfully at the book, a lovely faraway smile touched her lips.

"Why the smile?"

Her snow-white cheeks pinkened with surprise at his question—and at his obvious interest in her answer—and after a moment, and even more surprisingly, she heard herself confess, "Well, I suppose I was thinking about my weekend: choosing flowers and reading a romance."

"Not your usual weekend?"

"No." The single syllable was embellished by a soft laugh. "Not my usual weekend at all."

"But a nice one, I hope."

His voice was gentle, and serious, as if he truly did care that her weekend was nice. Without warning, a single powerful shiver swept through her.

"I'd better get going so you can take a long hot

shower. I'm Nicholas Gault, by the way." His voice made it sound like the most casual of revelations . . . but Nick felt very far from casual as he watched her reaction to his name. Nothing. Not a flicker of recognition. Either the name meant absolutely nothing to her or she was the best actress in this town of actresses. Nick guessed it was the former. His name wasn't that unusual. Indeed, according to his nine-year-old daughter, there were four Nick or Nicholas Gaults listed in the Greater Los Angeles phone book, none of whom were her father. And, although Eden Resort Hotels were widely known, his name was not. Satisfied that the necessary pretense could continue, he added, "I'm Nick to my friends."

"Hi."

"Hi, Nick," he clarified.

"Hi, Nick," she echoed with a soft smile of gratitude—and of surprise. As she realized what needed to come next, her smile faded and her slender body stiffened, as if steeling itself for an assault. Finally, lifting her chin bravely, she offered quietly, "I'm Raven."

The quiet revelation came as no surprise to Nick. Raven Winter, along with her address, had been written on the cardboard boxes.

I know your name, he thought. But what I don't know, and what I want to know, is why you look as if I'm going to mock you. And I *will* know . . . someday.

For now, Nick repeated softly, "Raven. That's a very beautiful name."

## ❀ 4 ❀

# ❀ 4 ❀

*Kodiak, Alaska*
*Friday, March Tenth*

The world outside was midnight black, and snow was falling in heavy curtains of crystal silence. It was a time when Holly should have been writing, should have been escaping her own anguished memories of snow and blackness by journeying into fictional worlds of love and romance and happy endings.

But tonight Holly could not escape from waking nightmares to faraway dreams. Tonight she had to face the long-ago memories of terror—and the terrifying recent memory: the promise made to Raven Winter that she would fly to Los Angeles to meet with Jason Cole.

For a very long time following the phone call, Holly hadn't even moved. She had simply stood by the living room window of her rustic cottage and gazed at the drama of sky and sea that unfolded before her. Finally, long after the soft pastels of the early spring twilight had given way to a night that was pure winter, she wandered to her bedroom and opened the cedar-fragrant closet, her pale hand trembling as she touched the single dress that hung there.

The ivory muslin was intricately embroidered with a meadow of wildflowers, delicate blossoms of pink, lavender, gold, and mauve. Its long sleeves were ruffled at the cuffs, and there was a high ruffled collar as well, and except for small darts at the bust it was as shapeless, as modest and demure, as a girl's nightgown. The dress was ten months older than Holly. It had been her mother's wedding dress, worn thirty-one years before, on Valentine's Day, when seventeen-year-olds Claire Johnson and Lawrence Elliott had become husband and wife.

As a little girl, Holly had tried the dress on many times. "You look so grown up, Holly Elizabeth Elliott—and so beautiful!" her parents had lovingly raved every time. Now it had been more than twenty years since she had last worn the dress, and over seventeen since she had vanished forever, taking with her the dress and the few other treasures that were mementos of a time when there had been such happiness and such joy . . .

"Her nose is so soft, Daddy!" three-year-old Holly exclaimed with delight as Lawrence held her so that her small eager hands could touch the nose of the palomino mare and she could feel for the first time the velvety softness of a horse's muzzle. "So soft."

Accompanying her father to the stable where he worked, one of the many jobs he held to support his family, was pure joy for Holly—as were all the moments of her young life. She was cloaked in the billowy softness of her parents' love and together the family of three made wonderful dreams.

Her daddy, the strong handsome man whose dark green eyes glittered with loving wonder every time he saw her, was going to be a veterinarian. It would take a while, because he was only able to attend college part-time, but eventually he would have his own clinic. He would care for all creatures, great and small, wild and tame; and her gracious and beautiful mother would be at the clinic too, greeting the "patients" and their owners; and Holly would be there as well, greeting their patients *and* helping her father.

Neither Claire Johnson nor Lawrence Elliott had had the kind of childhood that permitted them to believe in dreams; but because of their love for each other, and for their golden-haired daughter, it seemed as if dreams *were* possible, even for them. All hopes, all wishes *could* come true.

Even when Lawrence was drafted, and even when they knew that he would be going to Vietnam, he and Claire still dared to dream. He would return safe and sound, and he would go to college—full-time, on the GI bill— and by Holly's thirteenth birthday he would be a veterinarian.

But the wonderful dream wasn't to be. Two days before Lawrence's tour of duty in Vietnam was to end, his unit returned from the jungle without him. The somber report of his death came from fellow soldier Derek Burke. Derek had been right beside Lawrence when the bullet entered his chest, and it was Derek who had held Lawrence and listened to his dying words of love for his wife and daughter. Derek returned from the jungle with Lawrence's dog tags, but without Lawrence's body. It would have been impossible to carry the body out with the enemy in pursuit; and, the Army told Claire a few days later, it was unlikely that Lawrence's body would ever be recovered.

Seven months after Lawrence's death, Derek appeared on Claire's doorstep. He and Lawrence had been best friends, he told her, and with his dying breath Lawrence had implored his friend to promise that on his return to the States he would visit Claire, to make certain that she and Holly were all right, and to tell Claire to go on with her life, to find a new love, to be happy.

Derek was kind, and charming, and so wonderful with Holly. Claire never stopped missing Lawrence, not for a second, but when she was with Derek, who had loved Lawrence too, her immense pain was a little less.

Derek and Claire were married eighteen months after Lawrence's death. As Derek had promised before the wedding, they moved from the small apartment where Holly and Claire had lived with Lawrence to a spacious house with a big yard. The move was much farther than Claire had expected, though, to another state entirely, from Montana to Washington. It was a big move—and a nostalgic and somewhat eerie one—because part of the wonderful dream that Claire and Lawrence and Holly once had shared had involved relocating to Washington, where Lawrence would attend the excellent school of veterinary medicine at Washington State University in Pullman.

Now Derek had moved them to Washington, not to attend college, but to run a business, the precise nature of which he never revealed to Claire. She knew only that it was consultant work, based on expertise he had acquired in Vietnam, and that it required him to travel quite often.

For a long time, too long, Claire fought the deep quivers that tried to warn her that something was not quite right about the man she had married. Derek was so unpredictable, charming one moment, remote the next. But whenever her concerns crescendoed to the point at which she resolved to confront him, his moodiness would suddenly disappear. He would be wonderfully charming once again and her worries would be allayed.

And for a long time, too long, Claire permitted those worries to be allayed. She wanted to believe that everything was fine, that her concerns were foolish, that she had made the right choice for Holly . . . and for the twins, the son and daughter she had conceived with Derek.

If Derek had ever laid a hand on her children, or on her, even once, Claire would have left him instantly. But he never had. He must have known what she would do if he did—and Derek did not want to lose Claire. Despite his ever-increasing coldness toward her, he was far from indifferent. He wanted her. And he wanted to control her, to make her solely and irrevocably dependent on him. Claire yielded without resistance to Derek's obvious wish that she not make friends. She had her children, after all, three wonderful children with whom she wanted to spend every moment of her life.

Finally, because of those children, because the quivering warnings about Derek could no longer be denied, Claire made a bold decision of love.

I'm going to leave him, Lawrence, Claire's heart whispered to the only man she had ever loved. I know he was your friend, my darling, but he must have changed since you knew him. I think he's dangerous, and sometimes I even wonder if he's using drugs.

Leaving Derek required careful planning. Claire knew that she couldn't return to Montana. He would follow her there. Seattle, she decided. She and Lawrence had dreamed about living in Seattle someday . . .

Claire began saving money from the small household allowance that Derek gave her. It would take a while, but as soon as she had enough for bus tickets for four across the Cascades, and a little more with which they would live until she found work, they would leave.

Claire shared her brave plan with Holly. Her golden-haired daughter was thirteen now, and the young blue-green eyes which had once sparkled with radiant happiness and boundless dreams were wise, and sad, and solemn. Holly's eyes sparkled anew, however, when Claire told her that they would begin again in Seattle.

"We'll have enough money by April," Holly predicted with quiet joy. "Then, while Derek is off on one of his business trips, the four of us will escape."

But just as the dream of Lawrence's veterinary clinic was never to be, neither was the dream of Seattle—at least not for all of them. On a snowy day in February, the Valentine's Day that would have been Claire and Lawrence's fourteenth wedding anniversary, Derek went crazy.

He's on drugs, Claire thought with grim certainty and foreboding clarity when he arrived home. His dark eyes were wild; but it was some kind of drug that made him agitated not blurred, sharp not numb. The black eyes that focused on her weren't the least bit glazed, and his voice was shatteringly clear as he spoke the ominous words.

"Are you my Valentine, Claire?" he hissed softly as he shoved a bouquet of blood-red roses at her. "Or does your heart still belong to your precious Lawrence?"

As she smiled bravely and told him that she loved him, Claire realized with crescendoing terror that Derek had no interest whatsoever in her answer. His wild eyes glistened with lethal intent, and the hand that hadn't held the blood-red roses was clutching a hunting rifle, one of the many weapons that he owned. What she said didn't matter. Derek already had scripted his own scenario of horror.

"You want to be with him, don't you, Claire? You want to be with Lawrence."

Claire and Derek were in the kitchen. The children, in the living room, hadn't heard Derek return home. Nor did they hear the hushed words that were spoken—neither the quiet desperate pleas nor the resolute hisses of determined madness. The television was on, a rerun of the original Mickey Mouse Club. Holly sat on the couch with the twins. She had been doing her homework, but when "The Adventures of Corky and White Shadow" had begun, she joined her little brother and sister in watching the beloved story of the brave young girl and her brave white dog.

Holly heard nothing, none of them did, not even the swish of the kitchen door. But suddenly her mother and

Derek were there and Holly saw Claire's terror beneath her valiant attempt to stay calm for her children. And even though Holly could not have put a name to it, she saw Derek's madness and understood with amazing clarity what it meant.

"Hi, kids." Derek's voice was ominously pleasant. "How would you all like to go on a trip?"

The trip that Derek had planned was a journey to death for all of them—except Holly. For her it was simply a passport to the unspeakable memories that would play forever, in slow motion and in living—dying—color in her mind.

In Holly's memory, and in her nightmares, the terror and the carnage lasted forever. Every anguished expression and every frantic plea stretched into an eternity of despair. In truth, the horror for the victims—the ones who died, not Holly—was mercifully brief; and thankfully, the twins were too young to really comprehend what was happening.

But Claire and Holly knew. Claire tried frantically to save her children, pleading for their lives, offering her own in trade, standing between them and the rifle, shielding them from harm with her slender body. And when Derek tired of Claire's pleas and pulled the trigger, it was Holly who moved in front of the lethal weapon to shield her little sister and brother. She grasped the barrel with both hands, her fragile strength fortified by courage born of love.

Love should have been enough. For the first few years of her life Holly and her parents had lived in a world in which love was all powerful. But now, even though she was only thirteen, that wonderful world was a faraway memory; and now, even her most courageous love was a woefully delicate match for the crazed power of her stepfather.

Derek's wild eyes mocked her foolish bravery, then

became even more chilling, lethally cold and filled with hatred.

"You and your father," he scoffed.

As Derek hissed the inexplicable words, he grabbed Holly, imprisoning her beside him in such a way that she was forced to witness the murders of her little sister and brother. Their young eyes were so huge, so innocent, as they beheld the unfolding drama. It didn't seem real to them, something on television, the continuing saga of Corky and her dog.

Kill *me!* Holly's shattered heart pleaded when the three people she loved so much lay still and silent on the floor before her. Kill me now . . . *please.* Let me be with them—and with Daddy.

Holly had no fear of death. She welcomed it, wanted it; and as Derek released her from his grasp, she made no attempt to flee. She stood before him straight and proud, accepting her death with regal dignity.

Hurry, she pleaded silently. Let me be with them—*now.*

But Derek was moving in slow motion, savoring these final moments of torment and terror. He aimed the rifle at her heart, but even after endless moments, he didn't pull the trigger. Perhaps he realized that her heart was already shattered, that even the blast of a rifle fired at point blank range would cause no further harm. Slowly, so slowly, he raised the weapon from her heart to her face . . . to the eyes that were the remarkable blend of bright blue from Claire and the deep forest green that had belonged to Lawrence.

Did Derek want her to plead for her life? If so, it would never happen. Holly's life was already over. And if he wanted to see fear in the luminous blue-green eyes, he would have to wait forever. There was nothing left to fear. She had already lost all that she could lose.

Finally Derek smiled, and when he did, it was the charming smile he'd once used to convince Holly and

Claire that he was kind, and would take care of them—and that that was what Lawrence had wanted.

"Goodbye, Holly. *Enjoy.*"

With that mocking farewell, Derek Burke put the rifle to his own temple and pulled the trigger.

The thunder of the final shot faded swiftly and Holly was suddenly alone—except that now the voices from the television that had been lost amid the terror seemed to be shouting at her. Holly silenced those voices, her hand leaving a splatter of blood as she pressed the "off" button. Then she knelt down on the floor that was now the crimson of Valentine's Day roses and tenderly touched the small lifeless bodies of her little sister and brother.

"Holly . . . ?"

*"Mommy."*

In an instant, Claire was cradled in Holly's loving arms, and in another instant Holly realized that in order to save her beloved mother, she would need to abandon her loving grasp. "I have to call for an ambulance!"

"No, my precious love."

Claire's pale trembling hands reached to touch her daughter's cheeks. "Just listen to me, my darling. You can go on with your life. You're strong, and you were so very loved by your daddy and me. Will you remember that, Holly?"

"Yes, but—"

"And will you promise to be happy?"

"Yes, I promise," Holly whispered. "I love you, Mommy. Please don't die!"

"I love you always, Holly. Always."

Claire died then, having already lived far longer than her mortal wounds should have allowed. Her heart had simply, defiantly, refused to stop beating until she had whispered the words of love to her daughter.

\* \* \*

The police were summoned by neighbors concerned by the sound of gunfire coming from inside the house. They found Holly in the blood-splattered living room, cradling her mother still, rocking her gently and whispering words they could not hear. When they finally managed to pull her away, they saw even more blood. The cotton blouse that Holly wore was soaked through, her golden hair was streaked with crimson, and on her pale white cheeks there were bright red smudges where Claire's loving fingers had bid their final adieu.

Holly was in shock, unable to answer questions with more than a hopeless nod of her crimson-and-gold head. Her eyewitness testimony was almost unnecessary anyway. The bloody scene itself provided ample and gruesome evidence of what had happened.

But the crime scene could not answer the inevitable question, *Why?* Why would a man murder his wife, his children, and himself?

Because of Vietnam, the townspeople reasoned. The immorality of war created an immorality in its soldiers, a blood lust and a madness that were kept evergreen by vivid flashbacks of the carnage in the steamy heat of the faraway jungles of Southeast Asia. That a Vietnam vet had returned home a murderer was more than plausible. Indeed, many argued, how could he not have become one?

What was more perplexing was why the marauding soldier had spared his thirteen-year-old stepdaughter. After much discussion the townspeople decided that there could be only one reason: Holly herself. She was a lethal Lolita. She had preyed on the man who had become crazed by the war, inciting deep and forbidden passions within him; and then she had played with him, satiating his passions for as long as it amused her, and then, when she became bored with the game, she had rejected him without mercy.

Both Holly and her stepfather had committed crimes

of passion. But even in Derek's madness he could not murder the teenaged temptress he loved.

It made sense. Within forty-eight hours of the murder it was what most of the town believed—including the neighbors who had offered Holly temporary sanctuary.

Strands of police crime-scene tape still draped the house, a yellow web of death that fluoresced eerily beneath the pale winter moon. It was after midnight when Holly parted the ribbons that wrapped the front door and entered the house for the last time.

She had left the bedroom where she had stayed for the past three nights, not a prisoner but not a welcome guest either. The neighbors who now viewed her with unconcealed disdain would be relieved to find that she was gone—the whole town would be relieved; and Holly needed to escape from the hostility that surrounded her . . . and from the small army of reporters eager to hear from her own lips her story of seduction and murder. But most of all, she needed privacy for the despair that was almost beyond endurance.

Her mother and sister and brother were no longer lying on the living room floor, not really, but Holly saw their beloved images anyway; and the blood stains which, during the past three days, had become brown-black with age looked bright crimson to her still, and glistening.

"I'm going to take the money that we were saving, Mommy," she said softly to the empty room where her own life, too, had ended. "I'm going to Seattle, just like we planned. Maybe you'll be there waiting for me."

Her voice broke then. She needed so much to be touched, to be held and comforted. But she was all alone, and after a moment she reminded herself sternly, Mommy won't be waiting in Seattle. No one will be. You can't let yourself pretend anything else. "You won't really be there, Mommy, I know that. But you'll be with me. You and Daddy will be with me . . . always . . . won't you?"

Holly knew that if she permitted herself to believe in happy endings that could never be, she would go mad. And she knew something else, something far more immediate: If she didn't leave the blood-splattered living room right now she might act out the idea that had been dancing in her mind. She would get another one of Derek's guns and she would join her loved ones.

Holly turned to leave the room, her mind and heart uncertain where her trembling legs would carry her—upstairs, her destination when she had left the neighbors' house . . . or to Derek's study with its lethal racks of loaded guns.

"Promise me that you will go on, Holly. Promise me that you will be happy."

"Mommy!" The voice was so real. Holly spun, fully expecting to see Claire. "Mommy?"

But there was nothing—except for the brown-black stains that were silent and somber gravestones of all that had died.

Nothing—except for the solemn promise that she had made to her dying mother.

Holly's trembling legs carried her upstairs, to the place where the money that she and Claire had saved was so carefully hidden. It had almost been enough to provide safe passage and housing for a family of four. For a teenaged girl who was all alone, it would last for a very long time.

Holly packed her knapsack with some of her own clothes—sweaters and jeans—and on top she gently folded Claire's wedding dress. Then she found the photo album that had been hidden too, the only tangible proof of that joyous, faraway time when she and Lawrence and Claire had been a family.

There was no reason whatsoever for Holly not to take the entire album with her. She had room for it in her knapsack, she had left room, and there was no one else on earth to whom the photographs would have any meaning. Her parents were both dead, and there had never been any loving grandparents or aunts or uncles or cousins. No one.

But something very powerful, some invisible hand, stopped Holly from taking the entire album, compelling her instead to simply remove five of her favorite photographs: her parents' wedding picture, taken by the wife of the justice of the peace, a portrait of boundless love and brave hope; and a baby picture of her, being cradled by both of them; and another one of just Lawrence and Claire, gazing at the camera—at her—and smiling with love as her small eager fingers captured the shot; and one of her mother and her frosting her father's birthday cake; and finally, the photograph of Lawrence holding her as she patted the velvet-soft muzzle of the palomino mare.

Holly took those five precious treasures of that faraway time, and from an album that had not been hidden she took two pictures of the baby sister and brother who had died.

Then she left the house—and the town—forever.

"If we honor the names, if we are good and kind and careful with them, then it's okay, don't you think?" Claire had asked when she had explained to Holly that the way they were all going to disappear was by taking names of people who had died as children.

Holly remembered her mother's question as she wandered through the cemetery near Seattle's Volunteer Park on Capitol Hill. This is necessary, she told herself. Holly Elliott, the thirteen-year-old innocent believed by the world to be a Lolita, needed to vanish completely and forever; and she needed to be at least eighteen now, of legal age, old enough to live by herself and support herself.

Holly wandered slowly through the cemetery, solemnly studying each gravestone. Her somber wanderings eventually brought her to the grave of Mary Lynn Pierce. According to the dates chiseled into the shining granite, Mary had been born five years before Holly and had lived less than a month.

Holly vowed to honor and cherish her borrowed name. But she could not promise more. She could not promise the spirit of its original owner that she would take it with her on a magnificent journey of bountiful hopes and wondrous dreams. Indeed, most of Holly wanted to journey no farther. Most of her wished simply for the peace she found in the silent cemetery with its brilliant bouquets of springtime flowers.

From the King County bureau of vital statistics, Holly obtained a photostatic copy of Mary's birth certificate, which she used to apply for the Social Security card that she would need in order to get a job. Her next stop was an eye-care center, where she ordered a pair of gold wire-rimmed frames that would encase glass only, without magnification of any kind.

"My vision is fine," she explained to the surprised receptionist. "I'm an actress. I need the glasses for a prop in a play."

What Holly truly believed was that she needed a disguise for her potentially recognizable face, something more than the long golden hair that she now wore as a veil. And, she reasoned, the glasses might help her appear closer to the age that Mary Lynn Pierce would have been.

In truth, no one who met Holly had any trouble imagining her to be the almost nineteen years she claimed. What could be glimpsed of the solemn face beneath the veil of gold held such sad, mature wisdom. Indeed, the real difficulty would have come in trying to convince Holly's acquaintances that she had ever been the smiling pig-tailed teenager whose photograph—and unsavory but compelling story—had commanded the evening news until another tragedy had replaced it.

Holly wasn't recognized when the grisly story was still fresh in the news, and when a stunning twist resurrected it eight months later, even those who saw Mary Lynn Pierce every day never guessed that the shy and serious young woman they knew had ever been the much loved and radiantly happy Holly Elliott.

Holly found work in a bookstore on University Avenue. She worked tirelessly; and when she wasn't working, she read romantic fiction—happy endings only. And when her blue-green eyes became fatigued, but resisted sleep because of the nightmares that she knew awaited her there, her mind created its own stories, with happy endings only, necessary antidotes to the anguished memories that would have invaded her thoughts had she allowed them to be idle, even for a moment.

Two years after the murder of her family, Holly read a romance that was set in Alaska. After reading it three times she read everything else she could about the forty-ninth state. And when she did, the descriptions of the untamed natural beauty reminded her of Montana, where she and her mother and father had once been so very happy, and even Alaska's nickname—"The Last Frontier"—beckoned to her.

Holly booked one-way passage on a boat that would sail through the inland passage from Seattle to Anchorage. Before leaving Seattle, she got a letter of recommendation from the manager of the bookstore, a rave review for his quiet but competent employee; and since she didn't have a driver's license, no proof of who she was except for the copy of the birth certificate and her Social Security card, she decided to apply for a passport as well. Before completing the application, she made a modification in her name, officially changing Mary Lynn to Marilyn, because even though she would have never broken her promise to honor and cherish her borrowed name, she knew full well that she would never bring it joy. Holly wanted Mary Lynn Pierce to rest in peace amid the flowers in the cemetery, untormented any longer by the ghosts that would torment Holly always.

It was Marilyn Pierce who boarded the *Arctic Star* on that morning in May. According to the documents she had with her, she was twenty. That was Marilyn Pierce's age; but five months earlier, on Christmas day, Holly Elizabeth Elliott, who no longer existed, had turned fifteen.

Holly's arrival in Alaska coincided with the arrival of the midnight sun, and for that first summer, working in the cannery in Kodiak and living in a world that was illuminated almost constantly by a brilliant golden glow, Holly felt tiny rushes of hope.

Then winter came, bringing with it a silent snow and relentless darkness that reminded her of that Valentine's evening of death.

Holly could have returned to Seattle. She could have even traveled farther south, following the sun. But she had inherited strength and courage from her parents and it was a legacy that she would not deny—because it felt like them, alive, *living,* inside her. She needed to stay. She needed to find a way to live with the snow, with the darkness, *through* the darkness.

Holly spent the long dark winter nights reading, and eventually she began to write her own stories of love, losing herself in those stories and feeling far safer with them than with stories written by others. Holly had control over the imaginary worlds she created. No unforeseen tragedies would ever shatter the lives of her heroes and heroines. She wouldn't allow them to.

Holly wrote about people who were loving and kind, men and women who would never betray the solemn vows and reverent promises of love. Holly's heroes and heroines had problems, of course, deep tormenting secrets of the heart that sometimes seemed almost insurmountable. But invariably, all the secrets were revealed—the ghosts exorcised and the mistakes forgiven; and invariably, even the most insurmountable of obstacles was conquered—by hope, by courage . . . and by love.

Holly wrote her stories of love in long hand, in a girlish script that was so legible—and so earnest and compelling—that despite the inviolate rule that manuscripts submitted to publishers were to be neatly typed, especially ones sent from unpublished authors, her first book was read anyway.

Read . . . and published . . . and welcomed by readers, embraced by them with a sense of hope and joy.

The few townspeople in Kodiak who even knew Holly existed knew her only as Marilyn Pierce, the quiet young woman who lived four miles out of town, in a rustic cottage perched high above the sea. No one in Kodiak had any idea that Holly was really the bestselling novelist Lauren Sinclair. She kept only a small amount of money in the local bank, enough to live on. The rest was elsewhere, conservatively invested, and every year she made large anonymous contributions to organizations dedicated to the care of victims of violent crimes.

All her mail, including the many letters from her readers, arrived in Kodiak addressed to Marilyn Pierce. The latter were forwarded to her in large manila envelopes— or sometimes large cardboard boxes—from her publishing company in New York. Holly answered every letter from every reader; but her thoughtful replies were never mailed from Kodiak. Instead, Holly sent them to her publisher for mailing, and thus, they bore a New York City postmark.

It was a matter of privacy, Holly explained to her editor. She wanted no one to know where she lived, or even that Lauren Sinclair was a pseudonym.

Holly's world inside her small cottage was a silent one. Her heart still ached with the worry that had she not been watching television on that Valentine's night, had that sound not muffled the sounds that came from the kitchen, she might have known, might have been able to do something to avert the tragedy.

There was no television in Holly's cottage, nor was there a radio, nor did she receive a newspaper. When she walked to the grocery store in town, her blue-green eyes sometimes drifted to the bold-faced headlines on the newspapers, but she never bought one. The headlines were more than enough reality for her. She preferred to live in the worlds she created, worlds populated by kind and loving people for whom she could guarantee that there would be no senseless tragedies and no irrevocably shattered hearts.

During the few hours of daylight on the Christmas day that marked her twenty-sixth birthday, Holly decided to make the long walk into town. The sky above was a brilliant blue and the crystals of snow and ice glittered like diamonds as they captured the dazzling fire of the surprisingly warm and golden sun. As she wandered through town, she passed a movie theater and saw a poster advertising *Escape Artist,* a movie starring Jason Cole. For a very long time she simply stood, staring at his image. He seemed to be one of her heroes come to life, strong and gentle, loving and kind.

The theater was closed on that Christmas day, but Holly made the eight-mile round trip journey again the following day, when it was open. She saw that Jason Cole movie, more than once, and over the next four years, she saw every movie that came to town in which he starred, and every movie that came to town for which he was the director.

Holly never wavered from the firm belief that in real

life, the *real* Jason Cole was kind, and gentle, and strong, and heroic. But now she had been forced to face the bitter truth: the man whom she had cast as a romantic hero was in fact a cavalier rogue. Without a flicker of remorse or regret, Jason Cole was planning to destroy. He was planning to ruthlessly murder one of the people she had so lovingly created . . . a loving mother who wanted nothing more than the opportunity to spend her life loving her baby girl.

And now, in just seventeen days, Holly was going to meet the real Jason Cole. Somehow, somehow, she was going to find a way to tell him that he could not let that mother die.

Holly's delicate fingers trembled as she touched the ivory muslin of her mother's wedding dress, and as she traced the petals of the tiny embroidered flowers, she made a decision. She would wear the dress for her meeting with Jason Cole. She would wear it for luck, just as she would carry with her the five photographs she had taken, symbols of her family . . . precious symbols of precious love.

## ❀ 5 ❀

Despite the fact that Nicholas Gault had spent the weekend with his daughters in Santa Barbara, he had managed to learn more about Raven W. Winter. During the late-night hours while the girls slept, he made a few phone calls. None of Nick's sources could tell him what the middle "W" in her name stood for, but that was a trivial detail, a tiny mystery compared to the far more important and troubling ones.

She was nicknamed the "Snow White Shark," his sources told him. At thirty-three she was already regarded as one of the top entertainment attorneys in the entertainment capital of the world, the best of the best. Because she had a well-deserved reputation for devouring the competition, everyone in Hollywood wanted her on their side of the negotiating table. Raven had the luxury of selecting as clients only the ones she wished to represent, and she had chosen the very most talented and powerful.

That was Raven the lawyer. Tough. Shrewd. Brilliant. Successful. And Raven the woman? She had been linked, Nick discovered, to some of Hollywood's richest and most influential men—ardent sexual liaisons, apparently, none of which had ever led to matrimony.

Her most recent relationship, with producer-director Michael Andrews, had just ended. Andrews had returned from seven weeks on location in Spain and on the very night of his return had "tossed her out" of his mansion in Beverly Hills. There was another woman, of course, an enchanting and passionate ingenue. But Michael's affairs were nothing new, Nick was told. Throughout his almost three-year relationship with Raven, he had been with many other women.

And yet Raven had stayed with him, despite the public humiliation and betrayal.

Why? Nick wondered. Did the woman who had reached the pinnacle of a traditionally male-dominated profession somehow lack confidence? There was no doubt in the minds of any of those to whom Nick spoke that Raven Winter had earned—not slept—her way to the top. She had succeeded despite her astonishing beauty. She had made people look beyond her looks and take very seriously her considerable intelligence.

Raven hadn't compromised professionally, hadn't needed to, so why in the world did she make such personal compromises?

Had she loved Michael Andrews so much that she had forsaken herself—her dignity and her pride—and simply endured his repeated betrayals? Nick himself was an expert on the betrayal of love. From his own firsthand experience, once the betrayal was discovered the love ceased to exist. Did Raven love Michael so much, and have so little respect for herself, that she forgave him again and again?

It seemed implausible to Nick that Raven Winter could lack confidence, could consider herself so unworthy . . . and yet he remembered vividly the vulnerability of her brilliant blue eyes. Nick hated the thought that something so traumatic had happened in her past that she would doubt her own worth and accept humiliation and betrayal as if it were her due; but he hated almost more the other possible explanation for why she had tolerated Michael Andrews' infidelity without complaint: that love didn't really matter to her—only power and money did.

The brilliant entertainment attorney, the Snow White Shark, was wealthy and powerful in her own right. But Michael Andrews' wealth and power were of a different order of magnitude. His celluloid empire was immense . . . yet even its vastness paled in comparison to the kingdom of Nicholas Gault.

That he could buy and sell Michael Andrews many times over was a deeply troubling realization for Nick. If Raven had been willing to endure repeated humiliation and betrayal at the hands of Michael Andrews, what compromises would she make if she knew that Nick and Eden Enterprises were one and the same? What compromises, what magnificent seductions, what false and calculated promises of love?

When Nick had left her on Friday evening, the images of her lovely vulnerability had overshadowed the images of her expensive home, clothes, and car; and now, as he brought his truck to a stop in front of her house, and despite his worries about what he had learned over the weekend, the intriguing and enchanting images of vulnerability danced anew.

Raven had no idea who he really was, and for now that was the way it had to be. He would be Nick the Gardener, not Nick the hotel tycoon. And she wouldn't be the Snow White Shark . . . she would only be the lovely and vulnerable Snow White.

Assuming, Nick thought as his long strides carried him swiftly toward the house, I don't instantly realize that whatever it was I saw last Friday was merely an enchanting illusion . . .

\* \* \*

It wasn't.

Yes, this morning the apricot linen suit by Armani sent a clear message that appearances and money mattered very much to Raven Winter. But even the expensive outfit sent a message of uncertainty. It was perfectly—impeccably—accessorized, precisely the way the designer had planned, as if she were merely a model, merely a mannequin, not the rich self-made woman she truly was. Nick knew many rich and successful women, and he knew that every one of them would have embellished the outfit with some symbol of her own, some signature color or jewel that confidently celebrated her own unique style, her own personal flair.

Was Raven so unsure of herself? Was she truly so afraid of being even a little bit different, unique, *special?* Was that really authentic uncertainty that he saw now in her sapphire-blue eyes?

"Good morning," he greeted softly.

"Good morning."

"How are you?"

Her skinned and presumably bandaged knees were concealed by the mid-calf apricot skirt, but Nick turned his own hands palms up, a silent invitation for her to do the same.

Her palms were bandaged, snow-white gauze on snow-white skin, and when Nick saw the bandaging, something tugged deep inside him. The bandages were held in place by the white paper tape he had bought for her, but there were tiny creases in the tape and the squares of gauze were slightly askew—eloquent and touching testimony that even though she had use of her slender fingers it had been awkward—and difficult? and lonely?—for her to bandage her wounds by herself.

"May I look?" Nick asked, knowing he could lift a corner of the paper tape without disrupting anything.

As Raven nodded in reply, shimmering cascades of lustrous midnight-black hair danced around her face and caressed her shoulders. Surely the hairstyle usually worn at work by the Snow White Shark was far more severe, a sleek and shining knot tightly subdued at her nape. But that austere style demanded perfection, every black silken strand precisely in place, with not a hair askew—a task that was now beyond the ability of her badly injured hands.

Nick's long fingers lifted the paper tape as gently and carefully as three days before he had removed the front door key from deep inside her shorts' pocket. And now, as then, his exquisite and surprising tenderness made Raven tremble.

"What do you think?"

Nick heard the anxiety in her voice and reassured truthfully, "I think everything looks very good." Reassuring further, he embellished, "There's been quite a bit of healing already and I don't see any sign of infection whatsoever. What do you think?"

Raven hadn't known what to think about the wounds that had caused her to bleed more than she had ever bled before—far, far more than the scant menstrual periods that were monthly reminders of the barren iciness of her womb. Until now all the wounds of her life had been deep inside. She felt them—oh, how she felt them—but never before had they been visible.

Raven agreed with Nick that the wounds on her palms seemed to be healing. It was an astonishing realization . . . because none of the wounds inside her had ever healed, not one, not ever.

"I guess I think they're healing too."

"How is the pain?"

Raven smiled at last and admitted, "Much better."

"So you were able to turn the pages of *Gifts of Love?*"

"Yes." Raven's voice filled with quiet reverence. It was as if Lauren Sinclair had been writing specifically to her, to the wounds deep within her that had never healed. Lauren Sinclair had seemed to know that the wounds were there, and with her words she had sent a balming promise of hope to Raven: even her deepest wounds could heal. There could be happiness, there could be love . . . even for her.

"And?" Nick urged gently.

"And it was wonderful." With a thoughtful tilt of her dark black head, she added, "I was also able to turn the pages of the catalogs that you left for me. They were wonderful too. I have them in the kitchen and I made some coffee for us."

It was Nick who poured the coffee. When they each had full steaming mugs, he sat beside her at the table on which were neatly stacked all the catalogs he had left on her front porch early Saturday morning.

Pages, many many pages, were flagged with pale yellow Post-its. The small yellow markers were precisely aligned, at perfect right angles to the page. It was, Nick supposed, the impeccably orderly way that the bandages would have been placed on her palms had she been able to manage it.

"It looks as if you've found lots of flowers that you like."

"Yes . . . well, I thought I should choose options in case there are ones that don't go well together."

Nick gazed thoughtfully at the woman who, if today's outfit was any indication, didn't dare make a personal fashion statement, didn't dare embellish or countermand any of the choices the designer had made.

"All flowers go well together, Raven. There are no right answers and you really can't go wrong. Choose what you like the best. Be creative. Be daring."

Little by little, as his patient and unrelenting encouragement gave her increasing confidence, Raven discovered that she did have preferences, very definite ones. She wanted lilacs and roses—and nothing else—and when that pronouncement was greeted by Nick with what seemed like unreserved approval, she told him which colors of each she liked the best. For the lilacs, she wanted both traditional lavender and lacy, graceful white; and as for the roses her delicate fingers kept pointing to, and lingering on, the soft romantic blends of pink and cream.

"I love the names," she said impulsively, her snow-white cheeks coloring with a faint pink blush that was very reminiscent of the pink-on-white caress of Pristine, one of her favorite roses. "I'd never even realized that roses had names."

She is going to call her roses by their names, Nick realized with a bittersweet mix of emotions. He was glad that Raven was so enthusiastic about her garden of lilacs and roses. But he felt a deep sadness as his thought continued, She's going to call them by their names . . . as if they were her friends . . . as if they were her family.

Swiftly, too swiftly, the enchanted, make-believe time when they were Nick the Gardener and Snow White came to an end. It was almost nine. The Snow White Shark had a nine-thirty meeting in her penthouse office in Century City, and Nicholas Gault had a business meeting too, at ten, at his mansion in Bel Air.

"Sometime later this week I'll get rid of the weeds and prepare the soil for planting."

"This week?" Raven echoed, surprised but obviously pleased. "So soon?"

"Sure," Nick affirmed. "I should be able to get all the flowers by the end of this weekend, so if it's all right with you, I'll plan to spend next Monday planting them."

"Yes, that's fine."

Nick hesitated a moment, then said, "It would be nice if you could arrange to be here that day too."

"Me? Why?"

"So you can help me with the design." Nick greeted her startled expression with a smile. "I can obviously do it myself, but there are those extremely delicate questions of etiquette and protocol."

"Protocol?"

"You've invited Lady Diana and Queen Elizabeth and Princesse de Monaco and Barbara Bush into your garden. Who goes where? Who gets the location of honor? The most sunshine? The least shade?"

Raven was smiling now, too, and her sapphire eyes sparkled. But still she murmured, "I don't know."

"Well. Think about it. After all, it's your garden." Your family . . . your friends.

The telephone rang just moments after Nick left.

"Hello, Raven."

"Michael."

"Have I got a deal for you . . ."

Raven listened in silent and stunned amazement as the man who had thrown her out of his life less than a week before, and who had so cruelly mocked her brave suggestion that he had ever loved her, now spoke to her as if there had never been anything personal between them at all. His tone was exactly the same as it had been three years ago, when he had persuaded her to add his name to her elite list of clients.

He was calling her in that professional capacity now, wanting her to attend a meeting with him next Monday.

Raven felt the excruciating pain of the brutal truth: everything that Michael had yelled at her last week had been true. He had never loved her. He believed her to be a creation of pure ice—without heart, without feelings, and without any enduring interest or value to him . . . except, apparently, when it came to her indisputably brilliant legal mind.

Speaking at last, she echoed, "Next Monday?"

"I'll need you all day. I've already checked with your secretary. You have nothing scheduled for that day that can't easily be changed."

Oh but I do, Raven thought. The thought came with astonishing confidence—and astonishing calm.

"Actually, Michael, I have plans for next Monday that can't be changed."

"Plans can always be changed, Raven. This deal is almost as big as the four-picture deal you did for Jason with Gold Star. Hell, knowing you, maybe it will be even bigger."

"Sorry, Michael, but I'm simply not available." Then, into the shocked silence that greeted her words, she bravely issued even more shocking ones, "I think you'd better find someone else to represent you, and I'm not just talking about the meeting on Monday."

He swore at her then, a harsh and vulgar barrage that was painfully familiar. Raven was accustomed to such degradation—from Michael, from many other men. She had fully expected to hear such enraged and demeaning contempt from the man who, because of *her* carelessness, had almost struck her with his truck.

But Nick hadn't sworn at her.

Nick had only cared.

And just moments before, Nick had told her how nice it would be if she would help him design her garden of lilacs and roses.

And now it was the vivid—and gentle—memory of Nick that empowered her to defy Michael Andrews' malicious fury.

# Part Two

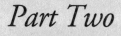

## * 6 *

As Caroline Hawthorne dressed for lunch at the Seattle Tennis Club, she listened to KBSG, one of Seattle's soft-rock stations that promised—and delivered—thirty-minute music sweeps of oldies but goodies: timelessly evocative songs of first love and forbidden love, of revolution and of peace, of chilly winters of heartache and endless summers of fun.

As Leslie Gore sang "It's My Party," Caroline clothed her slim body in linen and silk, the elegant simplicity of a tailored jade-green skirt and long-sleeved ivory blouse. During the Beach Boys' "Good Vibrations," she gave a final vigorous brush to the shoulder-length auburn hair which, with a minimum amount of coercion, framed her face in smooth, symmetrical twin commas of glittering golden-red fire. And while Roy Orbison crooned "Pretty Woman," she applied her makeup, adding only subtle embellishment to the naturally radiant coloring that sent a robust message of good health.

In two weeks Caroline would turn forty. This was how forty looked these days: healthy, energetic, fit. Yes, of course there were tiny wrinkles, proof positive that she had been on the planet for almost four decades, and that during

73

that time there had been laughter and tears, sorrow and joy. And yes, her emerald eyes had a solemn wisdom that hadn't been there when she was younger. But they sparkled too, with a brilliance that was far more confident now, more optimistic, than it had been in years.

During "Unchained Melody," Caroline stood by the window in the second-floor bedroom of her house on Queen Anne Hill and gazed at the wind-tossed splendor of the white-capped indigo water below as she listened to the haunting music—and the even more haunting words.

*I've hungered for your touch.* As always the words stirred a gnawing hunger deep within her. What would it be like to love so much? she wondered. What would it be like to *be* loved with such emotion, such wanting, such need?

It would probably be disastrous, Caroline told herself. Disastrous, and dangerous, and terribly precarious: a floating-on-air ecstasy that could crash without warning, an uncontrollable free fall to anguish, betrayal, and pain.

It was better, safer, to be content. Which Caroline Hawthorne was—at last. She had fought hard for contentment, for tranquillity, and her determined struggle had been more than rewarded, because she was more than content: she was happy. Happy, optimistic about life . . . and realistic about love. Still, as the song ended, she felt a slight wistfulness as she bid adieu to the dangerous but compelling hunger which the lyrics had once again evoked.

As Caroline started to turn off the radio in anticipation of leaving, her hand was stopped by the message of the disk jockey.

"The overnight mishap involving the oil tanker off the Washington coast has left an oil spill that is threatening sea life from Cape Flattery to Kalaloch. Emergency shelters have been set up in both Neah Bay and Moclips and the Coast Guard and other agencies are providing transport for the otters and birds. Volunteers are urgently needed to help remove the oil from the animals' coats when they arrive. For details, call the KBSG hotline at . . ."

Within fifteen minutes Caroline was in her car beginning the three-hour drive to Moclips. The small oceanside resort town was located thirty miles north of Hoquiam. Its local high school, closed for spring break, had been designated as one of the two emergency animal shelters.

Caroline's luncheon meeting at the Seattle Tennis Club hadn't been forgotten, only rescheduled. It was to have been a planning meeting for the Emerald City Ball, the charity event of the season for which Caroline was hostess. But because the ever-efficient Caroline Hawthorne was in charge, everything was already well in hand and the good friend with whom she was supposed to have dined greeted the call to cancel with a laugh of fondness—and no surprise—that Caroline was dashing off to the coast because of a needy cause that was far more urgent than the black-tie ball that was still months away.


"Welcome." The warm greeting came from a rosy-cheeked woman who stood in the foyer of the gymnasium of Moclips High. It was obvious from her demeanor, and the clipboard in her hand, that she was the triage officer for both animals and volunteers. "And thank you."

"I've never done this before," Caroline admitted. "But the person I spoke with at the radio station said they needed any hands—even inexperienced ones."

"Absolutely. Let's see." The woman consulted a sheet of paper. "Why don't we put you with Lawrence? He's set up in the boys' locker room. It's at the end of the gymnasium on your left. Before you go, let me get your name. There will be a room waiting for you—at no charge, of course—at the motel across the street. Even if you don't plan to spend the night, you're welcome to use it to freshen up before you leave."

Caroline had never before volunteered to remove oil from birds and otters, nor had she ever before been in a boys' locker room. As she wove through the maze of wooden benches and steel lockers, she was guided at first by the sound of splashing water, and then, as she neared the showers, by another sound, deep and calm and gentle: the sound of a male voice speaking soft reassurances.

He didn't hear her above the noise of the splashing water, so Caroline had a chance to watch him unobserved. It was a chance she needed, time she needed, because she recognized him at once.

During her journey from the foyer to the boys' locker room, it simply hadn't occurred to her that it would be he. Perhaps it should have. The rosy-cheeked triage officer had given her his first name after all, and from everything Caroline knew about Dr. Lawrence Elliott, it was very logical that the dedicated veterinarian would be here.

Everything she knew about him . . . that was why Caroline needed a few moments to adjust.

Until a month ago, when she had finally put a stop to it once and for all, there had been a relentless campaign among her "friends" to convince her to meet him. It was nothing as frivolous as matchmaking, of course. Caroline's friends knew not to do that to her, and no one would even attempt such frivolity with the man whose life had been so tragic.

No, the reason that Caroline Hawthorne was supposed to meet Dr. Lawrence Elliott was far more important than love.

"He needs to run for public office, Caroline. He needs to run for Senator, or Governor, or maybe even President. If there's anyone who can convince him of that, it's you."

Caroline was undeniably an expert at graciously convincing wealthy philanthropists to donate substantial sums of money to charity and the arts. But from the very beginning she had been skeptical that such expertise would translate into an ability to convince a man like Lawrence Elliott to donate his life to the public good; and as of a month ago, for another reason entirely, she had resolutely told her friends that under no circumstances would she ever even try.

Caroline's reason was Lawrence Elliott himself, what she had learned about him from the *20/20* telecast that had been purposefully aired to coincide with Valentine's Day because of the special meaning—the special horror—that day of romance held for him. She had been at the opera on the night of the telecast, so she had set her VCR and watched it later, more than once.

Caroline had to agree with her friends that Lawrence Elliott should be President, that his character and integrity and vision would be wonderful for the country. But she believed even more strongly that the Vietnam veteran, who had escaped seven years of captivity only to discover that his wife had been murdered and his teenaged daughter had disappeared, deserved his privacy. He had paid far more dearly than any man should have to pay for that unalienable right.

It had been obvious from the telecast how very private he was, how difficult it was for him to publicly reveal his anguished past. But he had done it. He had opened his veins for all to see, because far more important than Lawrence Elliott's privacy was his search still, after seventeen years, for the daughter who had vanished.

It was the search for his long-lost daughter, Caroline knew, that would make him say no to even the most persuasive pleas that he run for office. The girl who had fled in shame at a time when a Lolita was viewed as a villain, not a victim, might never return to her father, no matter what. But that she would hide forever seemed a virtual certainty if her father's address changed from Issaquah, the rural community eighteen miles east of Seattle, to the Governor's mansion . . . or the White House.

Before seeing the *20/20* segment, Caroline had thought it most unlikely that she would ever accede to the wishes of her friends and make the short drive to Issaquah to meet him. And after the telecast, even though something about

77

the anguished dark eyes made her want to meet him, for reasons very far away from politics, Caroline knew that she never would.

But now it was going to happen after all and Caroline felt a quiver of apprehension. What did she, what did anyone, have to say to him? Yes, there had been some sadness in her life. In fact, at the time, when she had been only twenty-one, her sadness at her parents' death had seemed insurmountable, an irrevocable end to the happiness that had virtually defined who she was from the moment of her birth . . . and for the seven years following that immense loss there had been even more shattering blows.

But the death of her beloved parents paled by comparison to the emotional upheaval faced by a young father and husband forced to go to war. And the seven years that Caroline Hawthorne had spent in a bad marriage, in the lap of luxury, was quite trivial when compared to seven years of imprisonment and torture in a faraway jungle.

Caroline had eventually adjusted to the death of her parents, and through sheer determination her broken heart and badly battered spirit had finally overcome the ravages of her loveless marriage; and now, twelve years later, she felt happy again.

But there were no happy endings for Lawrence Elliott. He had escaped seven years of horror only to find a greater horror awaiting him at home. And now, seventeen years later, his heart was still held captive to torment, still imprisoned, still tortured as he pursued his relentless search for his lost and much beloved daughter.

Even the career he had chosen had been because of his missing daughter. "It was our dream," he had quietly answered when the *20/20* reporter asked him why he'd become a veterinarian. He was searching for his child, and he was keeping their dream alive, and . . .

And what words can I possibly find to say to him? Caroline wondered. She didn't know, and he still hadn't realized she was here, so against the backdrop of the splashing water the only words that were spoken were his: soft words, gentle words, spoken with reassuring calm to a terrified seagull.

Caroline heard the gentleness of Lawrence's voice, and she saw the gentleness of the hands that held the bird's trembling body, a necessary but almost apologetic imprisonment as his long lean fingers carefully wiped off layer after layer of thick black oil. The gull was remarkably calm, trembling but not struggling, a wild creature in whom a deep contrary instinct sent the strange message that it was safe in the confines of these alien hands.

I'm not going to have to think of words to say to him, Caroline thought as she watched the expertise of the skilled and gentle hands. He doesn't need my help. I can just withdraw quietly and find someone else to assist.

But Caroline didn't withdraw, because it wasn't entirely true that Lawrence Elliott didn't need help. Thick strands of his dark brown hair had fallen onto his forehead, and despite their slight curl, the strands were long enough to obscure his vision. At least for a moment, Lawrence needed another hand. If she held the bird, or took over with the towel, then he could take a swipe at the unruly strands— another swipe, she amended as she noticed the smudges of oil already at his temple.

Caroline drew a steadying breath, and then, not wanting to startle either man or bird, she said quietly, "Hi."

It probably wasn't possible to startle Lawrence Elliott. The heart and nerves that had suffered unspeakable torture during his seven years of imprisonment, not to mention the horrors of the jungle warfare that had come before, were doubtless scarred beyond further injury, unshockable and numb.

For a moment Caroline wondered if he had even heard her quiet greeting. But he had, she realized. He was merely finishing a gentle pass of the towel on the oily feathers before looking up.

When he did look up, and directly at her, it was Caroline

who was startled. She had believed, from her repeated viewings of the *20/20* telecast, that she knew what he looked like. The show's producers had missed no opportunity to zoom in as close as possible to his solemnly handsome face. It was a remarkable face, a stunning portrait of strength, discipline—and pride. The pride wasn't arrogance. It was the naked dignity of a man who had been caged, but neither tamed nor broken; a very private man who had been stripped of everything that had meaning for him—but had his integrity, his nobility, still.

Caroline had believed that she knew what he looked like; but she had not anticipated the raw sensuality of him, and she had been entirely wrong about the color of his intense dark eyes. On camera, they had looked almost black; but she had assumed that, like his hair, they were actually a very dark brown. In truth Lawrence Elliott's eyes were green, not a brilliant emerald like her own, but the dark green of the most hidden places of a forest. Like those mysterious, primeval places, his eyes held shadowed secrets and ancient wisdoms; and like those places, which became enchanted, magical, when the sun's rays reached through the thick canopy of leaves, there was a golden light in the dark green depths.

The light was there now, and it cast its welcoming, golden, magical warmth for the trembling seagull . . . and for her.

"I'm Caroline. I'm here to help."

"I'm Lawrence, and I'm glad that you're here."

There had been no smiles during the *20/20* telecast, so Caroline was quite unprepared for what a smile would look like on his handsome face; and she was even less prepared for the effect it would have on her. It was only a slight smile, and it was offered without pretense or guile. There was no doubt that he intended it only to be welcoming—not sexy, not seductive—but as it caressed her, Caroline felt a rush of warmth.

*I've hungered for your touch.* The thought shocked her

almost as much as the warmth did . . . until she realized that in fact the two were quite linked. Here was this emotionally strong, privately tormented, and indisputably sexy man who had compelled his long-limbed body to endure seven years in a small cage because of his immense love for his wife. He had endured that imprisonment, and the accompanying torture, because his need to see her again, to touch her and love her was far more powerful than even the most unimaginable of physical pain.

If the lyrics of a song could stir her, it was small wonder that the sight of a man who was the embodiment of a boundless love could do the same. There. Caroline now had a diagnosis for—and control of—the surprising rush of warmth. Good.

Except that now another rush swept through her as the intense green eyes fell from her face to her body. She was still wearing ivory silk and jade-green linen, still dressed for a gourmet lunch at the Tennis Club in Seattle.

"I need to change," she murmured. "I brought jeans and a sweatshirt but the woman in the foyer said there were scrub suits?"

"Yes, scrub suits and smocks. They're on the bench on the other side of the first row of lockers."

The green eyes that had lifted to answer her question returned again to her body. They were appraising, a thoughtful and analytical appraisal, not a hungry and predatory one, but nonetheless the rushes over which Caroline apparently had no control swept through her still.

"The scrub suits are all in men's sizes," Lawrence said finally. "I think small would be right for you."

Given the choices, "small" was indeed the most appropriate size. Admittedly the top was a bit snug over her full breasts, and the drawstring bottoms were somewhat loose over her slender hips, but those imprecisions in fit didn't matter because, before emerging from behind the wall of lockers, Caroline covered the entire blue surgical ensemble with a disposable paper smock.

\* \*. \*

"You must be exhausted."

Lawrence's comment didn't break a silence. There had been words throughout the afternoon and evening, gentle words of reassurance to both Caroline and the oil-cloaked refugees that had been brought to them in a seemingly never-ending stream. "You're okay," he had said softly, sometimes to a trembling creature, sometimes to the hands that were uncertain about the way she was holding a wing or a flipper or a beak. "That's good," he would say, rearranging her gloved hands with his if need be. "There, that's exactly right."

Now, for the first time, his words were purely for her, because now, for the first time, they were truly alone. The final gull of the day was oil-free and had just been taken out of the locker room to be loaded onto the truck bound for the sanctuary where it would remain until the oil had left its home. No more birds or otters were waiting their turn. The process would begin again at daybreak, when it was light enough for the searchers to find more damaged animals, but for now Lawrence and Caroline's work was through.

"You must be exhausted too," Caroline countered quietly.

"I should have asked you hours ago if you wanted to take a break."

"I would have said no," Caroline told the man who had worked with tireless passion to save the animals, greeting each one with welcoming calm, frowning concern for their plight but never, not for a second, frowning because he himself was tired or hungry or thirsty. It had been almost three by the time she had arrived to help him, and she was certain that Lawrence had been there for hours before that, one of the first people called because it was known that he would come right away and stay for as long as he was needed.

"Will you join me for dinner?" Lawrence asked. "Or are you about to leave?"

"No, I'm planning to stay, to help again tomorrow. And yes, I'd like to have dinner with you."

They gathered their street clothes, to be put on after showers at the motel, and left the gym still wearing their scrub suits.

"What a glorious evening," Caroline enthused when they walked outside. The night sky glittered with an infinity of stars, twinkling silver sparkles around a golden moon, and the sea breeze was fragrant and warm. "It's not even cold. In fact, it's almost balmy."

Caroline heard Lawrence take a breath, as if in anticipation of speaking, but when no words came, she looked up at him—and in his dark green eyes, lighted now by moonlight, she saw hesitation . . . and uncertainty . . . and finally a decision.

"You said something about a sweatshirt and jeans," he began quietly. "If you're in the mood, we could have a picnic on the beach."

"I'm definitely in the mood."

"Then I'll have the kitchen prepare some sandwiches and chowder to go."

It was obviously a request of the motel kitchen that Lawrence had made before, during the last oil spill perhaps. But his hesitation before making the suggestion led Caroline to believe that the last time Lawrence Elliott had picnicked late at night on the moonlit beach he had been very much alone.

## ❀ 7 ❀

The beach was all theirs, and it was the most magnificent setting in which Caroline had ever dined. There was music, the soft serenade of lapping waves, and in the midst of the snow-white sand nature had placed a table of sun-bleached driftwood, and in lieu of the flickering light of tapered candles, their faces were illuminated by starlight and moon glow.

"Where do you live, Caroline?"

"In Seattle."

"I'm across the lake, in Issaquah." Lawrence paused, stopped by her frown. "Issaquah is about eighteen miles east of Seattle."

"Yes, I know. I know who you are, Lawrence. I saw the segment on *20/20.*"

Lawrence nodded solemnly, and his eyes darkened with deep, complicated shadows. Caroline couldn't read all the complex messages, but . . . was it actually possible that she saw a flicker of apology, regret that in his desperate search for his lost daughter he had exposed others to the tragedy of his own life?

Yes, she decided. Amid the dark, enigmatic shadows, there truly was apology.

But it was Caroline who offered quietly, "I'm very sorry about what happened to you . . . to your wife and daughter. Have you heard anything since the broadcast?"

"Thank you. No, I haven't heard anything."

His daughter is probably dead, Caroline's friends had offered with somber but sanguine confidence. But, they added, if by some miracle she *is* still alive, unless she herself has been imprisoned in a cage in a faraway jungle for the past seventeen years, she knows he's been looking for her and has chosen not to be found. It's time for him to give up the search.

From the moment Caroline had first seen him on television she had sensed that Lawrence Elliott was not about to stop searching for his missing child. And now she saw with brilliant moonlit clarity the magnitude of that commitment: Lawrence would search for Holly until the day he died.

"So, Caroline, you already know all about me," Lawrence said with quiet finality. "But all I know about you is that you're willing to take time to help injured animals."

Her willingness to help innocent creatures was obviously a very important credential to Lawrence, and Caroline hoped that it was all he knew about her. But what if the people who had been unsuccessful in their own attempts to convince him to run for office had mentioned her name? What if they had implored him to talk to the persuasive Caroline Hawthorne before making his final decision?

"My last name is Hawthorne." Her admission triggered interest, but no wariness, and as relief washed through her, she elaborated further. "My grandfather was Alistair Hawthorne."

Caroline spoke her grandfather's name with loving pride. Alistair Hawthorne had been a remarkable man, a penniless orphan who had created a shipbuilding empire and spent much of his adult life sharing the riches of that empire with his community—as a patron of the arts and a champion of worthy causes. He was a Seattle legend, a revered man whose legacy of generosity was immortalized not only in buildings, museums, and parks throughout the city, but in his company as well. Although Hawthorne Shipyards had been long since sold, the business still maintained both his name and his commitment of loyalty to its employees.

"Does that mean that you're a Seattle native?"

"No. Actually, I was born in Egypt." With a loving smile, Caroline explained, "My father was an archeologist. Not a dilettante, but a true scholar, with pure gold instincts and unrelenting wanderlust. I spent my childhood traveling all over the world with my parents, from dig to dig and treasure to treasure."

"And you loved it."

"Oh, yes. Every day was an adventure. My parents were both incurable romantics. Even the dustiest of digs, with no treasures whatsoever, was wonderful. There was a fairy-tale quality to all of it, too, because when we weren't sleeping in tents in some remote excavation site, we were usually guests in palaces of princes and kings. My father was disarmingly charming—but he was also as highly respected in the scientific community as my grandfather was in business."

"Did your grandfather wish that his son had followed in his footsteps?"

"If so, I never knew it. I think Grandfather was genuinely proud of Dad and quite happy that his money could help fund some of what turned out to be very significant explorations."

"And your mother?"

The sudden thoughtful tilt of Caroline's moonlit auburn head sent a shimmering burst of golden-red fire into the balmy night air, and her smiling emerald eyes gave radiant forewarning that a slightly embarrassing confession was about to be made—an embarrassment of riches. "My mother was a Raleigh, the only child of one of Seattle's other most prominent families. But she was a real trouper. She rolled up her sleeves and dug with the best of them. She loved Dad very much."

"And they both loved you very much."

Caroline gazed thoughtfully at the father whose love for his daughter was the compelling force in his life. "Yes, they did."

We were a team, Caroline thought but did not say. She knew from the *20/20* telecast that Lawrence, Claire, and Holly Elliott had once, too, been a joyous team of love.

"Caroline?" Lawrence asked as he saw her sudden sadness. "Something happened to your parents?"

"Yes," she answered. The sadness Lawrence had seen had been for his shattered family, not for hers, but now her voice grew solemn at the memory of her own loss. "All three of them—my parents and grandfather—were killed in a plane crash in West Africa. It was foggy, and they shouldn't have tried to land . . . but they did."

"Where were you?"

"In New York, in the midst of my junior year at Vassar. My education through high school had been informal but comprehensive thanks to a correspondence program customized just for me by a private school in Switzerland. When I was eighteen, we made a family decision that I should go to college. We knew we'd all feel sadness at being apart, but . . ."

"It was time for an adventure of your own?"

"Yes." Caroline laughed softly. "And it was an adventure. Since I'd spent my entire life in the company of adults, just being with girls my own age was new and exciting."

"And meeting boys your own age?"

"Daunting. Even after three years at Vassar, I was still a very naive twenty-one-year-old, and when my parents and grandfather died, I suddenly became an incredibly wealthy one." A wry smile touched her lips. "Enter Grant Gannon."

"The villain of the piece?"

"Yes—cleverly disguised as a white stallion riding hero. He was five years older than I, already an upwardly mobile Wall Street broker. He'd been dating my roommate at Vassar for six months, but the moment I became an heiress, he turned his full and undivided attention to me. He claimed that he could no longer pretend to want my roommate when from the first moment he had laid eyes on me, he had been infatuated. The chronology is painfully clear in retrospect, as is the obviousness of his plan, but at the time I was completely gullible, totally susceptible. Grant was older and terribly charming, and I was sad and lonely and needy."

Caroline stopped abruptly, and as a rush of heat filled her cheeks, her gaze fell away from his. Here she was telling Lawrence her story of betrayal, her experience with a charming man who had seduced her for her immense fortune. Grant Gannon had been a villain of sorts, but his self-absorbed greediness was absolutely trivial compared to the villainy of Derek Burke, the man who had shot Lawrence in cold blood, leaving him for dead in the jungle, and then seduced Lawrence's sad and lonely wife with stories of his great friendship with her beloved husband.

"Caroline?" His voice was soft, but Lawrence, who had not felt fear for a very long time, was suddenly fearful. *Don't stop talking to me, Caroline.* His voice was a little hoarse, a little urgent, a little raw, as he repeated, "Caroline?"

The emotion in his voice called to her, compelling her to look at him again. And when she did, when her brilliant emerald eyes met his shadowed forest ones, Caroline said quietly, "What happened to me, Lawrence, my marriage to a man who only wanted my money and social position is a trivial cliché, a foolish choice made by a naive girl, hardly worth talking about."

"You mean compared to what happened to Claire, don't you?"

"Yes."

"No." *No, don't withdraw from me!* Lawrence drew a steadying breath. But still he heard the rawness of his voice. "Betrayal is betrayal, Caroline. Loss is loss. Please don't stop talking to me because you think that what happened to me is more significant than what happened to you."

By any measure what had happened to Lawrence Elliott was *far* more significant. But Caroline understood his quietly impassioned plea. He wanted to be allowed to listen to someone else's anguish, however trivial, to be permitted to help, if he could, and not to be forever isolated because there were few tragedies that could compare to his.

Lawrence Elliott's story was an extraordinary one. Indeed, there were few that could rival it. And Lawrence Elliott himself was an extraordinary man. But now he was asking to be allowed to be normal, a sympathetic listener, nothing more.

Since his return from war, had anyone ever shared *their* troubles with Lawrence? Somehow Caroline doubted it, and she felt flattered that he was reaching out to her now.

Flattered . . . and as his dark green eyes banished their shadows, and she saw with breathtaking clarity how much he needed her to talk to him, *hungered* for her to, Caroline felt dangerous rushes of need and hunger too.

"Tell me, Caroline," Lawrence whispered. "Tell me how you felt about what he did to you."

Caroline had never really told anyone before. She had worked through her painful emotions by herself, tapping into a deep core of strength that promised her that with hard work and perseverance she would be better—happy—again.

Now, to the man who knew all about private struggles

and inner strength, she confessed, "I was confused, and very hurt. I didn't understand why Grant's charm and attentiveness simply vanished after we were married. I kept trying to figure out what it was that I'd done wrong, and trying as well to recapture the love I'd believed was real but which, of course, had merely been a charade."

"That must have been terribly difficult for you."

"It was," Caroline admitted. Not even a fraction as difficult as what you've been through, what you're going through still. The thought almost made her stop her trivial story of betrayal. But Lawrence seemed to read her thought, and his dark eyes commanded her to continue. It was a gentle yet hungry command, one that she had no choice but to obey. "The marriage lasted seven years, although it might have lasted forever. I was absolutely determined to make it work and he was quite happy with the way things were. One day, however, a disgruntled mistress—one of many, it turns out—called to regale me with the bitter truths about my husband. I was devastated, but I was also relieved to finally have an answer. It enabled me to act, and when I did, I modeled myself after my father, cutting my losses and moving on. I didn't do it with his boundless spirit of adventure, of course. I wasn't nearly that strong. But nonetheless I got a quick divorce and moved from New York to Seattle, where my parents and I often lighted between expeditions to regroup and make plans. When I made the move, I expected it would just be temporary, while I regrouped . . . but that was twelve years ago."

"Twelve years?" Lawrence echoed as he swiftly did the math. She'd been twenty-one when she married, and the marriage had lasted seven years, and that had been twelve years ago . . . "You're forty?"

"I will be, two weeks from today." She smiled at his surprise, and trembled at what else she saw. He had obviously assumed that she was much younger than he—too young?—and now he knew that their age difference wasn't that great. He seemed relieved at the revelation, *more* than relieved. Somehow she finally managed to embellish lightly, "Forty, and happy again, and optimistic."

And content and settled, she amended silently. At least she *had* been content and settled . . . before the appraising and approving forest-green eyes had stirred dangerous and ravenous longings.

"Because you're so strong."

It took Caroline a moment to realize what Lawrence meant, that she was happy and optimistic again because of some deep inner strength. Yes, she supposed, that was true. But, she decided, perhaps Lawrence needed to hear the most important truth, the *reason* for her strength: the immense gift that had been hers since the moment of her birth.

"I believe that what has helped me survive my various emotional upheavals was that I was so very loved when I was young. My parents' love gave me a confident and irrevocable memory of happiness and hope." Caroline hesitated only a heartbeat before offering quietly, "I think it's the same memory that you and Claire gave to Holly."

A thoughtful frown touched his brow, and after a moment he said very softly, "I hope so, Caroline. I hope so."

Lawrence's mind—and heart—drifted then to their own bittersweet memories; but because the golden light from the springtime moon would not permit privacy, Caroline saw his torment.

The presumptuousness of the golden moon was a bold yet gentle invasion, and its glowing boldness was somehow contagious, for suddenly Caroline heard herself issue a brave command. "Talk. Tell me about you, from the beginning. You were born forty-something years ago . . ."

For several heart-stopping moments Caroline thought

that he wasn't going to answer, that she had crossed way too far over the line, that the invasion of emotional privacy was permissible for trivial betrayals only—not for the kind of betrayal that had befallen him. She feared that she might see anger, or perhaps astonished contempt that she had dared to be as presumptuous as the moon.

Caroline *did* see astonishment, finally, just before Lawrence began to speak. But, she realized, his amazement was with himself, his own need, his own hunger to share at last what he had never shared before.

"I was born forty-eight years ago, in Texas. My mother left when I was five and for the next nine years I wandered with my cowboy father from job to job and rodeo to rodeo. When I was fourteen, he found work on a ranch in Montana. By the following spring he was restless to move on, but school had always mattered to me, and by then I had met Claire, so I stayed behind doing chores on the ranch in return for room and board. Claire and I planned to get married as soon as we graduated from high school, but because it became increasingly important to me to get her away from her stepfather, we got married three months before graduation—on Valentine's Day."

"She was killed on your wedding anniversary?" During the *20/20* telecast, much had been made of the fact that the tragedy had occurred on Valentine's Day, and that there had been blood-red roses scattered amid the crimson carnage. Had the final grim twist, that the murders had occurred on the anniversary of a marriage, been known to the show's producers? No, Caroline decided. Such a gruesome happenstance would certainly have made its way into the script if they had. Lawrence had kept that anguished irony very private—until now. "That's something that hasn't been known, hasn't been discovered, isn't it?"

"Yes."

With the single solemn syllable Lawrence's expression

changed from the gentle memories of love to something very powerful and very dark.

"Lawrence?"

"Derek knew that Valentine's Day was our wedding anniversary." Lawrence's voice was soft, and yet harsh, without even the faintest trace of gentleness. "After he shot me, he took off my wedding ring, read the inscription aloud, and then tossed it into the jungle."

Had the badly wounded young soldier struggled to find the band of gold amid the dense tropical vegetation? Caroline wondered. Believing that he was going to die, had he determined to keep death at bay until he held in his hand the golden symbol of love, of hope, of dreams? Was it the search for his wedding ring that had miraculously kept him alive?

Caroline guessed that Lawrence had been found by the enemy before he himself had found his ring. Otherwise, she thought, he would be wearing the golden band now, married to Claire still, searching for Holly, trying so desperately to save what was left of his small family.

When Lawrence spoke again, his voice was gentle, touched anew by memories of love. "Holly was born on Christmas Day, ten and a half months after we were married. She was very much a planned baby. As I think about it now, it amazes me that Claire and I had the courage to plan to have a family."

"Because neither of you had a happy childhood?"

Lawrence nodded, and what Caroline now recognized as stark rage returned to his eyes. "Derek never touched Holly, Caroline. Claire knew that horror from her own stepfather. She would not have permitted it. Maybe that's why she died . . ."

"Oh, Lawrence."

"I'm sorry."

*"You're* sorry?" Caroline echoed with disbelief. "Why?"

"Because it seems unfair to expose people to my

story," Lawrence said quietly. Then, even more quietly, "But it's my only hope of finding my daughter."

People don't mind being exposed to tragic stories, Caroline thought. In fact, there seems to be a morbid fascination with them.

As if he had read her thoughts, Lawrence explained, "I have very little control over when the telecasts are aired or what the journalists choose to say. From the very beginning, though, I have not let them portray Holly as a seductress."

"Seventeen years ago that must have been a battle."

"Yes." His solemn expression told her that it was a battle he had won . . . always . . . for Holly.

Lawrence was confident that Holly had not been abused by Derek, which meant that her life hadn't been spared because of a perverted notion of love, so . . .

"What, Caroline? What are you wondering?"

"Why Holly was spared? Do you have any idea?"

"Yes," he answered, his voice weighted with the immense heaviness of his own immense guilt. "She was spared because of me . . . because Derek wanted my daughter to watch the horror of what he did to her family and then to spend the rest of her life reliving that horror. During the telecast, they gave as his motive that he sensed—correctly—that I was suspicious that he was smuggling drugs. But it went deeper than that. Derek hated me, Caroline, a twisted vengeful hatred. He wanted us to be friends, but from the moment we met there were things about him that worried me."

"You were right."

"Yes . . . but I had no idea how pathologic he really was, how dangerous."

"How could you have known that, Lawrence?" Even before her question was finished, Caroline saw the silent answer in guilt-laden eyes. Lawrence obviously believed that he *should* have known, despite his own youth and the fact that he himself was caught in the midst of the craziness of war; and even after he had been left for dead in the jungle, he should have found a way to escape sooner to rescue his wife and daughter from Derek's lethal madness. That was Lawrence's answer. But, with quiet confidence, Caroline offered an answer of her own.

"You couldn't have known. You *couldn't* have."

Caroline saw gratitude for her words; but it was abundantly clear that even an infinity of such words would not erase the sense of responsibility Lawrence felt.

As they had talked, the world around them had changed, as if angered, too, by what had happened on that long-ago Valentine's Day. The waves that serenaded them had now become harsh, crashing, and the sea breeze that had been so balmy now held an unmistakable chill.

But the moon glowed brightly still. It hadn't lost a single carat of its golden boldness . . . and neither had Caroline. What Lawrence had said to the television cameras about his seven years of captivity had made her want to scream, and to weep; but she had sensed then, and she knew now, that whatever tortures he had revealed on the telecast had been merely the tip of the iceberg of horror, just enough to appease the bloodlust that drew viewers to the show. He hadn't wanted to shock, nor to sensationalize his own ordeal. He had only wanted to find his daughter.

Now softly, boldly, Caroline asked, "You told them very little about what really happened in the prisoner of war camp, didn't you?"

"What happened to me in Vietnam is nothing compared to what happened to my thirteen-year-old daughter on that Valentine's night."

Caroline nodded solemnly, and then waited. She didn't want to hear more about the torture, she had no bloodlust; and yet, if Lawrence wanted, needed, to speak those words aloud she would listen forever.

But Lawrence Elliott said nothing, nor did she see even the slightest hint of a silent debate.

Eventually, Caroline offered gently, "It's all right that the show was telecast on Valentine's Day, Lawrence. It was a Valentine, a most loving Valentine, from you to Holly."

"Thank you."

Caroline Hawthorne, champion of worthy causes, and heiress to many fortunes, and welcomed guest of emperors and presidents and kings and queens, gazed thoughtfully at the extraordinary man who sat across from her as she engaged in her own silent debate.

Finally she simply said, "Is there something I can do, Lawrence? I have contacts and . . ."

Somehow she couldn't say money. She just let him read it in her eyes.

And he wasn't offended. "I have contacts and money too, Caroline. The government has been extremely cooperative, and there was a remarkable amount of money in Derek's bank accounts when he died. In all likelihood he was still smuggling drugs, but since there was no actual proof that the money had been illegally obtained, the decision was made that I could use it in my search for Holly. I've spent a few fortunes in that search . . . and there's still plenty left." Lawrence frowned, and then confessed, "I can't help worrying that there's some obvious avenue I've missed, but I have no idea what it is. In addition to all the advertisements I've placed, and all the coverage in the media, and all the private investigators, her fingerprints are on file; and for the past seventeen years, both the Social Security and passport offices have routinely checked for applications made using her own birth certificate, or Claire's, or the one that belonged to her half-sister who died."

"It's difficult to envision what more you could do."

Caroline's words were honest, and they were meant to reassure, but they only forced Lawrence to speak even more painful truths. "I know there are those who believe that Holly was to blame for what happened, and that she's chosen to stay hidden because of that. But they're a small minority. Most people believe that she's dead." His anguished dark green eyes held hers, and they wouldn't let go, as he asked very softly, "What do you believe, Caroline?"

"I believe that you and Claire gave Holly a foundation of love and happiness. That's all you can give a child, Lawrence, and it's the greatest gift. I don't believe that she was in any way to blame for what happened, but . . ."

"But?"

She drew a steadying breath. "But it's just very hard to imagine that in all these years she hasn't realized that you've been searching for her. Especially in the beginning, when you first returned from Vietnam, the story was everywhere."

"You remember it from then?"

"Yes." Caroline remembered the headlines. They were difficult to miss. But she had been so preoccupied with her own problems—her loveless marriage—that she hadn't read all the grim details.

"So," Lawrence said slowly, "you think that Holly must be dead."

"I . . ." Yes, she thought apologetically. Her eyes didn't leave his, and she was certain that he must have read her thought. But his reaction was one of gentleness, not anger. Lawrence Elliott was a man who did not regard honesty as betrayal, and he was also a man who could face the truth. He had, after all, faced the most horrifying truths and had not been broken. Now he accepted without condemnation her belief that Holly had died, even though it was a belief which he obviously did not share. "What do you think, Lawrence?"

"It's not a thought, it's just a feeling. I *feel* that she's alive." He paused, debating for a moment, before elaborating, "But she's just barely alive, Caroline, just like I was only barely alive when I was in prison. She's in some sort of prison too, removed from the world but still in it." He stopped abruptly. "You must think I'm crazy."

"No." *I think you're wonderful.* Caroline didn't attempt to hide the thought. Indeed, had she not seen his surprise, proof-positive that he had read her bold thought correctly, she would have spoken the words aloud.

Hours before, Caroline had decided that it was probably impossible to startle Lawrence Elliott. But now she had. And, as she watched Lawrence adjust to the surprise, she saw the faintest whisper of a smile. It was a stunning smile, a little uncertain, but definitely flattered; unwittingly sexy . . . and disappointingly fleeting.

In an instant, the smile was gone. But the softness in his solemn voice when he spoke again, wanting to confide even more, made her heart race. "There's something else. By the time I returned from Vietnam the police had put everything that was in the house in boxes. One of them contained the photo album that Claire had made of our life, our family, before Derek. Five very special photographs had been removed, but the album itself was left behind."

"You think Holly took the photographs with her."

"Yes, and I also think she took Claire's wedding dress." Lawrence paused. And then to the woman who with silent yet dazzling eloquence had told him that she did not believe him to be crazy, he said, "There was no reason for Holly to believe that I was still alive, but there was no one else in the world for whom the album would have had meaning. It's as if she left it for me, to let me know that she hadn't forgotten the wonderful memories."

"She hadn't forgotten," Caroline affirmed swiftly. It was then, as she uttered that reassurance, that Caroline realized what had happened to their moonlit, seaswept world. The waves had gentled once again, singing anew; and the balmy warmth had returned to the caressing breeze; and the moonbeams fairly danced on the snow-white sand. After a reverent moment, she amended with soft confidence, "She hasn't forgotten, Lawrence. She *hasn't.*"

It was almost one when they said goodnight at the door of Caroline's motel room. They would see each other again, shortly after dawn, when the first rescued creatures of the morning would begin to reach the shelter.

But when Caroline arrived at the gymnasium, before any animals and before most of the other volunteers, she was greeted with the news that Lawrence was gone. He had been flown by helicopter directly to one of the Coast Guard boats. He was going to spend the day aboard the boat, caring for the animals that were so critically damaged that without immediate intervention they would not survive the journey to Moclips or Neah Bay.

Caroline fought her disappointment with a truth that would enable her dangerously soaring heart to land safely back on contentment. It was for the best, she told herself. In the golden enchantment of the presumptuous springtime moon she and Lawrence Elliott had undoubtedly already said all the words there were to say.

## ✿ 8 ✿

Nick and his truck filled with roses arrived at Raven's Brentwood bungalow at seven-thirty. Ten minutes later a truck from a Santa Monica nursery arrived with even more roses and all the lilacs. By eight-ten the plants from both trucks had been unloaded and the one from the nursery had rumbled away.

Raven hadn't gone outside to greet Nick when he first arrived, and she still had one more phone call to make before joining him for the day; but before making that call she gazed for a long thoughtful moment at the luxuriantly blooming flowers that were strewn on her emerald lawn.

It was as if someone had sent her the world's most extravagant bouquet, a fragrant tableau of ivory, pink, lavender, and cream. But that isn't what happened, Raven reminded herself sternly. You sent this beautiful pastel bouquet to yourself, and it is by far the most romantic gift of flowers that you've ever received.

Raven *had* received flowers in her lifetime, beginning at age thirteen, when a black orchid had appeared on her desk at school. It was the morning after she had lost—given—her virginity to Blane Calhoun. Her young heart had soared with hope when she had seen the rare and exotic flower. Surely it was a symbol of what Blane considered her to be: a rare and exotic black-haired flower who had blossomed from girlhood to womanhood just for him.

But the black flowers that made many encore appearances over the next few years, each time she gave herself to yet another golden heir, were simply gravestones of hope, symbols of shame and death, not of romance and love. She never knew if the raven-black orchids were sent by her ardent and then cruel lovers, or by their cruel and spiteful girlfriends; but despite the immense pain she felt every time one appeared on her desk at school, proof of betrayal again, Raven always pinned the flowers to her blouse and wore them proudly, just as she would have proudly worn a corsage to any of the dances to which she was never invited.

The black orchids given to the teenaged Raven by the heirs and heiresses who had been her classmates at Meadow Academy were the only flowers she was ever to receive. Later, when she was a grown woman and the object of almost obsessive desires of rich and powerful men, she had been lavished with glittering jewels, not delicate bouquets. Flowers would have meant far more to her. But something about her must have sent the signal that she was not the flower type. Because she herself seemed more diamond than rose? More fire-brilliant ice than soft, fragile beauty?

No man had ever sent her roses. No, Raven realized suddenly, that wasn't true. Jason Cole had sent her two dozen peach and cream roses as a thank-you for the four-picture deal she had negotiated for him with Gold Star.

Now she was conspiring to undermine the only man on earth who had ever thought her worthy of roses. Not undermine, Raven told herself as she walked resolutely toward the phone. She was simply going to help Lauren

Sinclair guide Jason to the important truth that *Gifts of Love* would be a far better movie if the happy ending was preserved as written.

Raven had been so moved by the book that she had bought all the other Lauren Sinclair novels she could find. She'd already read two more, and even though the plots were quite different the hopeful message, the wondrous promise, was the same: it was possible to be loved for who you really were, after all the shameful secrets were revealed, and all the dark shadows were exposed, and all the masks and disguises were cast away.

With every word she read, Raven felt ever closer to the brilliant author, and ever more surprised by the memory of the voice that had seemed so fragile and so wary. Given Lauren Sinclair's wondrous message of hope and love, and the confidence with which that message was conveyed in her books, her voice should have been brimming with happiness and joy.

As Raven dialed the number in Kodiak she hoped she would hear the expected joy—without a hint of sleepiness.

The phone was answered on the first ring, a wide-awake greeting, but a soft, surprised one. "Hello?"

"It's Raven Winter. I hope I didn't wake you."

"You didn't. I've been working for hours."

"Good. Since the last time we spoke, I've learned from Barbara Randall that Lauren Sinclair is a pseudonym and that your real name is Marilyn Pierce. Barbara wasn't sure which name you prefer."

"It really doesn't matter . . . either name is fine," Holly murmured distractedly. "Is there a problem, Raven?"

"No, not at all. I was just calling to touch base with you about your plans for next week, to offer to meet you at the airport and show you around Los Angeles if you'd like."

"That's so kind of you."

"Do you know yet when you'll be arriving?"

"No." It was a necessary lie. Holly was grateful for Raven's offer, but she knew that she needed to concentrate every ounce of energy on preparing for the meeting with Jason Cole. She needed to find whatever inner peace she could and to marshal whatever inner strength and courage she had. "I'm not exactly sure when, sometime Sunday of course, but it may be quite late. I have a deadline that I'm trying to meet, so please don't worry about me."

"Are you sure?" Raven asked, worrying anyway, because once again she heard fear in the faraway voice that should have been so fearless. "Why don't I plan to pick you up Monday morning? Do you know where you'll be staying?"

"No, not yet . . . and no, thank you. I have friends—acquaintances—in Los Angeles, and I may be staying with them, or in a hotel. I know the meeting is a week from today, and I must sound terribly disorganized." Holly's gaze drifted from the already purchased airline tickets on her desk to the maps and guide books of Los Angeles that lay on the floor. She wasn't disorganized at all. She was arriving in Los Angeles on Saturday afternoon. From the airport she would take a taxi, the first of her life, to the Hotel Bel-Air. The descriptions of the garden bungalows overlooking the ponds of swans had sounded idyllic, and the hotel's location seemed ideal. According to her careful measurements, it was only three miles from Gold Star Studios' address in the fourteen-hundred block of South Sepulveda in West L.A. There were always waiting taxis at the hotel, she had been assured when she called, and limousines too, both of which could be reserved in advance. "I will be organized, Raven, and I will be at Jason Cole's office at noon a week from today."

"I'm sure you will, but both my home and office numbers are listed, so please don't hesitate to call. Okay?"

"Yes. Thank you."

It was time to say goodbye to the wary voice, but Raven had a message of hope of her own to deliver. "I wanted you to know that I've just read *Gifts of Love*. It was really wonderful and I absolutely agree with you that the ending should not be changed."

"Will you tell Jason that?"

"Of course I will," Raven promised. "We both will."

After saying goodbye to Lauren Sinclair, Raven faced the implications of the conversation that had just transpired. She wasn't going to be spending this weekend hostessing the gifted author after all; which meant that except for her own lack of courage she had no reason to cancel the all-important trip to Chicago. She still had reservations for the suite at the Fairmont. But there was no Michael, there was no one, unless . . .

"Good morning."

"Good morning," Nick echoed, standing as he turned away from the pink and white splendor of Garden Party to the splendor of flushed pink cheeks and snow-white skin. Her midnight black hair was loosely captured in slightly lopsided ponytail, and beneath a large crimson sweatshirt she wore faded, baggy, generic jeans. His steel gray eyes glinted their approval and their welcome. "You decided to play hooky after all."

"Yes."

As she shrugged, Nick saw what else she wore: her brilliant but uncertain sapphire eyes.

"I'm glad," he said. "How are your palms?"

"Much better, thanks." Raven offered for his inspection the now unbandaged and definitely healing flesh of her graceful hands.

"They are better," Nick agreed. "You should have no trouble whatsoever pointing to where a given rose or lilac should be planted." He saw the flicker of worry, as if she wasn't truly comfortable playing the role of the grand duchess, and assured her softly, "That's your job today, Raven. You point and I plant."

"Well . . . these palms are now also completely capable of making—and pouring—coffee. In fact, they've already made some. Would you like a mug?"

"Sure. I like your jeans, by the way."

"Thanks, so do I."

"Old friends?"

"Yes. I guess. I've had them since high school." There it was, an effortless segue. All she had to do now was say, Speaking of high school . . .

Later, Raven promised herself. I will ask him—later.


It wasn't until much later, after all the plants had been put into the rich dark soil and her house was encircled by a breathtaking bounty of color and fragrance, that she found the courage to ask. She *had* to find the courage then because in a few moments he would have been gone forever.

Raven had been rehearsing various ways of asking him all day, but when the words finally came, they were entirely different from anything she had practiced.

"Do you dance?"

"Dance?"

"Yes, you know . . ." Raven faltered, the coherency of her thoughts suddenly sabotaged by his intense—and intensely interested—dark gray eyes.

"I can hold my own." The truth was that he was a magnificent dancer, at least that's what he'd been told many times by many women. He danced with the same unhurried sensuality, the same deep instinct for rhythm, that made him such a wonderful lover. Nick gazed at her lovely face, framed in soft tendrils of black silk and flushed pink with uncertainty, and asked softly, "Are you asking me to dance with you, Raven?"

*It's as if he's asking me to make love with him.*

Raven's stunning—and amazingly joyous—thought was swiftly shattered. How do *you* know? an icy voice taunted. True, you may see smoldering desire in the sensuous steel. In fact you probably do. But no man, not ever, has asked you to make love with him with such gentleness. *And no man ever will.*

Raven looked away, needed to, and focused on a white lilac, pure and lacy and brave.

"Yes," she confessed, speaking to the lilac. "I guess I am asking you to dance with me. Not now, of course, but this Saturday night."

Nick moved, blocking the line of sight between the apprehensive blue eyes and the delicate white lilac. When he had her full attention, he said quietly, "I accept."

"It's a formal dance. Black-tie. You'd have to rent a tuxedo, which I'd pay for, of course."

Nick had a tuxedo: in fact, he had two, both of them coal-black, timelessly elegant, and impeccably tailored. "I'll take care of the tuxedo rental."

Nick fought a rush of annoyance as he saw Raven's surprise, and then her worry. Was she wondering if—no matter who paid for the rental—she should at least designate the store? One in Beverly Hills, perhaps, at which she could leave explicit instructions in advance about precisely what kind of evening wear he was to be given?

Nick's annoyance was swiftly vanquished by something far more important: he wanted to dance with her. Then . . . and now. "I insist. I'll get something very traditional—black, conservative, not a ruffle anywhere."

When her worry didn't vanish at his assurance, Nick realized that its source was something more than the Snow White Shark's concern that Nick the Gardener might not select the most appropriate apparel for a black-tie affair. Her worry was something else entirely, something his lovely Snow White had yet to tell him. "What, Raven?"

"Well, the dance is in Chicago. It's a dinner dance, and

it begins at eight Saturday night, so we'd need to leave Los Angeles early that morning. I'd like to take the six-thirty flight to be sure that we're there in time." Raven paused for a necessary breath, and to give him a chance to say no before she forged even further into foolishness.

"And we'd fly back when?"

"Whenever you want. Saturday night is the most important, but there's also a luncheon buffet on Sunday. If we stayed for that, it would mean catching the four o'-clock flight, which would get us back to LAX at about seven."

Nick nodded, as if considering what she'd told him about the flight times. But in truth he was envisioning another schedule entirely. Being away on this particular Saturday would pose no problem at all. The girls were going to a birthday party that afternoon and a slumber party that evening. And as for Sunday? Deandra had called, claiming she wanted to see her daughters all day, up to and including dinner. Which meant that being away on Sunday would be no problem, either, as long as he was home in time to greet the girls when they returned from the unsettling hours spent with their mother.

Now it was Raven's turn to see worry, and when she did, she assured him swiftly, "I'd pay for all the expenses, of course, and since being away for the weekend would mean there would be jobs you would miss, I'd compensate you for them as well."

"Don't worry about that." If the charade of Nick the Gardener not Nick the CEO was to continue, and it had to, then he would have to let her pay for the expenses. But he was reluctant to let her pay for more. "I can easily make up the work."

"Yes, but I'd feel better if I paid you," she countered quietly. "Really."

"Okay," Nick agreed with matching quiet.

It was her uncertainty that made him accede to her wishes without further protest. This was not, Nick knew, a request made by the Snow White Shark. She was undoubtedly far more forceful, and far more confident, when she negotiated multimillion-dollar deals.

This request was made by Snow White, and it was laced with vulnerability.

Before speaking again, Nick thought for a moment about the arrangement to which he had just agreed. Quite obviously, this trip to Chicago was very important to her. And, quite obviously—and correctly—she had concluded that he would look more than acceptable in a tuxedo.

So he, Nicholas Gault, was being hired because of his good looks, because he would make a stunning escort for the stunningly beautiful woman who should not have needed to pay for such a service . . . but who was going to pay him, a virtual stranger, because she had no one else to ask.

"What's the occasion, Raven?"

"My fifteen-year high school reunion."

"Did you go to your tenth?"

"No. I haven't seen or spoken to any of my classmates since graduation."

But for some reason she needed to see them now, after all these years, and she didn't have the confidence to go alone, and Michael Andrews was no longer interested in being with her, so she had chosen him, because this woman who was an expert on appearances knew he would look rich and elegant and successful in a black silk tuxedo.

Was that the only reason she was asking him? Nick wondered. Because of appearances? Because she sensed how dazzling they would look together?

"Will we be sharing a hotel room?"

"A two-bedroom suite."

"I think you'd better tell me who you want me to be."

Nick assumed that she would have a ready answer for that. In fact, it seemed likely that she might even have come up with a disguise that was who he really was: a landscape architect who had designed some of the world's greatest gardens.

But Raven didn't have a ready answer. She hadn't already scripted a role for him to practice to perfection.

And when she finally spoke, her hesitant words truly stunned him. "I guess, if you can, I'd like you to pretend that you care about me."

"That we're lovers?"

"Yes."

"Okay," Nick agreed. Then, to the woman who seemed to believe that she had just made a request that would be virtually impossible to honor, he repeated very softly, very gently, "Okay, Raven. I can do that."

## ❧ *9* ❧

Nick had looked forward to the flight to Chicago with Raven, to conversations made private by the sound of engines and made festive by the champagne that flowed so freely in the first-class cabin.

But from the moment the DC-10 lifted off the tarmac in Los Angeles, Raven was very far away. And it wasn't merely that she was lost in the romance of Lauren Sinclair's *Happily Ever After*. Yes, she held the book in her white—and virtually healed—hands; and yes, her eyes were cast downward toward the page. But she had been gazing at the same page since take-off and it was abundantly obvious from the anguish Nick saw that her thoughts had nothing to do with the hopeful story of love.

Raven was in another place altogether, a real not fictional place of hopelessness and despair; and even though Nick didn't want her to be there, didn't want for her the sadness he saw on her beautiful face, something in the resolute set of her snow-white jaw sent the clear message that it was where she needed to be.

For some reason Raven Winter needed to take the clearly less-than-sentimental journey into her past.

But she needed a companion for that journey, didn't she?

No, Nick decided. At least she did not need him.

Raven had made that crystal clear thirty minutes earlier when he had gently intruded with a question that might logically have invited him into her past. Gesturing to the initials engraved in gold on her purse—RWW—he had asked, "What does the middle 'W' stand for?"

Her initial answer had been a frown, and Nick had realized then that it was something she didn't usually reveal.

Tell me, he had commanded silently. Trust me.

Raven had followed part of his command. She had told him. But the quiet confession had been one of resignation, of pain, not of trust.

"It stands for Willow."

"Is that a family name?"

"No," she had answered before returning to her solitary journey. "It's just a name."


Just a name. But long ago, for Raven, it had been a most enchanted name. Long before she actually knew what it meant to be conceived, her mother had told her the magical setting of her own conception: a springtime meadow in upstate New York, beneath a massive willow tree, as a raven soared in the brilliant blue sky overhead.

As a little girl Raven had loved the story and the mystical way in which Sheila Winter had recounted it. As a little girl she had loved being Raven Willow. But as she grew older, the names that had once seemed so enchanted were used against her, cruel taunts from cruel children who found clever ways of making the once-beloved names as sad and ugly as the little girl to whom they belonged.

Ravens were such creepy birds, they mocked with unconcealed disdain. Black, ugly birds of death. And willows were ugly too, and *so* droopy. If *their* parents had given *them* such horrible names—a death-bird and a despondent tree—they would cry and cry and cry.

"Weep, Willow!" the cruel children commanded with glee. "Weep for us, Vulture, weep, *weep!*"

Raven's young heart had wept at their merciless taunts, and anguished tears had spilled from her eyes. But she had hidden her tears from her classmates, and after revealing them once to her mother, she had thereafter kept them carefully hidden from Sheila as well.

As Raven grew older, her mother's memory of her conception became more vague and far less enchanted. Maybe there had been a springtime meadow, and a willow tree, and maybe a raven as black as her hair had flown across a sky the color of her eyes. But maybe the entire image had always been merely an hallucination, a vivid tableau painted in Sheila Winter's mind by the LSD she had taken almost daily during her pregnancy.

Raven Willow Winter was an acid baby. That, and that alone, was the only certainty. It was a truth that Raven didn't question. She had no doubt that very early on in her life a harsh and corrosive acid had found its way deep inside her.

The acid burned, *how it burned.* It seared the most fragile and delicate places within her, scarring and leaving old and barren the places that should have been young and filled with hope. Thick layers of ice eventually formed over the areas of greatest destruction. Raven would have welcomed the glacial coolness, the relentless numbness, but the ice didn't quell the fires beneath. The acid was there still, corrosive still, flaming still, burrowing ever deeper into her badly damaged heart.

Deep inside the acid baby the fiery pain blazed still . . . even though what the world saw was only the austere frigidity of ice.

Raven was an acid baby, and Sheila was a flower child, and even though when the mood struck her, Sheila could conjure a vivid image of a willow tree and a raven, she had no memory of, nor would she bother to create, an image of Raven's father. So Raven created her own.

After careful study of the Native American tribes of upstate New York, she decided that he was an Iroquois, proud, noble, and brave. It was he who had marveled at the splendor of the willow and the raven and the sky. It was he who had given her the enchanted name. Raven had inherited her midnight black hair from him as well, and her elegantly sculpted cheekbones, and her solemn reverence for nature.

And her snow-white skin? It was that which eventually forced her to abandon the wonderful myth that she was part Iroquois. Her real father had undoubtedly shared with all her mother's lovers the unhealthy pallor that came from a wanton life of sex and drugs.

When Raven was nine, she and her mother and Sheila's latest boyfriend moved from New York to Chicago. The boyfriend vanished swiftly, as Sheila's men always did, but by then Sheila had heard about Lake Michigan's glittering Gold Coast and the possibility of work in the stately lakeside mansions north of the city.

At first, Sheila worked for a maid service, cleaning a variety of homes, alert always for better—and easier—opportunities. When such a golden opportunity presented itself, Sheila promptly made the most of it. The live-in cook at Thornwood estate was retiring to Florida, thus vacating not only the wonderful job but the gatehouse on the estate's spacious grounds in which she lived.

Sheila portrayed herself as an excellent cook, cleverly covering the truth of her inexperience by suggesting that Thornwood's retiring cook show her precisely how to prepare the Wainwright family's favorite meals. The cook showed both mother and daughter, and at last Sheila discovered a good use for her silent and burdensome child. Raven's photographic memory recorded the cook's every instruction; and it was Raven, not Sheila, who prepared meals, the old favorites as well as an expanded repertoire of gourmet offerings she learned from reading cookbooks. The ruse worked beautifully, in large measure because there were other servants, ones dressed in crisp black-and-white uniforms, who actually served the food.

Raven didn't mind doing the cooking. It made her feel wanted—a little wanted—by the mother who had so clearly never wanted her before; and it gave them a wonderful place to live. Thornwood's gatehouse felt like a mansion to Raven, and it was located in a secluded corner of landscaped grounds that stretched like a plush emerald carpet toward the sparkling sapphire lake. There were willows on the parklike grounds. To Raven, the immense lacy trees possessed a proud, majestic beauty.

And what of Lake Meadow itself, the north shore hamlet that was to be their new home? It was a place of elegance and charm, of gracious, country living; and its wealthy citizens, most of them, were known for their compassion.

Raven's new life might have been perfect, if only she hadn't been so terribly bright. When the principal at the public school she attended in Chicago learned of her impending move to Lake Meadow, he promptly placed a call to the headmaster at Meadow Academy. If ever the small, private school was going to make good on its pledge to—someday—offer its excellent educational opportunities to a bright but economically disadvantaged child, now was the time . . . and Raven Winter was that child.

Raven became a student at "the Meadow." But she was not welcomed by her rich and privileged classmates. The cruel and relentless crusade against Raven was led by Victoria Wainwright, who lived with her parents at Thornwood, and for whom, every day, Raven prepared gourmet meals. Victoria's dislike of Raven was immediate and impassioned. By some sixth sense, perhaps, the spoiled heiress knew that one day she would truly have a reason for such hatred.

Because Victoria ruled the class—at least its female half—in her fierce campaign against Raven, she had many allies, an entire entourage of admiring and supportive friends. It was *beyond* impertinence for the illegitimate daughter of a servant to presume to mingle with *them,* Victoria proclaimed to those friends. The scrawny waif was a disgrace to them all: her tattered clothes; the Vaseline that coated her thin, bare legs when the winter wind off the lake was chillingly—killingly—cold; and, of course, her ridiculous name.

The rich girls in Raven's class at the Meadow had exotic names: Chelsea and Brittany, and Caitlin and Taylor, and there was even one girl who was named for a bird: Ptarmigan. They wore their names the same way that they wore their designer clothes, with pride and grace. Raven Willow Winter tried to wear her own exotic name with such proud grace; but Victoria and her friends wouldn't permit it. It was an ugly name, they taunted, as ugly as her threadbare clothes, her pale, skinny face, and her Vaseline-covered legs.

Raven was as white as snow, and very thin, and her solemn blue eyes were haunted and hopeless. She seemed destined to be an object of ridicule forever . . . but sometime during her twelfth summer Raven Willow Winter became beautiful. She might not have noticed the transformation, she rarely looked at herself, but its effect was dramatically mirrored in the astonished eyes of her classmates and reflected in the words they now spoke to her.

The taunts of the teenaged girls became even more vicious than before, and now they had a sexual edge to them. Raven the scrawny little girl had been a bird of death, a weeping witch, a bedraggled and scraggly tree. But Raven the bewitchingly beautiful young woman was a tramp, a slut, a *whore,* just like her mother.

And the boys? They had never been involved in the

crusade against Raven, they couldn't be bothered, but they were teenagers now, boys becoming men, and the young heirs stared, and wanted, and desired . . . and because for the first time in her life Raven saw what looked like caring, she allowed them to touch.

She was thirteen when she lost her virginity. Blane Calhoun was sixteen and to Raven it was not a loss but a joyous gift of love. And there would be more gifts for Blane, she vowed, wondrous gifts, because even then, even at thirteen, Raven wanted a baby.

Blane wove in and out of her life for the next five years, a golden thread of torment and pain. He wanted her beautiful body, just her body, not her, never her. He took her cruelly, and left her cruelly, and returned to her cruelly whenever he wanted her again. There were other boys as well, lots of them, and Raven gave herself to them all, hoping for love, hoping for a baby—and getting neither.

What did she expect? She was an acid baby, after all, irrevocably damaged from the moment of her not-so-magical conception. The fires blazed deep inside her still, but all that anyone saw—all that anyone wanted—was the ice sculpture perfection of her snow-white body. She was desired desperately; but when the desires had been satisfied her lovers vanished swiftly.

There was no love for Raven Willow Winter, and there was no baby. The acid scars had made a barren tundra of her womb, a cold and ravaged place where no new life could ever possibly survive.

Raven's bright mind and the sanctuary she found in her schoolwork served her well. Three months before graduation from Meadow Academy, she was accepted on full scholarship to UCLA. It was her first choice, and she was resolute in her decision despite pressure from the headmaster, who wanted the school's fabulously successful experiment to accept comparable offers of full scholarship support from Radcliffe, Vassar, or Yale.

But ever since she had carefully studied its catalog, UCLA had become a dream for Raven. It was warm there and free and easy. It wouldn't matter that she didn't have nylons. Her bare legs would never freeze. There was a dress code at Meadow Academy: no pants, ever, for the girls. But from the photographs in UCLA's catalog, Raven saw that even jeans were allowed.

She could wear her jeans, and she would make a sundress, and there would be so many students at UCLA, from such diverse backgrounds, that she would simply blend in, wouldn't she? She would be left alone to study in peace . . . and maybe, just maybe, among all those students there might be someone who would like her, someone who might even become her friend.

Raven planned to leave for Los Angeles the day after graduation. That goal, that golden light at the end of the dark tunnel of her life, gave her great hope. She could endure anything for three months, she told herself. She couldn't be hurt any more than she had already been.

But she was wrong. Six weeks before graduation, she arrived home from school to discover Sheila in the midst of packing. She and her current boyfriend were leaving Illinois, she told Raven. Sheila Winter didn't ask her daughter to accompany them, and she was extremely vague about where they were going, and she made no mention whatsoever of contacting Raven in the future. Sheila did offer a small motherly assurance: Mrs. Wainwright knew that Raven could handle the cooking for the family and had even graciously agreed to let Raven live in the gatehouse until graduation.

At midnight, seven hours after Sheila left, Raven was awakened by a loud knock. Her immediate thought was that it would be Blane. He was a student at Northwestern now, and for the past two years he and Victoria had been going steady. But often, after he had bid a chaste goodnight to his heiress girlfriend, he stopped by for more, much more, from Raven.

Raven moved toward the door with self-destructive resignation. She knew she would say yes to Blane, and she knew that afterward her heart would hurt again. But as she neared the door, that much abused heart suddenly soared with hope. It would be Sheila, not Blane. She would be returning, if only for a moment, because she had forgotten to hug her daughter goodbye, and to tell her that she loved her, and to figure out a way that they would keep in touch—always.

But the face at the door was neither the handsome visage of Blane Calhoun nor the drug- and tobacco-ravaged face of Sheila Winter. The silky smooth skin over the beautiful patrician bones belonged to Patrice Wainwright, Victoria's mother. The elegant face was very grim, so grim that Raven was suddenly gripped by the fear that she was bringing tragic news about her own mother, a car crash perhaps . . .

That fear was instantly and thankfully removed when Patrice Wainwright asked to speak with Sheila.

"She's already gone."

"Gone?"

"Yes." Patrice Wainwright's obvious surprise at the news sent an ominous warning to Raven: what she was about to learn was something she did not want to know. Continuing hurriedly, as if saying the words would make them true, she said, "She told you that she was leaving and that I would do the cooking for the next six weeks. I know how to cook. She told you that too."

Before Raven's eyes the amazed patrician face transformed to arch disdain and unspeakable contempt. It was an expression of extreme disgust that Raven knew very well. Victoria had worn the same look, many times, just for her.

"The only thing your mother ever told me about you, Raven, is how very troubled you are."

"Troubled?" As Raven echoed the word her heart quivered with delicate hope. Had her mother known about her torment? Had she cared?

"I know all about your drug abuse, and your nymphomania, and I also know that you are a thief."

For a stunned moment Raven was unable to speak. She had never used drugs, not ever; and although she had had sex many times, it had never been pleasurable for her, only a desperate attempt to be loved; and . . . "My mother told you that I was a thief?"

"Don't try to deny it. I know that you have stolen money from the house many times and I know why—to buy drugs and at least once to pay for an abortion."

No! Raven's heart screamed at the terrible accusations. It was her mother who had bought drugs . . . and it was her mother who had had an abortion. Raven hadn't learned about it until after it was over. And then, when she had learned that there had been for a while the wonderful hope of a little sister or brother, she had pleaded softly to Sheila, Why, why, why? Sheila had answered with astonished silence, embellished with a harsh look that told Raven with shattering clarity that her mother wished she had made the same decision about her.

"Until now I've overlooked what you've done. Your mother has served us well and I have great compassion for what a struggle it has been for her to deal with you. But Raven, I cannot and will not overlook the theft of three thousand dollars. Return the money to me now or I will call the police."

"But I don't have it!"

"I don't believe you." Patrice began to move toward the phone. "I had hoped that we could resolve this quietly, without the unpleasant publicity of the police. Frankly, I've hidden all the previous thefts from my husband because I knew he would insist that I fire your mother immediately. My problem is that I'm just a bleeding heart. I felt very sorry for her." She sighed, as if the burden of her own compassion was far weightier than the sordid dilemma in which unwed mother Sheila Winter had found herself. "I could have withheld her paycheck as a way of recovering what you had stolen, but I didn't even do that because I knew that she used most of what she earned to pay for therapy sessions for you. I don't blame her for leaving, but I can tell you she took my charity with her." Her voice hardened. "I want the money, Raven, and I want it now."

"But I don't have it," Raven reiterated softly. My mother has it. My mother is the thief. Raven couldn't say those words aloud. Despite Sheila's immense betrayal of her, she simply could not betray her mother in return. Raising her chin proudly she lied convincingly to the angry patrician face, "I already used it to pay the bills that had accumulated for my therapy sessions."

"An obvious waste of money. You're really incredible, you know that? Here you've been given this wonderful educational opportunity, welcomed into a world you never would have known, and you simply mock those who have tried so hard to help you improve."

At Patrice Wainwright's allusion to Meadow Academy, Raven's heart almost stopped. What if Mrs. Wainwright tried to block her graduation? What if she couldn't go to UCLA after all? Raven could not let that happen. Even thinking about it made the glowing golden light that was the beacon to her future begin to flicker and fade.

"I *appreciate* the opportunity, Mrs. Wainwright, I truly do. And I'm really much better now. Please believe me. I'm completely off drugs, and I'll pay you back, I promise. Every penny plus interest. Please don't call the police, *please.*"

Patrice sighed again, and this time it was the put-upon sigh of an aristocrat confronted with the unsavory reality of the underclass. The truth was that a great deal of her heavy sigh was actually relief. Her husband would have been absolutely furious had he known that she had permitted the thefts to occur simply because she hadn't wanted to lose the best cook they had ever had.

"All right, Raven. I won't call the police. But I want you off my property *now.*"

Raven left the sanctuary of the cottage at Thornwood, and for her final six weeks of school, she was homeless. But, she wondered, hadn't she really been homeless all her life?

She found work, two jobs, both in fast-food restaurants. She worked every day after school until closing time and two shifts each day on the weekends. Sometimes she slept in the restaurants, and sometimes in the park, and sometimes beneath the bleachers at school. And each school day, she awakened at dawn and showered in the girls' locker room before classes began.

In six weeks it was over. Raven Willow Winter graduated with highest honors and the following day she boarded a Greyhound bus bound for Los Angeles and the beckoning golden light.

At first, Raven believed that UCLA was all that she had dared to hope it would be. The air was fragrant and warm, and it hummed with the energy and laughter of youth. Surely here, in the midst of this small city of students, she could simply blend in.

But even in the melting pot of UCLA, Raven was different. Her snow-white skin would not tan, nor did it even burn, as if her slender beautifully sculpted limbs were made of marble not of flesh. She was noticed, and stared at, and envied and desired . . . because amid all the magnificent     golden     California     beauties,     her midnight-black hair and alabaster skin were exotic and unique.

No one made fun of her name, or of her clothes, but the women were wary of her, just as Victoria and her friends had been. And here, as at Meadow Academy, the men simply wanted her.

Raven saw the casual flow of smiles and laughter between couples in love, and she tried very hard to learn how to laugh and to flirt. But it wasn't possible. Such authentic joy did not flow from her badly wounded heart, and being loved was far too important to laugh about, and she was far too desperate to play flirtatious games.

Raven gave her perfect body to the men who wanted it. With each lover she prayed that the intense desire she saw in his eyes would someday become a gentle love. But it never did, and each man left her with the same disdainful parting shot: she was so icy, so serious, so stiff.

Couldn't they tell that her stiffness was just pure fear that she would be betrayed yet again? And didn't they understand that her seriousness was because love was so terribly important to her? And didn't they realize that beneath the serene iciness the acid flamed and seared still?

Raven kept her solemn promise to repay Patrice Wainwright every penny plus interest. Even before she left Lake Meadow, she had mailed the first of many envelopes to Thornwood estate. That envelope contained cash, and from Los Angeles, as an undergraduate, she sent money orders, and later, as a law student and then a lawyer, she sent checks that were imprinted with her name and address. Raven sent a total of twenty-five thousand dollars, an amount that was surely far in excess of what Sheila Winter had ever stolen.

The final payment had been sent eight years ago, during her first year of practice in entertainment law. As she had put that check in the mail, Raven had felt a sense of closure, her contact with that painful chapter of her life severed forever. And it seemed to be true, until six months ago when an envelope arrived from an address that was less than half a mile north of Thornwood. The envelope contained an engraved gilt-edged invitation to Meadow Academy's fifteen-year class reunion. The favor of a reply was requested, to the address near Thornwood, the estate where one of the reunion's cohostesses, the former Victoria Wainwright, now lived with her husband Blane Calhoun.

Victoria Wainwright Calhoun hadn't needed to send Raven an invitation to the black-tie gala at the Fairmont in Chicago. But she had. And it was the ultimate taunt. Raven had replied promptly with the requisite check for five hundred dollars, the price tag per couple for the elegant dinner dance on Saturday night and the lavish champagne brunch to take place the following morning.

Raven had money now, and she had designer clothes and glittering jewels. But her hard-earned wealth had not brought her happiness, nor had it gained her an entrée into golden circles of friendship or love. She was alone still, an outsider, and now she was using her money to buy companionship for this all-important weekend. She was paying Nicholas Gault to help her create the illusion of happiness and love, to show them all that she had succeeded far beyond their wildest expectations.

But as she looked up from an unread page of Lauren Sinclair's *Happily Ever After* to a sky that was the color of her eyes, she thought grimly, What I'm really paying for is to make certain that they have no idea that I've become exactly what they always knew me to be: a bird of death . . . a willow that weeps still . . . an acid baby in whom even the most icy of glaciers can't cool the blazing fires of pain.

## ❀ 10 ❀

The suite that Raven had reserved at the Fairmont was one of the hotel's very best. Between the two spacious master bedrooms was a lavish living room complete with a baby grand piano. Every room was decorated in subtle shades of mauve and cream, and from each was offered a panoramic view of Lake Michigan, or Grant or Lincoln Parks, or the famous skyline of Chicago's Miracle Mile.

Nick and Raven spent the three hours before the dance apart, in the luxurious privacy of their separate bedroom suites. Nick called home, to give his parents the number where he could be reached; and with his expert hotelier's eye, he appraised, approvingly, the quality of his surroundings; and he enjoyed the magnificent views. But mostly Nick spent those hours thinking about Raven, wondering about her, and worrying, and very much looking forward to their eight o'clock rendezvous in the living room.

Nick was already there, waiting, when Raven appeared. He had been there for a while, at first distracted by the blue and gray drama as day became night, and then, after answering the doorbell, distracted by what had been delivered: a corsage of black orchids.

Nick was frowning at the flowers when he heard her voice behind him.

"Oh, good."

Nick turned toward her and for a moment he simply gazed at the vision of silk and satin that stood before him. Her gown was black and white, a creation of regal elegance. It molded perfectly to her perfect body, and was provocative not in what was revealed but in what remained demurely hidden beneath.

Raven's lustrous black hair had been swept away from her snow-white face and swirled into a thick knot atop her lovely head. It was a crown, Nick thought. A crown of midnight that shone as if caressed by an invisible moon. The makeup she wore was subtle, as always, and her only jewels were sapphire earrings the precise brilliant blue of her eyes. And the expression she wore? It was, as always, a beguiling blend of uncertainty and courage.

Snow White looked magnificent, a fairytale princess in no need of further adornment—except for confidence —and most certainly not in need of the black orchids.

"Good?" Nick echoed finally. "You ordered these?"

"Yes." Raven shrugged. "It's sort of an inside joke."

But it's not really a joke, Nick thought. It's not funny at all, just terribly important. So important, he realized, that her gown had undoubtedly been selected—or perhaps had even been made—to perfectly accessorize the black orchid corsage.

"Shall I help you pin it on?"

"Oh," she answered, surprised by the offer. "Yes . . . thank you."

As Nick removed the black corsage from its white box, he silently admired the quality of the orchids. They were quite exquisite, quite rare, and they gleamed with an inner luster that matched the sheen of her glorious hair.

It was a magnificent corsage, indisputably very expensive, but . . .

"This is wrong."

"Wrong?"

"It's not going to add a thing to how you look. In fact, I think it might detract." In response to his words, her uncertain sapphire eyes flickered with what looked like relief. She doesn't want to wear the orchids, Nick realized. And I'm not going to let her wear them. "Trust me, Raven. When it comes to flowers, I'm an expert."

"Well . . ." She had been afraid that Victoria—or perhaps Blane—would present her with black orchids, and had decided that her best defense was to be already wearing them, mocking her one-time classmates before they had a chance to mock her. She had planned to wear the exotic flowers proudly, as she had always worn them at school, even though they were symbols of such shame. But now Nick had pronounced them to be wrong, and his steel gray eyes told her that he was resolute in that opinion, and Raven suddenly felt wondrously safe. Even if Victoria or Blane thrust a similar corsage at her, Nick would protect her, steadfastly refusing to pin the black badge of shame on the pure white satin. In another century would Nicholas Gault have gallantly ripped the scarlet A off the bodice of Hester Prynne's puritanical dress? Probably, Raven thought. *Yes.* "Okay. I won't wear it."

"Good." Nick smiled, and added gently, "You look very beautiful, by the way."

"Thank you," she murmured, feeling a sudden rush of heat fill her cheeks at his gentleness. Raven fought the heat with a stern reminder: she was paying him to pretend to care, *paying* him. When she spoke again, her voice was businesslike and cool. "That tuxedo looks very good on you."

"Thank you."

Nick gazed at the woman who had not needed rare and exotic flowers to embellish her rare and exotic beauty. But, he thought, Raven Willow Winter did need something more. Her lovely lips needed to smile and her blue eyes needed to sparkle with confidence. She had every reason to be brimming with confidence. She was a dazzling success. Nick doubted that any of the high school classmates assembled in the Imperial Ballroom below had accomplished more.

But Raven didn't exude confidence, nor was there even the serene calm that came from hard-earned and well-deserved success. She looked instead like someone who believed without question that she was nothing, that whatever she had accomplished didn't count.

On an impulse that he had no wish to stop, Nick gently touched her cheek. It was snow white again, drained of the pink that had tinted it so enchantingly in response to his compliment. As he touched her, he felt satin, and ice, and just beneath the cool surface he felt trembling heat.

"I don't know who they are or why they worry you so much, Raven, but I have a suggestion. Why don't we just go give 'em hell?"

Her eyes answered first, with surprised gratitude, and then she smiled—a soft, hopeful smile that was an even more magnificent adornment than he had imagined it would be—and finally she said quietly, "Okay, Nick. *Okay.*"


Victoria Wainwright Calhoun had been absolutely astonished when she received the check that confirmed Raven's intention to attend the reunion. Astonished, and then delighted. Raven's brazen nerviness in attending gave Victoria an opportunity to share with her friends the deliciously disgusting truth that her mother had only recently shared with her, when Patrice had been compelled to explain why she happened to know that Raven was an attorney in Los Angeles.

Being a thief was added to the long list of Raven's crimes, and in the months leading up to the reunion,

Victoria had elaborately embellished the story to include theft of jewels as well as money. That embellishment, which became more grand with each retelling, meant that on the night of the reunion, when they all wore fortunes in jewels, they could taunt Raven with silent but knowing contempt whenever her lustful blue eyes fell on their priceless gems.

Over the past fifteen years, many of Meadow Academy's graduates had remained in the Chicago area. Victoria and her friends were in constant communication with each other, and, with their respective spouses, dined together frequently. Without Raven, the black-tie gala at the Fairmont would have been just another night of gourmet food, designer dresses, and vintage champagne. But now, trashy Raven Winter was going to entertain them once more, providing them with anecdotes to savor in the future, just as over the past few months they had enjoyed resurrecting the sordid stories from their days, with Raven, at the Meadow. The stories were even more sordid, even more delicious, in their adult recounting. The men who had then been teenaged boys were now quite happy to reveal never before disclosed details of their intimacies with Raven—how willing she had always been, how eager, how wanton, how immoral.

Even Blane, who had always been forthcoming about the deflowering of Raven, now revealed the previously hidden truth that their sexual liaison had actually spanned five years, including two during which he and Victoria had been going steady. Blane deflected his wife's instant and savage rage by casting the blame entirely on Raven, her unrelenting seduction of him, her bewitching immorality—and by promising Victoria that he would put Raven in her place once and for all at the reunion.

Victoria and her friends anticipated the reappearance of Raven Winter with the same sinister relish that a hunter awaits the appearance of his prey. As an attorney she would have some money, of course, not the kind of money that they all had but surely enough to buy reasonable clothes. But, they predicted smugly, her gown would be absolutely tasteless. Velvet, low-cut, a decadent bordello crimson.

And, they forecast gleefully, the man with whom Raven would appear would definitely be many years from her age. He might be much younger, a male model or an aspiring actor, a "stud," a "hunk," extremely attractive in a sexy, sleazy, low-class kind of way. More likely, they decided, the man in Raven's life would be much older than she, and very rich. She would be his mistress, his trophy, and by walking in with her vulture talons clutched to his aged arm, she would prove without a doubt that she was still willing to do anything to ensnare a man with money.

The beady eyes of Victoria Calhoun and her friends were fixed on the entrance of the Imperial Ballroom. None of them wanted to miss even a moment of Raven's much-anticipated arrival. But still, despite their malicious attentiveness and despite the fact that they were indeed all watching the ballroom's arched entryway when Raven appeared, it was quite a while before any of them realized that she had arrived.

Their eyes were drawn by instinct to Nick. He looked like one of them, rich and powerful and confident. But the handsome face wasn't even remotely familiar. Was this tall, dark, mysterious stranger crashing their party? If so, he was more than welcome.

It was only as Victoria and Blane moved toward Nick that their gaze shifted to his beautiful companion. She was the perfect match for him, a stylish portrait of elegance and privilege. She was more than welcome too. Except that she was . . .

"Raven," Victoria whispered in hushed horror to Blane. The word was a hiss, escaping through perfect teeth that gritted beneath the perfect polite smile.

"Raven! We're all so delighted that you decided to come."

"Hello, Victoria," Raven said quietly. She saw the contempt in the heiress' smiling eyes, private disdain, just for her . . . and when her gaze shifted to Blane, Raven was greeted by a private message that was even more terrifying: desire.

Nick sensed the deep shiver that seemed to freeze Raven's ability to reply. He had already decided that unless pressed he would withhold his last name. Graduates of Meadow Academy grew up to be readers of *Fortune* and *The Wall Street Journal,* both of which had featured articles on Eden Enterprises and its powerful CEO. When he had assumed that he would be meeting Raven's friends, he had planned to be simply "Nick." But because it was painfully obvious that these people were far from friends, he extended a strong hand to Blane and greeted, "I'm Nicholas."

After shaking Nick's hand, Blane introduced his wife.

"Hello, Nicholas," Victoria purred, compelled to purr because the black-haired silver-eyed stranger was even more gorgeous at close range than he had been from across the room.

Victoria purred for Nicholas, but inside she twisted with anger: Raven should not have had Blane, and she most certainly should not have this elegant man. Once Nicholas learned the truth about Raven, he would drop her instantly and—Victoria hoped—*cruelly.* And he would learn the truth, she vowed. That would be her own private mission for the evening, and once accomplished the mission would more than offset the extreme disappointment she had felt at the sight of the presumptuous Raven Willow Winter, beautifully dressed and on the arm of a man who was so obviously deserving of someone far better than she.

There would be anecdotes to savor yet: Nicholas' horror and ultimately his gratitude when Raven the slut, the thief, was exposed. And although it was probably too much to hope for, Victoria allowed herself a tantalizing fantasy: a public scene in which, in disgust, aristocratic Nicholas cast aside the very trashy Raven Winter.

The deliciousness of Raven's imminent ruin coupled with the fact that she was still looking at Nick kept the soft purr in Victoria's voice as she announced, "I took the liberty of seating the two of you at our table. There will be two other couples as well." Taking her gaze from Nick with obvious regret, she turned to Raven and politely issued the taunting challenge, "I hope that's all right with you, Raven."

No, Raven's heart answered. The silent scream was proof that her heart beat still, searing pulses of pure fire beneath the glacier of ice that had frozen her limbs. How could she possibly dine with the woman who had once tormented her so viciously? And how, *how,* could she possibly dine with the man to whom she had once so willingly and so hopefully given everything she had to give—only to have him greedily take that precious gift, and mock her when he was through, and then take again and again when he wanted more.

Raven could not dine with Victoria and Blane. It was simply impossible. In their presence she still felt what they had always told her she was: nothing, less than nothing, undeserving of kindness or of love.

And . . . hadn't the past fifteen years proved them right?

Raven knew that she had to get away, and she was going to flee as soon as she could free herself from the immobilizing clutches of ice. In her mind's eye she already saw the image of herself running away, like Cinderella at the stroke of midnight . . . a Cinderella who had no reason to leave behind a glass slipper because there would be no Prince Charming following in loving pursuit.

The searing pulses of fiery pain suddenly became a

welcome inferno, melting the imprisoning ice; but as Raven started to turn, she was imprisoned again, by warmth this time, a strong yet gentle arm that encircled her slender waist.

The gray eyes that gazed at her were warm too, and gentle, and strong. Nick smiled, and then the smoldering steel shifted to Victoria as he answered for Raven, "We look forward to sitting with you at dinner, Victoria. Right now, though, I think we'll get some champagne and do a little mingling."

"I don't drink," Raven said when they reached the silver fountain from which cascaded honey-colored waterfalls of vintage champagne.

"I don't drink much either," Nick conceded as he reached for two already filled crystal flutes. Handing one of them to her, he said, "However, I have a feeling that tonight a little champagne might help." With a smile of reassurance, he continued, "I'm feeling a little unprepared for questions that might arise during the course of the evening. I need a crash course on Raven Willow Winter, beginning now."

"There's really not much to tell."

"Just answer my questions then. Question number one: what kind of work do you do?"

"I'm an attorney. I practice entertainment law."

"Meaning negotiating deals and drawing up contracts for actors, directors, writers, and studios?" Nick already knew the answer, of course, but he wanted to hear from Raven her impressive credentials.

"Yes."

"And among entertainment attorneys in Los Angeles, where would you place yourself? Be honest."

"At the top."

"The most distinguished client list? The biggest deals?"

"Yes. Both."

"Okay. Now, earlier we established how beautiful you are." Nick's eyes left her then, to look around the room. It was a leisurely and thorough perusal, and when he was through, and his appraising gray gaze had returned to her, he said gently, "You are, in fact, the most beautiful woman here—by many orders of magnitude. So . . ."

"So?" Raven echoed with quiet hope.

"So you're astonishingly beautiful and astonishingly successful. Which means that there is absolutely no rational reason for you to feel the least bit intimidated by anyone in this room. But," he added softly, "the reason isn't a rational one, is it?"

"No."

Nick wanted her to tell him everything, all the anguished emotions, but there were people approaching, phantoms from a past that had obviously caused her great pain. Now was not the time to ask more questions. Now was the time to smile, and gently touch crystal to crystal, and toast quietly, "To you, Raven. And to my plan, which is this: pretend that we're in Los Angeles and all these people have come to you because they need someone to negotiate multimillion-dollar deals for them . . . and they've heard that you're the best."

It wasn't the champagne. Raven knew that the few sips she had taken from the crystal flute weren't enough to cause any effect at all, much less the floating warmth she felt. The warmth, and the wonderful sense of safety, came from Nick, not from Dom Perignon. He was there, a strong, powerful presence who didn't leave her side; and when he touched her, his gently protective caresses spoke of something far more intimate than lust . . . they spoke of deep affection, of caring, of love.

Nick was pretending to be the lover she had asked him to be, was paying him to be. Raven knew that it was pure pretense, but she blocked the knowledge, *needed* to block it in order to survive.

The gourmet dinner began with Caesar salad and with a polite yet incisive cross-examination of her. Raven's "friends" wanted to know all about her work. The terms of the deals she negotiated were confidential—unless the parties chose to disclose them—but the deals themselves and her role as negotiator were in the public domain. They appeared routinely in the trade magazines, and often, because of their importance, they also got play in such forums as *People, Entertainment Tonight,* and *USA Today.*

Still, strangely, when pressed now to reveal names of the celebrities she represented, Raven demurred.

"So," Victoria concluded with barely concealed smugness, "no one we've ever heard of."

"No, Victoria," Nick countered with quietly impassioned calm. "That's wrong. Raven represents almost everyone you've ever heard of."

"Really."

Nick's steel gray eyes held Victoria's for several solemn moments before he affirmed, "Yes. Really."

"Well, very impressive, Raven," Victoria announced with forced gaiety. "That probably hasn't given you much time for a personal life, has it? Have you ever been married?"

Raven was supposed to be pretending that she was in Los Angeles, and that these people had come to her because of her expertise, but the pretense wasn't working. She wasn't in control—Victoria was—and she seemed quite powerless to stop her. "No, never married."

The answer seemed to please Victoria, in a dangerously satisfying way, and in another moment Raven knew why. It gave the heiress an opening in which to pose to the never-married woman, who as a girl had been relentlessly belittled about her own illegitimate birth, her next malicious question: "What about children, Raven? Do you have any?"

Nick wasn't touching Raven then, but he felt the effect of Victoria's question on her nonetheless. Raven stiffened, as if struck by a stunning blow, and when Nick found her hand, curling it gently into his, he felt trembling ice.

"No children, Victoria," he answered. Then, smiling lovingly at Raven, he added, "No children yet."

"Well," Victoria continued hurriedly, disappointed by the answer and annoyed at the obvious intimacy it had caused. "No wonder you're in such good shape, Raven."

The stunning impact of Victoria's question about her illegitimate children paled by comparison to the effect of Nick's words and his loving gray eyes. He's just pretending, Raven reminded herself. I'm paying him to pretend. Still, because no man had ever looked at her with such tenderness, for a wondrous moment Raven allowed herself to believe in the glorious dream.

As Nick saw with brilliant clarity the enchanting wishes of Raven's heart, he permitted himself to believe, too, in the illusion of their love. He would have been quite happy to be lost forever in the pretense, to journey with Raven to the faraway dream; but the crescendoing anger he felt toward Victoria kept him tightly tethered to reality—and to the conversation.

So it was Nick who once again answered a question that had been posed to Raven.

"Raven jogs," he explained as his fingers gently touched Raven's snow-white palm. The rawness was gone, but the healing satin was still a little tattered, a terrifying legacy of the way they had met. "And she also gardens."

"I know that there are those who wouldn't agree, but as far as I'm concerned, for almost half of the year around here it's either too hot or too cold to do either." Victoria's pronouncement came with a whisper of defiance, as if Chicagoland's extremes in climate were responsible for the fact that her own shape, although stylish and trim, wasn't what Raven's was. "Besides, the more I read about jogging, the less good it seems for you. What's the term? High impact?"

"That's right." The voice belonged to Sandra, the wife of one of Raven's "lovers" but a woman she had never met before this evening. Sandra's was a soft voice, graciously accented by a Southern drawl and quite untainted, it seemed, by any secret knowledge of Raven's past. "Jogging may cause too much wear and tear, but gardening is wonderful exercise. It's low impact and aerobic. Have any of you all heard of Eden exercise equipment?"

Five of the eight people at the table indicated that they had heard of Eden, and two others, Raven included, shrugged no. Only the eighth, Nick, was noncommittal.

"Well, it's simply wonderful," Sandra raved. "It was apparently designed by a gardener and it exactly reproduces all the motions of gardening—which, if done right, involve literally every muscle group in the body. The purpose is to firm and tone, without actually building up the muscles, but there are additional attachments for muscle-building if that's your goal. I guess that professional gardeners have rather magnificent bodies, just from the work they do. You would probably know the answer to that, Nicholas. You said earlier that you were a landscape architect?"

"Yes. But hardly a judge of magnificent male bodies."

"But have you heard of Eden exercise equipment?"

"Sure."

"And?"

"I think it has a lot to offer over the more traditional regimens of pumping iron." Nick's gaze had been focused on Sandra, but he had been touching, still, the rough satin of Raven's palm. He had felt her relax in response to his touch, and even to warm a little, and now he needed to see her face. Would she be lost still in the faraway dream? Or would her intelligent blue eyes have suddenly become quite shrewd, proof that she knew, had known all along, exactly who he was?

Nick looked at her then, and found eyes that were neither faraway nor shrewd, but dancing, sparkling, with some unspoken thought.

"Do you have an observation about the merits of pumping iron?" he asked softly.

"Not exactly." Raven smiled. "I was thinking, though, that given the choice between pumping iron or pumping roses, I'd pump roses any day."

## ❀ *11* ❀

"May I have this dance, Nicholas?" Victoria asked the moment the orchestra began to play. "You don't mind, do you, Raven? Besides, you and Blane should have at least one dance, shouldn't you, for old times' sake?"

Raven saw immediately that Victoria wanted her to dance with Blane, as if the heiress knew that Blane would make the dance a form of punishment. As she had anticipated this night, Raven had planned to dance with Blane, to dance with all of them. She had planned to let them all touch her once again, knowing they would want her still; and she had also planned to make it clear to all of them that what she felt for them now was pure contempt.

But now Raven didn't even want to dance with them. She didn't want their hands on her skin ever again. The wish came from strength, not from weakness. Once she had wanted so desperately to be accepted by them, to be included in their inner circle. Now that no longer mattered. It was as if somehow she had floated far above them, where always before she had been way beneath.

Raven did not want Blane Calhoun to touch her.

It was a wish that Nick read with stunning clarity.

"I don't think I'm willing to share Raven tonight, Victoria," he said. "We're both so busy that we rarely get a chance to go dancing together. This is a luxury for us and I don't want to squander one minute of it."

"But what about you, Raven?" Victoria challenged. "Are you willing to share Nicholas for just one dance? After all, there was a time when we all had to share—"

"Yes," Raven interjected swiftly, knowing exactly what Victoria had been about to say: After all, there was a time when we all had to share our boyfriends with you. It was a warning, and Raven suddenly realized that whether Victoria danced with Nick or not, her ancient enemy was going to be very certain that he learned all the shameful truths about her.

It doesn't matter if Nick learns the truth about me, Raven reminded herself. He's only pretending to care.

The pretense had been so wondrous . . . but Nick was a sensational actor, that was all, and now the act was going to be put to its ultimate test. Something very self-destructive within Raven wanted Victoria to tell Nick everything—because then the fantasy that had been dancing in her own mind, that maybe he did care, just a little, would be put to rest.

"Go ahead, Nick," she said quietly. "Dance with Victoria."


"You must be a very sexually confident man, Nicholas."

Nick answered Victoria's provocative remark, provocatively delivered, with a lazy smile—and without the slightest break in the rhythm of the slow dance they were dancing. "Oh? Why do you say that?"

"Because Raven has slept with—no, had sex with—virtually every man in this room."

Victoria's remark bothered him a great deal, for Raven; but, for Raven, Nick's smile held as he replied easily, "Over fifteen years ago."

"Yes, but—"

"I'm sorry, Victoria, but if you're going to test my sexual confidence, it's going to have to be with something a little more threatening than sex between teenagers years ago."

"You're not worried about smoldering flames of passion?"

I'm worried about black orchids, Nick thought. And snow-white fingers of ice, and lovely, uncertain sapphire eyes, and searing pain—not smoldering passion. And I'm also worried that you're trying to cause her even more pain by provoking me, by trying to turn me against her too.

Victoria's maliciousness enraged him, but Nick forced himself to remain unwaveringly calm. Victoria was obviously determined to reveal to him Raven's deepest flaws and most heinous crimes, and he was resolved to hear her out and to dispassionately discount each accusation one by one.

"I'm not the least bit worried about smoldering flames of passion, Victoria. Are you? I assume that Blane—"

"Raven was a slut, Nicholas, a nymphomaniac. She slept with anyone and everyone. She was poor, and the boys were rich, and it was the easiest way for her to get their money."

Easy? Nick's mind echoed silently. He was quite certain that for Snow White it had not been easy at all.

"She was trying to get pregnant, of course, to entrap one of them into marriage. Thank heavens it never happened."

"Why are you telling me this, Victoria? You think she's trying to entrap me too?"

"I think it's a distinct possibility."

"Well, I don't. Raven is a very rich woman. She doesn't need my money."

"Her desire for wealth may be as insatiable as her

desire for sex." Victoria would have said more, but his gray eyes had turned wintry, filled with icy warning. It was obvious that Nicholas had heard quite enough on the subject of Raven's sexual exploits. After a moment she said solemnly, "There's something else you should know about Raven, something else that she was fifteen years ago . . ."

At the table, while Nick and Victoria danced, Blane moved closer to her.

"Raven, Raven," he whispered softly, seductively. "We've never danced together, have we?"

Raven shuddered at his words, at his tone, at the horrible memories of what he had been to her. Raven Winter and Blane Calhoun had never danced, never dated, never even talked—except for a few words that were a preamble to sex. And after, most of the words spoken to her had been cruel.

"Dance with me, Raven."

"No."

"Well, then why don't we do something else? This is a reunion, after all. Why don't we reunite?"

His words were plainly, painfully clear. Even if they hadn't been, the demanding desire in his eyes was hauntingly familiar. Blane wanted to have sex, here, now. Where? Raven wondered. Behind one of the plush velvet drapes? Or upstairs, in his suite, or hers?

"Don't look so shocked, Raven," he admonished. "You know that I've always wanted you. And you're even more beautiful now, more sexy. We were always so good together—remember?"

Good together? Something deep within inside her twisted, a smoldering ember suddenly stirred, sparking and then bursting into blazing flames of pain. During the twenty years since she had joyfully given her virginity to

Blane there had been times, many times, especially in the beginning, when there had seemed to be authentic whispers of gentleness from her lovers. Raven had finally realized that it was only because they were grown men, not teenaged boys. The gentleness was something they had learned—or read about—something that women supposedly wanted. Her adult lovers had seduced her with veneers of gentleness, especially in the beginning; but the truth was that they had all really been just like Blane, wanting her for their pleasure with a desire that was harsh, desperate, and demanding.

Blane had never even pretended gentleness. Raven realized now that in the nakedness of his desire for her—and for his own pleasure—he had been the most honest of them all.

But she and Blane hadn't been good together. They had only been good for him. And after, for her, with Blane, and with all the others, Raven had only felt more empty, more isolated, and more alone than before.

"Come on, Raven," Blane urged, and there was a little gentleness now, something he, too, had learned. "Come on."

"No."

Her eyes left Blane then and traveled to Victoria and Nick. It was a reluctant voyage. Raven had no doubt that Victoria would tell Nick all the truths about her, regaling him with every sordid detail she knew. But, Raven realized as she watched them dance, the chronicle of her unsavory crimes had not yet begun. Nick's strong, lean body moved gracefully still, sensually, eloquent proof that he possessed an instinctive understanding of the way that male and female bodies were intended to move together—and eloquent proof as well that Victoria had yet to share with him the devastating truths. Raven would know precisely when that sharing began: the sensual grace would leave Nick's body as his taut muscles tightened with pure disgust.

"You think that lover boy would object?" Blane pressed.

No, Raven thought. Nick wouldn't care if she disappeared with Blane—especially not after Victoria finished regaling him with the exploits of her youth. Nick had taken his job very seriously so far, protecting her, being so gentle, far more gentle than any man ever had been. After a moment, even though Raven knew it was a lie, she solemnly answered Blane's question, "Yes. He would object. He would probably kill you with his bare hands."

Nick's face was somber, chiseled stone, as he followed Victoria from the dance floor back to the table.

He knows everything, Raven thought. No amount of money could make him stay with me now, pretending to care about me still. He has far too much pride for that. He is not a man who will tolerate being played for a fool. Maybe he will just keep walking, past the table and out of the ballroom . . .

In a way that would have been a relief, far easier to endure than his steel-hard anger.

But Nick stopped when he reached the table, and to the woman who greeted him with such apologetic apprehension, he smiled. "Let's dance, Raven."

He led her to a remote and shadowed corner of the ballroom. Once there, even though they were far away from prying eyes, he insisted that they dance as lovers would. After draping her slender arms around his neck, he encircled her waist with both of his.

Their bodies didn't touch. They didn't need to. They were confident lovers, not desperate and furtive ones. When they chose to be intimate it was always in private, not in a place where curious eyes might strain to see them even in the shadows.

They looked like lovers, swaying sensually to a romantic melody of love, but Nick felt the icy tension of the silent woman in his arms. Raven was stiff, wary, waiting.

"I had an interesting conversation with Victoria," he said finally. "Raven, look at me."

He waited very patiently until at last, and with obvious dread, the troubled face that had been staring at his chest followed his quiet command.

"Would you like to know what she said?"

"I'm sure I already know."

"You tell me then."

He was holding her gently, with his bare hands and his dark silver eyes. The hold was gentle, but neither the hands nor the eyes were going to let her go . . . and yet, somehow, Raven felt more free than imprisoned.

"She told you that I was very poor, and that much to her embarrassment, my mother and I lived on her family's estate, and that everyone hated me."

"Why, Raven? Why would everyone hate you?" After a moment he added very softly, "Why would anyone hate you?"

His gentleness made her tremble, made her confess, "I suppose it was because I was so different. They were rich and I was poor. My clothes were second-hand and tattered, and they all wore designer labels. And, of course, there was my name."

"What's wrong with your name?"

"They thought it was ugly. They teased me about being a bird of death . . . a weeping tree."

White-hot rage surged through Nick as he saw just how much the merciless taunts had wounded her. A powerful and primitive instinct urged him to destroy them all—right now. But something even more powerful stilled the warrior within him, and when he spoke again, all that Raven heard was exquisite tenderness.

"Raven is a very beautiful name, and so is Willow. In fact, it's a perfect name for a raven-haired willowy beauty."

"Thank you," she whispered, and for a wondrous moment Raven Willow Winter forgot all her shame . . . and all her pain. But quickly, too quickly, she remembered the stony solemnity of his face when he had finished dancing with Victoria. "What did Victoria tell you?"

"She said that I must be terribly sexually confident to be in a room filled with men who had been your lovers." Raven's head started to fall then, a descent of shame, but Nick caught her lovely chin with his finger, and lifted, and waited.

"They were never lovers," she said softly. "Yes, I slept with—had sex with—many of the men in this room. They were teenaged boys then and I was . . ."

"Lonely? Alone?" *Just like you are now?* "Looking for love in all the wrong places?"

"I'm not proud of what I did, Nick."

"They're the ones who shouldn't be proud."

"We were all teenagers."

"That may be an excuse for hormones—but not for cruelty. There's never any excuse for cruelty." The warrior within him was ready to do battle again and this time the edge of harshness, of tautly controlled rage, touched his voice as he asked, "Why are we here, Raven?"

"What do you mean?"

"I mean, why do you care what these people think of you? You don't need their approval, do you?"

"I thought I did."

"And now?"

"No." She smiled a brave lovely smile. After a moment it faded to wistful sadness. "We can leave if you want."

"I want to leave," Nick said. "But Raven, I don't want to stop dancing with you."

"Oh!" Her surprised sapphire eyes glowed with soft hope. "I don't want to stop dancing with you either."

"Then why don't we go upstairs, find a soft-rock station on the radio, and dance in private?"

# ❊ *12* ❊

Upstairs, on the plush carpet in the cream and mauve living room of the suite, they danced, their bodies swaying slowly in a chaste and gentle kiss.

Finally, compelled by bold whispers of desire, Raven lifted her face to him, inviting him; and when her lovely invitation was crystal clear, Nick bent to greet her mouth. His kiss was chaste and gentle, a warm hello; and even as his need for more of her crescendoed swiftly, his lips explored gently still, but more insistently; and when the hello became a question from him, it was answered immediately by soft lips which parted in joyous welcome.

Nick was steel, and Raven was ice, but there was nothing cold or unyielding about their caress. The molten heat that forged the steel that was Nick smoldered deep within him, just as beneath the glacial layers that were Raven blazed a brilliant, glittering fire.

And now, as their kiss deepened and she heard soft sighs of desire—his and hers—for the first time the flames within her didn't burn with pain, but with a glowing warmth, a shimmering heat that enveloped her as gently as his arms did, desiring her but not imprisoning.

"What do you want, Raven?" he asked softly. The intense glinting steel told her eloquently what he wanted, but the sensuous silver had another eloquent message as well: that the choice was hers.

Raven wanted to make love. It was something she had never really wanted before, nor had it ever really been a choice. It had been a compulsion instead, a desperate need to be accepted, to belong to some imaginary circle of love, to escape from her icy loneliness and fiery pain.

And what are you doing now? a soaring flame demanded, scorching her heart as it did. Aren't you desperately needing something from this seductive stranger who is so gentle, who knows your secret shames and seems to care still?

You're *paying* him to care, remember? the flame seared deeper. You're paying him to pretend to care, to pretend that you are lovers.

Was Nick simply playing the role to perfection? she wondered. Was he hoping for an extravagant tip? Or was his hope that she would recommend his services—gardening? making love?—to all her wealthy friends?

Raven pulled away.

"You don't have to do this, Nick. Downstairs, in front of all of them, I really appreciated how you pretended—"

Nick stopped her words with a gentle finger on her lips. He could have stopped them with the truth—*Yes, I do have to do this*—but he chose not to confess that he was drawn to her more powerfully than to any woman ever before, and he could not with absolute honesty proclaim that he wasn't pretending. His desire for her wasn't pretense, of course; but to Raven he was a gardener still, successful yes, but not the fabulously wealthy man he truly was. He wanted to believe what Raven had told him about her past, about the girls who had taunted her and the boys who had used her. His heart did believe. But Victoria Calhoun's warnings echoed in his mind: it was Raven who had been the user, Raven who had calculatedly seduced the rich young heirs in hopes of entrapping them.

Nick wanted Raven tonight, tomorrow night, for all

the days and nights of his life. It was a dangerous desire, and perhaps an impossible one, because there were other hearts—young and precious and fragile ones—to be considered. For them, for his beloved daughters who had been so brutally betrayed by a woman who had seduced to entrap, Nick had to keep pretending.

Nick needed Raven, and wanted her, and had fallen in love with her.

But he didn't really know if he could trust her.

"Tell me what you want, Raven," he repeated quietly.

"You," she whispered. It was a whisper that seemed to echo throughout time, far beyond tonight. "I want you, Nick."

Nick had made love to many women, before his marriage to Deandra and after his divorce. The women he had been with since his divorce knew all about him, all about his rules. He had no intention of remarrying, nor of becoming emotionally involved, nor of ever even introducing them to his two little girls. Nick's love, all of it, was for his daughters. The women he dated knew that, accepted it, and approached their relationship with him the way he did, as an impermanent liaison of companionship and pleasure, a gourmet feast to be savored, lingered over, and eventually forgotten.

Nick's lovers proclaimed him to be the best they'd known, the most expert and most talented, an explorer of the senses who knew the maps of pleasure by heart and made those breathtaking voyages with unwavering confidence and staggering control.

But now, with Raven, the journey upon which he was about to embark was entirely new, a voyage into wild and uncharted territories of desire, of passion . . . and of love. And how should he make this most important—and most dangerous—of all journeys?

Slowly, Nick told himself. One caress at a time, each

one a promise of forever. His lips would tenderly celebrate each discovery of her with a loving kiss. But, he knew, the prints left by his tender lips would be quite invisible. He would leave no tell-tale marks on her snow-white flesh, no signposts that he could follow should he become lost. Once begun, this was a journey from which there could be no turning back.

He needed her desperately.

But he wanted this first time to feel to her like the leisurely beginning of forever.

So slowly, slowly, he started to undress her, beginning with the pins that held the few strands of hair that hadn't escaped their lustrous crown while they had danced and kissed.

"What are you doing?"

"Undressing you."

Nick kissed goodbye, for the moment, to the snow-white neck that was now curtained by midnight-black silk. Then his long lean fingers and his darkly sensuous gray eyes turned their intense concentration to the slow and gentle removal of the sapphire jewels that adorned her ears.

"Hurry," she whispered.

"No."

"Nick . . ."

The urgency in her voice pulled his gaze from the glittering blue earrings to her shimmering blue eyes—and he saw her fear. She's never made this journey before either, he realized. She believes it's impossible, that something will happen to destroy it, that the dream has only a few moments in which to exist before being shattered.

"There are no pumpkins here, Cinderella," he said softly. "No white mice. It's only you and me . . . and we have all night."

He was reading her thoughts now, her desires and her

fears. Raven heard his reassuring words, but still she reached to begin undressing him in return.

"If you do that," he warned with gentle promise, "we won't have all night."

"You want me, too?"

"I want you, Raven."

Nick took her to the bedroom then, to her bedroom, and closed the heavy drapes, and smiled loving reassurance when he saw her worry as he reached to illuminate a porcelain lamp. The lamp was on the dresser, away from the bed, and its golden light was soft not glaring, their own private moon.

Nick undressed her, removing black silk and white satin until all the black-and-white silkiness that remained was Raven . . . and when she was naked, he kissed first the places that no other man ever would have—her palms and her knees, where her delicate flesh had been torn by the pavement as she had fallen to the ground. As he tenderly caressed the healing tatters, his lips and his heart sent an apology and a promise: I am so sorry that I hurt you. I will try very hard never to hurt you again.

"I need you, Nick. Please."

At her urgent words, Nick looked up from a tattered palm—and was greeted by blue eyes that glistened with confidence, not fear. Raven believed in the dream now, believed it wouldn't vanish, but there was urgency still—a glorious urgency compelled by pure desire.

"Undress me then."

She was trembling, quivering inside with warm heat, but her fingers were steady, and so confident, as they found the buttons of his shirt . . . and when she had finished undressing him, Nick laid her gently on the cool soft sheets . . . and as she welcomed him, he saw brave words in her glowing blue eyes . . . and they were the same joyous words that sang in his own heart: I love you. *I love you.*

\* \* \*

He had never felt such perfection, such peace. They were entwined—no, they were one—forged together still by the fire of their passion, melted into a lump of bliss in which there were no boundaries between his flesh and hers, his heart and hers.

Nick gently wove his long fingers through her love-tangled black hair, cradling her face, urging her to look at him, wanting to see how such perfection, such peace looked on her lovely face.

But when her head lifted, and he tenderly parted the black silk to see her eyes, what Nick saw was worry.

"What, Raven?"

"There's something else, something that Victoria probably didn't tell you."

"Oh?"

"She—and I assume all of her friends—believe that I'm a thief, that I stole money from her parents' home when my mother and I lived on the estate."

"And jewels," Nick embellished softly. Then, to the surprised eyes that were more brilliant than the most flawless of sapphires, he said, "She told me. You were young, Raven, and desperate and poor."

He already knew, and had already forgiven her, and his gentleness told her that it didn't matter. But it *did* matter, to her. She wanted him to know the truth. But in the silent moments before she began to speak, her heart twisted with a deep ache—because, even after all these years, her confession of that truth still felt like a betrayal of Sheila.

Nick's heart twisted, too, as he listened to Raven's quiet words; and he heard the apology in her voice, the guilt she felt for revealing the truth about the woman who had caused her such pain *but was her mother;* and when Raven's story was through, he offered, very gently, "You protected her."

Even though she never protected you, he amended silently. You're loyal to her still, even now. Just as, despite everything, something very deep compels my lovely little girls to love their mother. "You confessed, Raven. You accepted the blame for what she had done. Had charges been pressed, that would have been disastrous for you. It seems highly unlikely that a convicted felon would have been admitted to law school."

"But charges *weren't* pressed, and as promised, I eventually repaid Victoria's mother." A wry smile touched her lips. "In fact, investing in my future—by not ruining it—was a good investment for her. I sent her a total of twenty-five thousand dollars, which I'm sure is far more money than was ever taken . . . and Mrs. Wainwright never mentioned anything about missing jewels." Raven's smile faded and her own jewel-bright eyes were very grave. "I'm not a thief, Nick, I never was. I wanted you to know that."

Oh, but you are a thief, Nick thought. You, Raven Willow Winter, have stolen my heart. And I don't want it back. It's yours to keep.

"Now I know," he whispered softly against her lips, wanting her, needing her again, already. "And now I'm going to love you . . . very slowly . . . if I possibly can."

*Love you.* The words washed through her with a wave of heat more powerful than all the wondrous waves that had come before. Love you, Nick had said, not *make* love to you. To Raven, the distinction felt like the difference between make-believe and believe, between imagined and real.

He kissed hello to the parts of her that there had been no time to kiss the first time, and for the first time in her life of intimacy without gentleness, Raven was unafraid of such intimacy, and joyously unashamed. She gave herself to Nick as she had never given herself before, and as she heard his soft sighs of desire, for the first time she believed—and it wasn't make-believe—that she truly had gifts of her own . . . and that in the giving of those gifts, in the sharing, there was magnificence and splendor.


They floated from bliss to blissful dreams, but were awakened again and again by entwined bodies which even in sleep began anew their wondrous dance of love.

Eventually they were awakened by something far less enthralling: the strident sound of the telephone. Nick was closest to it, and as he moved to answer, he noticed the time on the bedside clock: eleven-fifteen.

"Good morning, Nicholas. It's Victoria. We're saving a place for the two of you at our table. It's a marvelous brunch and the champagne is flowing."

"Hold on a moment, Victoria." Nick covered the phone and looked at the lovely face that had filled with wariness at the mention of Victoria's name. Nick smiled at her, reminding her of *them,* and only when all the wariness had disappeared did he continue. "The brunch has started. Victoria and Blane are saving a place for us at their table."

"Are you hungry?"

"Only for you." With that Nick uncovered the mouthpiece of the phone. "I think that Raven and I will pass on the brunch, Victoria."

"So we won't get to see you again?"

"I'm afraid not."

"Is anything wrong, Nicholas?"

A rush of anger pulsed through him as he heard the hopefulness in Victoria's voice, a hope that he was going to hurt Raven, to cast her aside when he became bored with her perfect body. Nick blocked the quick, angry retort. Laughing softly, he answered, "No, Victoria, everything's absolutely terrific. Please send our apologies to the others."

After he replaced the receiver, Nick looked at Raven

and repeated with quiet passion, "I'm only hungry for you."

They were awakened next by the radio, the alarm that Nick had set before showing her how much he wanted her still, again, always. The alarm meant that it was one-thirty, time to shower and dress if they were to make the four o'clock flight to Los Angeles.

Nick kissed her lingeringly, then reluctantly left the bed, slipping into one of the terry cloth robes provided by the hotel as he crossed to open the heavy drapes. There was time, before getting ready to leave, to spend a few moments viewing together the magnificence of the lake and the sky.

But there was no lake, no sky. There was only a pristine white blur of swirling snowflakes. Just as Nick and Raven were making the dramatic discovery, the voice on the radio told them exactly what it meant. The spring snowstorm had appeared quite literally out of a clear blue sky. The city that was always prepared for winter snows had been caught off guard and was already paralyzed by the inches and inches that blanketed the ground. O'Hare was closed, at least until morning, after which, assuming it opened, there were bound to be long delays while all the stranded passengers were accommodated.

Nick and Raven were safe and warm in the midst of a fairyland, but both of them had solemn commitments half a continent away.

"I'm sorry," Raven murmured, and with the apology, she felt herself instinctively steeling for anger. It took her a moment to diagnose why. Because of Michael, she realized. He would have been so angry if this had happened. But she and Michael wouldn't have been stranded by the snowstorm. They would have left on an early morning flight, long before the storm hit. Michael and Victoria and Blane would have become friends, and Michael would have insisted that she dance with Blane and all her other old lovers while he charmed their wives, and when she finally convinced him that it was time for bed, because of their early flight, he would have satisfied himself sexually, a swift harsh union, and she would have felt lucky, grateful, that he had agreed to accompany her to this important reunion.

*She looks so sad,* Nick thought. So sad, so lost.

"Hey, Raven," he said softly. "It's not the end of the world. In fact, one could reasonably argue that it's more than a little romantic. I need to make a phone call and I assume you do too. So, how do phone calls, showers, and room service sound?"

He had wanted to vanquish her sadness, to rescue her; and he had. She greeted his suggestion with a lovely smile . . . but after a moment her expression changed again. This time, however, there was no sadness. Her intelligent face had merely become a portrait of intense concentration.

"Visualizing tomorrow's calendar?" he guessed.

"No. I'm actually trying to remember a phone number in Kodiak, Alaska. It belongs to Lauren Sinclair. She and Jason Cole and I are supposed to meet for lunch tomorrow to discuss the picture he's making from *Gifts of Love.*"

"She may already be on her way to Los Angeles."

"Yes, and I don't know where she's staying."

"Do you need to be at the meeting?"

"No, not really, but I'd like to be." And I think that she'd like me to be there. Raven didn't speak the thought aloud. It sounded so presumptuous. "She and I have to convince Jason not to change the happy ending of her book." Raven softly shook her love-tangled black hair. "I've called her twice, so I should be able to remember the number."

"Photographic memory."

156

"It used to be. As I've gotten older, I feel like I've run out of film—or at least have forgotten to load it."

"Directory Assistance? Or is Lauren Sinclair a pseudonym?"

"It is, but I know her real name. Still, she's so protective of her privacy, I'd be surprised if she's listed."

"I'll stop asking you questions so you can think. In fact, I'll go into the other bedroom and use the other line on the phone. And then shall I join you in the shower?"

"Yes . . . please."

## ❖ *13* ❖

Raven was quite certain that the telephone number she eventually remembered was correct, but when it rang unanswered, she checked with Directory Assistance in Kodiak, just in case. As she'd anticipated, however, there was no listing for either Lauren Sinclair or Marilyn Pierce; and, as Nick had suggested, the author was undoubtedly already en route to Los Angeles anyway.

Raven made one final call, to her own office high above the Avenue of the Stars, and left for her secretary the message that since she probably wouldn't be in at all tomorrow to please cancel the entire day's appointments first thing in the morning.

Then, her calls finished, Raven walked to the window and gazed at the drama of snow and wind. It was probably terribly cold in the midst of the storm. But, she thought, even if I were outside now, I would feel warm. Warm, wonderfully warm, and happy, truly happy, for the first time in my entire life . . .

Nick was staring outside too, marveling too at the drama and feeling wonderfully warm and truly happy. As he dialed the number to his mansion in Bel Air, expecting his call to be answered by one of his parents, he wondered if the happiness he felt would be apparent in his voice. If so, if it could possibly be detected, his mother would hear it instantly.

But the voice that answered the phone belonged to his twelve-year-old daughter. Samantha was home, which meant that Deandra had canceled their day together. Powerful emotions swept through Nick at the realization: hatred for Deandra and fiercely protective love for his daughter. Both of his girls had been betrayed by their mother, but only Samantha, the older of the two, had a memory of that betrayal.

Nick allowed only love to fill his voice when he spoke.

"Hello there," he said gently.

"Daddy!"

"Hi." And then, dealing with it directly, because it was the best way to get his sensitive daughter to talk, he asked, "What happened?"

"She said she had a bad cold." After a moment Samantha added softly, "Her voice sounded like she really did."

Fresh waves of hatred washed through him as he heard Samantha's soft defense of the mother who deserved no defending, who had abandoned her years ago and kept abandoning her still. Samantha didn't feel anger toward Deandra, not yet; although during the past year Nick believed that his eldest daughter's sensitive young heart was finally beginning to understand that the flaws lay with Deandra, not with her. Now, sometimes when Deandra canceled their time together, Samantha seemed more relieved than disappointed or hurt.

Nick was impatient for the day when the girls would simply decide that they no longer wanted their visits with their mother. It was a choice he would have made for them long ago. But he knew it would have been the wrong choice. To make Deandra forbidden to them would have made her more wanted—and somehow wonderful. In time, Nick prayed, his daughters would see their mother for what she was: selfish and unloving.

"Are you okay, honey?"

"Yes. Gran and Grandpa and I are playing canasta."

A loving smile touched Nick's face. He would never know if he could have raised his motherless daughters alone, if all his love would have been enough, because from the very moment he had needed them, his parents had been there, loving his little girls as fiercely as he did.

"Are you winning?"

His question had the hoped-for response: a young laugh at the other end of the phone.

"No! Gran is—of course."

"Of course," Nick echoed. It was a family tradition. Gran always won at canasta. No one wanted it any other way. And today, when Samantha's world had once again been shaken by the mother who didn't want her, everything needed to be normal and safe. "Where's Mel?"

"At Jessica's."

Nick wasn't surprised. On a day when she had been rejected again by Deandra, Samantha needed to be at home, with the grandparents whose love for her was boundless. But nine-year-old Melody, who would not even have been born had Deandra had her way, had no such need. Melody didn't know, would never know, how much her mother hadn't wanted her; and unlike Samantha, who had spent the first three years of her life with a mother who had only loved her when her father was present, Melody viewed her mother as little more than an occasional visitor in a world that was already filled, overflowing, with the immense love of her father, her grandparents, and her big sister.

"Are you on your way home, Daddy?"

"No," Nick admitted with quiet apology. He wanted to be there now, with her, probably far more than Samantha actually needed him to be. "In fact, it looks like I won't be home until tomorrow afternoon, maybe even tomorrow night. Do you want to know why?"

"Yes."

"Because all of a sudden, without any warning whatsoever, a huge snowstorm has hit Chicago."

"Snow?"

Nick smiled at the enthusiasm that had so swiftly replaced the disappointment in Samantha's voice. Both girls loved the snow. As soon as they had discovered its existence, they had wanted to see it, in person. For the past few years they had all spent the Christmas holidays at the Eden–Lake Tahoe, frolicking in the snow, going on sleigh rides, drinking mugs of hot chocolate dotted with marshmallows as they watched the snow fall outside.

"I wish you were here," Nick said softly. "Do you know what it feels like?"

"No, what?"

"It feels like I'm inside one of your snow globes and someone has just given it a good shake."

"Neat!"

"Very neat," Nick agreed, thinking as he did about the girls' collection of glass globes.

They were presents from him, from necessary business trips taken to oversee the creation of his hotels at Tahoe and Aspen and Chamonix and Gstaad. From his long trips, especially to faraway places, Nick always returned with presents; but from shorter trips, like the one this weekend, he returned with presents only if he saw something he thought the girls would like. Their life was about gifts of love, not gifts of money, and from this weekend in Chicago they would be most happy with his smiles, his hugs, and his detailed description of the snowstorm.

Nick hadn't planned to return from Chicago with presents for his daughters, but now his heart whispered something very dangerous: You could bring them the most magnificent present of all, the one gift you had never planned to give—a mother.

"Daddy?"

"Yes, darling?" he asked gently of the daughter
needed a mother, the little girl who was so rapidly—
rapidly—becoming a little woman.

"Gran has that look in her eye when she's about to
another natural."

Nick laughed. "You'd better go then. I love
honey. I'll see you tomorrow night."

"I love you too, Daddy."

*I love you, honey. I'll see you tomorrow night.* Th
were the words—devastating words spoken with s
tenderness—that Raven overheard just as she reac
the open doorway to Nick's bedroom.

Nick had told her precisely what he had wanted he
do: make her phone calls and then meet him in
shower. That was what she should have done. Hadn't
learned, over and over, that the men who had been
lovers expected her to follow their commands *to
letter?*

But the wonderful warmth had made her so brave,
the happiness she had felt had its own compel
commands: go to him, and marvel with him at
wonder of the snowstorm, and then, when it's tim
again marvel at other wonders, seduce him as he
seduced you all night long . . .

The warmth was gone now, replaced by ice, except
the sudden liquid heat that blurred her eyes. No one
her cry, not ever, and she wouldn't let Nick, of all peo
see her pain now. Her tears would be completely hid
by the time he joined her in the shower, shower dr
concealing teardrops. Not that Nick would spend m
time surveying her face anyway. There were other thi
obvious pleasures, that would occupy his concentrat

And that was what she wanted, Raven realized as

withdrew from the doorway. She wanted him to touch her, to love her.

You mean to *make* love, don't you?

Yes! I know now that it's all a pretense, a dream that will melt with the snow. But for now, for as long as it can last, I'm going to keep pretending . . .

"Raven?"

She was halfway across the living room, only halfway, so far—too far—from the shower that would veil her foolish tears. She wasn't going to turn around, she couldn't. But she couldn't stop him from moving in front of her, nor could she stop the strong fingers that lifted her chin and became so very gentle as they touched her tears.

"Whatever you overheard I'm pretty sure you misinterpreted. Tell me what you think you heard."

"I think I heard you talking to your girlfriend . . . or your wife."

"There's no girlfriend, Raven, and there's no wife," Nick said softly as he gazed at the eyes that had filled with tears because it had bothered her so much that there might be another woman to whom he said "I love you." She cares about you, Nick's heart whispered with dangerous joy. She wants to be your girlfriend—and maybe even your wife. Tell her she can be both, *ask* her to be. Nick subdued the dangerous wish with the memory of the precious young hearts that were so very vulnerable. "I was talking to my daughter."

"Your daughter?"

"Yes. I have two daughters. Samantha, to whom I was speaking, is twelve and my other daughter is nine. Two daughters, Raven, but no girlfriend, no wife."

"Did she die?" Raven asked softly.

"Who? Deandra?" Nick's laugh was short—and bitter. "No. My ex-wife is very much alive."

"She hurt you very deeply."

"No," Nick answered solemnly. "She hurt my daughters."

*"Oh."*

It was a single syllable, a soft whisper, but it spoke volumes to Nick's heart. Raven had been concerned about him, that he might have been hurt by Deandra, but even that deep concern paled in comparison to her worry about the harm Deandra might have caused his daughters.

*She would love them,* his heart proclaimed. This woman, who was so terribly harmed by her own mother, knows all about the fragile sensitivities of little girls.

But, caution warned, the great harm that was done to the once impoverished and outcast Raven has made her care about other things as well: wealth, appearance, acceptance into the innermost circles of privilege and power. Don't forget what Victoria said: Raven's desire for money is insatiable.

Most of Nick wanted to pull Raven close to him, to tell her in a rush all the truths about himself and his girls, to ask her to join *their* innermost circle—of love—forever. But it was far too soon. He had fallen in love with her, that was certain, and he believed that she was falling in love with him too. But for now the masquerade needed to continue.

Instead of encircling her in his arms, Nick created even more distance between them. He gestured for her to sit on the couch while he remained standing. It was a necessary distance because he was about to tell her the carefully worded—carefully edited—story of Deandra. If he had been touching Raven, she would have felt his rage; and if he had been touching her, his heart might have succeeded in its dangerous pleas to tell her all the truths.

"Deandra and I were married six months after we graduated from college. It wasn't an impulsive marriage. We had known each other for over two years and had talked at great length about our shared desire to have children. When Samantha was born sixteen months later, we were thrilled, at least I thought we were. Deandra was a doting mother when I was around, but as I discovered later, almost too late, she was simply a terrific actress. Whenever I wasn't there, she ignored Samantha altogether."

"I'm so sorry," Raven whispered, but Nick didn't seem to hear her. There was more to his story, more that needed to be told.

"About a year after Sam was born, we decided to start trying to have another baby. Deandra was an active participant in this decision, Raven. I wasn't a dictatorial husband imposing his will on a meek and oppressed wife. I believed that she wanted more children as much as I did, and we mourned together as month after month passed without conception."

Nick took a deep steadying breath. But the emotions that swirled within him weren't steadied and never would be. Not now, not after nine years, not ever.

Raven had seen rage before, contemptuous rage in the eyes of lovers frustrated by her iciness; but what she saw now far surpassed anything she had ever seen. Fire blazed in Nick's smoke-gray eyes. The inferno deep within, always so carefully contained, was contained no more, and the steel that was Nick had become molten, a silver river that threatened to destroy, to ravage, all that lay in its path.

But Raven, who had always been so fearful of the rage of men, was strangely unafraid.

"Nick?"

His eyes were focused far away, on an invisible image of hatred, but still, when he heard her concern—and her courage—a little gentleness surfaced from the fiery depths.

There was gentleness for Raven. But there was no gentleness whatsoever for the memory that danced vividly in his brain—and no gentleness in his voice when he told Raven about that long-ago day.

"One afternoon, when Samantha was almost three, I happened to come home early from work. The phone was ringing as I walked through the door. It was a call from a doctor's office, confirming the D and C that was scheduled for Deandra the following morning. She was pregnant, despite the IUD she'd had all those months when she pretended to be devastated that she couldn't conceive. She was planning to terminate the pregnancy and have a tubal ligation at the same time."

Raven's heart wept with sadness. How well she knew the anguish of betrayal. It had been a constant companion for her entire life.

But why, she wondered, had Deandra betrayed Nick? How could she have *not* wanted his baby? It hadn't been an impulsive betrayal, a sudden change of heart, but a calculated one—which, perhaps, had started even before their wedding.

Deandra had chosen to marry Nick, had wanted to. Indeed, her desire to marry him had been so strong that she had systematically lied to him, pretending to share with him his wish for a family.

*Why?*

For Raven, the answer was a simple one: because Deandra had loved Nick so much, *too* much. She had wanted his love desperately, but she had wanted to share it with no one, not even their babies.

"Deandra just wanted you."

No, Nick thought. Deandra just wanted my money. That was the bitter truth, but in Raven's soft pronouncement he heard a different, and quite wondrous, one: it made sense to Raven that Deandra could have wanted just him, loved him that much, without all his riches, all the glittering treasures his money could buy.

"What happened, Nick?"

"I convinced her to have the baby." I paid her to, he amended silently. The divorce settlement had been huge—but quite trivial compared to what it had bought . . . what it had saved. "Obviously, the marriage was over. It ended legally the day Melody was born."

"Melody."

Nick smiled lovingly. "It's the perfect name for her. She marches to her own drummer, but it's the happiest of marches—a joyful and exhilarating song that she seems to want to share with the world." Nick's smile faded and emotion filled his voice. "When I think what would have happened if I hadn't come home early that afternoon . . ."

"But you did," Raven reminded quietly as her thoughts drifted to her own never-born little sister or brother.

"Raven?"

Raven gave a soft shake of her head, shaking away his question and her own faraway thoughts. Then, looking up at him again, she asked, "Who's taking care of the girls this weekend?"

"My parents. We all live together. Deandra was supposed to have spent today with them, but she canceled at the last minute—not for the first time."

"So she's still in Los Angeles?"

"In Los Angeles, in New York, in Palm Beach. She married a wealthy man who already had all the family he wanted."

"Do you still love her?"

"I honestly can't remember having ever loved her, Raven. Whatever I felt for her was erased from my memory the moment I realized what she would have done if I hadn't discovered her plan."

Raven nodded solemnly, and for several moments there was silence. Finally, because he wanted, perhaps needed, to know, Nick asked, "Do you still love your mother, despite her betrayal of you?"

Raven carefully considered his question before answering, searching her heart for the truth that seemed so important to him. Finally she replied, "Still? No. But I did, for a very long time, even after she left. I realize now how deeply troubled she was, and I just feel sorry for her. She didn't love herself and that made her quite incapable of loving a child. Why are you asking me, Nick? Is it because of the way Samantha and Melody feel about Deandra?"

"Yes. Especially Sam. Even though she should have the most resentment, she's the most determined to preserve the mother-daughter bond which is tenuous at best and hurtful at worst."

"You need to let her preserve it, Nick, for as long as she wants to. When the time is right, she'll let it go."

Raven had understood his rage, and she had offered brave and gentle counsel about his daughters, and now, even though he wasn't touching her, the dangerous wishes of Nick's heart would not be still. "I'd like you to meet them."

"Oh," she whispered. "I'd love to."

"How about dinner one night this weekend?"

"Wonderful." Raven hesitated a moment. It had been a very long time since she had prepared a meal for anyone—fifteen years to be exact. That night, after her mother had left and before Patrice Wainwright had arrived at midnight to shatter her world, she had cooked for Victoria and her parents a gourmet's delight. "Why don't you come to my house? I'll cook."

"Are you sure?"

"Positive."

"Okay. We'll be there." Nick watched her tug thoughtfully at her lower lip, and when she didn't speak the thought aloud, he urged, "What?"

"I wondered if your parents would like to come too?"

Yes, Nick thought. His parents would *love* to come. His mother especially would be bursting with curiosity

168

about the woman whose rose garden he had planted and with whom he had gone to Chicago and to whom now, most astonishingly, he wanted to introduce his daughters.

"Thank you, but I think that meeting the girls will be enough for one night. There won't be any problem with Melody, but Samantha can be withdrawn, a little hostile even. She's a lovely girl, Raven, generous and loving with her sister and her grandparents and me, but beyond that circle of love she's quite wary, and she's ferociously protective of preserving the circle just as it is."

"I understand, Nick. I understand about betrayal and trust."

"I know you do," he said softly. I only hope that when you discover that I have withheld important truths from you, betraying your trust so that I didn't again betray the trust of my daughters, that you will understand . . . and forgive.

# Part Three

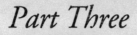

## ❀ *14* ❀

"Mr. Cole? This is Elaine at the reception desk. Raven Winter's secretary just called to cancel her luncheon meeting with you today. Apparently Ms. Winter is snowed in in Chicago."

"Okay. Thanks," Jason answered calmly, concealing his annoyance. He was not at all happy with the message but there was no need to kill—or even concern—the messenger.

Jason *was* annoyed though. In anticipation of his luncheon with Lauren Sinclair and Raven Winter, he had given Greta the day off. Following the lunch, he had reasoned, he would simply have gone home to work in his penthouse atop the Santa Monica Palisades until the limousine arrived at four forty-five to whisk him to the Dorothy Chandler Pavilion.

Jason hated wasting time. Indeed, he almost never did. Indisputably a creative genius, a director of unique and compelling vision, he differed from many creative personalities in that he did not lose touch with reality. He was focused, organized, and so much in control of his artistic vision that he routinely brought his multimillion-dollar masterpieces in ahead of time and under budget.

Now, within seconds of learning that his afternoon was

173

suddenly free, Jason swiftly shifted his attention to the next four days. On Thursday he was flying to Hong Kong, to film *The Jade Palace*. Between now and then numerous tasks needed to be accomplished. Some were trivial, almost optional, and others were of utmost importance. But Jason didn't differentiate. All would be completed before the Gold Star jet lifted off the tarmac at 3 P.M. Thursday afternoon.

During the hours that had just opened up for him, he would dispense with much of the correspondence that needed to be done. He would do the dictating, but with Greta gone, he would need someone else to transcribe his words. After only the slightest moment of hesitation, Jason dialed the familiar four-digit number that connected him to Gold Star's executive administrator. Margot's streamlined efficiency and no-nonsense organization perfectly complemented his; and Jason knew that despite the fact that Academy Award Day was an unofficial holiday in Hollywood, Margot would be in today—even though much of the usually large secretarial pool might not be.

"Help," he said without identifying himself.

"Oh, Jason, no. Today?"

"I know. If you can't get someone for me, I'll understand."

"Just *one* someone?" Margot asked hopefully. Usually when Jason requested extra help, he wanted several people *now*.

"Just one," Jason confirmed. "Just someone to do some transcription for me between noon and three."

"Not until noon?"

"I think I can keep myself busy until then. So? Possible?"

"I'll have someone there promptly at noon."

"Thanks."

"You're welcome. Oh, and Jason, good luck this evening."

\* \* \*

It was precisely noon when she appeared in his open doorway; but even though he had an internal clock that never lost track of time, it wasn't the awareness that it was noon, time for the promised secretary to arrive, that made Jason look up from his dictation. Nor was it anything that she herself did. She made no noise whatsoever, not even the softest of sighs to announce her arrival, and there was something so ethereal about her that it seemed unlikely that a change in shadow or light, signaling movement, had been what had alerted him.

Jason had no idea why he looked up when he did. He was compelled to, that was all, and when he did, the gifted actor somehow swiftly disguised his surprise.

Secretaries and receptionists who found work at the studios in Hollywood were often aspiring actresses. They usually wore stylish clothes in brilliantly memorable colors and cuts, and their makeup was always flawless, and they had unrelenting enthusiasm for every task, no matter how boring or repetitious it was, and their reactions to various events in the office ranged from anguish to ecstasy, an eloquent demonstration of their range of emotion.

The aspiring actresses who were secretaries in Hollywood were beautiful, talented, and savvy; and they all possessed the other ingredient necessary to survival in Tinseltown: confidence—or at least the illusion of same.

The woman who appeared in Jason's open doorway at precisely noon did not convey even the slightest illusion of confidence. Maybe she was an illusion herself, a mirage that would dissolve as mysteriously as she had appeared. She looked as if she wanted to disappear, Jason thought. Her face was already mostly hidden, curtained by a magnificent veil of golden hair. He caught intriguing glimpses of delicate features beneath, but when he searched for her eyes, all that answered were harsh reflections from the wire-rimmed glasses she wore.

When his searching gaze made the already hidden face withdraw even deeper, Jason shifted from her face to her clothes. Instead of the brilliantly colored plumage worn by most secretaries, in styles cut to show to best advantage shapely legs and lusciously curved bodies, the dress she wore was as concealing as the golden veil—a shapeless, floor-length creation embroidered with a meadow of wild-flowers.

The dress was quite beautiful, Jason decided, and it seemed to be a wholly authentic relic from another era—just as she was. The apparition who stood before him was a flower child, a most fragile blossom destined to be merci-lessly crushed by the changing tides of time. She should have been in a meadow herself, strumming an acoustic guitar and singing a poetic ballad of love; but instead she was here, torn from the pastoral tranquility where she belonged and transported across the decades to this fast-paced empire of glitter—and to him, the man who was its crown prince.

It seemed a horrible mistake for her to be here. But here she was, right on time, just as Margot had promised. She was his secretary for the afternoon, and if Jason needed further proof of her identity, he needed only to look at her hands. There, clutched tightly by fingers that should have been softly strumming a guitar, was a spiral notebook.

She was here, on time and ready to go to work.

She was not, however, an aspiring actress. Anyone of them would have killed for a chance to spend an afternoon helping Jason Cole. What better way to be discovered? What more powerful man in Hollywood was there? And even if nothing came of it, most were starstruck enough to have simply been delighted to have had the chance to spend a few hours with him.

There was no doubt in Jason's mind that the vision who stood in his open doorway was not delighted to be here. But, he decided, she was somehow bravely determined to be.

Was he really so terrifying? he wondered. Had his well-deserved reputation for uncompromising perfectionism somehow taken on a wholly undeserved dimension of cruelty toward those who didn't measure up?

Yes, he was demanding, *very* demanding. But no one had ever seen him lose his temper—not ever. Even now, even as he felt a powerful surge of angry frustration that the delicate flower who stood before him was so obviously afraid of him, Jason's voice was as pleasant and reassuring as his smile.

Standing, he greeted her. "Hello, please come in. You're right on time."

In response to the silent but masterful direction of the Academy Award-winning director, she entered the office and sat down in a chair directly in front of his desk. Now, separated from her only by the expanse of polished oak, Jason saw clearly the tips of her faintly trembling pale fingers, the nails chewed to nothing; and he also saw her eyes. They were an extraordinary combination of blue and green, their remarkable brilliance magnified by the corrective lenses she wore. And, he realized with another rush of anger, the remarkable blue-green eyes seemed to be trembling too.

He wanted to, had to, put her at ease. The quickest way was simply to show her how very easy he was to work for. He could have just given her the tape he had been dictating, to let her begin to transcribe that while he dictated more; but then she would have vanished into his secretary's office, and she would have waited there, trembling with fear that he would find fault with what she had typed.

Jason wasn't going to let her go until she knew she had no reason to fear him. He had been halfway through a letter when she had appeared. He would simply dictate the rest of it to her directly.

"Shall we get right to work?" When the golden veil shimmered assent, he suggested, "Why don't I just dictate something to you?"

Jason thought he saw a flicker of surprise, but he was only permitted a fleeting glance, because she quickly bent down to retrieve a pen from the woven yarn purse that lay beside her on the floor. It was a sixties purse. And, Jason realized as he noticed how tattered it was, it had obviously been a sixties purchase.

"Ready?" he asked when she held the pen in her hand and had opened her spiral notebook. After a slight nod sent more shimmering waves of gold, he said, "Okay. Please write this: Be very clear that, although I hold the option on the work, I am not sufficiently wedded to the project that I am willing to make any compromises about the ending—"

"Mr. Cole? I'm so sorry that I'm late!"

Although the breathless words promptly interrupted his dictation, it was a moment before Jason looked toward the intruder. He was quite mesmerized still by the vision before him, fascinated—and troubled—by what he saw. Her delicate fingers, with their mercilessly chewed nails, clutched the pen *so tightly* . . . and they seemed to be carefully writing down his words longhand, not the shorthand she should have known.

When he finally took his gaze from the pale fingers and looked beyond the moonlit veil, Jason saw in the doorway the woman who matched the breathless voice. She was stylishly clothed and very beautiful, and the instant she had the attention of his dark blue eyes, her lovely face began to eloquently convey for the maestro her dramatic range, from a frown of great sorrow at her tardiness to the wonderfully hopeful smile of an ingenue.

Here, breathless, beautiful, and indisputably talented, was his secretary for the afternoon.

Then who the hell was it who had been so painstakingly transcribing his words? Who was this pale and golden phantom from the sixties? And why did her luminous eyes flicker with relief as she looked at the beautiful woman in the doorway?

"Who are you?" Jason's question was to her, the vision, and it was a demand. She looked back toward him then, and when she did, fear replaced relief. Gently, so gently, he repeated, "Who are you?"

As he waited for her to speak, Jason realized that he had yet to hear her voice. Until now her communication had been silent, the messages of her fearful eyes and the shimmering nods of her golden head. He hadn't heard her voice, but he had imagined her in a faraway meadow in a faraway time softly singing a ballad of love . . .

The voice that finally answered his question was even more soft, more musical than he had imagined it would be.

"I'm Marilyn Pierce . . . Lauren Sinclair." Holly shrugged in soft apology to the dark blue eyes that seemed both disbelieving and angry at her revelation. "We had a luncheon meeting this afternoon. I mean I thought we did."

She faltered then, and gazed searchingly at the beautiful woman in the doorway—as if, somehow, the intruder could help her.

"She isn't Raven," Jason clarified. "Raven is snowed in in Chicago. And I obviously misinterpreted the message I received this morning from her office. I thought the entire meeting had been canceled. But all that's really happened is that Raven won't be joining us."

"Maybe we should reschedule."

That, Jason realized, was what she wanted. But if he complied with that wish, would he ever see her again? She undoubtedly believed that she had already gotten his answer to her request that he not change the ending of her book—that, in fact, he had made her write it down, like a schoolgirl being taught a humiliating lesson, compelled to write over and over on the blackboard: I am not sufficiently wedded to the project that I am willing to make compromises about the ending.

But the words he had dictated to her had been about another project entirely; and now, as he debated what to do, Jason's eyes met hers with gentle apology. Jason Cole rarely found himself in a position of needing to apologize, and gentleness and vulnerability were usually reserved for the camera, for one of his many Academy Award-winning roles.

But he wasn't acting now. An astonishing and unfamiliar emotion accompanied the gentleness, and as he made himself vulnerable to Lauren Sinclair, he wondered if he was about to discover that she was a talented actress after all, having worn both the tattered sixties attire and the flower child fragility as a costume, because *Gifts of Love* was a period piece.

When she saw his apology, would her remarkable aquamarine eyes suddenly flash with triumph? Would they blaze with the confidence—and petulance—that he had expected from the best-selling author?

Jason waited. But the gentleness of his stare seemed to cause even greater uncertainty than his anger had. Finally he shifted his gaze and addressed the gorgeous woman who was to have been his secretary for the afternoon. "I'm afraid there's been a mix-up. My luncheon meeting wasn't truly canceled, so I won't be needing your help after all."

The aspiring actress handled her disappointment brilliantly, concealing it completely under a beautiful smile before making her graceful exit. She was very good, Jason thought. He would make sure that she got a screen test.

When he and Lauren Sinclair were alone again, he said gently, solemnly, "I didn't know who you were. The letter I was in the midst of dictating had nothing to do with *Gifts of Love.*" With a smile, he added, "I must have known that you were coming, though, because I didn't cancel our luncheon reservations."

## ❋ *15* ❋

Jason had made reservations at the Bel Air Hunt Club. On this day, when Los Angeles was flooded with reporters from around the world, luncheon at any of the usual celebrity restaurants would have been constantly disrupted by both well-wishers and journalists hoping for his last-minute predictions about how many of the seven nominated categories he would actually win.

The Bel Air Hunt club offered privacy. Its rich and famous members demanded it, and they respected it among themselves. As the maître d' led them through the lavish dining room filled with Hollywood's most glittering stars, Jason was greeted by many knowing smiles. But he was not ambushed by anyone demanding more.

The table he had reserved was one of the dining room's most private, secluded in its own alcove. They were inside, but the spotless glass surrounding them gave the illusion that they were sitting in the midst of the rose garden itself, an illusion enhanced by the fragrance of the bountiful bouquets of roses that bloomed within.

Had he been dining with anyone but her, Jason, who rarely bothered with lunch at all, would have ordered only a small Caesar salad. But here she was, looking as if she rarely bothered with food *ever*. She ate her fingernails, that was certain; but, he decided, beneath her billowy dress was a fragile, painfully thin body.

"Everything here is wonderful," Jason said as he watched her study the menu.

"I'm sure it is. I'm not very . . . I usually don't eat lunch."

*And today, because of me, you're far too nervous to eat anyway.* "Shall we just have warm rolls and salad then?"

"Yes," she answered with obvious relief.

As she answered, her eyes met his, and now, in this intimate alcove of roses, Jason saw that the glasses she wore were just glass, merely a disguise. Her blue-green eyes weren't magnified at all, not enhanced or embellished in any way. They were truly luminous, truly shimmering . . . and truly dark-circled, as if she hadn't slept for days in anticipation of this fearful encounter with him.

Jason realized then that some part of him had been waiting, albeit reluctantly, for the charade to come to an end. Raven and the real—glamorous and confident—Lauren Sinclair would suddenly appear, and after congratulating the actress seated before him for her compelling performance, they would force him to admit that yes, it was a mistake to alter storylines, to change endings.

Jason did not want the charade to end, and now, as he gazed at her, he realized that it wouldn't. This was no carefully crafted masquerade. She, this diffident woman *and no one else* had written the words that had enchanted him so. Her writing was poetic, lyrical, otherworldly—just as she was. There was no dazzling glamour to her romantic stories, no glittering confidence. There was only a courageous hopefulness: joyous and innocent . . . as innocent as she.

There was sex in her stories of love, of course, but it was never explicit . . . as if she had no actual experience . . . as if she had only the brave and hopeful belief that making love was the ultimate union of hearts and minds and spirits and souls. In a Lauren Sinclair novel, sex was the gift-wrapping for love, the beribboned adornment that came last, after the true gift—the one inside—had been chosen with joyous care.

A thousand questions filled Jason's mind. He wanted to know everything about her. Why she wrote what she wrote. Why she was who she was. Where she had been in all the years since the sixties. He wanted to know the real Lauren Sinclair. No, he amended silently. Not Lauren Sinclair, but the woman hidden *behind* the costume glasses.

"Your real name is Marilyn Pierce?"

How long had her heart been fluttering? Holly wondered. The life-defying pace had begun the moment Raven had first suggested the meeting with Jason, and it had increased with each passing day until it had reached a plateau beyond which further fluttering seemed simply impossible. The racing heartbeats had prevented sleep, and she couldn't eat even the small amounts of food that usually sustained her, and at times she had wondered if she could actually survive until today.

But she had survived. And as the taxi had swiftly transported her from the Hotel Bel-Air to Gold Star Studios, she had told herself that she would survive the dreaded meeting itself. The past seventeen days had proven how strong her frail body really was. She didn't need food, or sleep, and her heart could race at a seemingly impossible speed without failing.

But when his eyes had lifted to her, sensing her presence the moment she arrived, and the intense blue had made her feel as if he been waiting for her, searching for her, all his life, her fluttering heart took flight and her starved mind soared with it.

She was alive still, in a magical floating place that she knew to be an illusion, and which was probably just this side of death. Now he was asking her, so gently, what name he should call her—and she wanted, for this magical time, for as long as it could last, to be called a name that she had shared with no one else.

"Marilyn Pierce is my legal name, but I'm Holly."

"Holly," he echoed. "Were you a Christmas baby?"

"Yes," she breathed, barely, because of the gentle wonder with which he had spoken her name.

"How many Christmases ago?"

"Thirty. I was thirty last Christmas."

Holly frowned slightly at the admission. Part of her truly believed that she was thirty-five, the age that Marilyn Pierce would have been. Part of her truly believed that she had already reached the place that was considered midway through life, that she was halfway there, halfway home . . .

"Holly?" Jason asked softly when he saw what looked like pure anguish in her beautiful eyes. What causes you such pain? And what compels you to hide behind golden hair and costume glasses? "Holly?"

She had drifted away from the magic—to visions of death, past and future—but now the tender concern in his voice returned her to the present, terrifying and wondrous.

"Yes?"

"What were you thinking just then?"

"Nothing." Then, not happy with the lie, not wanting to lie to him, not able to, she added, "A faraway memory."

"Can you tell me about it? Will you?"

No, Holly thought swiftly. She knew that it would be impossible for her to ever share with another living soul the memories of that snowy Valentine's night. She knew with absolute certainty that if she ever even started to recount the unspeakable details of that horror that the anguish that had lived inside her would suddenly gush out, a scream that would never stop. She wouldn't die, she would just scream forever—contaminating with evil whoever happened to overhear her screams. Holly knew that her memories of beloved faces and desperate pleas and unrelenting madness must remain forever within, forever silent. She had no right to share such evil or such horror.

"I can't," she answered finally.

Meaning you won't, Jason amended silently, his heart aching as he witnessed the transformation in her beautiful eyes. They were gray now, opaque and deathlike. You need to tell someone, Holly. Whatever it is, you need to speak the words aloud.

But why would she tell *him?* Why would she tell the man whose decision to change the happy ending of her story had forced her to leave the sanctuary of her romantic writing and the cocoonlike safety of the time warp in which she so obviously dwelled?

Jason already knew that he was going to tell Holly that the movie version of *Gifts of Love* would be absolutely identical to her wonderfully hopeful book of love. But if he told her that now, she would leave, wouldn't she? She would simply vanish, floating away as mysteriously as she had appeared.

Jason didn't want her to leave. He wanted to see again her shimmering blue-green eyes, and the beautiful smile that had touched her lips when she had confessed that she was indeed a Christmas baby, and he wanted to hear again the affection in her voice at that gentle memory.

Jason wanted that—and much more. The man whose greatest passion and most unselfish energy had always been devoted to his movies, not to the glamorous and confident women with whom he had shared his bed, wanted much more from Holly . . . for Holly . . . with Holly. He wanted the magnificent gift of love about which she wrote.

The realization was stunning. Jason Cole had a lifelong history of getting what he wanted. Nothing, however, had been handed to him on a silver platter. The triumphs that appeared effortless to the outside world were, in fact, won with hard work, tireless energy, and demanding determination.

But never before had Jason Cole wanted love. And never before had what he wanted seemed so totally out of his control.

And so impossible? he wondered as he gazed at the cloudy eyes which now shut him out completely.

But which *had* shimmered, he reminded himself. And which had filled with a brave and hopeful intimacy when she had confessed to him that her real name was Holly.

"Holly?" Jason heard the emotion in his own voice, the gentle plea, and Holly heard it too, because suddenly she seemed to be struggling to find her way through the dense fog, to reach him, to see clearly what had caused his emotion.

"Yes?"

Do you feel it too? his heart asked as from deep within the foggy gray he began to see delicate wisps of blue and of green—for him. Do you feel the magic?

Yes, *yes,* the shimmering colors seemed to answer before they were stolen from his view, suddenly hidden beneath pale, downcast lids.

She felt the magic, Jason knew that she did, but it terrified her. So he found a topic that was far safer than the one his heart wanted him to pursue.

"I've never been to Alaska."

"It's very beautiful."

"Will you tell me about it?" Will you look at me? And talk to me? Holly? Please?

Yes, her eyes answered as they opened to him once again. *Yes.*

At first, her words where halting and uncertain, but eventually the naturally gifted storyteller that lived within her took over. She told him of glaciers and forests, of green seas and indigo skies, of majestic bears and soaring eagles. And of the people: the richness and grandeur of the Native Alaskan culture.

Holly paused occasionally in her eloquent story, as if uncertain that he really wanted to hear more, but he always encouraged her to continue, not wanting the enchantment ever to end. The clouds had vanished from her eyes, and there was such affection in her voice.

And sometimes she even smiled.

But, eventually, her story of Alaska came to a close. *Her* story? No, Jason realized. Nothing of what she had told him had been about her.

"How long have you lived in Alaska?"

"Fifteen years."

"It sounds as if you've traveled all over the state."

Holly nodded, but a frown touched her face. "I used to travel a lot, in the beginning, when I first moved there." But now I rarely leave my cottage, she thought. Now even the journey into town seems a monumental undertaking, made only when necessary—for groceries, to mail a manuscript, to see if a Jason Cole movie is playing at the theater.

"Did you have a favorite place?" Jason asked, rescuing her, rescuing both of them, as she began to drift again from the magic of their present to the grayness of her own faraway memories of the past.

"Barrow," she answered with a soft grateful smile. "I used to go there every summer."

"Because?"

"Because in summer, between May and August, the sun never quite sets. It begins to set, falling like any other setting sun, but just before it touches the horizon, it starts to rise again, a ball of fire bouncing back up to the sky."

As she spoke, her eyes glowed with remembered wonder; and there was more wonder, present wonder, as Jason said, "I'd love to see it."

And then the dark blue eyes that had won Academy

Awards for their silent eloquence sent a message of future wonder: I would love to see it with you.

It was the most important message his eyes had ever sent, and Holly read it with brilliant clarity. Her pale cheeks flushed a soft pink; but she did not look away. Her eyes glowed in answer; and they were even more luminous now, far more shimmering, than when she'd described the wonder of the summer sun's dazzling pirouette in the midnight skies above Barrow.

As boldly as the summer sun flirted with the horizon in Barrow, Holly and Jason talked about magic—the magical splendor of nature and the technological magic that created motion pictures. Neither mentioned the magic of love, but they both knew that in those enchanted hours they were living it, falling in love, like the glorious summer sun that began to fall only to bounce back up again, soaring with joy, its golden brilliance unwilling to fade.

The magic should have gone on forever, that was what they both wanted, but the part of Jason that was tethered to reality suddenly kicked in with a jolt, forcing him to glance at his watch.

It was almost four. The limousine that would whisk him—a tuxedoed version—to the Dorothy Chandler Pavilion would be arriving at his penthouse in less than an hour.

"I have to go," he apologized quietly. "The Award ceremony begins promptly at six and I need to be there at least twenty minutes before it starts."

"Award ceremony?"

It was clear that Holly truly had no idea what he was talking about, and somehow Jason managed to swiftly suppress his surprise. But he was surprised—and worried.

Perhaps the Oscars weren't major news in Kodiak; but

she had told him that she'd been in Los Angeles since Saturday. Had she not turned on the television in those two days, or read a newspaper, or even glanced at a headline? Holly had been in Los Angeles. But, Jason wondered, where had she really been? Lost somewhere in the sixties? Or in the latest romance novel she was writing? Or in the gray anguish that he wanted so much to banish forever?

"The Academy Awards are tonight," he answered finally, gently. Then, even more gently, he said, "When I RSVP'd, I told the ceremony organizers that I would be coming alone. However, if I showed up with someone—you—they would find seats for us. Would you like to come with me this evening, Holly?"

"Oh, no," she whispered. Then, almost urgently, she amended, "I mean I'd like to . . ." She faltered, she had to, because the next words would have been "be with you." Holly knew the next words because the shy heroines she created became infinitely brave when the heroes—strong and gentle men like Jason—gazed at them the way he was gazing at her now. Her heroines would have uttered the brave words, and her heroes would have echoed them, but . . . "But I don't think so. Thank you."

Jason didn't push. He wanted to be with her, of course; but alone, in their magical world. And if she accompanied him tonight, to Hollywood's most glamorous gala, their privacy would be invaded by a legion of photographers, zooming in for a closer look at Jason Cole's mystery woman.


"We still need to talk about your book," Jason said when they reached the Hotel Bel-Air. "Why don't we have breakfast together tomorrow morning?"

"With Raven?"

Jason fought a sudden rush of frustration. At the

mention of her book, Holly's expression had become shadowed with worry, and now it was obvious that she wanted Raven at the meeting—Raven, who would be on her side.

*I'm on your side, Holly.* "I think the two of us can discuss it, Holly, but if you want Raven there, I'll see if she's back and can join us."

"No, it's okay."

"Good." Then, because he didn't want her to spend another night sleepless with worry, he said, "I want to discuss your book with you, Holly, but I promise you I won't change a word, not a syllable, if you don't want me to. So . . . I'll pick you up at nine. We'll go to Malibu. There's a restaurant there, overlooking the water, that I think you'll like."

## ❀ *16* ❀

Holly had not watched television for over seventeen years, not since the snowy evening when the happy voice of the fictional Corky had drowned out the real-life lethal whispers between her mother and Derek. If she hadn't been watching television, if she and the twins had been quietly playing a board game instead, then she might have heard the whispers, might have been able to call for help, might have been able to save the beloved lives which had been lost.

The private and solitary world in which Holly had lived since that Valentine's evening had been a silent one. There was no television, or radio, or stereo in her cabin in Kodiak, no sounds whatsoever to muffle even the softest of whispers—whispers that she strained to hear still, long after they had been silenced forever.

For a very long time Holly simply stared at the television in her luxurious room at the Hotel Bel-Air. It was silent, dormant, but beckoning. The Academy Award ceremony would surely be televised. Indeed, she had vague memories of watching the glittering glamour of Oscar night as a little girl.

For so many years a television had been an enemy, a co-conspirator in Derek's gruesome madness, but now it was an ally to the fluttering heart that needed to see more of him . . .

Holly's fingers trembled as she turned on the power and she steeled herself for a noise that in her memory was harsh, strident, deafening. But the volume was set low, and it seemed as if the beautiful reporter who stood outside the Dorothy Chandler Pavilion on the red carpet on which the celebrities walked after emerging from their limousines was talking just to her.

Holly watched the screen and listened to the reporter chronicle the arrival of each new star; but until Jason appeared, part of Holly—most of Holly—was listening for the faraway whispers that were the prelude to death.

The moment he appeared, the moment he gracefully unfolded his long tuxedoed form from the limousine, the futile vigil for the lethal whispers of the past was vanquished by the recent memories of their magical afternoon. Holly's fluttering heart now fought a new voice, one that reminded her that the afternoon's magic had merely been an illusion, a dazzling trick conjured by Hollywood's most gifted actor.

He was dazzling you, the voice said. He was seducing you with his gentle eyes in order to get what he wants: no resistance whatsoever to the changes he plans to make in *Gifts of Love.* The sincerity on his face when he asked you to accompany him to the Award ceremony tonight, as if he, too, didn't want the magic to end, was the pièce de résistance of his command performance. He knew that you would say no. He could see at once that you've never been on a date in your entire life and that it was beyond the realm of possibility that you would say yes to him today.

You'll see. He's getting out of the limousine now and in a moment he will turn to gallantly offer his hand to his date. She'll be unbelievably confident and beautiful, a woman as glamorous as he is dashing, his girlfriend, his lover . . .

But as soon as Jason was out of the limousine, the

We have 4 FREE BOOKS for you
as your introduction to
KENSINGTON CHOICE
To get your FREE BOOKS, worth
up to $23.96, mail the card below.

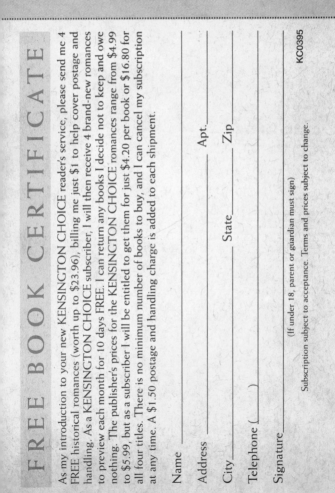

# FREE BOOK CERTIFICATE

As my introduction to your new KENSINGTON CHOICE reader's service, please send me 4 FREE historical romances (worth up to $23.96), billing me just $1 to help cover postage and handling. As a KENSINGTON CHOICE subscriber, I will then receive 4 brand-new romances to preview each month for 10 days FREE. I can return any books I decide not to keep and owe nothing. The publisher's prices for the KENSINGTON CHOICE romances range from $4.99 to $5.99, but as a subscriber I will be entitled to get them for just $4.20 per book or $16.80 for all four titles. There is no minimum number of books to buy, and I can cancel my subscription at any time. A $1.50 postage and handling charge is added to each shipment.

Name _____

Address _____ Apt. _____

City _____ State _____ Zip _____

Telephone (____) _____

Signature _____

(If under 18, parent or guardian must sign)

Subscription subject to acceptance. Terms and prices subject to change.

KC0395

We have
4
**FREE**
Historical
Romances
for you!

(worth up
to $23.96!)

*Details inside!*

**KENSINGTON CHOICE**
Reader's Service
120 Brighton Road
P.O.Box 5214
Clifton, NJ 07015-5214

curbside valet closed the car door behind him and the limousine pulled away.

Jason had come to the Dorothy Chandler Pavilion alone, a fact that prompted a carefully *sotto voce* observation from the reporter as he approached. "There was a great deal of speculation that Jason Cole would be arriving with Nicole Haviland, his *Without Warning* costar and, rumor has it, his leading lady off camera as well. But Jason is quite obviously flying solo tonight, leaving one to wonder if Nicole is *home alone.*"

The cattiness of the reporter's whisper held something else, a flicker of satisfaction, as if she herself had been left home alone by Jason and was quite delighted that even one of Hollywood's most glamorous actresses had obviously gotten the same cavalier treatment. The impression that she had known Jason intimately was underscored by the coy smile that touched her lips as he approached for his brief but requisite interview.

"So Jason," she purred. "How does it feel to have seven nominations including Best Actor, Best Director, and Best Picture?"

"It feels very good."

"All the other nominees that I've talked to tonight have said that winning the golden statue doesn't really matter. It's the honor of the nomination itself that counts. Do you agree?"

A bemused and *so sexy* smile touched his handsome face. "The nomination matters. And winning matters even more." The smile vanished as he added solemnly, "But what matters most is making a picture in which you believe . . . and making it the best picture you possibly can."

Caroline's smile was one of pure approval as she watched the interplay—with its obvious undercurrents of intimacy—between the beautiful reporter and Jason

Cole. Good for him, she thought when he answered the clichéd question with what was undoubtedly an honest reply.

Forthright and honest. Qualities she admired. Qualities that Caroline Hawthorne valued in herself.

The suddenly ringing phone, which she made no move whatsoever to answer, forced Caroline to admit that tonight she was being slightly less than forthright. Her honesty was still intact, however—yes, admittedly, it was hanging on only by the thread of a technicality.

She *did* have plans for her fortieth birthday. That was the truth, a completely honest statement of fact. She had faltered slightly, however, in the forthrightness department. She had not specifically spelled out to the friends, who had wanted to host a gala celebration in honor of the momentous occasion, the precise nature of those plans: to spend the evening by herself, watching the Academy Awards, drinking some of the champagne that even now was chilling, and nibbling on the thumbprint cookies she had bought earlier this afternoon.

That was how Caroline wanted to spend her birthday, and was going to; but since the various friends she had told that she already had plans undoubtedly assumed that those plans included, at the very least, an evening out on the town, she could not now answer the ringing phone.

Whoever was calling waited through the four unanswered rings and was waiting still as her answering machine greeted, "Hi. It's Caroline. I can't come to the phone right now but if you'll leave a message at the beep I'll get back to you as soon as possible. Thanks!"

She heard the beep, and then the deep, solemn voice that she had wondered if she would ever hear again—except, of course, on the videotape which she had played often in the past ten days.

"Hello, Caroline. It's Lawrence Elliott. I just wanted to wish you—"

"Lawrence! Hi."

"Hi. You're there. Happy birthday."

"Thank you."

"You sound a little breathless. Were you halfway out the door en route to a birthday celebration?"

"No. I just don't have the answering machine in a very convenient location." It was a partial truth. The whole truth was that the breathlessness had started the moment she had heard his voice, long before making her mad dash to the phone. Honesty, forthrightness, she reminded herself sternly, and then confessed, "I'm having a fairly low-key celebration. Here, by myself, watching the Academy Awards."

"Which is your first choice for the evening? Ahead of a big party thrown by your friends?"

"Yes." *First* choice? Not really, but every time her mind had wandered to what she had really wanted, she had firmly intercepted the musings. But now he was calling. "I miscalculated a little on the champagne and thumbprint cookies—too much of both for one person, but probably the right amount for two . . . if you would be interested."

There it was, a forthright invitation, to which Lawrence Elliott responded with what felt to her like endless silence.

"Have you had any of the champagne yet?" he asked finally.

"No."

"Well, then, if you'd like, you could come here. I have a TV. So, in between helping me deliver ten springer spaniel puppies, you could watch the Academy Awards."

"You're delivering puppies tonight?"

"Actually, a black and white springer spaniel named Katie is delivering them." The sudden gentleness in his voice told Caroline that Katie was obviously right there, her head probably cocked in inquisitive response to her name. "I'm just helping. She had the first puppy about five minutes ago."

"And you said that she is going to have ten? How do you know?"

"I took an x-ray."

"It wouldn't bother her if I watched?"

"I don't think so. Some springers are very high strung, but not Katie. Mellow is her middle name. Actually, I'm expecting quite a few observers. Katie lives about five miles away, in a neighborhood with lots of kids, many of whom are going to get pups from the litter and all of whom have been planning to watch the delivery for quite some time. The original plan had been for me to go to Katie's house, but three days ago her owner injured her back and is on strict bed rest for at least two more days. So, Katie's here, and in a few minutes, the kids—and their parents—will begin to arrive."

"It's awfully nice of you to shift the whole show to your place."

"It's no problem. The children are very excited, and I think it's a fairly remarkable event for them to see."

"An event which, in forty years, I've never seen—and would love to."

"Good." After Lawrence gave her detailed instructions to his home on the outskirts of Issaquah, he added, "The door nearest the driveway will be open, so just come on in."


Katie's second puppy was being born just as Caroline walked into the bright and spacious kitchen. A handwritten sign inside the doorway requested that shoes be removed, which she did, adding hers to the rows of large and small ones that already lined the foyer.

On her way to Issaquah, she had stopped at her favorite bakery on Queen Anne Hill and bought cookies, additional thumbprints, chocolate chips, and snicker doodles. As she placed the fragrant white sack on the kitchen counter, she saw another handwritten sign, requesting this time that she wash her hands. After complying promptly and thoroughly, she spent several moments studying the x-ray illuminated by a radiology view box. She counted ten tiny sets of skulls, spinal columns, and limbs, then followed the sound of hushed but excited whispers into the adjacent family room.

Young heads peered with wide-eyed wonder into the whelping box where Katie was energetically licking her just-born puppy. The aggressive lapping was far more than a vigorous welcome from a mother to her baby. It was the way in which she stimulated the newborn's tiny lungs to make the necessary transition from the world in which they were bathed in fluid to the one in which they must—quickly—learn to breathe nourishing air on their own.

As Katie licked, Lawrence suctioned the tiny newborn mouth with a bulb syringe, clearing the puppy's throat of remnants of its fluid world; and when that was done, he expertly placed a single suture around the small umbilical cord to stop the lingering seepage of blood.

The wide-eyed wonder wasn't limited to the assembled children. Caroline and the parents watched with comparable awe—and with reverent sighs of relief when, quite suddenly, the small motionless creature became animated, sneezing first and then breathing. Remarkably, that hurdle conquered, the new little life promptly began to walk, unsteadily, yes, but with valiant determination. Before their eyes, the lifeless body had become a puppy. Its black-and-white fur, which had glistened with amniotic fluid, was now tongue-dried by its mother; and its nose was bright pink from the oxygen in its blood; and its tail wagged, quite by accident, for balance, as its legs sought stable footing on the thick towels in the box.

When the puppy was dry and breathing, Lawrence

gently moved it from the whelping box into a smaller one in which its sibling already slept, safe and warm. Katie offered no protest. Later, when all the babies were born, she would care very much about their whereabouts; but for now, while she was in labor, the instinct to protect and nurture was put into necessary abeyance.

As Lawrence gently transferred the newborn puppy, Caroline felt an invisible magnet pulling at every one of them, luring their eager hands to reach for the tiny creature, to cradle it as Lawrence was.

"We can't hold the puppies yet." The voice that spoke was very young and very emphatic. Obviously someone—the combination of Lawrence and their parents—had discussed in advance with the children the issue of holding the babies. "We have to wait until they are at least one week old."

"That's right, Jenny," Lawrence agreed, smiling at the little girl whose curly blond head nodded in reply. "It would make Katie much too nervous, and we don't want her to be nervous, do we?"

"No." Jenny embellished her response with an emphatic shake of her golden curls.

"No," Lawrence echoed softly. After a moment he looked up, and when he did, his searching green eyes seemed slightly worried . . . until they found Caroline. "Hi. You made it."

"Yes. I stopped on the way to pick up some cookies." Caroline gave an easy shrug as her eyes fell on the platters of cookies on a nearby table. "Coals to Newcastle, I see."

"There's probably no such thing as too many cookies," Lawrence answered with a smile. Then, sensing that for the adults the appearance of the mystery woman was almost as fascinating as the delivery of Katie's puppies, he offered casually, "This is Caroline."

It was time to socialize then, while Katie rested until new contractions, signaling the imminent arrival of the next puppy, began again. Caroline exchanged first-name greetings with the adults, and chatted with the children, and felt the undeniable heat of an undeniable stare.

The unconcealed appraisal came from a pretty blonde, who, even had her daughter not called her "Mommy," Caroline would have known to be Jenny's mother. Her name was Eileen, and she wore no wedding rings, and it was she who had also brought cookies. Eileen was very interested in Lawrence, that was obvious; and she had a great deal to offer him: herself, young, pretty, vivacious . . . and her lovely blond-haired daughter, a little girl who looked very much like the daughter Lawrence had lost.

Were Eileen and Lawrence lovers? Caroline wondered. From Lawrence's behavior, it was impossible to tell. Despite Eileen's obvious interest in him, he interacted with her in the same friendly yet detached way that he interacted with all the parents.

But that was Lawrence, Caroline thought. Even if he and Eileen were intimately involved, he would protect the privacy of that very private truth.

It was then that Caroline felt a new heat, a different heat, and when she turned toward it, she was greeted by the dark intensity of dark green eyes. They were staring at her, and they were far from detached. They seemed to hold private messages—intimate ones—just for her.

The caress stole her breath, swirled her thoughts, and filled her with the euphoric warmth of hastily swallowed champagne. Still, amid the dizzying swirl, Caroline managed to plan a brave answering smile.

Before the plan reached her lips, however, his gaze was gone. An eagerly impatient child had tugged at his shirt sleeve to ask when Katie would have another puppy . . . and almost on cue Katie began to have that puppy.

And by the time Lawrence's eyes found Caroline's again, their dark green desire was merely a bewitching memory—perhaps even a mirage. They were friendly now, smiling, as Lawrence asked if she would help him, as she had in the boys' gymnasium at Moclips High. Caroline became his able assistant, charged this time with the small but important tasks of handing him bulb syringes, sutures, and hemostats.

"I have another project for you," Lawrence said quietly as he watched her carefully place the fourth healthy puppy beside its three sleeping siblings.

"Okay."

"Somewhere beyond that door is a blond cocker spaniel who needs to go outside for a few minutes before she settles down for the night. She's probably asleep on one of the living room couches but she could already be curled up on her pillow on the bedroom floor."

"That seems like awfully calm behavior given the activity that's been going on in here."

"If she knew, believe me, she would be wriggling to be part of it. She's fifteen, and very lively, but also very deaf." Lawrence's smile eased the sudden frown from Caroline's face. "Her deafness doesn't bother her in the least. In fact, according to her owners, she has been feigning deafness for years."

"Her owners? She's not yours?"

"No. I don't have any pets of my own, just guests who stay here when their families are on vacation and strays who need a place until my partners and I can find homes for them."

Lawrence told Caroline that the cocker's name was Mindy, and that she had a habit of bringing a small rock inside with her every time she came in, and that there was a supply of them beside the door. And just as she was about to leave in search of the deaf but lively cocker spaniel, he added, "It startles her to be touched if she hasn't seen or sensed your approach. So if she's awake, let her see you first, and if she's asleep, hold your hand near her nose so that she's awakened by your scent. And talk to her. She may be deaf, but she does read lips."

What a nice man you are, Lawrence Elliott, Caroline thought as she left the family room to find Mindy. Nice, kind, gentle . . . and tormented.

In the family room, fragrant with freshly baked cookies and crowded with enraptured children, there had been a feeling of warmth and community. But as she left that vibrant gaiety and entered the starkness of the living room, Caroline was confronted with the truth: Lawrence's world was an isolated one. He was detached, alone, focused on his relentless and essentially solitary search for his own golden-haired daughter.

Caroline was struck by the starkness of the living room, but also by its spaciousness. High-ceilinged with large skylights and walls of windows, it was, she decided grimly, precisely the kind of room that would be chosen—built?—by a man who had spent seven years of his life in a cage.

The starkness, the absence of any personal adornment whatsoever, seemed imprisoning in itself; but as her eyes fell on the floor-to-ceiling bookshelves that lined the room's inner walls, she realized that he found at least a little escape. Lawrence was a reader, as was she, and as Caroline glanced at the many titles that filled the shelves, she discovered that his tastes in reading were as varied and eclectic as hers.

This is something we share, she thought, and with the thought came a wonderful image. This spacious living room, with its sparse furnishings and stone fireplace would lose all its starkness, all its aching loneliness, with two people in it. Two people, reading in front of a roaring fire, drinking hot chocolate, listening to the rain pelting against the skylights . . . and if, in the midst of

that warm coziness, the dark green eyes stared at her
the intimate hunger she had seen earlier—

Stop, Caroline commanded the imagination that
so brazenly donned rose-colored glasses.

The rosy hue disappeared at her stern command,
she saw again only the starkness that was a symbo
how Lawrence Elliott lived his life. Alone. Imprisone
his memories and by his desperate search. Yes
sometimes offered his gentle expertise—and even
home—to other people's children and other peo
pets; but they were guests only, nothing more, not
permanent, just visitors.

There was no blond cocker spaniel in the living ro
although there were a number of telltale rocks, nor
she in the spacious study filled with neat stack
veterinary journals and even more books, nor was sl
the first bedroom to which Caroline wandered. It w
delightful room, different from the others she had s
brightly decorated and filled with warmth and welco

It was, Caroline realized with a deep twisting sadr
a place that symbolized Lawrence's only true es(
from his prison . . . the room that would be Holly's w
she returned.

Oh, Lawrence. You have to live your life. You hav
let something—someone—touch you.

Maybe he does, she thought as she moved toward
open door that had to be the master bedroom. Mayb
there I will discover some proof that the tormented
so sexy man has at least permitted his physical desir
little freedom. Maybe there will be a bottle of perfum
the dresser, or a romance novel left by a lover on
nightstand beside the bed.

But Lawrence's bedroom held only more starkr
and it would have been the greatest starkness of all,
most loneliness, if it hadn't been for the blond co(
spaniel sleeping blissfully not on her pillow on the f
but in the center of Lawrence's bed.

I hope you sleep with him, Caroline thought. A soft smile touched her lips as she decided that the golden ball of fluff undoubtedly did sleep with Lawrence, that he would never relegate her to the floor if she preferred the bed. I hope you curl very close to him. I hope he feels your companionship and your warmth.

Before moving to the bed to offer a fragrance that would gently awaken Mindy from her deep sleep, Caroline cast a final glance around the room. It wasn't an invasion of privacy because here, as in all the rooms, nothing private was revealed.

Here, as in the other rooms, there were no pictures of his own family, not even a single framed photograph from the album that Holly had so mysteriously left behind before vanishing forever.

The photographs were somewhere, and perhaps when his absolute privacy was assured, they were on display. But not tonight, not when his home was open to the obviously admiring but definitely curious eyes of strangers. Dr. Lawrence Elliott was Issaquah's local hero, a Pied Piper who was immensely respected and seductively intriguing. They knew all about him, of course. They had all watched him open his veins on national television.

Lawrence had very little privacy left. But what he had, the precious photographs of his own family, were for his dark green eyes only.


By ten-fifteen, only six of the ten puppies had been delivered. But it was a school night, and all children had long since been taken home, and Lawrence and Caroline were alone.

Katie wanted to go out, so they accompanied her, and as Lawrence's powerful flashlight cast golden beams into the darkness, Caroline saw that the fenced yard in which Mindy had safely romped was only a small part of his property. The family room door opened to a vast meadow. There was a stable in one corner, and a fenced paddock, but with the exception of those man-made structures, the naturally landscaped sea of shrubs and wildflowers swept unimpeded to a forest of pines.

How very peaceful, Caroline mused as they stood in the night's enveloping stillness. I hope he finds at least a little peace here from his many haunting ghosts.

At eleven forty-five Katie delivered her final puppy. As she had watched each of the other puppies being born, there had been for Caroline a breath-held moment of worry between the time when Katie licked the small motionless bodies free of their amniotic sacs and the moment that their small lungs courageously took their first gulps of air.

But by this last puppy, her worry had almost vanished. The others had all made the transition from life in the womb to life on their own without difficulty. Yes, Lawrence had tied sutures around several umbilical cords and had encouraged the first breath by gentle suction with a bulb syringe. But, by his own admission, those modern medical interventions had largely been unnecessary.

But this last baby needed his help . . . her help.

Katie was exhausted. Still, sensing this final puppy's distress, the unwillingness of the motionless body to come to life, she licked more frantically, more vigorously than ever. The force of her mother's rough tongue rolled the little body over and over on the towels, but it failed to ignite any spark of life from within.

Lawrence's strong and gentle fingers stroked the puppy too, matching Katie's rigorous effort, and after handing Lawrence the bulb syringe, Caroline's own fingers joined the cause.

Come on, she urged silently as she stroked the delicate

rib cage, hoping to stimulate the lungs beneath to take a first valiant gasp. Come on, *breathe*.

It was then, as Lawrence turned the tiny head to insert the syringe into the mouth, that Caroline saw the puppy's nose. She had seen the noses of the other puppies during the precarious moments when their lifeline to the oxygen in their mother's blood had been severed and they hadn't yet discovered the oxygen in the air. Those noses had been a little dusky, a soft pastel blending of pink and blue.

But with this puppy, as each second passed without the replenishment of oxygen, the pink disappeared entirely, leaving only cold, dark, ominous blue.

"Come on," she whispered. "Come *on,* little one."

"Caroline," Lawrence began, his handsome face filled with worry, his voice gentle with apology.

He was about to tell her what she already knew, that nature was about survival of the fittest, and not all could survive; but before he could speak, the puppy sputtered at last, and then gasped, and then breathed.

And before their eyes, the cyanotic nose became rosy pink, and in another instant the small legs began to move with surprising sturdiness. Katie kept licking, but not so frantically now, and as he had done with all the other puppies, Lawrence began to dry the wet fur with a soft cloth.

He was behaving as if this puppy, who had been so very close to eternal lifelessness, was just like the others. Indeed, with each passing moment, the newborn seemed to be as robustly healthy as her sibs. She was walking now, resiliently righting herself whenever a rigorous lick made her tumble and roll.

"She certainly looks good," Caroline offered hopefully.

Lawrence smiled. "She'll be just fine. Once they breathe, once they cross that invisible barrier, puppies are remarkably hardy."

When the puppy was dry, Lawrence handed the small wriggling body to Caroline, as he'd handed the other puppies before, allowing her to make the transfer to the other box. But this transfer took longer than the others, because Caroline had a special message for this newborn.

"You gave us—at least me—quite a scare," she said softly to the black-and-white face. "You do seem awfully frisky now, though."

"I think she should be yours."

Caroline looked up from the little canine face to the very serious human one. "What?"

"Katie's owner has offered me pick of the litter." Lawrence stroked the small body that Caroline held, and although his fingers didn't actually touch hers, she felt their gentleness . . . and their heat. "I think I should pick this little one for you, for your fortieth birthday. If you want her, that is. You don't have to decide now. She'll need to be with Katie for at least two months, and there will be no problem finding her a home if you decide you don't want her."

*But I do want her.* The thought was instant and confident. Caroline knew that assuming responsibility for a puppy—and then a dog—was solemn, not to made impulsively. But this didn't feel impulsive at all. With a deep and confident calm, she felt the willingness to make a long-term commitment to the tiny creature cradled gently in her hands. True, she did have the odd board meeting and gala charity event—to both plan and attend; but those were merely brief forays away from her house. Mostly she was at home, or could be, and as for traveling, her journey to Moclips to help the oil-cloaked otters and gulls was the farthest she'd ventured in a very long time.

She would be at home, and in the next two months she could fence the yard, and puppy-proof the house, and when the short sturdy legs became graceful and strong

they could go for walks all over Queen Anne Hill, and
. . .

Caroline knew she wouldn't waver on her decision to
welcome this puppy into her life. But she thought about
a blond cocker spaniel asleep on a nearby bed, and about
the affection that had touched Lawrence's voice as he
had told her about Mindy's deafness and her rocks, and
after a moment she said quietly, "I think this would be a
wonderful home for her, right here. With you."

"No." His answer came swiftly, almost harshly. Then,
more gently, he offered, "But I'll be happy to puppy-sit
her whenever you like."

"Okay," Caroline agreed softly, a little stunned by the
implications of his offer, the link it would create between
them, the bond that would span years. "I want her,
Lawrence, and I don't need two months to decide. I
won't change my mind."

After memorizing the distinctive markings of her
puppy, the five white freckles on the velvet black face and
the snow-white left front paw, Caroline snuggled her next
to the others. Then, while Lawrence gave Katie a bath in
the laundry room, she removed the birthing towels from
the whelping box and put in a thick layer of fresh ones.

By the time Lawrence had finished drying Katie, all ten
puppies were awake, eagerly awaiting the reunion with
their mother and their first meal. It was sheer instinct,
maternal and infant. Katie lay on her side, a portrait of
serenity and calm, and her puppies, their eyes still tightly
closed, moved unerringly to her nurturing nipples.

"Pretty remarkable," Caroline murmured, smiling as
she watched *her* puppy move as determinedly as the rest.
"A pretty memorable way to spend my fortieth
birthday."

"I never did turn on the television for you, did I?"

"It doesn't matter. I assume that Jason Cole's *Without
Warning* swept the awards. And if it didn't, I'm glad I
didn't watch anyway."

They fell silent then, and for a while were serenaded by the sounds of energetic suckling, and the odd squeal that would eventually mature into a determined bark, and an occasional sigh from a placid but exhausted mother. This was how the puppies were going to spend their night, and they didn't really need witnesses, and it was already after one . . .

"Well," Caroline said quietly. "I suppose I should be going."

"If you like, I'll call with progress reports on your puppy," Lawrence offered as he walked her to her car.

"Yes . . . please."

"And maybe I could take you to a belated birthday dinner?"

"Yes." Please, Caroline added silently as, with forthright honesty, her expression told him how delighted she was by his invitation.

Lawrence smiled, and despite the night's concealing shadows, Caroline saw the hunger, the intimacy in his eyes. Now, as earlier, his intense dark-green caress stole her breath, and cloaked her in sudden warmth, and made her tremble deep within. And this time no eager child would break the spell. Nothing would.

This time, Lawrence would see her brave, welcoming smile.

Throughout the evening Caroline had witnessed the drama of birth, the remarkable moment when stillness became motion, when what had looked like death magically came to life.

Now, without warning, she witnessed the exact opposite of that magnificent drama. The seductive green eyes that had filled with such breathtaking intimacy, such vital desire, seemed suddenly to lose all traces of that vibrancy. The loss was greater even than death, however, because where there might have been nothingness, emptiness, Caroline saw raw pain.

And was there even terror amid the anguish? she wondered as she stared at him. Had Lawrence, gazing at her with unconcealed hunger, suddenly seen the image of the only woman he had ever loved? And had that image been an image of horror, the police photographs taken of Claire just minutes after her brutal death?

"Lawrence?" Then, before posing her next question, Caroline drew a steadying breath—and with that breath, the question she had planned mysteriously changed. Instead of asking "Is it Claire?" Caroline heard herself ask, "Is it Holly?"

His dark head answered with a slight nod, and then a disbelieving shake.

"What is it Lawrence? What happened?" *Happened,* past tense, because, Caroline realized, whatever it was that had stolen the life from his eyes had vanished now. It had released its grip of terror and left in its wake a legacy of disbelief.

"I . . ." He shook his head again and said with soft apology, "It sounds crazy."

"Tell me. Please."

After a long shadowed moment he confessed slowly, "I suddenly felt as if she were dying. I told you before that sometimes I have the strong feeling that she is alive but somehow imprisoned. This was different, Caroline. This was something I've never felt before."

"Is the feeling gone now?"

"Yes." Gone but not forgotten, not the feeling, and not his confession to her. He said very quietly, "I really don't want you to think I'm crazy."

Caroline wanted to respond at once. But the way he'd said "you"—as if what he really meant to say was "you, of all people"—halted her swift reply. In the end, the slight delay was better, because it gave him time to see her absolute confidence in her answer, *and in him,* even before she spoke.

"Well," she said softly, "I really don't."

## ❀ *17* ❀

Holly believed that she had died, and in that moment of death, when her fluttering heart had suddenly stopped, she had felt relief.

It made sense that her heart would finally fail. For years it had beat with the measured calm of suspended animation, the never-never land between life and death. Then the call had come from Raven that she needed to leave her cocoon of solitary silence and travel to Los Angeles, and her heart, unceremoniously forced to emerge from its safe hibernation, had begun its unhealthy fluttering. It seemed impossible that it could race any faster, but it had, the moment she had first seen the gentle concern in his dark blue eyes.

It made sense that the fluttering alone would eventually be fatal, and what had happened this afternoon had only hastened that inevitable demise. For a very long time her fragile heart had been filled to overflowing with sadness. But this afternoon, with Jason, other astonishing emotions had vied for room in its anguished chambers. Holly had joyously welcomed those wondrous, unfamiliar emotions . . . even though she had known that they would kill her. Her fluttering heart, so dangerously overfilled, would surely burst.

Holly wasn't surprised when it happened, when at last the heart whose every racing beat she had felt for the past

211

two weeks had suddenly stopped. The fragile fluttering thing that had been soaring so high above the ground, amid terrifying and then wondrous clouds, had finally exploded in midair; and when it did, Holly felt relief that it was over, relief that she would die quickly, long before she felt the shattering fall to earth.

But the anguished heart which for weeks had fluttered without failing betrayed her now: *it did not die.* It merely stopped fluttering. It merely abandoned its breakneck pace and resumed the slowly measured calm of that place between life and death where she had dwelt for the past seventeen years.

Her heart was beating as if it were back in the safe sanctuary of her cocoon in Kodiak. But she wasn't there—and her heart would not truly be safe until she was—and in just a few hours she was supposed to see Jason again, to discuss with him the ending of *Gifts of Love.*

Jason had told her, had promised her, that he wouldn't change a word, not a syllable, if that was what she wanted. Even if that were true, there was still an insurmountable obstacle: he would want her to tell him *why* the happy ending was so terribly important to her.

Before leaving Kodiak, Holly had armed herself with data about her book—royalty statements documenting the millions of copies that she had sold, the wonderful reviews it had received, the months and months that it had topped the bestseller lists, the deluge of letters from more-than-satisfied readers.

She had planned to present Jason with those facts, proof positive that her story had worked, had succeeded, as written. And she had even imagined that when the time came, when he told her that her ending was hopelessly romantic for a saga of war, she might somehow be able to become one of her own heroines.

With quiet courage she would meet his skeptical and so seductive blue eyes and ask him if, perhaps, the *real* cliché wasn't the compulsion to make bittersweet all stories about war. Everyone knows the anguished lessons of war, she would say. Mightn't there be a new lesson to be learned, a triumphant one, the conquest of hope and love over all?

Her heart had now resumed its slow steady pace, plummeting from the clouds to the place where it belonged, and now it was promising her that it would not soar again, that it would flutter no more. It was exhausted, beyond exhaustion. It would dabble no more in such wondrous folly.

And even if her heart was telling her the truth, even if it wouldn't suddenly race at the sight of him, there was the greater truth: the man who had just won seven Academy Awards would listen calmly to the dazzling data she presented him, and he might even accept her philosophical stance on the lessons to be learned from war, but he would sense that he had yet to hear the real reason she cared so very much about her happy ending.

Gently, so gently, he would command her to tell him.

And she couldn't.

She could not say to Jason Cole that the reason that she didn't want Savannah to die was because her fictional character was real to her. She was a beloved friend, as all her characters were, the only friends she had.

He would think she was crazy.

And he would be right.

She *was* crazy. Holly knew that now. It was a slow, silent madness, but a relentless one, becoming ever more entrenched with each passing day. She had deluded herself into believing that she was alive, surviving. But it wasn't true. She was only barely alive . . . and she was quite mad. She rarely left her cabin anymore, and more rarely still ever permitted her thoughts to leave the imaginary lives she created.

Jason had undoubtedly already diagnosed her as slightly crazy, in a charming, hopelessly eccentric kind of way. He had even been a little intrigued by that eccentricity and had probably concluded that it was some quaint fascination with the sixties that compelled her to choose the flower-child dress, to wear in joyous celebration of the era gone by.

But Holly knew all too well that there had been neither choice nor celebration. The lovely dress was merely an exquisitely accurate symbol of how out of touch she was, how truly vast was the distance between reality and herself.

Holly didn't want Jason to know of her madness.

She *would not* let him know.


"Miss Pierce checked out early this morning, Mr. Cole." The Hotel Bel-Air desk clerk's radiant smile faltered when she saw the reaction on his famous face. "But," she offered hopefully, "she left you a note."

Jason took the sealed envelope and walked outside. The sun shone brightly and the warm air was scented with the intoxicating fragrance of gardenias. Leaving the hotel's arched main entrance, he strode down a path toward a pond.

White and ebony swans glided languidly across the tranquil surface, but except for the graceful birds, Jason was quite alone. The hotel was full, of course, but at 9 A.M. on this Tuesday its celebrated overnight guests were all asleep, having lingered until dawn at the many champagne-drenched galas that had followed the Academy Awards.

Jason hadn't slept at all, but his sleeplessness had nothing to do with the lavish parties or the seven golden statues he had won. What had kept Jason awake was restlessness, wanting to see her again, needing to. Between three, when he had left the party at Spago, and seven, when he had returned to his penthouse to shower and change, Jason had been at the beach, walking up and down the sandy shoreline, pacing away the endless moments, his mind spinning with questions that only she could answer.

Who are you, Holly? What makes me want to hold you and never let you go? And why am I so fearful that even my most tender touch might make you run away?

The questions had spun without answers, but with a haunting prophecy . . . because now, even before he had ever touched her, Holly had, indeed, run away.

And now, after having spent an evening in which the famous words—"The envelope, please"—had heralded monumental golden success for him, Jason's lean agile fingers tore open the only envelope that really mattered.

Dear Jason,

I have to get back to Alaska. Please do whatever you think is best with *Gifts of Love.* I know I'll like whatever you choose to do. Thank you again for yesterday afternoon.

Holly

Jason stared at the note, the only tangible proof he had that she actually existed at all. Her handwriting was clear, girlishly simple and completely unadorned. As he searched for even greater clarity in the eminently legible words, he found himself discovering deep layers of mystery and worry.

*I have to get back to Alaska,* she had written. But Jason read "have to" as "need to" and he sensed in that distinction urgency—and even despair. And Holly had capitulated entirely on the ending of the movie, without even discussing it with him, even though it had been her fierce protectiveness of that ending that had compelled her to journey to Los Angeles in the first place.

*Thank you again for yesterday afternoon.* Those words alone gave Jason hope. Holly was thanking him for far more than lunch—because yesterday afternoon had nothing to do with lunch at all. It had to do with magic, with falling in love . . . and even though something terrified her so much that she had run away from him, Holly knew it too.

"Jason!" Raven greeted the moment her secretary announced his unexpected arrival. "Congratulations . . . what's wrong?"

"I need your help."

"Okay." Raven had never seen Jason look this worried, this distracted, this serious—not even in the midst of negotiations that would materially affect his entire career. "What is it, Jason? What's happened?"

"I need you to get Holly's address for me."

"Holly? Who's Holly?"

"Marilyn Pierce. Lauren Sinclair."

"Didn't you meet with her yesterday?"

"Yes, and we were supposed to meet again this morning, but she's gone back to Alaska."

"You want to send something to her?"

"No. I want to tell her, in person, that I'm not going to change the ending of her book. I also want to convince her to write the screenplay for me. I thought you could handle that contract for her."

Raven knew that in two days, Jason Cole was leaving for Hong Kong. There were undoubtedly numerous matters which required his attention before his departure. But now he was going to drop everything and travel to Alaska? That revelation was amazing enough, and Raven had just begun adjusting to it when Jason shared the rest of his plan. Without bothering to conceal her surprise, she clarified, "You want me to negotiate the contract for *her*? Not for *you*?"

"I'll pay her whatever tough but fair price you come

up with. So, Raven, will you call her publishing company and tell them that you need her address?" Jason could have gotten Holly's address from the desk clerk at the Hotel Bel-Air. She would have been breaking the rules, of course, but he had no doubt she would have done it for him. He hadn't asked, though, because he abhorred the VIP mentality of stars who truly believed that the rules were for everyone but them. Jason knew that Raven wouldn't cave in to a request that was unreasonable, not even for him, her most powerful client. "If they won't release it, they won't, but my reasons for wanting it are quite legitimate."

As Raven realized that there were reasons—astonishing ones—beyond what Jason had articulated, her mind drifted to the soft voice in Kodiak and her hopeful books of love . . . and to the astonishing weekend that she herself had just spent with Nick.

Finally, with a lovely smile, Raven gave Jason his answer. "I'll give it my best shot."

Raven's best shot yielded Holly's address with a minimum of resistance.

"I'm impressed," Jason said as she handed him the piece of paper that was—hopefully—his passport to another journey to magic.

"It's not often that I get a blank check from you for a screenplay," Raven teased. Then, suddenly solemn, she added, "I hope it works out."

"Thanks. So do I."

Jason was in a hurry to leave, to arrange for the studio jet to take him to Kodiak and for the car and hotel room that he would need when he arrived. But halfway to the door, he turned back toward her.

"Raven."

"Yes?" she queried, quite aware that for the first time she truly had the undivided and undistracted attention of his dark blue eyes.

"You look ... happy. Something's happened—but not with Michael."

"Yes. Something wonderful has happened. And not with Michael." Raven tilted her head and said softly, "I hope something as wonderful happens to you."

# ❧ *18* ❧

It was almost midnight by the time Jason checked into Kodiak's Westmark Hotel. After a brief internal debate, he succumbed to the restless impulse to at least see where she lived, to drive past her home in the hope that he could sense that she was there, safe, asleep, peacefully dreaming happy dreams.

Holly's rustic cottage was located four miles outside of town at the end of a narrow road which was half a mile beyond its nearest neighbor. The road wove through a dense forest of towering pines, and it wasn't until he reached her cottage, perched high on a cliff, that Jason realized how closely the wooded road had hugged the island's coastline. The sea below rippled silver, caressed by moonbeams that filtered through a fleecy veil of clouds.

As Jason had driven through the forested darkness to the isolated spot where Holly lived, he had hoped that when he reached the cottage he would be greeted by glowing porch lights, golden sentinels meant to discourage unwelcome intrusions. What greeted him was even more reassuring: bright lights, lots of them. The cottage was brilliantly illuminated from within, a blazing glow of warmth, and its curtains were all opened wide, as if in welcome.

Jason saw Holly at once. Her golden hair glittered, the brightest beacon of all, beckoning to him. She was on a couch in the living room, dressed in a mauve and lavender bathrobe. The robe must be down-filled, he decided, because it gave a luxuriant plumpness to what he knew to be her very thin body.

She was curled in a tight ball. Very tight, Jason realized. It was a tense and rigid tightness, not a languid cozy curl. Her head was bent, her forehead resting on knees that were hugged as close to her body as possible, held there, clutched there, by her arms.

Jason couldn't see her face. It was hidden behind the golden veil of silk. But there was absolutely no doubt that Holly was wide awake, alert and wary, every cell of her body on guard. Against what? Jason wondered. What frightened her so? From his vantage point, Holly seemed quite alone.

Instead of going to the door, Jason decided to knock softly on the plate glass window. That way she would see instantly that it was he—not the invisible midnight menace she so obviously feared.

His knock was soft and gentle, but her reaction was instant and stunning. The body that was already rigid with terror suddenly became even more taut—so taut that it was trembling; and the pale hands that had been clutched together, thus ensuring the tightest ball possible, released their viselike grip and reached out imploringly to the apparition he could not see. As her golden head lifted, Jason caught a brief glimpse of her eyes. They were quite gray, colorless stormy eyes that didn't even begin to turn toward the sound of his gentle knock. Instead, they stared straight ahead, toward whatever it was to which her pale hands so frantically implored.

It was then that Jason heard the sound, a cry so anguished that at first he didn't believe it to be human. It was the wind, he decided, hissing through the trees. Or the haunting call of a faraway gull. Or the wise yet ghostly screech of a distant owl.

A wilderness sound, Jason thought. A noise of nature.

But the sound didn't come from the vast silver shadows of the cloud-misted night. It came instead from within the brightly lighted cottage, piercing through the window with agonizing clarity—and, Jason realized, with desperate words.

"Please," Holly cried. "Please don't kill her!"

Jason knocked again, more loudly this time, urgently trying to distract her from whatever it was that caused such terror. "Holly!"

She didn't seem to hear his voice and the knocking seemed only to trigger even more frantic pleas.

"Please stop, *please.*"

Academy Award-winning director Jason Cole was witnessing a scene over which he had no control. The realization sent a rare feeling of helplessness rippling through him. Conquering it swiftly, he moved decisively toward the door. No matter how securely it was locked, it would yield to the power of his determination to be with her, to join her in the scene of terror, to make it end.

But the door was unlocked, a symbol that Holly had no fear of human intruders, of thieves, rapists, or murderers who might prey upon a woman alone in a remote cottage in the woods. The unlocked door was also a symbol that Holly knew that whatever it was that now held her prisoner to unspeakable terror could not be stopped by such man-made contrivances as deadbolts or chains.

For a moment Jason wondered if he would find a human intruder after all, a man who had been hidden from his view. It was a surprisingly hopeful thought, an enemy far more easily conquered than the apparition he could not see.

But except for Holly the living room was quite empty.

She wasn't screaming any longer, only whimpering, soft whispers of endless despair as her gray eyes bore witness to what could only have been a scene of death.

Jason knelt before her, putting himself between her and the ghastly vision that only she could see. Her wire-rimmed glasses were gone, permitting him an undisguised look at her colorless eyes . . . and at the dark circles that bespoke days, perhaps weeks, of little sleep.

"Holly, it's me. It's Jason."

She was quite blind to him, seeing beyond him—through him—as if it were he, not the apparition, who wasn't real. Some part of her, however, did hear his words. But, Jason realized, it wasn't a part that remembered the magic, but rather the place that had been filled with fear.

Don't be afraid of me, he commanded silently even as he confronted the disturbing truth: Holly was pleading desperately for someone's life, some woman's life, and it was he who had planned so cavalierly to kill off the heroine of her book. It seemed impossible that her immense anguish could be because of that, because of *him*.

But if it was, he could swiftly vanquish it.

"Holly, listen to me. Savannah isn't going to die. That's why I'm here. That's what I came to tell you. She will live happily ever after, just the way you wanted her to." His words, or perhaps simply the gentleness of his tone, seemed to calm her, luring her a little from the imagined to the real. "Whatever you're seeing, Holly, it's just a mirage. It's nothing real, nothing that can hurt you. You obviously haven't slept for a very long time, and I have a feeling that you haven't eaten either, and somehow the fatigue, the exhaustion . . ." Jason took her hands then, curling the icy paleness in his warm strength. "Holly? I think you can hear me. It's Jason, Holly, and I'm here because—"

"Jason?"

"Hi," he greeted softly. "I'm real, Holly. And I'm

really here, in your cottage in Kodiak. The other . . . whatever it was . . . wasn't real."

*Yes it was!* The thought came with immense power as her starving and exhausted brain struggled for clarity—a struggle made more difficult because the heart that had promised never again to flutter was fluttering now and she was beginning to float toward the clouds . . . toward the magic.

Her eyes fell from his gentle smile to the startling warmth of her hands—his hands. The last hands that had touched her had been her mother's, tenderly cupping her face as she had bid her daughter goodbye. Now, after seventeen years, Holly Elliott was being touched again, and there was such tenderness, such loving warmth.

Suddenly, as if the warmth were a blazing fire, she pulled her hands away.

I'm *crazy,* she reminded herself. And now my madness is fully exposed.

She realized vaguely that what had sounded to her like gunshots had been his knocking on the windowpane; but that realization was simply a faint glimmer of sanity in the midst of madness. She had been so lost in her faraway memories that she had been quite unable to discern the imagined from the real.

For seventeen years, Holly had been able to keep the memories under control. She had been able to make them hibernate, to dwell in that same place between life and death where she herself had dwelled. But on her return to Kodiak, the memories had been wide-awake, revived, energized, and aggressive. They had greeted her with a vengeance, brazenly escaping the confinement of her mind entirely and coming to living, breathing, terrifying life.

She had been hallucinating. Derek and her mother and the twins had all been in the room with her, life-sized, three-dimensional, and even more vividly clear now than they had been on that long-ago night of death. She had seen them. She had heard them. And even though she had heard as well a gentle voice telling her that her vision—her hallucination—was merely a phantom of a starved and exhausted mind, Holly knew the truth: she was quite mad.

"Holly? Do you remember what happened? Can you tell me?"

Her answering shrug was evasive.

*Tell him,* the memories taunted. Tell him everything. Let him see for himself your madness.

The memories wanted the gentleness to vanish from Jason's eyes, just as they wanted him to vanish from the cottage. They wanted Holly all to themselves, a captive audience for whom they could perform their bloody scene of terror and death *forever*.

"You were pleading for someone, a woman, not to be killed. Was it Savannah, Holly? Because if it was, you don't have to worry. That's why I'm here, to be sure that you know that I'm not going to change the happy ending of your book."

"It wasn't Savannah." True, she had gone to Los Angeles to plead with him to spare her heroine's life. But she hadn't. She had known in time how crazy those pleas would have sounded. There had been, in Los Angeles, islands of sanity amid the sea of madness. "Thank you, but . . . you shouldn't do that because of me. You should do what you want, what you think is best."

"That *is* what I think is best." And as for what he wanted? So much: her trust, and glowing sparkles of blue and green where now there was only gray, and radiant smiles of happiness and love, and the feel of her hands cradled inside his . . . and the feel of the two of them cradled together. Jason gazed at her exhausted face and sensed the great effort she was making even to speak. "What I also think is best is for you to get some sleep— lots of it."

Holly nodded a fragile nod of hope. It had been so very

long since she had slept. Perhaps if she had not deprived the memories of their nightly forays into her dreams, they would not have escaped the confines of her conscious mind. Perhaps, with sleep, she could contain her madness once again.

"If you don't mind, Holly, I'd like to stay here tonight. This couch looks quite comfortable."

Holly frowned, a hostess worrying about her guest's comfort—but not, Jason realized, worrying because she did not want him to stay.

"I'm quite accustomed to sleeping on couches, in the studio, when we're in the midst of editing. This will be just fine. Okay?"

She didn't respond at once, but when she did, with a nod of her golden head, Jason felt a powerful rush of pure joy.

She was letting him stay without the slightest protest. It seemed to him the wondrous beginning of trust.

## ❀ *19* ❀

As Holly awakened from her deep sleep, an unfamiliar feeling awakened with her. It felt like hope.

Hope? That seemed impossible. Why would it come to her now, bravely invading all the places where for so long only sadness had dwelled?

As her astonished mind tried to make sense of it, her thoughts drifted to a once-beloved fairy tale: *Sleeping Beauty*. She had been asleep for years, condemned to that lingering slumber by a wicked spell, until a valiant prince had slashed through the thick walls of thorny brambles to find her, to rescue her with his gentle kiss . . .

The memories came flooding back then, and they seemed so real. But they weren't. They *couldn't* be. She'd had a nightmare about death, that was all, and she had been rescued from that torment by a wondrous dream—so powerful that it had resurrected a feeling of pure hopefulness that she'd believed was dead, brutally murdered on that snowy Valentine's night.

In Los Angeles, Holly had felt a floating euphoric magic she could not name, and now a dream about the magician himself had brought back to life a once familiar friend. The magic had been an illusion, created by Jason and unable to exist without him. But, Holly knew, the exuberant hopefulness she felt now belonged to her—at least it had when she was little. It had lived within her

226

then, a constant companion, and now because of an extraordinary dream it had been returned to her.

The hopefulness was a magnificent gift, miraculously hers again, and Holly wasn't going to let it go. Even if they were merely frolicking symbols of her madness, she was going to find a way to persuade the sparkles of golden light that danced within her never to leave again.

I will treasure you! she promised. Please stay.

The golden sparkles answered by urging her to leap out of bed, throw open the curtains, and joyously embrace the glorious new day. Holly followed the command to leave her bed, but she did not leap. Despite the twirling exuberance within, she moved slowly, carefully, making absolutely certain that the hopefulness was with her each step of the way, not wanting to lose it as Peter Pan had once lost his own shadow.

*Stay with me, please.*

The hopefulness obeyed. It was with her as she opened the curtains to a day more glorious than all the days of the past seventeen years, and it was with her still as she walked, barefoot and clad only in her cotton nightgown, into the living room.

"Good morning," Jason said softly to the lovely vision of tangled golden hair and glowing blue-green eyes.

"Oh," Holly whispered. Oh, *no*. It wasn't a dream. He witnessed my madness, and it was his gentleness that rescued me and this wondrous feeling of hope. But my hopefulness is all an illusion, just as the magic was. It belongs to Jason . . . and it will vanish with him.

You're not going to let your hopefulness vanish, Holly, *and you're not mad.* The voice came from deep within her, strong and confident—and loving. Whose voice was it? she wondered. Her mother's? Her father's?

"Did you sleep well?" Jason asked.

"Yes, very well. Did you?"

"All that I needed." He hadn't slept at all, of course. He had chosen instead to spend the night keeping vigil over Holly. That was what he wanted, far more than sleep, and as he had quietly paced all night long, a sentry on guard against an invisible intruder, he had learned more about her . . .

The world inside her cottage, the spartan world in which she lived, was more office than home. Equipped with state-of-the-art computer, printer, and fax, it was quite barren of personal embellishments of any kind. Nothing hung on the walls, not posters of the sun bouncing off the horizon at Barrow, nor blowups of covers of her books, nor photographs of family or friends, nor even a framed copy of the *New York Times* bestseller list the week that *Gifts of Love* had hit number one.

Holly had not adorned the walls with mementos, nor had she put them anywhere else. There was no television, Jason noticed. Nor could he find either a radio or stereo. And although there were books everywhere, he discovered no newspapers or magazines, no links of any sort to the current affairs of the outside world.

There were novels, all with happy endings, and there were reference books: the *Encyclopedia Britannica,* and dictionaries in seven languages, and a thesaurus, and guides to proper English usage. Her collection of reference books on Vietnam was vast, and an entire bookcase was filled with travel books, exotic and glamorous destinations—including, he noted, a recently published and obviously read book about Los Angeles.

Jason had greatly enjoyed reading the bestselling novels of Lauren Sinclair set in London and Paris. When he removed from a bookshelf the Fodor's guides for those cities, he saw that although they had clearly been read, there was no writing in the margins, no hastily scribbled notes made as she herself had shopped in Highgrove or marveled at the wonders of the Louvre.

Holly took her readers on magnificent journeys to enchanted places, the most magnificent and enchanted of which was love. Now Jason knew the truth about the exotic locales in which she set her novels. Although her descriptions were remarkably authentic, the detail richly textured, they were places to which she herself had never traveled.

Was the same true of her journeys to love? Did she have no firsthand experience either with that enchanted place?

During the dark arctic night, Jason had learned that the cottage where Holly lived was more office than home, and at dawn, when he decided it was time for coffee, he had made another troubling discovery. The stark white kitchen housed appliances that were as high quality and state-of-the-art as her computer and fax, and there were brightly gleaming Revere Ware pans, an extensive array of utensils, and complete sets of flatware and dishes. But it was as if Holly had stocked the kitchen for someone else, some future tenant, because it was obvious that nothing had ever been used.

And as for food? All that Jason found were breakfast bars, boxes of them, all the same flavor, and beside the boxes was a large jar of vitamins. Jason tried to tell himself that this was a temporary situation. After all, when he was deeply involved in a project, he rarely paid any attention to what he ate, absentmindedly devouring whatever was handy when his brain demanded fresh fuel.

Jason wanted to believe that the cold, monotonous diet was simply a symbol of a recent deadline. But the never-used pots, pans, oven, and microwave told a different tale: no hot meals had ever been prepared here—not ever—not even a bowl of soup. And there was no hot chocolate, no coffee, no tea.

During his wanderings, Jason had discovered the attached garage. There were snowshoes there, and a reassuringly large supply of neatly stacked firewood, but no car. Was Holly's spartan—and easy-to-carry—diet of breakfast bars because of the long walk into town? No, he had decided grimly. The local grocery would surely be happy to deliver, and if not, she could always hire a cab.

This was simply how the fragile arctic flower lived, cold food always, even in the dead of Alaska's deadliest winters; food consumed without pleasure, as nutrition only, just enough to keep her thin body alive.

Jason was so very aware of her thin body now. Except for her pale white face, hands, and feet, it was amply hidden beneath the modest flannel nightgown. But he sensed its trembling thinness nonetheless.

Gently, he began, "I went into town earlier, to shower and change at the hotel. While there, I picked up some food. I hope you don't mind."

He knows that all I ever eat are breakfast bars. With that thought, Holly felt the newfound hopefulness trying to escape, to leap as far away as possible, as if she were a sinking ship about to disappear forever into the dark depths of an icy sea.

Please don't! she pleaded silently to the mutinous feelings. I *know* you need more nutrition than I've been giving you. To sustain your dancing golden sparkles, you need hot meals and vegetables and fruit. You'll have them from now on, I *promise*. The bars were all I needed before, when I thought you were dead. They were more than enough to sustain the slow heartbeat and icy metabolism of my hibernation . . . and my sadness.

"Holly?"

"No, Jason, I don't mind. Thank you."


While Holly showered and dressed, Jason set the table, chilled the orange juice, made the hot chocolate, and heated the blueberry muffins and chocolate-filled croissants he had gotten from the Westmark's fragrant kitchen. The hotel chef had also willingly supplied him with food for later: tomato soup, an assortment of sandwiches, a crab and cheddar casserole, and a blackberry pie. Yes, the cook assured him, this was a service that the hotel was quite happy to provide; and yes, they would be delighted to deliver entrées to any address in Kodiak.

Jason had seen Holly only in long flowing gowns. Both the sixties' dress and the modest nightgown had given her an enchanting quaintness. The Holly who joined him for breakfast had a different look entirely: jeans, turtleneck, pullover sweater, and cowboy boots. The hair that had been a shimmering veil was pulled away from her beautiful face and braided into a single thick golden rope. She gazed at him with what seemed like courage, and despite the thinness that was more apparent than ever, she seemed strong and proud, a brave pioneer on America's last frontier.

These were her at-home clothes, and her at-home hairstyle, and seeing her this way made Jason realize that this spartan cottage *was* her home, a place where, until the invisible intruders of last night, she had felt comfortable and safe.

She looked delicate but courageous. And something else: she looked like who she was—a woman who had survived the thirty years of her life without him. More than survived. The frontierswoman who stood before him routinely walked eight miles for her groceries, in all seasons of sun and snow and darkness and light, and in between those necessary journeys she wrote the stories of hope and love which had garnered her immense fame and more than a small fortune.

Holly had brilliantly survived thirty years of life without him. But now, as Jason gazed at her proud and determined eyes, he wondered if she was trying to prove something still. To him? To herself? Was the defiant aquamarine really saying to him—to both of them—that she could survive the next thirty years perfectly well without him too?

Something had happened to her during the night, in

her dreams. Something that she was clinging to with the ferocity with which Jason had hoped she would cling to him. What was it? he wondered. Her life? Her love? Her privacy? Her trust? He didn't know. But he sensed that whatever it was she guarded so fiercely was somehow threatened by him, as if he might steal it from her if he ever had the chance.

I'm not going to steal anything from you, Jason vowed silently to the brave yet wary pioneer. But there is so very much I want to give you . . . if only you'll let me.

"I told you last night that the reason I followed you here was to make certain you understood that I'm not going to make any changes in *Gifts of Love*. But that's only part of the reason. I was also hoping I could convince you to write the screenplay for me."

"The screenplay? But I've never done anything like that. I have no idea if I could."

"I'm not worried about the 'could.' Your dialogue is terrific and that's essentially what a screenplay is."

"But the pacing in a movie is so different from in a book," she protested softly. "And movies are also so visual."

"Are you a movie buff, Holly? I didn't see a television, so I wasn't sure how many movies you'd seen."

"There's a theater in town," she said as the battle that raged within her became even more intense. Her fluttering heart wanted to soar to the magic created by Jason while her mind fought against the powerful urge with a determined mantra, The hopefulness belongs to me; to me, *to me*. To us! her heart sang as it soared, compelling her to confess, "I don't go to many movies . . . but I have seen all of yours."

The hopefulness leapt from her to him then, arcing like a sparkling current of electricity. Holly felt its glittering leap, and waited to feel her own loss, but the dancing hopefulness only seemed enhanced by the sharing . . . and he seemed so surprised and so pleased to learn that she had walked, sometimes trudged, eight miles to see the movies he made.

"You've seen *Bayou?*"

"Oh yes."

"Well," Jason said softly, losing his place in the conversation, suddenly quite lost in the luminous depths of her beautiful eyes. He would have been content to stay there forever, but when it seemed that she was about to look away, as if suddenly remembering that he was a thief to be feared, he quickly refocused. "You're right about the pacing in a movie. For a feature film, it's best not to exceed the two-hour format, which means that when you're adapting a book, there may be entire scenes that need to be cut, condensed, or blended together."

"I understand that, and it doesn't worry me. Except that I'm not sure how to do it."

Jason smiled. "That's where I come in. If you don't mind, I'd like to give you an outline of the movie as I envision it, the scenes I perceive as absolutely essential. The reason I asked about *Bayou* is because it was also adapted from a long and complex book. If you remember, I used a collage of scenes set to music as a way of including yet condensing some of the storylines."

"I remember. It was very effective . . . very evocative."

"Thanks. So, Holly, are you willing to be my screenwriter?"

He seemed to be promising that the magic would last forever, that he wouldn't take it away, and Holly answered that promise with a brave one of her own. "I'm willing to try."

"Good. I'm glad." Jason had two films to make before *Gifts of Love,* and since he had planned to write the screenplay himself, he hadn't yet given any thought to the scene-by-scene outline. But now the screenplay was a link to Holly. "I'm leaving for Hong Kong tomorrow, but before I go I'll arrange to have some books on script writing, as well as a copy of the screenplay for *Bayou,* shipped to you. By Sunday or Monday I should be able to fax you the outline from Hong Kong. It will just be a rough draft and I will definitely want your input on it."

He was leaving for Hong Kong? *Tomorrow?* The magic wasn't going to last forever, after all. Very soon, oh too soon, it all would end. And what of the joyous hopefulness? Would Jason take that with him too? No, Holly vowed. I won't let that happen.

"Hong Kong?" she echoed finally. *Tomorrow?*

"I have to go," Jason said, very softly, as he gazed at lovely eyes that seemed to miss him already.

How he wanted to stay. But Jason Cole could not delay his journey to Hong Kong by even one hour. Too many people were relying on him. All of them, the cast and crew, had set aside this time in their talented lives to make what was destined to be his most stunning blockbuster yet.

This morning, as he had watched the sun shine its golden smile on the indigo sea, he had thought about asking Holly to go with him, to share with him the rich, exotic splendor that was Hong Kong. But the delicate arctic flower had almost not survived her journey to Los Angeles. Someday, *someday,* when Holly felt safe with him, they would see together all the glittering treasures of the world.

"How long will you be gone?"

Jason hesitated before answering. Eight weeks had been budgeted for the Hong Kong shoot, although he'd already told Gold Star's executives that, with luck, he could probably wrap in seven. But now he heard himself saying, and it sounded very much like a solemn promise, "I'll be back in six weeks. Back here, if that's okay with you."

"Of course," she whispered. "And we'll discuss the screenplay then?"

"Yes, although depending on your publishing commitments, we could do some of that during the next six weeks. The combination of the time difference and my filming schedule may make it a little difficult for you to reliably reach me by phone." Jason saw at once that his words caused worry. And, he decided, it had nothing whatsoever to do with movies or time zones. It had to do with calling a man, in his hotel room, even on business. "You should never hesitate to call, Holly, no matter what time it is. And if I'm not there, you can send a fax. I'll have a machine in my room."

"Really?"

"It's not an uncommon option in hotels these days, especially in Hong Kong, where the pace is so fast that even faxing seems too slow. So, I'll be expecting calls—or faxes—with your thoughts and suggestions about the outline. Okay?"

"Yes." Her worry vanished then, in a dazzling sparkle of blue and green. "My editor would be so impressed."

Wanting the blue-green sparkles to dance forever, Jason asked softly, "Why?"

"Well, the only reason I even have the fax machine is because she said it would be nice if I had one, so she could send me things like advertising copy and hot-off-the-press reviews." Holly smiled. "I don't think she really believed such advanced technology would be available in Kodiak."

"But it is, along with a very state-of-the-art computer system."

"Which I'm just beginning to learn how to use."

"Is there something I can help you with? I'm pretty comfortable with most computer systems."

"Actually, what I'm trying to learn is how to type." Holly shrugged. "I wrote my first book, *Forever and Always,* by hand, and because I really didn't know any better, I bound it with colorful ribbons and mailed it to the publishing company that had published what was then my favorite novel."

"You sent an unagented and handwritten copy of

*Forever and Always* over the transom?" Jason's amazement showed that he knew enough about publishing to know that most books sent over the transom were instantly relegated to the slush pile, where they might languish, unread, forever. It was rare for one to be published, much less to become a bestseller, as *Forever and Always* had been; and now Holly was telling him something more extraordinary still: that the manuscript had been handwritten, presumably on lined paper from a spiral notebook like the one she had carried into his office. "That's pretty remarkable."

"It was luck."

"More than luck."

"Well . . . it was lucky that the ribbons caught my editor's attention and even more lucky that she bothered to begin to read the book."

"Your handwriting is very legible."

"That's what she said."

"Someone has been typing your manuscripts ever since?"

"Yes, my publisher has made arrangement with a typist in New York. They're happy to stick with that system forever, but it seems silly for me not to deliver a typed manuscript like everyone else."

"Are you going to be able to create your stories directly into the word processor?"

"I don't think so. I'm too accustomed to writing them by hand, and that's how I like to do it."

"Is it really cost-effective for you to transcribe what you've handwritten onto disks?"

"I don't mind." Holly's shrug attempted, unsuccessfully, to toss off a thought that threatened to weigh her down, suffocating the magic and crushing the hope. *I don't mind spending endless hours painstakingly transferring my words from script to type. I have nothing else to do with my time, nothing better; but it's more than that, part of my madness: I love being with my* characters, living in their worlds, and escaping from mine. *You're not mad.* The inner voice was confident still, but so soft, a mere whisper amid the sudden thunder.

"Holly?" The eyes that answered his gentle question sent a silent plea: Rescue me from these frightening thoughts. Please? But don't ask me to talk about them. Complying swiftly, Jason suggested, "After we've finished with breakfast, maybe we should take a nice long walk before lunch. I'd love a guided tour of this end of the island."

"Yes, of course," she agreed with soft gratitude, and then glowing surprise. "Lunch?"

Jason smiled. "There's dinner in the refrigerator too." His smile faded. "I'm afraid that I won't be able to share that with you, though. Six is the latest the studio's jet can leave here and still have enough time in Los Angeles for proper servicing—not to mention required rest for the crew—before departing for Hong Kong tomorrow afternoon."

## ❀ 20 ❀

"In summer there's a pod of whales that frolics right out there." As Holly pointed to the sparkling indigo sea, her eyes were more blue than green, and they sparkled like the sea as they envisioned the families of ocean mammals that played every summer in the waters of the gulf.

"Where are the whales now?"

"In Hawaii. Having babies."

They had walked for almost two hours, a leisurely meandering stroll that took them through the majestic forest, and across a vast meadow that was just beginning to bloom with wildflowers, and finally onto the snow-white beach. Holly showed him her world and all of its magnificent treasures.

As Jason smiled at this most magnificent treasure, the most breathtakingly arctic wildflower of them all, he saw the interplay of sea breeze and golden silk. The breeze seemed intent on freeing every strand from the tight confinement of the long thick braid. The effort to date had met with some success. Tendrils now framed her face, and they seemed to dance in joyful celebration of their daring escape.

The breeze was doing what his fingers longed to do. But Jason no longer secretly wished that the entire braid would come loose. He liked being able to see her eyes.

Except that now the radiant sparkles of those

unhidden eyes had vanished behind a cloud of uncertainty.

"I need to explain to you about last night." I need you to know that I am not truly mad. It was a bold assertion. But in the golden light of this glorious day, *with him,* it was a truth which Holly had permitted herself to believe. "As you suggested, I hadn't slept well or eaten very much for quite a while. I suppose that made me more susceptible to the memories."

"Terrible memories."

"Yes."

She had already decided that she would tell him just the facts, without any descriptions at all. That way she could hold the screams inside, couldn't she? And he would know the reason for her terror without himself becoming tainted by its evil. Holly knew that she had to tell him. The hopefulness that was dancing within her still was now putting a nonnegotiable stipulation on its willingness to stay: she had to be honest with him.

When she finally spoke, her voice was calm, flat, unemotional. In a few sentences that were as spartan and impersonal as her home, she told Jason that her father had been killed in Vietnam and that the stepfather who had seemed so charming at first was in fact a monster.

"He killed my mother and sister and brother—and then himself. But he made no attempt to kill me. I have no idea why he didn't, but it made the police and our neighbors believe that I was somehow responsible for what he did. So I left, and as soon as I could, I changed my name."

She had been speaking to the indigo sea, not his indigo eyes, but now she turned and looked up at him with brave triumph. *She had done it.* She had told her story, and her own screams had been kept at bay, and she had not imparted to him the horrific details that would have irrevocably contaminated him with Derek's evil. "I've never told anyone—until now."

For many moments, Jason didn't speak. He was engaged in a hidden struggle between what he wanted and what he believed was best for her.

What Jason wanted for Holly was a blissfully happy childhood, unshadowed by sadness of any kind—much less darkened by the immense tragedy that she had just so calmly described. That was what Jason wanted. But it wasn't to be.

And what about what was best for Holly? Jason didn't know. But it couldn't be best for her to keep everything locked inside, could it? Wouldn't it be better for her to tell him, really tell him, about the memories of that night? Wasn't that the only hope of exorcising the ghosts that were so vivid, so powerful that they could imprison her in sheer terror?

Finally, very quietly, he said, "You still haven't told me."

"What do you mean?"

"I mean," he clarified softly, "you haven't told me what happened that night."

"Yes, I have!"

"I know that you remember everything, Holly. Every word, every expression. That's what you were seeing—and maybe even hearing—when I arrived last night . . . wasn't it? When I knocked on the window, I think it must have sounded to you like gunshots." The brave triumph had long since disappeared and what Jason saw now was simply fear. "Don't you think it might help to talk about it?"

Her golden head shook softly, a gentle no, even as she confessed quietly, "I don't know."

"Well," Jason admitted, "neither do I. But I do believe that keeping the memories and their emotions locked up inside can't be good."

Locked up. The words echoed in Holly's mind. Shouldn't memories and emotions like hers *be* locked up,

like the most vicious of criminals, prohibited forever
from any freedom at all?

No, she realized with surprising confidence. *No . . .*
because the memories weren't criminals. Only Derek
was. And amid the anguished memories, there was so
much more, forgotten until now, crushed by the
remembered horror. But on that evening, as on all
evenings, there had also been great love.

"It had snowed that day," Holly began softly as that
memory of pristine beauty filled her mind. "There was a
tree in our backyard, a noble fir, and I remember my
mother and I talking about the way it looked, so delicate
and lacy, as if it were a bride . . ."

Holly spoke to the sea, to the place in the rippling blue
water where families of humpbacks would cavort in the
summer, and as she did, every second of that evening
came back to her: what Claire had been cooking for
dinner; and the smiling conversation they'd had about
the snow; and what she and her brother and sister had
talked about—*laughed* about—during the commercials;
and even the details of the episode of "Corky and White
Shadow" that they had been watching.

How happy it all had been, how normal.

As the precious remembered moments of love moved
too quickly toward the instant when Derek made his
ominous appearance, Holly felt the welling up within
her, the screams that would suddenly gush forth, spilling,
flooding, drowning . . .

But there were no screams.

There were only tears, seventeen years of them. Always
before they had only spilled within, never once flooding
her eyes, puddling in her heart instead, drowning her in
sadness.

She was going to cry, not scream, and even before the
hot tears began to fall onto her cheeks, she was somehow
in his arms.

"Holly," Jason whispered, his lips gently caressing her silky hair as he spoke.

"I do need to tell you, Jason."

"And I need to have you tell me."

Her tears fell still, a warm, silent rain that nourished the delicate roots of hope in her heart; and as they spilled, the golden tendrils that had so recently danced with joy danced no more. They were soggy now, weighted with tears, drenched by the immense sadness which, at long last, had found escape.

But there was a new dance now, and it was far more magnificent than the dance of sea breeze and golden silk. It was the dance of a woman and a man, of their hearts and their souls, an exquisite, emotional minuet of anguish and of love.

There were times, as Holly told her story, when she needed to be in his arms, cloaked by his warmth and his strength. But there were other times, when she needed distance from him, just a little, to be near him still but separate.

Neither Jason nor Holly had ever danced this dance before. But they did so flawlessly, without the slightest falter, because this extraordinary *pas de deux* was choreographed by the confident mandates of love. Jason did not try to stop her when she needed to pull away. Nor did he move to capture the pale hands that twisted so mercilessly as the images of death came to her. But he was there, his loving arms aching to hold her again, when she needed to return to the sanctuary of his embrace.

Most of the words were hers, but there were times when he sensed that she had seen a memory too awful to share and had gone on without sharing it. It was then that he spoke, commanding very gently, "Tell me, Holly. Tell me everything."

And she did tell him—everything. And no detail of those moments of terror was missed . . . because the images that came to her in living—and dying—color came in excruciatingly slow motion as well.

When at last she was through, Jason held her fragile and trembling body close to his, and for a very long time, as she wept still, Holly was serenaded by the powerful beating of his heart. And when at last her tears finally began to abate, she looked up—and saw the emotion in his dark blue eyes. She had not tainted him with Derek's evil, nor with what she had once believed to be her own madness; but somehow the immense sadness that had dwelled within her for all these years had overflowed to him.

Her delicate fingers reached for his face then and as she touched him, she whispered, "I'm sorry."

"Sorry?" he echoed softly. "For what, Holly? For trusting me?"

"No."

Jason tenderly moved a tear-dampened strand of golden silk away from her eyes. "For letting me touch you?"

Her cheeks answered first, with a rush of warmth and glowing pink. "No."

"Don't ever be sorry for having told me, Holly. I'm not." His gentle smile filled with love. "Okay?"

"Yes," she whispered. "Okay."


By the time they returned to Holly's cottage, it was almost time for Jason to leave for the airport. She convinced him to take two of the sandwiches with him and promised in return that over the next few days she would eat everything else.

Then it was time for him to go.

"I'm going to send you at least one fax a day and call you whenever I can," he promised. "Will you write or call me every day, too?"

"Yes, of course, but . . ."

"But? You don't think I'm talking about daily progress reports on the screenplay, do you?"

"I wasn't sure."

"Well, be sure, Holly," he said solemnly. And only when she seemed certain, when her beautiful eyes shimmered with hope, did he continue. "I know you're practicing your typing skills, but will you write to me by hand?"

It was a request for intimacy, as much intimacy as was possible given the separation of space and time that was about to begin.

"Yes." Her reply, embellished by a soft nod, caused golden tendrils, no longer soggy with tears, to dance anew . . . a new dance, more free now, and more joyful than ever before.

His goodbye kiss was a tender caress of gentle fingers on her lovely face, and of even gentler dark blue eyes on her lovely heart.

Then he was gone, and as Holly watched his car disappear into the pines, she held her breath. The wondrous hopefulness was with her still, and there was magic too, but any moment both of them would see his car disappearing into the forest and make a mad dash to be with him.

But it didn't happen. Not then, and not forty-five minutes later when she was lured outside by the sound of a low-flying plane. The sleek jet was a silver silhouette in the night-dark sky, and she was a small figure illuminated by porchlight, and it seemed a little foolish, but still she waved . . . and the silhouette dipped a silvery wing in reply.

Only when the jet had vanished into the blackness did Holly—and the hopefulness and the magic—go back into the cottage. There, in her bedroom, she reached thoughtfully for the woven purse that had accompanied

244

her to Los Angeles. She removed the wire-rimmed glasses, never to be worn again, and she removed as well the photographs of her beloved family. She wanted to share these happy images with Jason . . . and she would.

In six weeks, when he returned from Hong Kong, she would show him.


On Monday morning, when he had been told that his luncheon meeting with Raven Winter—and presumably Lauren Sinclair—had been canceled, Jason had quickly transformed the annoyance he had felt into something far more productive, a plan to use the suddenly freed hours to begin to address the many issues that needed to be resolved before his Thursday afternoon departure for Hong Kong.

Now it was Wednesday evening. The jet had just bid its final adieu to Holly, and he was speeding swiftly away from her toward Los Angeles—and Hong Kong—and Jason was left with the astonishing truth: since the moment Holly had appeared in his doorway, he had made no headway whatsoever in the mounds of paperwork that needed his attention.

A bulging briefcase lay in the adjacent seat, just as it had yesterday, during the flight to Kodiak. Yesterday, he hadn't even tried to work. He had spent the entire flight thinking about her, worrying about her—and hoping.

He could easily spend the return flight lost in thought as well, such hopeful thoughts. But Jason imposed discipline on his fatigued mind. He had to make thoughtful decisions regarding every item in his bulging briefcase. And he would, even if it meant another night without sleep.

So what if he didn't sleep for three nights, or four, or five? It was all so very trivial compared to seventeen years of nightmares.

*Stop thinking about her,* the disciplined part of Jason Cole commanded.

I will, he vowed. But a soft smile touched his face as he thought, Holly will sleep better tonight. The memories that have terrorized her for so long won't be so confident of their dominion over her anymore. Their secret is exposed now, and shared, and even though her great sadness at the loss of her loved ones remains, and always will, at least the tormenting memories can no longer make her a private hostage to their evil terror.

For four hours Jason worked with unfailing concentration and remarkable efficiency. Then, quite suddenly, as if despite his conscious discipline it had been relentlessly building, the thought literally exploded: Something's wrong. Something's *missing* from what Holly told you.

The extraordinary thought came with extraordinary conviction—despite the fact that it was hard to imagine that Holly had omitted anything at all.

True, except for Derek, she had not mentioned proper names. But that had been an omission of love, of family, because she remembered her loved ones as she had known them, as her mother, her sister, her brother.

Besides, Jason realized, it wasn't the missing names that had caused the thought to explode. It was something else, something hidden deep in his own mind, his own memory.

Jason had absolutely no idea what it could be. He had no conscious memory of the *Time* magazine article he had read during his sophomore year at UCLA. But the story of the massacre that had occurred on Valentine's Day and the seven years' imprisonment of the father who had returned from the dead—a miracle that had come eight months too late—had made an impact on him. Even then, at age nineteen, Jason had known that one day he would be a director; and even then his creative mind envisioned almost everything in terms of film, how he would bring a given story to life, the visual statement he would make.

The story in *Time* was intriguing, but ultimately not satisfying. Until the teenaged daughter who had vanished was found—dead or alive—the story was unfinished. Perhaps that was why it stayed with him, stored deep in his memory.

Jason didn't consciously remember the article, nor had he seen the recent *20/20* telecast. On that Valentine's night, he had been with Nicole Haviland, an evening of passion and pleasure, not romance and love; an evening that ended with petulance when he left at midnight because he had work to do.

Jason stared at the work he was supposed to be doing now. Once again the work that had always been so important to him, his greatest passion, had been wholly preempted by Holly and the strong feeling that there was a missing piece to what she had told him . . . a missing piece which, somehow, he already knew.

"The stepfather's name was Derek, and the girl who survived was Holly, and neither has a last name that we know of," Beth Robinson recapped, making no effort as she did to conceal her skepticism.

Although Beth's skepticism was obvious, it undermined neither her fondness for Jason nor her appreciation that he had come to her with this remarkable assignment.

Until three months ago Beth had been Gold Star's best and therefore busiest researcher. She loved the job, but left without a backward glance when her obstetrician told her that her unborn baby son—and his forty-three-year-old mother—needed to spend the final three months of pregnancy resting at home.

She was almost eight months along now, and felt far *too* rested, so she'd leapt at the chance to do some work for Jason. Yes, she had assured him swiftly. It was quite safe. Especially if all he really wanted her to do was make phone calls.

He had come to her house, en route to the airport, to Hong Kong, and presented her with the prospect of researching a crime that had taken place years before somewhere in the state of Washington.

"Do you have any idea when the murders were committed, Jason? What year, or even what time of year?"

"In winter," he answered, recalling Holly's description of the noble fir lacily dressed with freshly fallen snow. Then, as he thought about how many years ago it had been, he reasoned, Holly is thirty now, and she was a teenager then, but a teenager who was old enough to vanish—and survive—on her own. She must have been at least fifteen, hopefully even older. "I don't know the year, but it was probably no more than fifteen years ago."

"Okay." Beth might have teased that this project truly redefined "challenge." But Jason was so somber, so serious, that she merely carefully reconfirmed his instructions. "My story, if anyone wants to know, is that we're thinking about doing a documentary on domestic violence?"

"That's right, that's the story, but it's actually a personal project, Beth, not a studio one. I want you to keep track of your time and bill me directly. I'll give you my own telephone credit card number to use for all the calls and my Visa card number in case there's information that needs to be sent by courier. Okay?"

"Okay. I'll begin to let my fingers do the walking to police, newspapers, and television stations at eight tomorrow morning. Any idea which side of the state I should begin with?"

It was a question that Jason had already considered. The fact of snow wasn't a major clue. The area east of the Cascades had the harsher winters, but any part of the state could get snowfall. The fact that Holly and her mother had specifically talked about the snow, however, seemed to favor an area where it wasn't so common. That, coupled with the fact that she had chosen to live in Kodiak, with a panoramic view of the sea, made him conclude, "If I had to guess, I'd say the western part of the state. Seattle, maybe, or one of the smaller towns along the coast."

"I'll start with Seattle then. There's a man I've worked with before at the *Seattle Times*. He's always been very helpful."

# Part Four

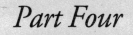

## ❈ 21 ❈

The Space Needle, Caroline had told him when he called Tuesday night to report on the puppies—all thriving—and to ask her where and when she would like to go for her birthday dinner. They had decided the "when" first: Friday night. Mindy's owners were going to retrieve her that morning, and Katie and her puppies would be leaving the day before.

Lawrence and Caroline made plans for her birthday dinner when he called on Tuesday, and they reconfirmed those plans on the following two nights. Lawrence's phone calls came at eleven, after he had settled his twelve canine house guests for the night.

Caroline assured him that eleven—or even later—wasn't too late to call. In truth, before Lawrence, she would have been asleep by then. But that week, even though she awakened early as always, she was wide awake when he called, alive with anticipation and energy. She would curl in the cozy warmth of her bed as they talked, and close her eyes to concentrate fully on his voice, but during those long late-night calls, fatigue stayed very far away.

They talked for hours, conversations that flowed effortlessly from topic to topic, although afterward, as Caroline

253

reflected on what they had discussed, she had trouble recalling precisely how a discussion of the Emerald City Ball had segued so seamlessly to one about the pyramids in Egypt, or how almost any topic, no matter how far afield it seemed, somehow managed to meander back to the recurring issue of great importance: what to name her puppy.

They spent hours on that, discussing the pros and cons of "Freckles" and "Ginger," "Duchess" and "Cleopatra," "Clover" and "Muffin." She needed his advice, of course. As a veterinarian he was in the position of knowing which canine names were in and which ones were out. They gave each name its due, and never once did Lawrence become impatient with the process.

Never once did Lawrence Elliott say that it was *her* decision, *her* puppy . . . as if that assertion would not have been true, as if the responsibility for the new little life was really *theirs*.

"Juliet," they decided before wishing each other good night at two Thursday morning. Not Romeo's Juliet, of course, just Juliet—a name that was both pretty and strong, and which, depending on the personality of the valiant creature who had survived her precarious birth, could soften to "Julie" or become sleek to "Jules."


"Are you still happy with 'Juliet'?" Lawrence asked as they drove the short distance between her house on Queen Anne and the Seattle Center.

"I am. How about you?"

"I like it."

Their reservation at the Emerald Suite, the elegant revolving restaurant atop the Space Needle, was for eight o'clock. They had known, of course, when they'd decided on that time, that the curtain of darkness would have long since fallen on the drama of the pastel spring twilight upon the glistening white mountains. But, they knew, there would still be the jewel-bright magic of the Emerald City at night.

On this rainy night, however, even if they'd come at twilight, there would have been no mountains to see. The Olympics, Cascades, and Mount Rainier would have all been cloaked in the thick gray mantle of clouds that had blanketed Puget Sound since dawn.

There were those, Caroline supposed, who would have canceled their reservations because of the rain. But not she. And now, as she gazed from the slowly revolving perch high above the city, she decided that this was perhaps the perfect way to see its splendor. The falling rain both muted and magnified, gently blurring the sharp silhouettes of buildings while capturing their glittering lights. And as if each raindrop were a soggy storm and each beam of light a fiery sun determined to conquer it, the night sky sparkled with an infinity of tiny rainbows.

"Beautiful," Caroline murmured as her emerald eyes beheld the magnificent play of water and light.

"Yes," Lawrence agreed quietly. "Very beautiful."

His voice was deep, and rich, and gentle, the same voice into which she had curled herself in the midnight darkness during the past few nights. She had heard him with such clarity then, his gentleness and his strength. And sometimes, she was quite certain, she had actually *heard* his sexy smile. And a few times, wonderful times, there had been his soft, surprised laughter, imprisoned for so long, escaping at last.

Now, as Caroline heard Lawrence agree with her about the beauty of this soggy night, she started to turn from that glistening beauty to him. But she got only as far as the inside of the glass window. There, in a reflection illuminated by candlelight, she saw him, gazing at her, just as he had been when he'd said, so softly, "Very beautiful."

The breath Caroline took was for her heart, to give it oxygen, or try to. And, perhaps, there was courage in this rarefied air high above the ground, because, quite suddenly, she found herself completing the turn toward him and greeting with sheer bravery the dark green desire that was awaiting her.

"You're very beautiful, Caroline."

Had the words been spoken by anyone else, she would have teased gaily, Beautiful? *Moi?* No! Wholesome, yes, and fairly well preserved for forty. And, maybe, even a little striking in a patrician sort of way. But not beautiful. It's just an optical illusion, she would have merrily proclaimed. Just an optical *de*lusion.

But the dark green eyes that were caressing her now did not seem deluded in the least. And for the first time in her entire life, Caroline Hawthorne truly did feel beautiful.

"Thank you," she said softly. If I'm beautiful, Lawrence, it's because of you . . . for you.


No one rushed them on the soggy springtime evening months before the tourist season would begin. There was no one waiting impatiently for them to vacate their windowside perch above the world. The courses came at leisurely intervals, and Caroline and Lawrence consumed them slowly, far more interested in talking—and smiling and discovering—than in eating.

Her wonderful birthday dinner did not go untouched. But still, with each passing moment, they became ever more hungry—for each other.

Finally breaking a long silence that had been filled with brave smiles and wholly unconcealed desire, Lawrence whispered huskily, "Let's go."


"Well, well, isn't this a wonderful surprise!" The voice belonged to Martin Sawyer, the influential businessman who, when his own attempts to convince Lawrence Elliott to run for political office had failed, had approached Caroline to see if she would be willing to use her remarkable powers of persuasion on the recalcitrant candidate. "Caroline and Lawrence—together at last . . . and obviously getting along splendidly."

The last was in reference to Lawrence's arm, which was draped around Caroline in a manner that suggested far more than the simple politeness of guiding her through the restaurant toward the elevator: it suggested intimacy.

"Lawrence and I met quite by accident, Martin," Caroline clarified urgently. But too late, she realized as she felt Lawrence release what had been a wonderfully possessive hold.

"But you met. That's the important part."

Martin's wife interceded then, because the maître d' was waiting to escort them to their table. Moments later Lawrence and Caroline boarded the elevator that transported them swiftly down to earth.

Then they were on the ground, and desire's ravenous spell was completely shattered, and the raindrops which had celebrated the nighttime brilliance by creating their own little rainbows were quite colorless now . . . very cold . . . and very wet.


Caroline wanted to blurt a thousand explanations into the silence. But Lawrence was concentrating on his driving, and that was where his undivided attention needed to be, on the dark and treacherous rain-slick streets.

The intelligent green eyes were intently focused on the road, never once drifting toward her. But as Caroline saw the taut rippling of the powerful muscles in his neck and jaw, she knew that at least some of his thoughts were still at the top of the Space Needle and Martin Sawyer's obvious delight that she had taken up the cause of convincing Lawrence Elliott to run for office, his missing daughter be damned!

"Please come in," she urged quietly when Lawrence had

brought the car to a surprisingly gentle stop in front of her house.

His solemn nod told her that he had already been planning to do just that, to speak to her the words that had been under such taut control during the drive.

"You need to know that we did meet by accident," Caroline began, following him into the living room after they had shed their rain-damp coats. He stood by the window, looking out. The view was of the Space Needle, gracefully stretching toward the sky . . . and toward the candlelit desire that now seemed an impossible dream. "Yes, Martin had approached me about trying to persuade you to run for political office. And yes, that was the reason that I had watched the *20/20* segment and knew who you were. But Lawrence, even before I met you, I had told him no. That's why he was so very surprised to see us together tonight. Please believe me. Please believe that I wasn't using you. I never would."

He spun to face her then, and when he did, his face wore an expression that Caroline had not seen before. His dark green eyes were almost black, and as shadowed as midnight, and the angular planes of his strong face had hardened with uncompromising resolve. And when at last he spoke, the voice that could be so very gentle was bitter cold.

"Using *me?*" His demand came with a harsh laugh. This laugh had been imprisoned, too, along with the soft ones she had heard late at night, and now it sent a fierce reminder of that anguished captivity. "You're not using me, Caroline. You couldn't possibly. I have nothing to give, nothing that would be of any use to anyone, not a damned thing. I'm the user, Caroline. I'm the one who's been using you."

"That's not true!"

"Yes it is. You've been giving, and I've been taking, and I've known all along how selfish it was. But"—his voice softened then—"do you have any idea how wonderful it has been for me to talk to you, to be with you?"

"I do know," she replied with matching softness. "I know because that's how it's been for me as well."

For a moment, he seemed to hear her words, and Caroline even saw a glimmer of dark green desire, and her heart began to soar to the candlelit magic of the Emerald Suite. But, too quickly, the shadows returned.

"I'm empty, Caroline. You know that, and you know why. You've been filling me up with your happiness, your enthusiasm, your joy, and I've allowed you to do it."

Caroline heard his words, but they made no sense, and she resolutely refused to abandon the memory of the magic. Softly, bravely, she offered, "As we were leaving the restaurant, before we ran into Martin, it seemed as if there was going to be more . . . that that's what we both wanted."

"Yes," Lawrence agreed gently. "But seeing Martin reminded me of who I really am, the true me, not the man I become when I'm with you. Because of you."

"There's nothing wrong with the man you are when you're with me."

"Except that he's not real. He's an empty shell, completely filled by you."

"But you're wrong! You're kind, and gentle, and . . . none of that has anything to do with me."

"Yes it does. Whatever kindness or gentleness you see in me is simply a reflection of yourself. Trust me, Caroline. I've lived with myself long enough to know."

He's saying goodbye, Caroline realized. He honestly believes that he has nothing to offer. He's going to leave, and he's never going to come back.

As the realization traveled from her brain to her heart, Caroline began to learn about the excruciating pain of losing someone you loved. She felt such emptiness, such loneliness; but she knew, it was absolutely inconsequential when compared to what he had felt, what he had lived, for all these years. Caroline didn't want the aching emptiness for herself. And she most surely did not want it for him.

But he was leaving, walking now toward the closet to retrieve his soggy coat.

"Lawrence, please!" It was a soft cry of despair, and it stopped him. And when he turned toward her, his worried eyes were very gentle. "Please don't leave. If being with me makes you feel less lonely, less empty, then—"

"Being with you makes me feel wonderful, Caroline," he clarified softly. "Wonderful."

"That's how being with you makes me feel, too. It's not just me seeing my own reflection, either, because I don't feel this way—this wonderful—when I'm alone."

"Oh, Caroline." His whisper was both soft and harsh, desire and despair. "I don't want to hurt you."

How could you possibly hurt me? The question was destined to silence because Caroline already knew its ominous answer. It was more than possible for Lawrence to hurt her. He'd already told her that he had nothing to give; but the truth was that he had nothing to give *her*. His heart had long since been given to Claire, and she owned it still. Claire, for whom he had endured seven years of torture and imprisonment. Claire, to whom, even after her death, he had made the solemn promise to find their missing daughter.

Caroline knew that she could be very hurt. Lawrence represented an immense danger to the contentment she had fought so hard to find.

But still she walked to him, and when she stood in front of him, she looked up to his tormented—and beckoning—green eyes and confessed, "I'm not afraid of being hurt, Lawrence, but I'm truly terrified that you might leave now and never come back. Please don't do that. Please stay . . . all night . . . with me."

"Oh, Caroline," he whispered, reaching for her then, gently weaving his strong fingers into her silky auburn hair. Just before kissing his first hello to her welcoming lips, he whispered again, *"Caroline."*

As his fingers wove caressingly and his lips kissed the

gentlest of hellos, wondrous sensations awakened within her. Caroline had never felt such sensations before, but still her floating mind found words for them: desire, passion, need. They were words that Caroline Hawthorne could have defined, as precisely as the dictionary did, but they were words whose meanings she had never truly understood until now.

*Oh, my love, I've hungered for your touch.* She had always loved the hauntingly poignant lyrics; and now they were alive within her, dancing with wonder and with joy.

Caroline had been married for seven years, and during the twelve years since her divorce, she'd had several physical relationships. Each had started out as a perfectly good friendship; but each had become cluttered, and ultimately not enhanced, by sex. She was forty years old, and from the standpoint of something as unemotional as a dictionary, she even fit the definition of "sexually experienced."

But these magnificent feelings—*this warmth, this hunger, this need*—were entirely new to her.

But not to Lawrence. He knew what it was to give all of himself to a woman he loved. Claire and Lawrence Elliott had made love for the last time just hours before he began the journey that would end in the jungles of Vietnam, and since that long-ago night of love, such intimacy had been only a memory. The man whose extraordinary discipline had enabled him to endure for seven years the folding of his long body into a small cage had imposed similar discipline on his own sexual needs.

But now those imprisoned desires were free, and they felt different now, more powerful than he remembered, no doubt enhanced by the many years of harsh denial. And yet . . . they seemed different in another way as well. Despite their breathtaking intensity, they felt more controllable now, as if more certain of their purpose.

Purpose? the question echoed briefly in his mind before being answered by his heart. To give. To share. To entwine far more than impassioned limbs . . . to unite far more than caressing bodies . . . to forge into one far more than molten desires.

They made love in the bed where for the past three nights Caroline had curled into a warm ball as she had curled into the warmth of his voice. Caroline had wanted darkness then, when she could see him only in her mind's eye, and she wanted darkness now.

Discovering this man and their passion through all her other senses in itself seemed almost too much. It was far too soon, too overwhelming, to imagine his hungry green eyes traveling with leisurely but ravenous desire over her nakedness. And Caroline needed to learn as well about her own awakened desires. What did they want? How far would they go? How brave would they be?

*Brave.* So very brave.

Theirs wasn't a single dance of love, but many dances, each one more joyous than the last, more intimate, more confident, more bold. The music came from within, but they both heard it, and the only words they spoke, the only lyrics to the magnificent melody of their loving, were each other's names, a gentle chorus that was whispered over and over and over again.

Caroline awakened at six. The bed in which she had fallen asleep had been tousled by love. But now the bedding was quite smooth, as if there had never been a night of passion, and she herself was tucked in, cozy and warm beneath her quilted comforter.

Pale gold slivers of sunlight peered around the edges of the curtains. It was dawn, just dawn, *and he was gone.*

On sudden impulse, Caroline threw back the covers and rushed to the window. Pulling back an edge of curtain, enough to see the street below, she was greeted by a day that was precisely what the weather forecasters had promised. Last night's storm was a distant memory. The freshly washed world was bright, sparkling clean, a perfect spring day.

Lawrence's car was still parked on the street below. But the message of the carefully smoothed covers was as crystal clear as the sky outside. He was planning to leave, before she awakened, and he would leave without a trace, as if he had never been there at all.

But he had not left yet.

Caroline grabbed her floral bathrobe from a nearby chair. She cinched it tightly, almost punishingly, around her slender waist, and without even stopping to brush her love-tangled auburn hair, she moved swiftly out of the bedroom and toward the staircase.

She was halfway down the stairs when her footsteps, absolutely silent on the thick carpet, were slowed by her thoughts: Lawrence tried to leave last night, and you pleaded with him to stay, and it didn't take a great deal of convincing because, let's face it, the physical attraction is really quite extraordinary. But now he's trying to leave again, and now his passion must surely be sated, and . . .

And I'm *not* going to plead. I just want to say goodbye.

Lawrence was in the kitchen, bending over the counter, writing. For several silent moments, Caroline simply looked at him, this harshly handsome man who under cover of darkness had ignited within her what no man ever had. He was dressed now, except for the jacket of his charcoal-gray suit, but Caroline was acutely aware of the taut, lean body beneath. She hadn't actually *seen* Lawrence's body, of course. But she knew intimately its power, its passion . . . and the texture and contour of its many scars.

"Hi."

As Lawrence straightened and turned toward her, the lips that had caressed her with such tenderness curved into a surprised yet welcoming smile. And the voice that had whispered her name over and over, never faltering once, never once even beginning to whisper *Claire,* greeted softly, "Good morning."

Last night, Caroline had wanted darkness because of her own self-consciousness, because it seemed that the hunger in his eyes might be too much to bear. And now, as she looked at the man who knew everything about her, every intimate passion and unashamed desire, she saw hunger still, wanting more, even more.

She trembled. But his dark green eyes would not permit her to feel self-conscious.

"I was writing you a note."

Caroline nodded solemnly. He was leaving her a polite goodbye. It was, she realized, something he would do. And there was something she needed to do, too, before he left, a polite reassurance. "I wasn't using any contraception last night, but—"

*"We* weren't using any contraception."

"No, well, I just wanted to be sure that you knew there's no need to worry." Caroline stopped abruptly, was stopped, by what she saw: sadness, not relief, as if he hadn't been worrying at all, as if perhaps he had even been *hoping.*

It was as if their loving—without contraception—had been for Lawrence, as it had been for her, not the carelessness of passion but the deep responsibility of choice. Last night, despite the astonishing commands of her awakened desires, Caroline had been very much aware that they would be using no protection.

Protection from what? she had wondered. Protection from conceiving a child with this remarkable man, this extraordinary father? Why on earth would I want to be protected from something so wonderful as that?

I *wouldn't,* she had decided with quiet joy. But before an internal dialogue about the consequences of such a choice could even begin, reality had intervened with a sobering crash. There was no way that even the most remarkable night of passion was going to create a new little life. Yes, it was said that one could theoretically get pregnant on any day of her menstrual cycle; but Caroline knew that to be a slightly exaggerated truth, an admonishment given to reckless teenagers. For this month, for her, the chance of conception had passed. Already she felt the changes that signaled a womb that had abandoned hope.

Caroline had known in advance that their loving would not create a new life. But Lawrence had not. At seventeen, he had been so very careful not to begin his family until after he was married. Now, thirty years later, had he become careless? Or was it a choice for him too? A forbidden wish which he would permit to escape, just once, in concealing darkness . . . just as he would permit his long-imprisoned passion one night of exuberant freedom.

Last night, perhaps, Lawrence had given brief freedom to a captive wish to have another child. But now, in the bright light of day, that wish was imprisoned once again. It had to be—for it was a betrayal of another child, the beloved daughter for whom he would search forever. And now, in Caroline's sunlit kitchen, the sadness she had seen swiftly disappeared.

"Wrong time of the month?"

"Yes," she answered. "My cycle is about as reliable as the moon. My period's due to begin on Monday, and it *will* begin because I already have the telltale symptoms."

"Such as?"

Caroline trembled, as if he were touching her, as if he were beginning anew the magnificent journey that began with a gentle hello and traveled to ecstasy. Why did she feel as if Lawrence were caressing her now? Because, she realized, there was such intimacy to his question. He wanted to know more about her: the mysteries of her womb, and how it told her so clearly that it was too late this month to conceive a child.

"Such as . . . swelling of my lower abdomen." It was immediately, breathtakingly, obvious that the man with whom Caroline had just spent the night did not concur with her quiet assertion. In a rush, she added, "And because my breasts are tender."

Lawrence's gentle smile vanished then, replaced by concern that was as fierce—and as tender—as his loving had been. "Did I hurt you last night, Caroline?"

"No," she assured swiftly, trembling anew as she remembered his caresses. She had been ravished by him, devoured and cherished; but despite the power of his strong body and the even greater power of his passion, she had not, not even for an instant, been hurt. "No, Lawrence, you didn't hurt me."

"It had been a very long time for me."

"For me too." Caroline smiled. "I do, however, have access to a diaphragm. My gynecologist, who is also a friend, makes a point of keeping me supplied with a current prescription, just in case. So as soon as the pharmacy opens for the day . . ."

Caroline's words faded, as did her smile. Lawrence had been planning to leave without awakening her, and she had come downstairs to say goodbye, and their conversation had been so gentle and so intimate that she had forgotten those truths. And now she was presumptuously talking about getting her prescription filled as soon as possible.

"Shall I tell you what I was going to say in the note?" he asked softly. When even the softness in his voice didn't erase the frown from her face, he added, "It was going to be an invitation, Caroline."

"Then tell me."

"Okay. Well, it was going to be an invitation to a number of things, from which you could choose the ones that appealed. So, let's see. Now that you're awake, I'll start with an invitation I hadn't even planned. I'm not officially on call this weekend, but I've agreed to make one house call, one barn call, and one stable call beginning at eight-thirty this morning. I'd be delighted to have an assistant." Lawrence smiled at the beautiful emerald eyes that were already sparkling *yes.* "After that, I thought it would be nice to visit Juliet. You'll be amazed how much she's grown in just six days. Then we could go to the shopping center, and you could fill your prescription while I get some food for a picnic lunch. You saw the meadow the other night, but I'd like you to see it in daylight, and there's another meadow beyond the stream and through the woods. No one knows about it, just me and the deer. It's very private, Caroline, and very beautiful."

Lawrence paused then, not for her answer, but to silently embellish with his forest green eyes what they would do in the private meadow. *We'll make love there, Caroline, in broad daylight, in a sea of wildflowers. Our loving will be like last night, only better, because we know each other better now, and trust each other even more. The air will be scented with the fragrance of flowers—and of freshly washed pines—and it will be warmed by the gentle caresses of the springtime sun. And today, Caroline, we will look at each other as we love.*

"And later, for dinner, we could go to Snoqualmie Falls, and tomorrow morning, if I can get out of bed without awakening you, I'll go out to get the paper, and lattes and croissants, and . . . Caroline?" Lawrence believed that he already knew her answer, that it glowed in her emerald eyes. But still, softly, somehow needing her words, he pressed, "Does any of this appeal to you?"

Caroline didn't answer right away, *couldn't.* She was far away, in the meadow of wildflowers, and she was being caressed by the sun, and his talented lips, and his hungry eyes. He would see her naked passion, and she would see the truth of his scars, and—

Quite suddenly, Caroline was drawn from sunlit images of pine-scented loving to the dark shadows of his green eyes. Lawrence was still waiting for her answer, and for an extraordinary moment, Caroline saw uncertainty . . . as if

267

he, too, worried about the naked revelations of daylight
. . . as if she might be repulsed by what she saw.

"It all appeals to me, Lawrence," she whispered softly.
"All of it."

* *22* *

*Brentwood, California*
*Sunday, April Second*

After pulling to a stop in Raven's driveway, but before making a move to get out, Nick looked at his two daughters, smiled, and said, "This is going to be fun."

They were in the truck, a decision their father seemed to have made quite casually, and one with which they willingly complied. Nick had told Samantha and Melody only the truth about Raven: how they had met, the garden he had planted for her, what she did for a living, the fifteenth high school reunion they'd attended in Chicago, and her invitation to all of them to come to dinner at her house tonight.

Nick had not told his daughters that Raven believed him to be a full-time gardener, not a sometimes gardener *and* CEO of Eden Enterprises. He had no intention of involving his girls in the subterfuge. And if, during the course of the evening, the truth slipped out? Then so be it. But Nick doubted it would. His unpretentious daughters spent very little time talking about money, or designer labels, or expensive restaurants. They cared as little about those topics as they cared about whether they traveled in the truck or the Lexus.

In fact, Samantha and Melody preferred the truck. They

liked the high perch, the bounciness of the springs, and most of all, they liked the spaciousness of the cab that enabled both of them to sit up front with their father.

Now, as they all sat together in that cab, Nick had smilingly announced, not for the first time, that the evening that lay ahead was going to be fun. The announcement was greeted by genuine enthusiasm from one daughter—and by genuine displeasure from her older sister.

"Really fun, Sam," Nick gently teased his scowling daughter. "Really, *really* fun."

Samantha's scowl could not last for her father. They both knew it. But even as her eyes began to twinkle for him, Nick worried anew about her reaction to Raven.

It's all right, Raven had assured him when they'd discussed the very real possibility that Samantha might maintain a solemn silence throughout the entire evening. I understand her wariness, Nick. I really do.

Raven was fully prepared for a taciturn Samantha; just as, Nick knew, she would be fully prepared for their arrival promptly at six.

But when she opened the door, she looked flushed and frazzled.

"Are we early?"

"No. You're right on time. Please come in." As they entered the house, Raven smiled at the girls, both of whom were staring at her, but only one of whom smiled in return. "Hi. I'm Raven."

"I'm Melody."

"Hello, Melody." As promised, Nick's nine-year-old daughter was pure sunshine. Her eyes glowed the brightest of blue and her unaffected smile was positively radiant. Even her startlingly red hair was brilliant, its unruly curls luxuriant spirals of glittering fire. It was hard not to want to bask in the warmth of that happy face, to marvel at its innocent joy. But after only a few beats of sunshine, Raven turned her full attention to Nick's other daughter.

*She could be mine.* The thought was stunning and emotional, for the resemblance between Samantha and Raven went far beyond midnight black hair and dark blue eyes. Samantha's solemn expression was Raven's too, identical to the one she had worn as a twelve-year-old, a look that said the world was a very serious place, filled with people who might easily break her heart.

Raven wanted to put her arms around Samantha, to assure her that she would no more hurt her than her father would. But instead she simply smiled and greeted, "And you must be Samantha. Hi."

"Hi."

Raven fought to hide her disappointment at Samantha's response. Instead of being reassured by Raven's welcoming warmth, Samantha seemed to become even more wary, more suspicious.

"So, Raven," Nick said softly. "What happened?"

Raven had promised herself that she was going to laugh about it, to make it an amusing anecdote for the girls, but now she allowed the frown she honestly felt to cloud her face.

"I dropped the casserole."

"I'm sorry." Nick's voice filled with quiet sympathy. He knew how nervous Raven had been about this dinner, wanting to serve something the girls would like, rejecting his repeated suggestions that maybe it would be easier—the first time—for them just to go out somewhere. But Raven had been insistent that she wanted to cook for them. "And it shattered?"

"Actually, the baking dish itself was quite durable. It simply bounced." She smiled wryly. "The casserole, however, did shatter."

"All over your spotless kitchen floor? I would think it's still pretty edible."

Raven's floor *was* spotless, of course, and as she had picked up the spilt food, she had washed it off and put it in microwave containers for future use.

"Edible, yes, and it won't go to waste. But I'm not going

to serve it to guests." She turned then to those most important young guests. "So, it's not very fancy, but I was thinking about ordering some pizza?"

"We *love* pizza," Melody offered swiftly.

Raven already knew that. Nick had suggested pizza more than once. But now she smiled gratefully at the little girl who was so instinctively gracious, who had so quickly wanted her to feel better about the mishap. "You do? Good. Then that's settled."

"In fact, we have a favorite pizza place not very far from here," Nick said. "Why don't I go pick something up while the three of you get better acquainted?"

Raven waited for Samantha to insist that she go with her father. But Samantha remained silent. So, knowing full well that both the enthusiastic Melody and her terribly serious twelve-year-old sister enjoyed cooking, Raven said, "I still haven't made the tossed salad. Maybe you two could help me with that? Maybe, with your help, I can even keep it from falling on the floor."

Samantha's response to Raven's attempt at humor was a look of surprise. Melody's was a lovely cascade of giggles.

"My dad isn't looking for a wife."

Somehow, remarkably, as Raven turned toward the voice, she managed to prevent the knife with which she had been slicing tomatoes from swerving off course and into her fingers.

The voice was barely familiar, having scarcely spoken. Not that the process of salad making had been silent, far from it. Melody had chattered, happy, interested, enthusiastic words.

But now, as her older sister made the stunning pronouncement, Melody gasped and fell silent.

Raven was at the sink, slicing the tomatoes, and the girls were seated at the table, where, until Samantha's comment brought all tasks to a shuddering halt, they had been grating cheese.

And now, as Raven turned toward Samantha, she saw both courage and fear. Nick's daughter was so afraid of losing her father that she had overcome her innate shyness to bravely issue the remarkable statement. How well Raven knew the source of both the courage and the fear: desperation . . . because the stakes were so terribly high, so terribly serious.

Before Raven could formulate a reply, Nick's twelve-year-old daughter spoke again, a devastating embellishment to what had come before.

"He's a man, so he has needs. That's why he sees women, lots and lots of them."

Samantha's second sentence would be remembered later; for now Raven's mind reeled from the first: He's a man, so he has needs.

As she stared at the desperate young girl who reminded her so much of herself, suddenly, horribly, the image became even more real. In just a few months Samantha would turn thirteen. That was the age at which Raven had lost her virginity, had given it away, because she had been so desperate for love . . . and because from her mother she had gleaned the destructive and demeaning belief that men had needs which women were obliged to fulfill. She had felt so old at thirteen, so exhausted somehow. But in fact she had only been a little girl; and Blane, the sixteen-year-old "man" who had wanted her, because he had needs, had seemed terribly mature.

But we were still *children,* Raven thought. I was a child, just as Samantha is, and there was no one to love or protect me.

But Samantha was loved, deeply, fiercely, protectively. And yet she had just solemnly spoken words that no loving father would ever permit his beloved daughter to believe.

"I can't believe that your dad told you that men have needs. Did he?"

"Not exactly," Samantha admitted. "No."

"Good." Raven crossed to the kitchen table and sat down, her expression now more solemn than Sam's. "Please don't ever believe that there is something about men, or boys, that gives them the right to make demands on you. Please don't ever, *ever,* think you have to do what a man wants you to do just because he wants it. Everyone wants to be liked, to be loved, and everyone has a right to be. But it's something that has to be earned, not taken, not expected, not demanded." Raven paused for a necessary breath, realized that Samantha's eyes were wide with surprise, and wondered if Samantha had concluded that she was utterly crazy—or utterly presumptuous. Maybe, Raven thought, this lovely young girl has absolutely no idea what I'm even talking about. Raven had no intention of being more explicit. Maybe, to Samantha, the "needs" about which she had spoken with such authority merely meant adult companionship, not sex. "Maybe what I'm saying doesn't even make sense."

"Yes it does!" Melody exclaimed. "It's *exactly* what Daddy told us after he heard Jeannette telling us that the reason he was seeing her was because men have needs." Melody's shrug indicated quite clearly that "needs" was a euphemism for something that made no sense to her at all. But her bright eyes sent the message that she had nonetheless listened with great interest to what her father had had to say on the subject. "We didn't even know Jeannette before then. She just showed up at the house one day, as a surprise, and that made him mad enough, but when she said that other stuff, he became *really* furious. He told her that it was completely inappropriate for her to have said something like that to us."

"Well, I agree with him. It was."

"I'm sure he never saw her again after that," Melody added.

Good, Raven thought. That Nick would protect his beloved daughters from anyone who would taint their belief system with such blatant sexism was no surprise. Nor was it, she realized, a surprise to Samantha. What had Nick's eldest daughter been trying to accomplish with her statement? Had she been hoping to entrap Raven into agreeing that men did indeed have needs, so that she could then report that inappropriate—and relationship-ending—belief to her father?

Perhaps. But now it was clear that Raven had truly shocked her by reacting with an impassioned protectiveness that apparently rivaled Nick's. Raven saw confusion, and maybe even a little hope, and suggested softly, "I think what you really meant to say, Samantha, is that you don't need—or want—a new mother."

"Oh," Melody whispered, her bright blue eyes widening with amazement as she looked from Raven to her older sister.

Samantha said nothing. She didn't need to. Her sadness said it all.

"Listen to me, Samantha, please. I'm not trying to become your mother. I'd never even presume to try. Besides, I'm not the least bit sure that I *could* be a mother, that I would be any good at it. In fact, I probably wouldn't be."

"Why not?" Melody asked.

Before answering, Raven thought about the unloved acid baby who had tried for such a long time to become a mother, because against all odds she had dared to believe that she would be a loving one. But nature had known best.

"It's too hard to explain," she said finally, gently, to the concerned young face. "It's just something that I've come to believe is true."

"Oh. Okay." Then, brightening, Melody asked, "What's your mother like?"

"Well, first of all, I haven't even seen her for fifteen years. A few weeks before I graduated from high school, she decided to go away. I never had a dad, or any sisters or brothers, so when she left, I was all alone. For a very long time I believed that she had left because of me, because there was something terribly wrong with me."

"But there wasn't," Melody countered instantly.

And almost as instantly, but far more quietly, Samantha said, "There wasn't anything wrong with you at all."

"No, there wasn't," Raven answered, not truly believing it for herself, of course, but believing it with all her heart for them. "I finally understood that the reason she left had far more to do with her than with me. By any way of measuring, she wouldn't get a very high score in the mother department, but I truly think she did the best she could." All three pairs of blue eyes were solemn now, even the ones that were the brightest blue, and for many heartbeats of silence they were simply three girls who had been abandoned by their mothers. Then Raven became a grown woman once again, and with insight born of pain, she offered softly, "Not everyone is cut out to be a mother. It's no one's fault. That's just the way it is."

By the time Nick returned with the pizza, the topic being discussed in the kitchen had shifted from mothers and daughters to the girls' favorite musical groups, and for the remainder of the evening, Samantha's darkest scowl never reappeared. Indeed, there were even glimpses of her lovely smile and her sparkling blue eyes. But mostly she was quiet, observant, watching Raven from a vantage point that was somewhere between disbelief and hope.

Even before the evening started, Raven had known what time it would end: at eight-thirty, if not before. It was a school night, Nick had explained, and nine o'clock was Melody's bedtime. After a hesitant moment he had added another truth, something that committed them even more rigidly to the eight-thirty departure. In response to the news of the dinner party, Samantha had announced that she herself wanted to go to bed by nine, at the latest, because she was going to get up early to do some last-minute study-ing for an exam.

But eight-thirty came—and went. When Nick quietly announced the time, both girls shrugged dismissive shrugs, made no move whatsoever to stand up, and remained in-tently focused on Raven. She was telling them about the snowy winters in Chicago, lavishly romanticizing what in truth had been, for the little girl who wore Vaseline on her thin bare legs, bitterly cold reminders of just how un-loved—and how unlovable—she truly was.

At nine-fifteen Nick reluctantly insisted that they call it a night. He could see that despite her valiant attempt not to, his youngest and most high-energy daughter was begin-ning to fade; and he knew from experience that she needed a good night's sleep to fully recharge her lively batteries.

Without any prompting from their father whatsoever, both girls politely thanked Raven for the evening. Melody's thank-you was embellished with an exuberant hug. For a wonderful moment it seemed as if Samantha's slender body was going to move forward too, and Raven was ready, at even the slightest indication, to welcome the embrace.

But Samantha stood her ground, and she seemed even to stiffen a little. Finally she said, "I'm sorry about what I said to you earlier."

They still didn't touch, but Raven embraced her then, with her smile and her eyes, an invisible yet tight embrace of the heart.

"I'm not sorry, Samantha. It gave us a chance to talk."

Raven waved goodbye from her front porch as they pulled out of the driveway, and they all waved back. Then the bright headlights of Nick's truck disappeared into the darkness . . .

And she started to cry. It wasn't the gentle mist that might have been predicted, a slight liquid runoff from an evening of welled up emotions. Instead, quite literally, quite suddenly, and totally unexpectedly, Raven Willow Winter burst into tears.

As the tears flooded and spilled, Raven's drowning mind clung frantically to a rescuing truth: shattered casserole notwithstanding, the evening had gone very well, far better than either she or Nick had imagined it would.

But even that reassuring truth was no match for the silent cries that burst from the same place that had given such precipitous birth to the torrent of tears.

Don't leave me behind! Take me with you! Please! We could be a family. We could talk, and laugh, and work through even the most difficult problems together . . . couldn't we?

The words were stunning, stinging, shocking. And according to a voice that sounded very much like Victoria Wainwright Calhoun, they were also astonishingly foolish. Nick is not going to entrust the care of his precious daughters to just anyone. Yes, he wanted you to meet them, and yes, he left you alone with them while he went out to get pizza. But you said it yourself: there is no reason whatsoever to think that you would be a good mother—and plenty of reasons to know that you would not.

And what's more, Nick hasn't given you any reason to think he's interested in anything more than a few nights of passion. Samantha was right: he's not looking for a wife, nor is he looking for a mother for his daughters.

Raven shuddered as she remembered what else Samantha had said. Nick had needs, and lots and lots of women who were more than happy to satisfy them, and even though both Nick and Raven wanted to make certain that his very loved daughters would never devalue themselves, never give themselves away, Raven had spent her entire life doing just that . . . because she had wanted so desperately to be loved.

And wasn't the place deep within her that had just burst into tears, and frantically pleaded not to be left behind, the most desperate place of all?

Yes—and no. Yes, she wanted to be loved; but now there was much more: she wanted *to* love. That was why she had always wanted a baby, because some defiant part of her had always believed in her ability to love, to protect, to cherish. And now, astonishingly, she felt quite confident of that belief.

I do have something to give. *I know I do.*


They had planned in advance that, as he had done every other night this week, Nick would return as soon as the girls were asleep. This night would be different, however, the last they would spend together for the next ten days. Nick's parents, who had kept vigil over the sleeping girls, were leaving for Denver in the morning, to visit their daughter and meet their first grandson.

On every other night this week, Nick had arrived shortly after ten. But tonight, as eleven became eleven-thirty, Raven's hopes began to die . . . and even when the bright lights of his truck finally illuminated her driveway, she believed at first that it was merely a golden mirage.

"Nobody could go to sleep," Nick said when she opened the door to him. "They were both far too keyed up. They were dazzled by you, Raven, even Sam—maybe especially Sam."

His hands gently cupped her face, and he smiled with unconcealed tenderness, and his steel gray eyes smoldered with desire—and with what looked to her like love.

Without any warning whatsoever, Raven burst again, an almost violent explosion of hot tears and silent cries of despair.

"Raven? What's wrong?"

*I want you and your lovely daughters. I want us to be a family. I want that so much . . . too much.*

"Raven?" Nick pulled her to him, cloaking her in his strength. "What is it? Everything went so well. Don't you know that?"

She heard his gentleness, and his words made it sound as if they were a team, parents approaching together the fragile sensitivities of their beloved children.

*Stop*, a voice warned. *You need him, but he doesn't need you, not really, except in bed. And when he gets tired of that, or when he finds your inexplicable tears themselves excessively tiresome, well, there are lots and lots of other women who would want Nicholas Gault.*

"Maybe it really didn't go well for you," Nick murmured into her silky black hair. "Samantha obviously said something that hurt your feelings."

Raven willed the tears to stop then, warning them that if they didn't, Nick would vanish forever. When they seemed under control, she looked up at him and answered emphatically, "No, she didn't. Everything did go well, Nick, very well. They're really lovely little girls."

"Then tell me why you're crying."

Raven smiled a wobbly smile. "I honestly don't know. Some sort of nervous energy, I guess. I was tense about this evening, probably more tense than I realized, and I didn't have time to cry over the spilt casserole, so it's all pouring out now."

Nick gazed thoughtfully at her beautiful face as one finger gently traced the tracks of a recent tear. He knew that she was telling him only a partial truth, that she was holding back from him something very important.

*So we're both keeping secrets now.*

On the way back to her tonight, Nick had confronted the idea that had been dancing in his mind all evening. *Tell her that you love her*, it prompted. *Tell her that you want her in your life—and the lives of your girls—forever.*

Nick had imagined speaking those words to her, and Raven's joyous reply, and then he had envisioned an earnest conversation in which they would quietly acknowledge that even though this evening had gone very well, it was far too soon to mention any specific plans to the girls. They would need to spend much more time together, and to weather together the relapses that were bound to occur, times when Samantha's longstanding fear outweighed her nascent hope. But eventually, they would be a family.

And somewhere during that earnest—and joyous—conversation, he would casually mention that he was worth many, many millions . . . and Raven's sapphire eyes would sparkle with pure surprise . . . and he would see at once that she hadn't known about his wealth—and didn't care.

It was a wonderful dream, and Nick hoped with all his heart that one day it would be real. But as he gazed at sapphire that was shadowed with its own important secrets, he realized that it was far too soon to reveal his own.

We need more time, he decided. We all need much more time.

## ❀ 23 ❀

At one o'clock Friday afternoon, five days after their pizza dinner, Raven's secretary announced through the intercom that there was a call from a Samantha Gault.

"I'll take it," Raven replied swiftly. Then, depressing the blinking light on her phone, she greeted warmly, "Hello, Samantha."

"Hi."

It was just a single syllable, quietly spoken, but Raven detected its trembling uncertainty nonetheless. Concealing her own sudden worry, she asked gently, "What's wrong?"

"Nothing. I mean . . . my grandparents are in Denver, and my dad has an important meeting this afternoon." Samantha stopped with what sounded to Raven like a gasp.

"Samantha?"

"This is so stupid! You probably have an important meeting this afternoon too."

"As a matter of fact, I don't," Raven answered without giving her afternoon's calendar a moment's thought. Of course she had meetings, but without even calling them to mind, she knew that none was as important as Samantha. Nor, she mused, were any of the multimillion-dollar projects that might have been on her agenda nearly as important as whatever it was Nick was doing: tending a garden, or learning about a new variety of rose, or designing a future tableau of color and fragrance. "So I'm all yours. What can I do?"

"Could you give me a ride home from school?"

"Of course. Just say where and when."

"I go to Westlake. It's on North Faring Avenue in Holmby Hills."

"I know exactly where is it." Raven also knew that Westlake School for Girls was one of the best private schools in the area—and one of the most expensive. "It's not far from here at all, less than fifteen minutes."

"Would it be possible for you to come now?"

"Absolutely. The second we hang up, I'll be on my way. Are you sick, Samantha? Should I take you to a doctor? I'd be very happy to."

"No, thank you. I just need to go home."


Raven spotted Samantha the moment she turned into Westlake's tree-shaded circular drive. She was standing on the curb in front of the main entrance and she was not alone. A woman stood beside her, protectively near, and as Raven pulled to a gentle stop in front of them, she saw the concerned expression on the woman's face and the apprehensive one on Samantha's.

It was immediately apparent that Samantha wasn't simply going to hop into the car—the woman wasn't going to permit it—so Raven turned off the ignition, got out, and smiling confident reassurance to Samantha, she extended a hand to the woman and greeted, "Hello. I'm Raven Winter."

The woman introduced herself as the school's headmistress and promptly explained her presence. "I'm afraid we have a bit of a problem, Ms. Winter. We had assumed that when Samantha called for a ride home, it would have been to someone who's listed as an authorized guardian in her file. We have a fairly firm policy about not releasing students to anyone whose name doesn't appear on that list."

I'm sure you do, Raven thought.

It was an important policy, of course, one of which she wholeheartedly approved. Westlake was populated largely by young heiresses from the Platinum Triangle, innocent little girls who might be stolen and held in exchange for some of their parents' vast fortunes. Samantha was the much-beloved daughter of a gardener whose success was such that he was obviously able to afford the school's expensive tuition; but of all the school's students who could be kidnapped, Samantha seemed an unlikely target.

Raven was impressed that the administration was concerned about the welfare of all its charges, no matter how wealthy, and she had no intention of arguing in front of Samantha that, although a priceless treasure to her father, her worth to a potential criminal might be somewhat less than that of her classmates. She tried another approach instead: to prove that she herself was quite safe, virtually a member of the family.

"I admit the situation is a bit unique. But as I'm sure Samantha has told you, her grandparents are visiting their daughter and her family in Denver, which is why they aren't available. And since Nick's—Mr. Gault's—schedule this afternoon is less flexible than mine, Samantha called me."

"I guess I'm still a little unclear as to your relationship to Samantha."

"I'm her friend," Raven said quietly, smiling at that young friend. Samantha's blue eyes answered with gratitude, and with such shimmering hope that Raven became even more determined to resolve the impasse as soon as possible. "I understand your concern, and her family and I fully support and appreciate the school's policy. But isn't its true purpose to prevent unknown people from showing up out of the blue and under false pretenses? I'm here today because Samantha called me. She obviously knows me, and—"

"And I trust her," Samantha interjected softly. Turning to the headmistress, she implored, "It's okay, really it is."

"All right." The headmistress smiled at last. "I just wanted to be sure. And now I am."

"Thank you," Raven said as an amazed Samantha began to move toward her, passing right through the invisible wall which, moments earlier, had seemed absolutely impenetrable. Raven curled a welcoming arm around her young charge, but before guiding her to the car, she removed one of her engraved business cards from her purse and handed it to the headmistress. "I'd like you to have this for Samantha's file."

"Hi," Raven greeted when they were both in her Jaguar. They had buckled their seat belts, but she hadn't yet turned the ignition key.

"Hi." Samantha's dark blue eyes glowed with admiration. "You were really great, Raven. I didn't think she'd let me go with you."

"Well, since I had no intention of leaving without you, it would have been a losing battle on her part."

"Thanks."

"You're welcome. So . . . are you sick?"

"It's not really an illness, I know that, and maybe I shouldn't even be going home. The school nurse thought it would be okay, though, just this one time, this *first* time." Samantha stopped her breathless preamble, shrugged, and admitted quietly, "I started having my period today."

"Really? Well, I agree with the nurse, I think it's fine to take the rest of the day off. Starting your period is normal and natural, of course, but it's also a big deal." Raven's thoughts traveled to Nick, to his reaction to Samantha's news. He would be quietly emotional, his gray eyes reassuring yet solemn as he reflected on what this signaled, his daughter's inevitable transition from little girl to young woman. On the drive over to Westlake, Raven had decided that Nick would be very pleased that Samantha had called her, that she had felt safe enough to do so. And now? Would he still be pleased? Raven hoped so. She hoped Nick would understand that Samantha had no idea how significant this life-changing event would be for him. How this was really girl stuff, friend stuff . . . mother and daughter stuff. With a thoughtful tilt of her head, Raven asked softly, maternally, "And maybe a little bit scary?"

"Were you scared?"

"I was terrified. I had no idea what was happening."

"You didn't? Didn't your mother tell you about it?"

"No." Raven kept the bitterness from her voice and even found herself offering an apology for Sheila Winter. "I was quite young when I first started. She hadn't told me yet because she thought there was still lots of time before I would need to know."

Raven hid her bitterness, but the memory, with all its emotion, suddenly returned in full force. She had been *so scared.* The bleeding had been brisk, and the cramps had been severe, and she had thought that she was dying. She had left school without telling a soul, running and stumbling to get home, as if she had a mother there who would comfort her, explain to her, care about her.

On that afternoon Sheila had been in bed with that month's boyfriend, and they both had stared at Raven with anger when she had burst in, and then her mother had added shame to her fear by forcing her to admit—in front of both of them—what was wrong. Her mother's lover had sworn lavishly, mockingly, at the confession, and her mother had sworn as well. And then, laughing her raspy cigarette cough, she had said, "So you have the curse. Terrific. Just one more cost of having a kid."

But the cost of Raven's menstrual periods had ultimately been quite trivial. The bleeding and cramping that had heralded her first period disappeared almost entirely by the second. Raven had no idea how atypical her periods were until college, when she overheard classmates bemoaning theirs. And when she went to the student health center for her first gynecological exam and described the duration of cramping in minutes not hours, and the bleeding in hours not days, the nurse told her how very lucky she was.

But even then Raven had known that she wasn't lucky at all. She had an acid baby's womb, so scarred and barren that it didn't devote the better part of each month to creating the layers of rich, nutritious tissue that were necessary to welcome and sustain a tiny new life. Her scant and painless periods were further proof of how very damaged she was.

Raven's first period had been terrifying and traumatic, and although she saw neither terror nor trauma on Samantha's young face, she asked again the question to which she had yet to hear the answer. "It's not scary for you?"

"I guess I feel sort of strange, but not scared. They taught us about periods in class, and some of my friends have already started, and Gran and I have talked about it."

"Not too much bleeding or pain?"

"I don't think so. The cramps just feel like a squeeze deep inside and I don't feel dizzy or anything." An impish smile touched her pretty face. "I'm pretty sure I'm not going to swoon."

"Swoon?" Raven echoed with a soft laugh.

Samantha's cheeks became rosy. "I know it's sort of an old-fashioned word, but my friends and I really like it."

"So do I," Raven assured swiftly, suddenly remembering the twelve-year-old girl she'd wanted so desperately to be, a girl who had friends, a circle of laughter and secrets in which the archaic term "swoon" had been carefully chosen because it had exactly the right amount of drama and charm. Her fingers trembled slightly as she turned the ignition key. "Let's get you home. Should we stop for supplies at a pharmacy along the way?"

"No. Gran and I got everything I would need a few months ago."

"Okay. So, where am I going?"

"Do you know how to get to the East Gate of Bel Air?"

"Sure."

"That's where we turn in."

"I have a confession to make," Samantha said quietly just before they turned off Sunset into Bel Air. "What I said Sunday night about my dad seeing lots and lots of women? It's not true. He never sees anybody. When he's not working, he's always home with us. I just wanted you to know."

Raven knew perfectly well that Nick wasn't *always* home at night. But still, for the moment, she allowed herself the wonderful luxury of believing that Nick's late-night visits to her were most unusual. "Thanks. That's nice of you to tell me."

Then they were in Bel Air. Samantha gave directions and Raven concentrated on driving carefully along the narrow winding roads amid the mansions. She assumed that they were heading for a gardener's cottage located on one of the magnificent estates. Here, as in Lake Meadow, the servants' quarters were often more than large enough to house a man, his two daughters, and his parents.

But when they finally turned into a private driveway, and climbed the final ascent to the top of the hill, Raven began to feel stirrings of worry. The mansion was a stately white colonial trimmed in teal, and it was surrounded by landscaping that was undoubtedly of Nick's creation.

But there was no gardener's cottage.

"Your dad must be home after all. His truck's here."

"No. He's not home." Samantha's blue eyes widened with surprise. "He usually doesn't take the truck to work."

"What does he take?"

"The Lexus."

\* \* \*

Samantha disarmed the mansion's state-of-the-art alarm system with an agile dance of fingers over a panel of numbers. Then she led Raven into the marbled elegance of the foyer. An antique mirror would have reflected Raven's image, had she glanced at it, but she didn't. Ever since Samantha's call, she had been someone else, someone who might have been a mother; but now, as she walked into the mansion and understood the depth of Nick's betrayal, she didn't need to look at her reflection to remind herself of who she really was: an exquisite creature of ice to be used, enjoyed, and then discarded.

"Can you stay for a while, Raven? We could have some cookies and lemonade."

"I'd like that, Samantha," Raven answered, self-destructive as always. She would stay a little longer, pretend a little longer, further fanning the already searing fires of pain. "If you show me where the kitchen is, I'll fix the lemonade while you change out of your school clothes."

As Samantha led the way to the kitchen, Raven found herself wondering who Nicholas Gault really was. Because of his parents' trip to Denver, they hadn't seen each other since he had left at dawn on Monday. But they had talked often, every night after the girls went to bed and several times each day, brief calls made by him to her on her private line. Raven had had the impression that Nick had been calling from phone booths as he traveled from one garden to the next. Obviously, that was very far from true.

"Where was your dad's important meeting this afternoon?" she asked, as casually as possible, just as they reached the kitchen.

"Let's see." Samantha plopped her notebook onto a nearby counter and withdrew from its inside flap a notecard-sized piece of paper. "The Westwood Marquis." Then, before going upstairs to change, she handed the paper to Raven. "Here's his schedule for today."

The neatly typed card provided Nick's hour-by-hour engagements, complete with pertinent telephone numbers. Presumably typed by his secretary, it had clearly been prepared for his daughter, in case she needed to reach him. At the top of the card was the elegantly engraved answer to who he really was: Nicholas Gault, President and CEO of Eden Enterprises. The address of his corporate offices on Wilshire Boulevard was engraved just below.

As Raven scanned the day's agenda, she realized that when Nick had called her just before ten, he had been about to begin the meeting at the Marquis. The topic, it seemed, was the Eden Resort that Nicholas Gault was planning to build on Maui. The meeting was scheduled from ten until two-thirty and the typed line that followed, the final entry for the day, read, "3 P.M.—Home." Nick obviously planned to be home before the girls, so they wouldn't return to an empty house . . . an empty mansion.

Raven glanced at the clock on the stove. Nick would be home in forty-five minutes. And she would still be here, she realized; and it had nothing to do with her own self-destructive impulses. It had to do with the little girl who was becoming a little woman. Nick would not leave his precious daughter home by herself, and neither would she.

Would his steel gray eyes blaze with fury that his pretense had been discovered? Raven wondered. Probably. *Yes*. But not in front of Samantha, not until she and Nick were alone.

He'll see my fury then too, Raven promised her breaking heart. My fury, not my pain, because I cannot, will not, put myself in the position of hearing his mocking words of pure contempt, *Love* you, Raven? Love *you*?

As Raven made lemonade and arranged a small platter of cookies, she felt the irony of where she was and what she was doing: preparing food in the kitchen of a magnificent mansion. Raven had been in many mansions in Bel Air, of course, as a welcomed guest. But Nicholas Gault had not wanted her here, not welcomed her in his home. She was here quite by mistake—mistaken for someone who might be a mother as well as an expert on menstrual periods. She was, of course, an impostor on both counts. For twenty years she had tried to conceive, and had failed; and she had no useful information to impart about menstrual periods, not normal ones, not the kind experienced by girls who weren't acid babies.

The acid baby suddenly felt terribly young, and terribly fragile. She was back in Lake Meadow, the girl who had been permitted in the kitchen to prepare meals for the Wainwright family, but who had never been allowed access to the rest of their magnificent house.

It was a young and fragile Samantha who returned to the kitchen.

Perhaps, Raven thought, the deeper meaning of what had happened today was beginning to settle. With the onset of her period, Samantha had irreversibly crossed the invisible line that separates little girls from little women. Maybe part of her wanted to turn back, to be purely that little girl again, still, always.

Raven waited to pursue the topic until—at Samantha's suggestion—they had taken their lemonade and cookies outside, to the verandah beyond the living room, and were seated at a teal-blue wrought-iron table. The verandah overlooked gardens of roses, and from its commanding perch afforded as well one of Southern California's most spectacular views: the City of Angels sprawling below, the bright blue Pacific shimmering beyond.

"Are you feeling okay, Samantha?"

Samantha nodded, but frowned.

"Does it all seem scarier now?"

"I guess so. It seems more real."

"And more irrevocable?" Raven smiled at Samantha's obvious relief that she understood. "The event is an irrevocable one, but you don't change, not really. Inside, you stay the same."

"You're the same as you were when you were my age?"

"In many ways, yes, I am." Raven smiled, because her words were meant to reassure Samantha. But her thoughts taunted, You're *exactly* the same. Afraid, vulnerable, wanting desperately to be loved, but so woefully undeserving. You're good enough—for a while—to satisfy a man's physical needs. But that's all. As Raven felt her smile begin to falter, and feared that Samantha might see the sadness in her eyes, she focused on Samantha's T-shirt. Bright green, it bore the words, emblazoned in gold, "Santa Barbara Polo Club." Looking up again, Raven asked, "Do you ride?"

"Yes. Not polo, of course. Do you?"

"I've never been on a horse."

"Then you have to! You'd love it. You'll have to come with us to Santa Barbara."

As Samantha expanded enthusiastically on the plan to have Raven join them for a weekend at their ranch in Santa Barbara, Raven's fingers curled ever more tightly around her glass of lemonade. It was as if her fingers were seeking the iciness, hoping it would be contagious, hoping it would freeze the heart that was burning up with pain.

When Nick saw Raven's Jaguar in his driveway, he felt a little surprise, a little worry, but mostly relief. The latter wouldn't be complete until he had finished explaining, of course, until the flashing sapphire eyes had softened into understanding . . . and love?

Nick glanced at his watch. Samantha wasn't due home for at least thirty minutes and Melody had ballet lessons until five. That gave them a little time to talk, to begin talking.

As Nick walked toward the west side of the mansion, somehow confident that Raven would have discovered the rose-fragrant verandah, his heart set a new pace, anticipation and worry, eager to see her and wanting the next thirty minutes to be behind them, safely navigated, so that the rest of their lives together could lie ahead.

A smile touched his lips when he saw her midnight-black hair shining in the sunlight. But there was another dark head, and it was she who saw him first, she who sprung from her chair to greet him.

"Daddy!"

"Sam," Nick answered softly, surprised to see her and surprised that the daughter who in the past year had made the monumental switch from "Daddy" to "Dad"—with regressions only in times of greatest emotion—had regressed now. He returned Samantha's exuberant hug, then knelt so that his eyes were exactly level with hers. "What's going on?"

The rush of pink in Samantha's cheeks answered before she did, and in that moment of hesitation, Nick's gaze drifted to Raven. It wasn't a reassuring glance. Raven looked very sad.

"I started my period today," Samantha blurted out finally. "I called Raven, and she gave me a ride home."

"Well," Nick murmured, suddenly emotionally ambushed. His little girl was growing up. Already it had been happening far too quickly, and now his heart felt the future: Samantha becoming a young woman, Samantha falling in love.

As Raven saw Nick's emotion, saw him struggling to find the next words, she felt a powerful rush of love. Love, not hate? Yes, because she didn't hate Nick, not really, *not at all*. How could she? She only, always, hated herself. Now she even hated herself for having unwittingly stolen this afternoon from Nick, and for having felt such joy that Samantha had trusted her. With quiet apology she offered, "Samantha called me because she somehow cleverly figured out that I didn't have much on my schedule this afternoon."

Her words were answered by a slightly shaky but grateful smile from the man she loved. And there was even more than gratitude on his handsome face. Nick seemed proud, of *her,* that she had so clearly won the confidence of his terribly wary daughter.

He's pretending, Raven reminded herself. The master of pretense and deception is pretending now because of Samantha. Somehow pretending too, Raven added breezily, "And also, I think, because this was girl stuff."

Sensing that her father felt a little left out, that this was all far more important to him than she had imagined, Samantha began to recount the events he had missed. "Since Raven's name wasn't in my file, she had to convince the headmistress that she wasn't a kidnapper."

"She was obviously very convincing."

"She was great!"

Nick's smile sent the wondrous message that he wasn't surprised, that he already knew how terrific Raven was. After a moment, and very softly, he asked of his daughter, "And how are you, Sam?"

"I'm *fine,"* she replied swiftly, reassuring both her father and herself. She was fine now, because of what Raven had said: despite the monumental event, she was still the same inside.

They sat at the wrought-iron table on the rose-fragrant verandah and talked about a variety of things, none of which had anything to do with menstrual periods. Eventually, when it occurred to Samantha that school was out, she stood to leave, to begin to share with her friends what she now regarded as rather exciting news.

"What about Gran?" Nick asked.

An expression of love touched the lovely young face. "I'll call her first."

Samantha looked at Raven then, and the lovely expres-

sion held as she said bravely, "Thanks for coming to get me
. . . and for everything."

"You're very welcome."

As soon as Samantha was out of sight, Raven, too,
began to leave.

"Don't, Raven," Nick commanded quietly. "Not without letting me explain."

Raven stopped her hasty retreat but didn't turn toward
him. "I'm a smart woman, Nick. I really don't need an
explanation."

"I think you do," he said softly. He moved in front of her
and spoke to the top of the shining black head that
wouldn't lift to look at him. "Just listen to me, please.
When I told you about Deandra, I let you assume that we
were college sweethearts who were beginning with nothing
and planning to build a future together. The truth is that I
was already very rich by the time we met. My wealth mattered to Deandra, it was all that really mattered, and even
though I was neither naive nor desperately in love, she
fooled me. She really convinced me that she loved me and
shared my dream of having children."

*She really convinced me.* The words plunged like jagged-
edged knives into Raven's heart. Just moments before,
Nick had learned how very convincing she herself had been
with Westlake's headmistress. She had convinced the
woman that she was virtually a member of the family, part
of the inner circle of love, not a thief, not someone who
would steal a child because of her own desperate need for
money.

It had been a lie, of course. Raven Winter was *not* a
member of the Gault family. Indeed, Nick had very carefully kept her far away from the truth, fearing that if she
knew about his immense wealth, she would steal whatever
was necessary, including the hearts of his daughters, to get
what she wanted.

In a shattering instant Raven understood everything.
When Nick had met her, in her designer-label jogging

clothes, he had deduced swiftly—and correctly—that appearances mattered to her. Then she had told him the truth about the little girl who had been so tormented because of her poverty and who wanted so desperately to be accepted that she had gone to her high school reunion with the hope of impressing her tormentors at last. And Nick had concluded that, like Deandra, if she knew of his riches, she would do everything possible to insinuate herself permanently into his life.

And was that such an illogical conclusion? Hadn't Raven Willow Winter spent most of her life trying to do just that?

*Yes,* but it had never been about money. From the very beginning, it had only been about love.

How could she blame Nick for mistrusting her? How could she convince him that she was anything but a beautiful woman who gave her body to the richest man who wanted her? How could she tell him that all she wanted was love, and that she had never really known what it was until him, had never really believed that her icy heart had delicate places within it that could melt into happiness and joy . . .

She couldn't, and now the tears that had been so close to the surface ever since Sunday evening began to spill again.

"I have to go."

Nick caught her before she made a move and held her with gentle strength as he said solemnly, "I had to know how you felt about me and the girls before I told you about my wealth."

"You know how I feel about you and the girls."

Her head was still bowed, her gaze focused on his chest. With great tenderness, Nick cupped her chin and lifted until he could see her glistening sapphire eyes.

"I thought I knew how you felt about us, Raven, but now you keep trying to leave. Please don't leave. Please come to dinner with us tonight, a celebration for Sam." As he saw flickers of hope through her tears, Nick placed gentle kisses on her damp cheeks. "Okay?"

Raven nodded. She didn't have a choice. Because it seemed like an invitation to far more than dinner. To Raven, to her heart, it felt as if Nick were inviting her to become a part of his family.

# Part Five

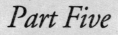

## ❀ *24* ❀

"Hi Raven, it's Sam. Dad wants to talk to you but there's something I want to ask first. We're going to Santa Barbara this weekend, to the ranch, and we wondered if you would like to come too."

"We?" Raven echoed.

"It will be my grandparents, and Melody and I are each bringing a friend, and you and Dad."

"I'd love to." *Assuming Nick knows about this,* she thought. *Assuming it's all right with him.*

"Great! I can teach you how to ride."

Raven hesitated before responding to Samantha's enthusiastic offer. *There's a tiny new life inside me, you see, Sam, your baby sister or brother, and I have to be so very careful with this miracle.*

The brave little life inside her *was* a miracle, of course; a miracle that had been confirmed just three hours before. Now she had the wondrous explanation for the sudden tearbursts, and for the voice deep inside that had cried on that Sunday evening, *Don't leave me! Take me with you! I'm part of your family!*

It seemed impossible that something so small could have had such a profound effect so quickly, and she had even

301

wondered if the baby was Michael's, a legacy of their final night together, conceived over two months before she and Nick had first made love.

No, the obstetrician had told her. The tiny life inside her was not more than six or seven weeks old.

The baby was Nick's, and now Nick's twelve-year-old daughter was asking her to spend a family weekend in Santa Barbara and offering to teach her how to ride horseback.

"Maybe I'll just watch you ride this weekend, Sam."

"Really? Well, whatever you want. I know that you'd love it if you tried. Oh-oh, Dad's reaching for the phone now. See you Friday!"

"Friday?"

Raven's question was answered not by Samantha but by Nick. "We thought we'd try to leave between three and three-thirty Friday afternoon. Hi."

"Hi. Is this all right?"

In the weeks since his parents' return from Denver, Nick and Raven had spent almost every night—at least the hours between 10 P.M. and dawn—together. There were a few exceptions: two nights when Melody had a sore throat and Nick wanted to be near her, three nights when Nick had been in Dallas, four when Raven had been in New York, and four more, including last night, when she had inexplicably—but now she knew why—felt so fatigued that she was asleep by seven.

The girls still knew nothing of the nights Nick spent with Raven. They knew only that at least twice a week the four of them did something together, and that recently their grandparents had joined them as well. Melody and Samantha knew how much they liked Raven, and that their dad must obviously like her too, even though he never even touched her in front of them.

"Yes," Nick answered. "This is just fine."

As strongly as Nick felt about not flaunting the sexual aspects of their relationship in front of his daughters,

Raven's feelings were even stronger. She had such vivid and painful memories of how inaccessible her mother had been to her when she had been entertaining her many lovers. "Meaning that your parents approve and that there is a guest room somewhere I can stay?"

"Meaning both of those things," Nick affirmed, his soft laugh telling her that smart young ears were close by. "So, can you shake free Friday afternoon? If not, it's no problem. We'll be taking two cars, so one can leave later if need be."

"I'll be ready by three."

"Good. How was your day?"

Raven knew that Nick was asking about her day, but also about their night, if she was exhausted still or if he could come over. She wanted him to come over, and she wanted to tell him about his baby. But, she knew, it was far too soon. The doctor had gently warned that first trimester miscarriages, especially in primiparous women, were very common.

That was one reason not to tell him, and there was the other reason: he might be furious. He might believe that she had become pregnant in order to entrap him, because she knew that he would never turn his back on his child.

Raven fought her fear with the memory of the tiny life that had had the courage to find a home in the womb where no other baby had ever dared. Smiling softly, she finally answered, "My day was wonderful, Nick, and it would end absolutely perfectly if you would come over tonight."


During the past five weeks, every time Jason returned to his suite in Hong Kong's Regent Hotel, his gaze swept immediately to the fax machine that had been installed beside the desk. No matter how tired he was, the sight of fresh pages written in her distinctive script was energizing. He would read what she had written, and depending on what time it was in Kodiak, he would either call or send an answering fax.

It was a high-tech romance, of fax and phone, but despite the thousands of miles that separated the Gulf of Alaska from the South China Sea there was an immediacy to their long-distance communication—and a surprising intimacy. A fax transmission had the intimacy of a letter, but in a way it was even more private, touched only by electronic fingers and with no possibility of being lost, misplaced, or read by a stranger.

Jason and Holly wrote to each other every day. Their letters were diaries of their lives, intricately—and interestingly—detailed chronicles of how they were spending their time apart. Jason sent her copies of the script pages that had been filmed that day—and more: in the margins and on additional sheets of papers, he recreated the drama of the set, the frustrations, the successes, the amusing anecdotes. He also wrote to her about Hong Kong, the enchanting sights and sounds and fragrances of that exotic place where East met West, where mystical dragon and majestic lion lived together in such resplendent harmony.

Eventually, at his gentle but persistent urging, Holly had responded in kind. She was in the middle of her new book, but she summarized the beginning for him, lovingly describing the characters, their hopes, their dreams, their secrets, their fears; and after that she sent him each new scene as soon as it was written. The pages Holly sent were annotated as well, notes about the drama of the writing process; and like Jason, she wrote about her world, painting with the delicate brushstrokes of her words a portrait of the arctic beauty in which she lived.

Jason was in Hong Kong, a place of vibrant energy and dazzling glamour, and Holly was in Kodiak. But she found as many treasures there, as spring came to sky and sea and meadow and forest, as Jason found in Hong Kong; and she shared them with him as enthusiastically as he shared with her the many brilliant jewels in the British colony's glittering crown.

Holly and Jason exchanged the daily diaries of their lives, and he called her whenever he could, and by week's end he would wrap the Hong Kong shoot, his impossible six-week schedule met after all. He planned to fly directly to Kodiak, arriving late Friday afternoon and staying until Sunday evening, when he would leave to make a brief stop in Los Angeles before flying to Dallas to film the scenes that took place there.

When Jason returned to his suite at midnight Tuesday, his gaze went immediately to the handwritten pages that awaited him; but as he moved toward the desk, his attention was drawn to the message light on the phone. The blinking red wouldn't signal a message from Holly. Despite his repeated urgings, she never called. It would be something about tomorrow's shoot, a small detail that might blossom into a major problem if not promptly nipped in the bud.

Jason wanted to reach for the pages from Holly, but he reached for the phone instead, because in a way it was reaching for her: the more smoothly the next two days went, the sooner he would see her again.

But the message wasn't about *The Jade Palace* at all. It was from Beth Robinson in Los Angeles, and she requested that he return her call as soon as possible, no matter what the time.

Jason frowned as he transcribed the phone number provided to him by the hotel operator. He had not expected to hear from Beth. Six hours after he had given her the virtually impossible task of finding out about the murders committed somewhere in Washington by a psychopath named Derek, Beth had suddenly developed a severe headache. As she had been rushed to the hospital, her mental status had deteriorated from alertness to delirium, and on arrival in the ER her blood pressure had been found to be sky high.

Jason had gotten the news from his secretary, and she

had kept him posted on Beth's subsequent progress: three precarious weeks in the intensive care unit at Cedars-Sinai, after which her son was delivered by Caesarean section. The baby was fine, and Beth's recovery was gradual, but the hopeful report from last week was that she was going home, dramatically improved.

Jason had sent flowers and a gift for the baby, but he hadn't expected to hear from her. He assumed she had forgotten entirely about the private research project he'd given her—and that was fine. He would learn what he needed to know from Holly, when he saw her again.

But now Beth had called, and it seemed urgent. It took Jason no time to calculate the time difference. Midnight on Tuesday in Hong Kong was seven Monday evening in Kodiak and an hour later in L.A.

"I'm fine, Jason, and I have a beautiful baby boy. He's absolutely perfect and such a good little sleeper that I'm getting lots of rest—too much. I decided that I needed a project, so on impulse I placed a call to the reporter I told you about at the *Seattle Times*. He knew right away about the story of a murderer named Derek and his stepdaughter Holly."

"He *did?*"

"Yes, and I'm sure it's the same case you told me about, except for one very important difference."

"Which is?"

"Which is that Holly's father, Lawrence Elliott, did not die in Vietnam. Based on Derek's testimony, everyone believed that he'd been killed by enemy fire, when in truth it was Derek who shot him and left him for dead. He was taken captive by the Vietcong and held prisoner for seven years."

With Beth's words, the memories that had been lurking in Jason's subconscious mind suddenly surfaced. He remembered reading about the tragedy in *Time*—and he remembered, too, that for him, the future filmmaker, the compelling story had been unsatisfying, unfinished, because the missing daughter had not been found.

But now she was found, wasn't she?

"You said her father's name was Lawrence? What about her mother? Was she named Holly?"

"No. Let's see. Here it is. Her name was Claire."

Lawrence and Claire . . . Lawrenceandclaire . . . Lauren Sinclair.

Yes, at last the missing daughter was found.

Now the compelling story could be finished.

But only, Jason vowed, if it had a happy ending for Holly.

"Where is Lawrence Elliott now?"

"In a place called Issaquah, a small community just outside of Seattle. He's a veterinarian there, very well liked and respected. Everyone knows about his tragedy, which is why the reporter recognized the story right away. He has been searching for his daughter ever since his return from Vietnam. In fact, just this past Valentine's Day, *20/20* did a segment on the murders and his search."

"I'd very much like to see that."

"I thought that you would. I've already contacted the research department at the network. They've made copies of all the information they have—newspaper and magazine articles dating back to the crime itself—as well as a copy of the videotape. Even as we speak, a very heavy box is on a United flight, getting frequent flier miles for you, from New York to LAX. Your secretary said you'd be in your office for a few hours this Monday, but I'm calling because I wondered if you want the box to be waiting for you here or if you want me to have it put on one of United's morning flights to Hong Kong."

"Please send it here."

"Will do."

"Did anyone ask why you were calling?"

"No. I told them what we agreed, that we were thinking

about doing a documentary on domestic violence, and that perfectly plausible explanation triggered no curiosity at all. The reporter at the *Times* gave me Lawrence Elliott's phone numbers in case we wanted to interview him directly. They'll be included in the information coming from the network, of course, but shall I give them to you now?"

"Please."

After Beth had given him the numbers for Lawrence Elliott's office, answering service, and home phone, she asked softly, "Holly is alive, isn't she, Jason? You know where she is."

Jason didn't hesitate. He trusted Beth without reservation. "Yes, she is alive and I do know where she is."

"And she has no idea that her father is alive? That seems improbable, Jason, almost impossible. My impression from talking to both the *Times* reporter and the network researcher was that from the beginning this has been a high-profile case, a high-profile search. Everyone I spoke with likes Lawrence Elliott very much and is sympathetic toward him, but without exception they believe that either Holly died years ago or for whatever reason does not want to see her father again."

"She's alive," Jason repeated quietly. Then, as he thought about Holly's cabin, without newspapers or television or radio, he added, "And I'm pretty sure that she has no idea that her father is alive and has been searching for her."

"That's really astonishing."

"What's really astonishing, Beth, is that you discovered all this."

"Not my most dazzling feat, Jason. Just one simple phone call."

"Well," he said softly, "I'm very grateful."

Long after the conversation ended, Jason still had not read what Holly had sent him today, nor had he called her, nor had he dialed any of Lawrence Elliott's numbers in Issaquah.

He was lost in thought, and emotion, and worry. As a director with multimillion-dollar budgets, Jason Cole had the wonderful luxury of shooting a scene over and over. From take to take, he could make whatever changes he chose, improving, perfecting, until it was absolutely right.

The long-unfinished story of the Valentine's Eve murders was now complete. All the facts were known—at least to Jason—and the missing daughter was finally found. The story was complete. But the final scene, the all-important ending, had yet to be scripted.

There would be only one take on this scene, only one chance to get it exactly right. It had to be planned very carefully, and Jason had to be prepared to scrap it all, if that was what his instincts—his heart—told him to do . . . for Holly.

## ❦ *25* ❧

For many years, except for food, Holly had made all her
purchases through mail-order catalogs. From computer
and fax, to bedding and books, to Revere Ware and
microwave, it was by far the most practical way for her
to shop. No matter how bulky or heavy, the items were
delivered directly to her cottage. And ordering through
the mail was also the easiest way to shop, the most
anonymous.

She could study the catalogs carefully, privately, and
then Marilyn Pierce, armed with a credit card, could call
and talk to one of the always-pleasant voices that
answered the 800 numbers.

All of Holly's clothes came from catalogs. Lands End,
Orvis, and L.L. Bean provided everything she ever
needed for the seasons in Kodiak: jeans, sweaters, flannel
nightgowns, thermal underwear, and arctic parkas. They
offered skirts and dresses too, Holly knew, and there
were even more glamorous offerings in the catalogs she
received from Neiman-Marcus, Saks, and Horchow. She
knew very well the contents of all the catalogs. She
studied them carefully, using them to dress her heroines,
attending to that detail with the same meticulous care
with which she attended to all details in the imaginary
worlds she created.

The day after Jason left for Hong Kong, Holly perused

the catalogs for clothes for herself. She wanted something other than jeans, and a dress other than her mother's wedding dress, to wear for Jason when he returned.

Not just for Jason, she amended swiftly. For herself, for the Holly who was awakening at last and welcoming with joy the hopefulness that had been hidden for so long.

Some of Lauren Sinclair's heroines could actually wear sequins by Cassini and gowns of chiffon and satin by Chanel. But others, the ones most like herself, could not. They preferred a more quiet style, flowing tea-length skirts with soft silk blouses or demure shirtwaist dresses in delicate floral prints.

The clothes looked wonderful on the models in the catalogs, but as Holly placed the orders, she had no idea how they would look on her . . . and she still had no idea, five days before Jason's return, even though some of the many packages had arrived weeks ago. She had opened each package as it arrived, hanging or refolding the contents carefully, frowning thoughtfully when she felt the silky softness of some of the items she had ordered. For *me,* she reminded herself. For the gentleness against my skin, for the way it will make me feel: feminine, womanly, hopeful.

Holly hadn't tried anything on yet, had not even slipped a curious foot into one of the new shoes; because even though she was the awakening Holly, and even though with each springtime dawn the hopefulness seemed ever more at home within her, she felt uncertainty still—and fear.

She knew the reason for her fear, of course, knew that the moment she tried on the clothes all the wonderful illusions might suddenly shatter. She would be forced to look at herself in the mirror then—really *look*—and she hadn't done that, except to be certain that she was adequately disguised, for a very long time.

As a little girl, Holly had never really looked at herself in the mirror. She had never needed to. The love in her parents' eyes had been the only mirror that ever mattered. She hadn't really known what she looked like then. She had only known that, whatever it was they saw, she was loved.

For the first five years of her life, her mother and father had been her mirror, and after that her mother had been, and since that snowy Valentine's night there had been no other mirrors, neither glass nor human, until Jason.

And he likes what he sees. You *know* he does.

Yes, but . . . *I* have to like what *I* see. I have to look at myself and like who I am.

And the little girl who had tried so desperately to save her family—and had failed—was very fearful that she would hate the face that gazed back at her from the mirror.

She managed to spend quite a while in front of the mirror without looking at her face. Her focus was on the outfits, intent, analytical, and finally smiling. She liked the cream-colored silk blouse with the sage and mauve skirt, and the ensemble that was shades of honey and butterscotch and gold, and the ivory dress with its delicate lavender flowers, and . . .

And finally it was time for Holly to look at her face. Except for the invisible obstacles placed by her own emotions, the view would be quite unobstructed. Her hair was pulled away, in the style she always wore when she wrote, the heavy braided rope of gold that fell almost to her waist.

Holly drew a steadying breath, then raised her eyes to her own reflection. It was a grown woman who returned her gaze, not a thirteen-year-old girl who had failed to save her family, and in that woman's face Holly saw an image that she had to like . . . had to love . . . because it was the image of her beloved parents.

Holly looked like neither Lawrence nor Claire, but a composite of both of them, every feature a harmony of their loving union. Just as her eyes were a remarkable blend of her mother's brilliant azure and her father's dark forest, the rest of her face was a living symbol too of the gifts they had given her: delicacy and strength, determination and pride, generosity and courage.

She was their creation, their baby, their joy, their hope.

As Holly stared into the mirror, her own face blurred slightly, shifting, transforming, until the face before her, the one that gazed at her with such love, belonged to Claire. Listen to me, my darling. You can go on with your life. You're strong, and you were so very loved by your daddy and me. Will you remember that, Holly? Will you promise to be happy?

Holly had made that solemn promise to her dying mother, and for the past seventeen years she had kept it the only way she could—by creating imaginary worlds of happiness and love.

But now, at last, she was emerging from the enveloping cocoon in which she had lived for so long, the necessary place where she had dwelt while her shattered heart regained its courage and strength.

*You might never have emerged if it hadn't been for Jason.*

Holly stared at the sudden taunting thought as bravely as she had met her own image in the mirror.

That's true, she conceded.

And if he wasn't writing to you every day, and calling almost that often, you would be back in your cocoon again, lost forever in imaginary worlds.

*No,* she challenged firmly. Admittedly, it was because of Jason that I rediscovered the hopefulness inside me. But it was there long before I ever met him, a wondrous gift of love from my parents. No matter what happens with Jason, I will treasure it . . . just as my parents treasured me.

Holly stared down the taunting thought, and when at last it was gone, she looked again at the image in the mirror—and saw Holly, not Claire. After a solemn moment, she smiled a soft, forgiving welcome to the woman she had become.

It was then that Holly became aware of a heaviness at the back of her head, as if an iron hand from the past was pulling at her, trying to prevent her from going forward with her life. The iron hand was her golden braid, the thick rope that sometimes served as a concealing veil.

I don't need you any longer, she thought. I don't need a rope that pulls me backward, or a veil that hides me from the world.

Holly found a pair of scissors and, with a confidence that amazed her, cut the thick braid two feet above its golden tail. As the silken strands untwined themselves, she realized that her hair, like all her features, was a blend of gifts from both parents. The color was pure Claire, brilliant gold unshadowed by her father's darkness, but the halo of soft curls around her face, that dancing life, had been inherited from Lawrence.

The dancing curls concealed the unevenness of the cut she had made. But tomorrow she would go to the beauty salon in town and have it trimmed and shaped, and she would buy clear polish for the nails that had been allowed to grow, and perhaps some light pink lipstick and maybe even a wand of mascara.

Caroline reached the end of chapter eight in Lauren Sinclair's *Gifts of Love* and closed the book. The temptation to begin chapter nine was strong, but Lawrence would be off the phone soon, and then they would go to bed, and that was a temptation to which she was definitely going to succumb.

Caroline put the book on the coffee table and smiled as she surveyed the living room. On the night when Katie had given birth to her puppies, Caroline's imagination had gone wild, envisioning a scene in which the stark room was magically transformed to a cozy one by the simple addition of a roaring fire and the two of them, together, reading.

It had seemed an impossible flight of fancy—of fantasy—but tonight, until the phone had rung, that had been exactly the scene. And in another week, when eight-week-old Juliet arrived, it would even be cozier—and livelier.

Fantasy. That was what the past weeks had felt like, a wondrous, dangerous fantasy of love. It still amazed her how effortlessly their two lives, private and solitary for so long, had become one, how easily they had adjusted. They could spend a quiet evening reading, never fearing the silence, and the next night they could talk until dawn, sharing deep, quiet truths, and having no fear, either, of them.

Lawrence would tease her about how young she was—only forty! But without any teasing whatsoever he would also tell her how beautiful she was. Then he would show her the passionate proof of his tender words. Caroline's entire being trembled still at their extraordinary passion and the immense hunger of his dark green eyes. And her heart trembled, too, with happiness, when he entrusted her with a secret truth, or when she could make him smile . . . or even laugh. Laughter still came as a surprise to him, and when he heard the foreign sound and felt its soaring hope, his eyes filled with gratitude, and desire, and love.

They were virtually living together, something which had happened more by default than by discussion. Every morning, they would make plans the coming night, when and where they would be together, never *if*. They spent most nights here, because of his work, his night call—and the many calls that came even when he was officially "off."

Caroline would live this life with Lawrence forever, never demanding commitments for the future from the man who was still so committed to his past. But recently, despite his attempts to hide it, Lawrence had seemed troubled, conflicted, a dark torment of desire and despair. It had to do with them, Caroline knew. His belief, perhaps, that their love could not last. And his loving was more desperate, too, the fiercely tender passion of a man who knew that very soon he would be saying goodbye.

So stop thinking presumptuous thoughts like how cozy it will be a week from now with Juliet frolicking around the house. You knew how dangerous this was, remember? And it isn't as though Lawrence didn't warn you as well . . .

Caroline decided to stop thinking at all and was about to reach for *Gifts of Love,* to begin chapter nine, when Lawrence appeared. His expression was obviously troubled, but it was a worry that he made no attempt to conceal.

So, Caroline decided, it's not about us. Making a logical guess, she asked gently, "An injured animal?"

"No." He frowned. "On the night Katie had her puppies, you said it didn't matter that you'd missed the Academy Awards, that you were certain that someone had won everything and, if he hadn't, you were glad you hadn't watched anyway. It was Jason Cole, wasn't it? That was the name."

"Yes. Why?"

"That was who just called."

"Jason Cole? *Why?*"

"Because he's planning to make a documentary on missing children and is thinking about including a segment about Holly. He'll be here this weekend to talk to me."

316

"Here? You mean Seattle?"

"No, here. The house. He's in Hong Kong now, but he plans to be here at nine Saturday morning."

This should have been hopeful news. But Caroline saw dark shadows in his dark green eyes. Softly, she offered, "You seemed so worried."

"It's just that the conversation was so awkward. I was surprised by the call, and there were satellite delays in our voices. I don't know if I really communicated to him how much this would mean to me, how grateful I am for any help."

"You must have communicated something," Caroline assured gently. "I would be very surprised if Jason Cole makes a habit of visiting people in their homes, much less traveling all the way from Hong Kong to do so."

"I got the impression that the reason he wants to meet me is to see if I'm really serious about finding Holly. If he decides that I'm not, I imagine he won't include her in the documentary."

Caroline felt a sudden and powerful rush of anger. How *dare* Jason Cole make the man she loved jump through even more emotional hoops. What was Lawrence supposed to do? *Prove* his anguish? Open his veins one more time? For what purpose? To convince the brilliant director that the anguish was somehow worthy of his attention and his help?

"Maybe . . ."

"Maybe what, Caroline? Maybe I should tell him no? I can't do that. I can't ever turn down any chance of finding her."

"I know." And I also know that unless Jason Cole is the most insensitive man on earth, just one look at you will tell him all he needs to know about your love for your daughter.

\* \* \*

Jason swore silently at the vast echoing space that lay between them. It was as if the revelation that Lawrence Elliott was alive had jolted the planet, making it spin slightly out of kilter, tilting it away from the Trans-Pacific telecommunication satellite just enough to sabotage what until now had been crystal clear and instantaneous telephone links between Hong Kong and the United States.

The earth-jarring conversation itself, with Beth Robinson, had been flawless, as if the two of them had been in the same room. But every call Jason had made since had been an infuriating blend of echoes and delays: the one to his secretary at her home in Los Angeles to ask her to arrange lodging near Issaquah; the one to Lawrence Elliott during which, because of his own frustration with the tricks being played with their voices, he had sounded far more harsh than he had intended; and now, in this one, the all-important conversation with Holly.

They had been talking, trying to talk, for almost twenty minutes. Jason had already told her that he hoped to arrive in Kodiak late Friday afternoon, just as he had been promising for weeks. But for a very long time after he said the next, "I need to meet with a man in Seattle Saturday morning," Jason heard only hisses and silence, echoes and emptiness from the vast blackness of space.

Where were his words? Jason wondered. Were they blithely ricocheting from satellite to satellite like a rogue pinball? Or had even the allusion to Lawrence Elliott—"a man in Seattle"—caused another jolt, another tilt of the earth, so that his words had missed the satellites entirely and were now traveling on a forever journey toward a faraway star?

Or, he wondered, had Holly heard his words clearly and there was something about Seattle, something about a man in Seattle . . .

"Holly?"

"Yes?" The syllable came back with no delay whatsoever, an eloquent transmission from a wounded heart.

All that Jason knew about Holly's relationship with her father was what she had said when she had given him the swift and skeletal version of her past: "My father was killed in Vietnam." When Jason had convinced her to tell him the details of the snowy night of murder, that horror was all that they discussed. Jason knew of Holly's great love for her mother. But what if she *hated* her father? What if she had reason to hate him? What if she knew that he was alive, and in Seattle, and lived in fear that someday he might find her?

Jason needed to know. He needed just a few more seconds of flawless communication: his question, her answer, without delay.

"Would you rather not go to Seattle, Holly?"

"You want me to go with you?"

The satellites did their job, and what Jason heard with brilliant clarity was the sound of a wounded heart healing swiftly with relief. It was not a faraway memory of her father that had caused her sudden hurt. It was *he* who had wounded her.

*Oh, Holly. How very far you are from understanding how I truly feel about you.*

"Of course I do." His voice was as soft, as tender as if he had just confessed to her his love. "Of course I do."

# ❊ 26 ❊

The spotting began in the early evening, twenty minutes before Nick's call. Raven fought her fear with the gentleness of his voice and with a promise to the tiny life inside. We will be spending this weekend with your family, little one, your *family*.

When Nick asked if he should come over, Raven pleaded fatigue; and then, forcing a smile into her voice, she added that she wanted to be very well rested for Santa Barbara. The smile vanished the moment she said goodbye, and as she replaced the receiver, she felt the first cramp.

The pain was piercing, as if the sharp talons of a bird of prey were clawing deep into her womb, determined to pluck from its sanctuary the tiny life that was dwelling there.

Vulture! Buzzard! Dark black bird of death!

Nevermore, Raven. *Nevermore.*

The ancient taunts circled overhead all night, vultures themselves, waiting for death. Raven didn't sleep, didn't even try. She needed to keep a constant vigil over her precious baby, warding off the predators as best she could. Despite her loving vigil, they swooped still, in

320

sudden breathtaking clutches of pain. She fought them, compelling them to soar away, and when they did, she would dare to hope . . .

But the sharp greedy claws would return, clutching more ferociously than before and mocking her for her foolishness.


At ten o'clock Friday morning, as soon as she had completed the pelvic exam, Dr. Sara Rockwell shared the findings with Raven.

"The cervical os is closed. What that means is that for the moment we assume the pregnancy is still viable. The cramping and bleeding you've had may indicate that you are in the process of miscarrying—"

"May? But not necessarily?"

"No, not necessarily. The bleeding may be coming from a place away from the baby, a remote edge of the placenta that's readjusting its attachment to the uterus. What I want to do is get a quantitative serum pregnancy test to compare with the one drawn on Monday. If the hormone level is higher than it was five days ago, then everything is still progressing quite normally."

"And if it's lower?"

"Then the pregnancy is no longer viable, and depending on what happens over the next couple of days—whether or not there is passage of tissue—a D and C might be indicated."

"How soon will you know the results of the blood test?"

"I'll have it run stat, so I should have the result to you by this afternoon." Sara Rockwell gazed with sympathetic concern at Raven's exhausted face. "In the meantime, you should rest."

"I will."

Raven's solemn answer sounded like a promise, and there was such hopefulness in her voice that Sara knew she needed to clarify. "The rest is for you, Raven, not for the baby. There's really no convincing scientific data to support the notion that rest—or anything for that matter—will avert an inevitable miscarriage. Please remember that if you do miscarry, it's because something wasn't right with the pregnancy, not because you did something wrong. As I told you on Monday, first trimester miscarriages are quite common in women who've never been pregnant before."

"Yes, I know." It's just that I know that there's nothing wrong with this baby. I've felt its strength, its will to live, its determination to survive against all odds. There's nothing wrong with the baby. There's only something wrong with me, with the home in which I have given it to grow, the womb that is so badly scarred with acid and with ice.

"The level is identical to the one from Monday."

Dr. Rockwell had explained the significance of a higher hormone level or a lower one, but not of one that was the same. "Identical? What does that mean?"

"It means that we don't know, that we have to continue to follow your progress. It means, Raven, that only time will tell. How have the last four hours been?"

A battle, Raven thought. A fierce, raging battle between the scarred womb that was trying to expel the baby and the baby who was fighting so valiantly for its life.

"There's been more bleeding and cramping."

"Have you passed any tissue?"

"I don't think so. No."

"Okay. I'm on call this weekend. You can reach me any time. If you do pass tissue, or if the bleeding suddenly increases, or if there are any other changes that worry you, I want you to call me right away."

"All right. Do you want to repeat the blood test?"

"Definitely. Even if the bleeding and cramping subside

entirely over the weekend, I'd like you to come in first thing Monday morning."

We can't go to Santa Barbara, Raven silently told the little life inside her. And we can't let your daddy or your sisters know what's really happening. But we have to go see them now, to explain in person that we're too sick to go with them, even though we want to . . . so badly.

Raven gasped then, as sharp claws of excruciating pain dug deep into the flesh that was now a raw aching wound. It was as if the claws were trying to prevent her from going to the mansion in Bel Air, as if the forces that were trying to expel the new life from the acid womb knew that if the baby was permitted to get near its family, close to that powerful circle of love, its valiant will would be fortified even more.

We're going to Bel Air, Raven promised both her baby and the merciless claws of pain.

The journey had originally been planned because of Samantha, because Raven wanted to be very certain that Sam didn't confuse her with the mother who made promises she didn't keep, who feigned illness when she could not be bothered with her daughters. But now the journey was for two young, fragile hearts . . . Samantha's and that of her unborn little sib.

The short drive from Brentwood to Bel Air had been astonishingly free of pain, as if the claws were going to allow her mission after all. But just as Raven turned into the rose-lined drive that led to Nick's mansion, the cramping returned with a vengeance.

She needed time to recover, to force herself to breathe, and then even to smile. But it wasn't going to happen. Nick and Samantha were in the driveway, loading his car, and as soon as they saw her, they began walking toward her.

Raven turned off the ignition, and as Nick opened the car door for her, she simply forced both the breath and the smile.

"Hi," she greeted, standing—and then swaying.

*"Raven."* Nick had her in his arms in an instant. Her snow-white skin was cool and damp, and the pain was obvious on her taut ashen face and in her dark-circled sapphire eyes.

"What's wrong?" Samantha's expression of concern mirrored her father's.

"Food poisoning," Raven managed. She smiled bravely at Nick, then freed herself from his grasp, stepping back until she found support against her car. "I'm okay." Smiling still, she said to Samantha, "I am *not* going to swoon."

"Food poisoning?" Nick pressed.

"That's what the doctor says. The culprit's probably a sandwich I picked up on my way home last night. It's neither serious nor contagious, but . . ." Raven paused, gazed gently at the girl who had been abandoned by her mother, and continued with soft apology, "I'm afraid I'm not in any shape to make the trip to Santa Barbara."

"But you're definitely going to be okay?" Samantha asked, whatever disappointment she felt about the canceled weekend greatly overshadowed by her worry about Raven.

"Yes, definitely," Raven promised. "A little time, rest, and fluids and I'll be back to normal—"

The claws stole her breath then. Liar! It's not food poisoning, it's *acid* poisoning, and you're never going to be back to normal, because you've never *been* normal.

"Raven?"

"I'm okay, Nick. Every so often my stomach twists. It will pass."

"Maybe we shouldn't go to Santa Barbara this weekend," Samantha said suddenly. "Maybe you should stay here and we should take care of you."

"Oh, Sam, that's such a nice offer. But it's not one that I can accept. I'm just going to be curled up in bed, thinking positive thoughts, and you know what? Thinking of you galloping along the beach in Santa Barbara is one of the very most positive of those thoughts."

"I think Samantha's right, Raven," Nick said softly. "Why don't you—"

"No, Nick. Really. Please?"

It was a quiet plea, but a compelling one. Raven was asking that he accept her decision without further protest, without making her expend her limited energy by arguing with him. It was a plea to which Nick had to acquiesce, because he loved her, because he wasn't going to impose his will on hers . . . and because he was so very grateful for what she had done for his daughter.

"Okay," he agreed. "We'll go to Santa Barbara and you'll convalesce in your own home, to which I will drive you right now."

"No," Raven answered swiftly. She might need her car. She and the baby might want to celebrate its triumph over the birds of death by driving to the top of a hill at dawn and watching the golden sun rise in the east. "I'd like to have my car. Who knows, maybe I'll wake up tomorrow morning completely well and want to drive to Santa Barbara."

This time Nick could not so easily acquiesce to Raven's wishes. It was simply too dangerous.

"I'll drive you home in your car and have my father follow us over in his." Not waiting for Raven's reply, he said to Samantha, "Would you dash inside and tell Grandpa that he and I have an important mission?"

"Sure." Before she left, however, Samantha smiled encouragingly at Raven. "I hope you feel better very soon."

* * *

Her fingernails dug into her palms as punishingly as the claws dug into her womb.

Nick felt her pain, her battle with it, and as she confronted the waves of discomfort, he confronted his own helplessness. There was nothing he could do, except what he was doing: being very certain that she got home safely, that a sudden twist inside her didn't cause her to swerve the car as she navigated the treacherously winding roads of Bel Air.

Sensing that even a one-syllable response would be a great effort for her, Nick didn't speak until they neared the Brentwood Marketplace on San Vicente. Then he asked, "Do you have plenty of fluids at your house, Raven? Soft drinks? Soup?"

"Yes." It was the truth. She had food, and she was forcing herself to eat, because of the baby. She smiled a wobbly smile. "Thanks."

"Thank you, Raven," Nick countered softly. "It meant a lot to Sam, to both of us, that you came over."

"I just wanted her to know that I'm not Deand—"

Not Deandra? the pain queried, returning then, piercing more harshly than before. You want Samantha to know that you're a good mother, not a terrible one? Another lie! What's going on inside you now is absolute proof of what a neglectful and unworthy mother you are!

"Oh, Raven," Nick whispered as he watched the pain steal her breath, her color, and for a horrible moment what looked like her life. "What can I do for you? There must be some medicine I could get."

"No . . . thank you. I just need to get into bed."

Nick wanted to tuck her into bed, put a chilled bottle of 7UP on her nightstand, and tenderly kiss her damp ashen face until she fell asleep. But Raven wouldn't let him past the front door. When he gently kissed her clammy temple, she trembled, and tears threatened, and before he could even ask her to promise to call him at the ranch tonight, tomorrow, every time she awakened, she whispered a quiet goodbye . . . and vanished.


There weren't many people at the small airport on Kodiak Island, but it still took Jason a few moments to realize it was she. His eyes were drawn immediately to her, of course, the beautiful woman dressed in rich golden shades of the moon: butterscotch, topaz, and amber. Her hair was the most brilliant gold of all, a glittering halo of curls around a lovely face . . . with its remarkable aquamarine eyes.

For weeks Jason had imagined this reunion, awaited it with a restlessness unparalleled in his restless life. In the letters she had written, and in the quiet voice that had traveled thousands of miles to reach him, Jason had sensed the blossoming of happiness, of hope, of joy.

And of love? he had wondered. Did Holly feel what he felt? Did she believe in the magic? Was she as desperate as he to be together again?

"Holly," he greeted softly.

He was unable to embrace her. Her hands were full, curled around a garment bag and a carry-on. As Jason took the luggage from her, his eyes embraced her instead, and he was greeted by a wondrous shimmer of magic, and then a lovely frown of confusion . . . and then, although she didn't actually move away, she seemed to put a little distance between them, as if protecting herself *from him.* It was as if she wanted to believe in the magic, and yet fought it, fearful of giving herself wholly to its splendor.

It was about trust, Jason knew. Holly's life was filled with grim lessons: everyone she had ever loved had been taken away, brutal, violent thefts that had stolen so much from her heart, her spirit, and her soul. Jason understood why she was holding back, why she had to keep some-

thing that would be hers even if their love died. But hi
heart raced restlessly for the time when she was con
vinced that it was safe—and wondrous—to believe.

"You look wonderful, Holly. Very beautiful."

"More modern anyway."

"Very beautiful," Jason repeated. Very beautiful, an
so much healthier now. Nourished by more balance
meals, he guessed. And nourished by us. Nourished b
our magical love.

Jason wanted to speak those words beginning now
while the plane was refueling for the flight to Seattle, an
he wanted to say them over and over as they flew to th
Emerald City, and he wanted to spend all weeken
gently, tenderly convincing her of his love.

But Jason didn't have all weekend. He only had th
next few hours. And he knew that during those preciou
hours, they needed to live the magic, not talk about it.

And besides, how could he possibly spend those hour
asking her to trust him? How could he promise never to
betray her love even as he kept from her a secret tha
would change her entire life?

It was almost midnight by the time Jason and Holly
retired to their adjacent rooms at The Salish Lodge. Nestled beside the Snoqualmie Falls, the elegant country
hotel had vaulted from local prominence to worldwide
fame by being featured in the opening montage of *Twin
Peaks*. Before wishing her a gentle good night, Jason told
her that he would see her again at about ten-thirty, after
he had concluded his meeting with the man who was the
reason they were spending the weekend here instead of
Kodiak.

That man was just a few miles away, and as Holly and
Jason were bidding each other good night, he was walking across the meadow in the midnight darkness, returning from the stable to the house.

Lawrence wasn't officially on call, but the frantic call had come directly to him nonetheless. The anxious caller was eleven years old. A year ago he had saved her dog, so this time Becky called him even before calling her parents, far more concerned about her horse's injuries than her own. She had been on the bridle trails at a nearby riding academy, and something had spooked Summertime, and there had been a barbed wire fence, and the golden flesh on the palomino's powerful flank had been shredded and pierced.

Lawrence and Caroline had rushed to the riding academy, not knowing how grim the prognosis might be. The flesh was badly torn, but the vital underlying structures—muscles, tendons, arteries, and bone—had thankfully been spared. The greatest risk to Summertime's survival, and it wasn't a small one, would be infection.

Lawrence could have cleansed the wounds, and sutured the ones that could safely be sutured, and administered the first injection of antibiotics in the mare's stall at the academy. But he preferred to transport her to his own stable instead. He could watch her more closely there, more frequently.

Lawrence gave the frightened palomino a mild sedative before even attempting to transport her and boosted the dose before beginning the necessarily aggressive cleansing of the wounds. With Caroline's help, by 10 P.M. they were done, and Becky and her family had been given the report that all was well.

Now, at midnight, Lawrence was returning from checking on his equine patient one final time before bedtime.

Caroline was in the kitchen, seated at the table, waiting for him. A cookbook lay open in front of her, but she had long since committed to memory the recipe for blueberry muffins that she planned to make in the morning . . . assuming she was still here. Caroline sighed at the troubling thought just as Lawrence walked in.

"How is she?"

"The sedation has worn off, but she seems very calm."

"Good." Caroline took a steadying breath. It was time. She had promised herself that she would do this tonight. Promised? It seemed the wrong word for something that filled her which such dread. "How are you, Lawrence?"

"A little tired."

"And very worried," Caroline embellished softly. She was seated still, and he was leaning against the counter, clad in denim, effortlessly sexy . . . but distant. A lone cowboy. A cowboy who, perhaps, longed once again to be alone. "I think that what's worrying you is more than tomorrow's meeting with Jason Cole. I think that because it started even before you got his call."

"It?"

"You've seemed distracted lately, preoccupied, and I've gotten the impression that it's had to do with us." Caroline saw at once that she was right. Black shadows flickered in his dark green eyes, and she saw the now familiar conflict between desire and despair . . . hello and goodbye. "I guess I've been wondering if you'd prefer that I left."

"Oh, Caroline," he whispered. "I'm so sorry that you've been worrying."

"It doesn't hurt me to worry," she said quietly. "But I do better with the truth."

"The truth?" he echoed gently. Then, with exquisite tenderness, he told her that truth. "I haven't been thinking about wanting you to leave, Caroline. I've been thinking about wanting you to stay."

"All right," she replied with soft soaring hope. "I will. I'll stay for as long as you want me to."

"As my wife?"

*You have a wife.* The thought came swiftly, stunningly. Claire was his wife. It was a truth that Caroline had long since made herself accept, a necessary but fragile shield against the immense danger into which she had placed her heart by loving him.

Lawrence saw her confusion and offered gently, "Maybe it's too soon for me to ask."

"No, it's not too soon. I just can't believe that you want to marry me."

"You can't? Well, I do, very much." His loving smile began to erase the shadows of confusion. "I've been in love before, Caroline. I know what it feels like. I never believed it would happen again, never believed it possibly could. But it has."

"You're in love with me?"

"I am very much in love with you." His soft words vanquished the last shadows and her emerald eyes glowed now, shimmered with love. "I love you, Caroline, and I need your love."

"You have my love. I've never been in love before, but I am now, and I'm very certain." Her eyes glowed still, but a thoughtful frown touched her face. "But you've seemed so troubled by this. Is it because of Holly and Claire? Because it feels like a betrayal of them?"

"Mostly a betrayal of Holly," he answered very quietly.

"We'll never stop searching for her, Lawrence. Not ever."

"No, but . . ."

Caroline understood then, understood with brilliant clarity the hello she had seen, and the goodbye. The goodbye hadn't been for her but for Holly.

Softly, gently, Caroline spoke the words that Lawrence could not say, "You want us to have children."

"If you want to."

Caroline gazed at the man she loved. I need your love, he had told her, and now she could answer that need, making the decision more hers than his, making the betrayal he felt seem less.

"I want to have children, Lawrence. I've always

wanted them. I just wasn't sure that I'd ever find their father. But now I have." She walked over to him then, and when she was in the gentle embrace of his loving arms, she looked up and said, "It's not really a betrayal, you know. It's really just more proof of how very much you loved them both. By wanting to remarry and by wanting more children, what you're saying is that the time in your life when you had your family was wonderful—so wonderful that despite the immense pain you're willing to try again."

His dark green eyes filled with emotion then, and gratitude, and finally a smile of love. "How can someone so young be so wise?"

"Because she loves you," Caroline answered softly. "Because she loves you with all her heart."

## ❧ *27* ❧

The telephone rang fifteen seconds before the doorbell did. The call was for Lawrence, a feline patient's chatty owner calling to report the good news that just as Lawrence had predicted Mittens was much better.

So it was Caroline who opened the door to Jason Cole. She had seen his films, and photographs of him in *People* and on *Entertainment Tonight*. In all those formats he had seemed a commanding presence; but she had nonetheless convinced herself that, as top stars often were, he would be surprisingly short. And because of the tone of his call to Lawrence from Hong Kong, she had also decided that he would be impossibly arrogant.

But Jason Cole was as tall as Lawrence, and he was even more handsome in living color than in Technicolor, and in the solemn smile that greeted her, Caroline saw apprehension not arrogance.

"I'm Jason Cole."

Caroline's answering laugh was a merry release of nervous energy and relief. "I know. I'm Caroline Hawthorne. Please come in."

She led the way to the living room, and when they heard the sound of Lawrence's pleasant and patient voice coming from the kitchen, she explained, "Lawrence isn't officially on call this weekend, but it's pretty typical for him to get a steady stream of unofficial calls anyway."

"Which he doesn't mind getting?"

"Not at all. Except, right now, as calm as he sounds, I'm sure he's concerned about keeping you waiting."

"I'm in no hurry."

"Well, it shouldn't be long. Would you like some coffee? Blueberry muffins?"

"Coffee would be great. Black. Thanks."

The coffeepot, three mugs, sugar, milk, and muffins were already on the coffee table, around which had been carefully arranged the chairs in which they all would sit. Caroline handed Jason a mug of coffee, but she didn't suggest that he be seated. She sensed that he wanted to prowl a little, to scan the titles in the walls of books perhaps, or to wander to the window and gaze at the meadow.

She would have been quite happy to give him a guided tour, beginning with "As you can see, Lawrence reads a lot" and ending with the names of the wildflowers that now bloomed so brilliantly outside. But before Caroline said a word, Jason had picked up the copy of *Gifts of Love* that had been lying where she'd left it beside her chair.

"Is Lawrence reading this?"

"No. I am."

"What do you think of it?"

"That it's her best yet. I have about thirty pages left, and I'm counting heavily on a happy ending." Caroline smiled and added, "There had better be one."

"You must be very involved with her characters."

"Absolutely."

"Do you want an answer to whether the ending is happy?"

"You've read the book?"

"A few times. I recently bought the movie rights and am in the process of collaborating with Lauren Sinclair on the screenplay."

"So there really is a Lauren Sinclair?"

"Why wouldn't there be?" Jason asked with Oscar-winning casualness.

"Well, since none of her books ever has an author photograph or biography, I thought she might be a team of writers."

"No. She's herself."

"What's she like?"

"What do you think?"

Caroline considered his question carefully before answering. Finally, she began, "I guess I think that she's had a hard life. Her books are obviously very romantic and idealistic, but there's a poignancy to them, as if even though what she writes about is how things should be, how people should treat one another and how generous love should be, she knows deep down that it isn't always that way. I think she's been hurt, but instead of becoming bitter or disillusioned, she's chosen to hope." Caroline smiled. "So, now tell me that she doesn't put one bit of her own heart or soul in her books, and couldn't care less about any of the characters she creates, and that she's just a very savvy businesswoman who calculatedly plucks heartstrings to make loads of money."

"No, I'm not going to tell you that," Jason said quietly. "She is very much what you imagine her to be."

"Which means that *Gifts of Love* will end happily."

"Both the book and the movie," Jason confirmed. After a brief pause, he asked, "Have you thought about suggesting to Lawrence that he read the book?"

The question caught Caroline by surprise. Jason Cole knew all about Lawrence's ordeal in Vietnam, and all that he had lost while he was at war. And yet now he was wondering if she had suggested to Lawrence that he read the Vietnam love story with its happy ending.

There was nothing cruel in Jason's tone as he asked the question; in fact, it seemed very gentle, so gentle, so concerned that Caroline confessed, "Yes, I actually have thought about it. I've wondered if he might find it healing."

Jason's reply was preempted, because it was then that Lawrence appeared, offering both greeting and apology to Jason as the two of them shook hands.

What transpired over the next forty-five minutes was quite baffling to Caroline. Except for one question at the end, Jason asked nothing about the murders, or about Lawrence's imprisonment in Vietnam, or even about the years of searching for Holly since. Instead, Jason wanted to hear about a time that had ended twenty-five years before, the first five years of Holly's life, the five precious years during which father and daughter had been together.

Until he had met Caroline, Lawrence hadn't talked to anyone about those years, even though it was that memory that had kept him alive in Vietnam and had kept him searching for Holly ever since. Until now, except for Caroline, no one had ever asked him about that time. As far as the media was concerned, when compared to the horror and drama of war, and the horror and drama that had greeted him on his return home, those five years were positively boring, not sensational in the least.

Not sensational to the press, but wondrous to Lawrence still, their joy evergreen in his loving heart.

Jason wanted to know about those years, and Lawrence didn't question his reasons. He was grateful that Jason wanted to hear about the happiness, not merely the despair. And when it became obvious that Jason's interest in the happy years was more than a polite prologue before querying Lawrence about the endless chapters of grief, Lawrence quietly mentioned that he had photographs.

Caroline held her breath as she waited for Jason to dismiss the quiet offer, or to pretend he hadn't even heard it. But he picked up on it instantly, wanting to see the precious family pictures which, until now, Lawrence had shared only with her.

He's not feigning interest, Caroline decided as she watched Jason study the photo album. In fact, she realized, he seemed very interested indeed . . . and as he gazed at the photographs of the young and radiantly happy Holly, a look of pure tenderness touched his handsome face.

When Jason wondered about the five missing photographs, Lawrence described them for him: a wedding picture, the only one ever taken; a photograph of mother, father, and daughter when Holly was a baby; one of Lawrence and Claire smiling lovingly at the camera held by their lively child; one of Holly and Claire frosting a birthday cake for Lawrence; and finally one of Lawrence holding his golden-haired daughter as she touched the velvet-soft muzzle of a palomino mare. After describing the missing photographs, Lawrence softly confessed his belief that Holly had taken them with her because they were treasured symbols of a time when there had been great happiness.

There were two albums, one containing the Elliott family photographs and the other the family that had been created after Lawrence's reported death in Vietnam. Caroline expected Jason to be interested in the second album as well, if nothing else to see if Lawrence had destroyed the images of Derek. He hadn't, Caroline knew, and she knew why: it would have been merely an impotent expression of his rage. It would not have removed from either his memory or his heart the vivid images of the psychopath.

But Jason did not want to look at the other album. And, Caroline realized, he wasn't about to launch into the usual questions about the murders themselves. In fact, he seemed suddenly restless, ready to leave, his questions all answered—save one.

Jason phrased his final question with nineties insight,

not the unenlightened viewpoint that had cast Holly as seductress not victim two decades before. "Apparently there was speculation that Derek might have been sexually abusing Holly. From the *20/20* segment, as well as the other articles I've read, I've gotten the distinct impression that you consider that unlikely."

It took Lawrence a few moments to shake free of the wonderful memories evoked by the album and focus on the grim truth of what had happened to the little girl whose smile had radiated with such boundless joy.

"Claire had been abused by her stepfather," he answered finally. "I know that sometimes the cycle repeats itself, but I'm absolutely confident that Claire would not have let it happen to our daughter."

Caroline believed she saw relief in Jason's dark blue eyes. But the impression was short-lived. Quite suddenly, the famous actor's expression changed from warm and interested to distant and cool.

"Well, I think that's all I need for now." As Jason stood, he added, "If I do think of something else, will you be here today, at least for the next few hours?"

"We'll be here all day," Lawrence assured.

"Do you think you'll include Holly in your documentary?" The question was Caroline's. It was the first time she had spoken in forty-five minutes and now she was posing the all-important question—one which, she guessed, Lawrence never would.

"At this point, yes, I think so," Jason replied. "I'll call in a few weeks to give you the definitive answer."

He's lying, Caroline thought as she met his unreadable blue eyes. He's lying, damn him. But why?


After Jason left, Lawrence extended his arms to her, and for a very long time they simply held each other. Finally he asked, "What did you think? The truth."

"I liked him very much . . . and then I hated him very much."

"You don't think he's planning to include Holly in his documentary."

"Do you?"

"No." Lawrence gazed at her with great tenderness. Her entire being quaked with anger—with outrage—for him. Fighting his own immense disappointment, he reassured, "It's okay, Caroline. We can't force him to make a decision he doesn't want to make, and there are so many missing children, so many desperately searching parents."

But it's *not* okay, Caroline thought. And more: it didn't even make any sense. If Jason Cole's purpose in meeting Lawrence had been to see proof of his love for his daughter, he could not have seen more.

How could the famous dark blue eyes have been so blind? she wondered. And how could the Oscar-winning actor have been so incapable of concealing the fact that he himself was lying?

Perhaps Jason Cole wasn't accustomed to lying in real life. Or perhaps because Lawrence had been so very honest with him, Jason felt uneasy, truly guilty, about lying in return.

Caroline sighed. "It just doesn't make any sense."

"No, it doesn't. But it's over." Lawrence spoke with the quiet resolve of a man who knew the irreparable damage that could be caused by permitting things that could not be changed to gnaw relentlessly at one's heart. "I need to go check on Summertime."

"Okay."

Caroline knew that Lawrence was going to check the wound, and change the bandages, and give the horse another shot of antibiotics. And although he would not refuse her offer of help, he didn't need it.

Caroline didn't even offer. She wanted to stay in the

house, in case Jason Cole called; because something deep inside her defiantly insisted that it wasn't really over.

There was something more. There had to be. Another chapter, a different . . . and happier . . . ending.

## ❋ 28 ❋

"Good morning," Jason greeted the womanly version of the lovely little girl whose photographs he had just seen.

Her hair was only slightly longer now than it had been then, and the curls that framed her face were a little more soft and loose, but the gold itself was quite untarnished by the passage of time.

And her eyes? The sparkling innocence that had smiled gaily at the camera was lost forever. But there was a deep luster in the aquamarine eyes that greeted him now, a radiant courage, a glowing welcome.

Jason needed to talk to her in absolute private, which meant in his room or hers. With a questioning tilt of his head, he asked, "May I come in?"

"Of course."

As Jason entered Holly's room, the mirror image of his own, he saw that she had probably been expecting him. Housekeeping had not yet been in his room, nor in Holly's, but the bed in which she had slept was neatly made.

The alcove overlooking the falls was furnished with a round oak table and chairs. It was obvious that Holly had been sitting there. One of the chairs was askew, her spiral notebook lay open, and her pens were on the table.

"Have you been writing?" Jason knew exactly where she was in her new book. He had read every word within

hours of her writing it and had become very involved
with the story. A wave of sadness swept through him as
he realized that it had undoubtedly been what her
characters had done today, not the sight of him, that had
put the lovely glow in her beautiful eyes.

"No," she admitted softly. "I've just been sitting here,
watching the sky, and the clouds, and the forest, and the
waterfall."

"And thinking happy thoughts."

"Yes." She met his gaze, and her own didn't falter as
she eloquently completed the confession with only her
expressive eyes, *Thinking about you.*

It was the moment that Jason had wished for, when
she truly believed—and trusted—the magic of their love.
It was a wondrous moment . . . and a fragile one. Like a
delicate sandcastle mercilessly obliterated by a giant
wave, it could vanish swiftly and without a trace. Jason
knew that the menacing waves were ever-present in
Holly's heart. They could surge without warning, a
sudden rush of fear that would remind her how terribly
dangerous it was to love, how very precarious were the
happinesses that she did not create with her own gifted
pen.

Jason wanted so much to seize this magnificent
moment, to hold her and love her until the waves of fear
were calmed forever. It was a powerful wish, but a selfish
one.

With great effort, and with a gentle smile that
promised there would be a next time, Jason broke the
spell. He left her beautiful face and gazed at the waterfall
that was a cascade of thunder just below them.

"There's something I've wanted to ask you about," he
began quietly, speaking to the churning thunder,
wondering what turbulent torment he was about to
unleash within the woman he loved. When Holly didn't
answer, he looked back at her and saw the harm he had
already done. She had been so bold, bravely confessing

her wish for their love, but now she was uncertain again. "Something that's been troubling me."

"Yes?"

"When you told me about what happened to you, about that snowy night when your family was killed, you mentioned that your father had died in Vietnam." Jason waited until Holly confirmed with a slight nod of her dancing golden curls that that was indeed what she believed. "But you never told me anything about him. Do you remember him?"

Jason's plan had been to be as certain as possible that both father and daughter wanted the reunion. His meeting with Lawrence had so convinced him that there had been great love that on the drive back from Issaquah he had almost decided that it was unnecessary to question Holly about her feelings toward her father at all. There would be no emotional skeletons, no unspeakable trauma, no devastating abuse. The photographs he had seen could not have been so gloriously joyous if there were.

Or could they? he wondered with a jolt as Holly answered his question by abruptly turning away. She crossed the room to the dresser, removed an envelope from her purse, hesitated for several heartbeats, then turned and faced him.

Her eyes were brave again, trusting him again. Him, not the magic, but him: the kind and gentle man with whom she had shared the truth about her past.

"After you left last time, I realized that I hadn't shown you these. They're pictures of my family."

"I want to see them," Jason encouraged quietly as she returned to the alcove.

Once they were both seated, Holly removed the treasured photographs from the envelope. There were seven pictures in all, the five described by Lawrence and two others, taken long after he had been left for dead in Vietnam, of Holly's little brother and sister.

"Are these the only pictures you have?"

"Yes. There were two photo albums, and I could've taken them with me, but . . ." Holly frowned. "I really don't know why I didn't."

Because, Jason thought, somehow you knew that he was still alive.

With loving emotion that was so very much like her father's, Holly began telling him about the pictures. "This was their wedding picture. There was just this one, taken by the wife of the Justice of the Peace. They were young, but very much in love."

The love on the young faces of Lawrence and Claire was obvious in the photograph, and Jason forced himself to smile even as his heart ached at what else the photograph revealed: Claire's wedding dress, the same dress that Holly had worn when she made her journey to Los Angeles to save the life of her imaginary heroine.

She's so much better now, Jason reminded himself. She's leaving the cocoon of her past behind her, a valiant effort of courage and hope, and now I'm about to immerse her in an entirely new sadness, a suffocating torrent of regret and loss.

"This was the first time I ever patted a horse's nose. I was only three and I think they were both a little worried that the horse might take an accidental nibble." Love filled her voice as her delicate fingers touched the image of Lawrence holding her so that she could reach the palomino's velvet-soft muzzle. "But there was no need to worry. My father had an uncanny instinct with animals, both wild and tame. He was so gentle with them, and they trusted him."

"It sounds as if you loved him very much."

"Oh, yes," she answered softly. "As I've gotten older, I've come to realize how truly remarkable he was. He was only seventeen when he married and only eighteen when I was born. But he had such a sense of responsibility to my mother and me. He held several jobs, and went to school part-time, and yet when I remember those years, I don't ever remember him being gone. I just remember him being there, loving me, protecting me, always having time for me and making me feel like I was the most important thing in his life."

"You were," Jason said quietly.

"Well." Holly smiled a trembling smile. "That's how he made me feel."

"There's something I need to tell you, Holly. Something you don't know."

She frowned at the sudden solemnity of his voice, and Jason saw that just as Lawrence had, she wanted to linger a little longer in the wonderful memories of the past. With gently loving patience, he waited while she made the journey back to the present.

When she was focused on him again, her eyes clear and trusting, he said, "When you told me what had happened to you, it triggered a vague and distant memory. I didn't know what it was, but because it troubled me, I asked someone to look into it. Your father didn't die in Vietnam, Holly. Derek shot him, and left him for dead, but he was found and taken prisoner. He escaped eight months after you vanished."

"No," she whispered. It was a soft plea of despair, a fearful protest against the truth—not the joyous truth that her father had survived but the devastating one that she hadn't known and that in vanishing from the world she had unwittingly hidden from him as well. "He tried to find me then, didn't he? But he couldn't."

"He's never stopped searching for you, Holly," Jason said softly. "He's never stopped believing that one day he would find you."

Emotion flooded her, drowning thought, suffocating breath, soaking her heart with grief and spilling from her anguished eyes. She might have died, lethally immersed in sadness, but quite suddenly her drowning thoughts came gasping to the surface, clinging to Jason's last words as if they were life buoys in a storm tossed sea.

*He's never stopped searching for you.*

"He's alive," she whispered. Then, urgently, "Where is he, Jason? Do you know?"

"He lives a few miles from here."

"That's who you went to see this morning."

"Yes."

"So he knows," she said softly. Then, standing, she added anxiously, "And he's waiting for me now."

"No," Jason countered quietly, standing too. "He doesn't know that you're here, or even that I know you."

"You didn't tell him?"

"No. I wanted to be sure that you wanted to see him first."

"But why wouldn't I want to see him?"

"It doesn't matter, and you obviously do want to, so why don't I drive you there right now?"


During the short drive, Jason told her what he knew about Lawrence, and he told her as well about Caroline, that she and Lawrence obviously cared very deeply about each other. As Jason answered Holly's questions about her father, he was acutely aware of the subtext, the questions that taunted her but remained unasked.

Why hadn't he told her the real reason for their trip to Seattle?

And why hadn't he told Lawrence that his missing daughter was only a few miles away?

And what would have happened if she'd had no memory of her father, or if what she recalled most vividly were the long absences when he was working so hard to make life safe and wonderful for her?

And the most troubling question of all, What if even the tiniest part of her memory of her father had been slightly tarnished, something even a little bit less than pure shimmering love?

Jason felt Holly's troubling yet silent questions, and as she began to find her own answers to them, he felt her withdrawing from him, uncertain once again, and fearful, and wary.

The troubling questions and answers were there, creating confusion on her lovely face and distance between them. But mostly, as they drove to Issaquah, Holly's thoughts and emotions were focused on the father she was about to see.

When they reached the house, she turned to Jason, and for a moment the shadows of mistrust left her beautiful eyes.

"Thank you, Jason," she whispered. "Thank you for finding him."


Something deep within Caroline had defiantly hoped for a different and better ending to Jason Cole's visit. *Hoped,* but not truly believed, because when she saw his car pull to a stop in the driveway, her heart raced with surprise. And when she saw him open the car door for the young woman with soft golden curls, her racing heart took flight and hot tears flooded her eyes.

And when she opened the front door to that beloved young woman, all Caroline could manage was a trembling whisper. *"Holly."*

"Caroline?" Holly asked softly, the pure joy in Caroline's glistening eyes shaking further her already precarious emotions.

Caroline's normally fluent speech returned then, a rush of words that came of their own accord, honest and stunning. "Yes, I'm Caroline, and I love your father very much, and I would have given my own life for this moment—for him." Then, with a tear-dampened smile, and without further ado, she led the way to the living room, opened the outside door, and pointed to the building that stood across the colorful meadow of wildflowers. "He's there, Holly, in the stable. Why don't you go to him?"

Twenty-seven years before there had been a stable, and it had been filled exactly as this stable in Issaquah was, with the warm sweet fragrance of freshly mown hay. The fragrance transported Holly to that long-ago time even before she saw the palomino mare. The golden horse had been in that long-ago stable, too, as had her beloved father.

Holly saw him then, and he was the same father from that faraway day, tall and strong and speaking gentle reassurances in response to the questioning whinnies of the majestic animal. His back was to Holly, his dark head bent as he jotted down the careful record of Summertime's progress.

Holly had no conscious memory of the six words she had uttered with such joyful wonder as a three-year-old, when her small eager fingers had touched the velvet softness of the palomino's nose. She didn't consciously remember the words; but now, as her delicate fingers caressed that extraordinary velvet once again, she spoke the first five of those six words exactly as she had then.

"Her nose is so soft."

Lawrence's strong back stiffened at the sound, and at what it meant. He was being visited by the ghost of a memory. It wasn't surprising that he should hear her voice here, and now, because he had been thinking about her and about that day. Holly had taken the photograph with her, but it didn't matter. He didn't need it. The glittering image of the golden-haired girl and the golden-haired horse was engraved in his mind forever.

It wasn't surprising that he should hear again, now, the same words that Holly had spoken that day. But what was surprising was the voice. There were two voices really, but when they spoke it was with perfect harmony—a melodic blend of the high soprano of a little girl and the softer, subdued music of a woman fully grown.

Girl and woman, past and present.

Lawrence spun in the direction of the voices.

And as his dark green eyes filled with immeasurable joy, his golden-haired daughter spoke the sixth word she had uttered on that long-ago day. "Daddy."

## ❀ 29 ❀

They walked through the meadow of wildflowers and sat on the sun-warmed grass beside the stream. Sunlight caressed the water, dappling it with glittering bursts of untarnished gold.

There, amid the fragrance of wildflowers and beside the sapphire river filled with gold, Holly and Lawrence quietly told each other the truths that could be shared, those which could be lovingly gift-wrapped until they were almost happy ones. And there, where the watery depths could not be seen because of the golden brilliance of the springtime sun, Holly and Lawrence lovingly hid from each other the truths that would only cause great pain.

Lawrence told her about becoming the veterinarian they had always dreamed he would be, and about the valiant and lively Juliet, and eventually about his love for Caroline. But he did not tell Holly, not in any detail, about his years of imprisonment in a small cage in the jungle; nor did he tell her about the endless weeks and months that he had spent wandering the streets of strange cities looking for her, his heart racing with hope whenever he caught a glimpse of golden hair, only to be shattered when he saw that the face did not belong to her.

And Holly told her father about becoming a writer, and about living in the magnificent splendor of Alaska, and about being one of the volunteers who had traveled to Prince William Sound to help the oil-soaked creatures of the sea who had fallen victim to the spill of the Exxon *Valdez*. But she did not tell Lawrence that during those years she had been barely alive, surviving only because of the imaginary worlds she created, her heart's only sustenance coming from the stories of love that she wrote.

And Holly didn't tell him, not in any detail, about the night that Derek had murdered their dreams. Lawrence had asked about that night, wondering quietly if it might help her to tell him about it, his love for the daughter who might need to talk far outweighing his own fear of hearing about the brutal murder of the woman he loved.

But, because of Jason, Holly had already spoken aloud those words of horror, had already exorcised those menacing ghosts. She had no need to share that anguished pain with her father, and she would not. Assuring gently, lovingly, she told him only that it had all happened very quickly.

It was a lie, and yet it didn't feel like one. Was that because it was true? Holly wondered. Because even though for her the horror had seemed to last forever, an endless slow motion scene of carnage and terror, it had in truth happened very quickly? Perhaps. But maybe, she thought as she saw her father's relief, there were lies of love that were just as important as all its wondrous promises.

Many hours passed. For Holly and Lawrence its passage was measured only in love, in healing, and in hope. It wasn't until they decided that it was time to return to the house that they saw what had happened to the golden river that flowed at their feet. The shining bright gold of morning was long gone, deepened to the rich burnished shades of late afternoon.

\* \* \*

As they neared the house, Caroline walked out into the meadow to meet them. Her hair gleamed copper in the afternoon sun, and her emerald eyes shone with happiness for them, but the questioning tilt of her sun-caressed auburn head betrayed her own uncertainty.

"I hear that you two are getting married," Holly greeted warmly. "I'm so glad."

"Thank you," Caroline said softly, obviously relieved. Then leaving the smiling eyes of the daughter, she looked up at the man she loved. "I am too."

"As am I," Lawrence assured, his tenderness promptly vanquishing all lingering vestiges of uncertainty.

They were talking about a man and woman who loved each other, so in Caroline's mind what she said next was still very much on the topic at hand.

"Jason stayed until we saw you leaving the stable and walking toward the stream." *Until he knew that you were fine, safe and loved.* "Then he left, to fly back to Los Angeles."

"Oh," Holly murmured. "I see."

"He gave me some phone numbers to give to you." Caroline withdrew a piece of paper from a pocket and handed it to Holly. "The first is his home and the second is the private line in his office. He said he'll be home all weekend and in his office until three Monday afternoon, when he has to leave for Dallas."

As Holly took the piece of paper, Caroline saw dark shadows of worry that were very much like the surprising shadows she'd seen in Jason's eyes just moments before he left.

"Jason seemed very eager to have you call him, Holly." *And terribly worried that you wouldn't.* "He should be in Los Angeles by now. There are plenty of phones in the house."

"And absolute privacy," Lawrence added. "Caroline and I are going to go check on Summertime, aren't we?"

"Indeed we are."

352

"Thank you." Holly shrugged. "But I don't think I'll call him right now."


"She's never going to call him," Caroline said many hours later. It was the middle of the night. She and Lawrence were in bed, awake still, marveling still at the wonder of the day.

Holly was in the cheerfully decorated room that had been waiting for her for so many years. She probably wasn't sleeping either, Caroline decided. She was probably marveling, too, at the day—and staring with worry at the telephone that Caroline had put on her nightstand. Holly's worried stare would have nothing to do with concern that a late-night phone call might disturb anyone. As she'd plugged the extension into the wall, Caroline had made it crystal clear that Holly's room and the master bedroom were separated by a distance that was far beyond the range of even the most superhuman ears.

"And she needs to talk to him, doesn't she?" Lawrence asked softly. "She's in love with him."

Caroline propped up on an elbow and gazed at him with loving surprise and unconcealed pride. "What an insightful father you are. You never even saw the two of them together."

"No, but every time his name comes up—and let's face it, my love, at least one of us has been mentioning his name fairly often—her expression changes. She loves him, but something's wrong."

"Yes," Caroline agreed quietly. "And he loves her too, Lawrence. I realize now that that's what I was seeing as I watched the two of you look at the photo album, and it was very obvious when he returned with her. Jason loves Holly very much, but he knows that something is wrong, and I think he's afraid that whatever it is can't be fixed, that Holly will never call."

"But you're not going to let that happen."

"Are you?"

"No," Lawrence assured her. "No I am not."


"Three o'clock," Caroline announced when she rejoined them in the kitchen.

It was almost noon, and even though none of them had really slept, they'd all been up for hours. They had eaten day-old but still wonderful blueberry muffins for breakfast and had been leisurely assembling something for lunch when, by a silent signal between Lawrence and Caroline, Caroline had precipitously vanished.

And now she was back, smiling mysteriously.

"Caroline and I have made an important decision," Lawrence explained to Holly.

Holly answered with a beautiful smile. "You're getting married today at three."

"No," Lawrence replied. "This is something more important, or at least more urgent, even than that. Caroline has just booked you on a three o'clock flight to Los Angeles."

"But I've only just gotten here. I've only just found you!"

Lawrence's voice filled with love. "We've found each other forever, Holly. But Jason is leaving tomorrow for Dallas, and Caroline and I think that you need to talk to him—in person—before he goes. Don't you?"

After a long thoughtful moment, Holly agreed quietly, "Yes, I do need to talk to him. And I suppose it would be better to do it in person . . . and before he's involved in filming again."

"Then that's settled. We should leave for the airport in about an hour."

Holly nodded, then frowned with a new worry. "I don't know where he lives."

Lawrence smiled. "But you have his phone number. You could call him and find out, or one of us could."

Holly gave a soft shake of her golden head. If she was going to hear his honest and unrehearsed answers to the tormenting questions she needed to ask, then her appearance on his doorstep had to be a surprise.

But how? Holly had no idea how she tumbled to the solution so quickly, but she did. "Raven might know."

"Raven?"

"She's an entertainment attorney in Los Angeles. She's negotiated Jason's biggest movie deals and she's the one who drew up the contract for me to write the screenplay for *Gifts of Love*. I've never met her, but she's always been so nice, so helpful. She once told me that all her phone numbers, even her home phone, are listed."

The fierce battle between her brave unborn baby and her scarred and hostile womb was over . . . and the precious little life had lost. It had ended an hour ago, in a final piercing stab of pain and a hot gush of tissue and blood. Now there was only stillness, the breath-held quiet that followed a devastating storm, the eerily calm silence that shrouded death.

Her baby had died, and most of Raven had died with it, and she wished that all of her had died, because the voice that was alive inside her still, the only sign of life, was a whisper of ice that hissed relentlessly, The acid baby killed the baby of love. The bird of death killed the courageous hope of life.

Raven had tried *so hard* to help the tiny life that had been struggling for survival deep inside her. She had armed it with everything she had to give—all her hope, all her love, all her prayers; and she had even made a promise that she would keep, no matter the cost to her: You will be with your daddy, my little love, your daddy and your sisters and your grandparents.

Raven knew without question that Nick would want his baby, and during the past three sleepless nights of pain, as she had lived with the excruciating proof that she wasn't meant to be a mother, she had bargained with her own heart. If somehow her womb could nurture the tiny life for just nine months, if for only nine months of her life she could be a mother, then that would be enough. She would give her newborn infant to its father and make no claims whatsoever of her own.

Raven had given all she had to give, every promise of love that she could make. But it hadn't been enough.

The acid baby had killed the baby of love.

The ringing phone seemed like a death knell.

It would be Nick, Raven knew; and she knew also that she had to answer. If she didn't, he would only keep calling, and if she never answered, he might even make the trip home from Santa Barbara early and appear at her door step without warning. She had called him last night, forcing brave cheer into her voice as she proclaimed herself to be a little bit better.

But the caller wasn't Nick. It was Holly, who, after identifying herself, apologized for having bothered her at home on a Sunday.

"It's okay," Raven assured truthfully. It *was* okay. In fact it was good. Each of the several times that she and Holly had spoken, Raven had felt a surprising warmth, a remarkable closeness—and trust. Was this what friendship felt like? she wondered. "It's no bother at all."

"Oh. Good. Raven, I wondered if you know where Jason lives?"

"Yes, in fact he lives about a mile from here." Raven frowned. "But aren't you with him right now? When I spoke with his secretary earlier this week, she said that he'd be back here tomorrow but in Kodiak this weekend."

"I'm actually in Seattle now, and he and I were both here until yesterday. It's a very long story, but . . . Jason

left his unlisted home phone number for me and said that
he wanted me to call him, but what I'd really like to do
is fly down this afternoon and talk to him in person.''

Without his knowing in advance that you're coming,
Raven thought, realizing that that was precisely what
Jason had wanted when he had asked her help in finding
Holly's address in Kodiak.

Holly's quiet voice spoke into the sudden silence, "If
you don't feel comfortable telling me, Raven, I'll understand.''

"No," Raven assured swiftly and with absolute confidence. "I feel completely comfortable about it, Holly. If
you'll just hold on a moment, I need to find my briefcase.''

As Raven stood, she reflexively braced herself for the
wave of dizziness that had been there for the past three
days and nights. The swirling dizziness would be there
still, because even though the battle was over, it would
take a while to replenish the blood that she had lost.

But there was no dizziness. It was as if there had never
been a baby, never been a courageous struggle of love at
all.

She was recovered.

Recovered? Never. It was just that she didn't need as
much blood now to keep her alive. She no longer needed
rich red nourishment for hope—because the hope was
dead.

There was no dizziness, nor was there even a twinge of
the clawing pain. But there was a new pain, more excruciating than all that had come before, a knife-like scream
of loss as her heart felt the inevitable death of its most
precious, hopeful places.

Raven forced herself beyond herself, to the love of
Jason and Holly. It *was* love, she knew. She had seen it
in Jason's eyes the day he had asked her to get Holly's
address for him; and she had heard it in Holly's voice

every time they had discussed the contract for the screenplay Jason wanted her to write.

Now something had happened to that love, and Raven very much needed to believe that whatever it was, it was not irrevocable. There might never be happiness for the acid baby, but there should be happiness, there had to be, for the woman who wove magnificent dreams of love and the man who brought such wondrous dreams to life.

Raven's briefcase was in the living room, where she had dropped it when she arrived home Thursday evening. She had been exhausted then, a joyous fatigue, a symbol of her healthy pregnancy. Raven blocked the memory as she retrieved her address book from the bulging briefcase and returned to the phone in the bedroom.

After Raven gave her Jason's address, and she had repeated it back for accuracy, Holly asked quietly, "Are you all right, Raven? You sound . . . sad."

Denial rushed swiftly to Raven's lips, but before she spoke, something intervened and she heard herself confessing, "I am sad, Holly."

"Can you tell me about it?" Holly asked gently. "I'm due to arrive in Los Angeles about five-thirty. Shall I come visit you before I see Jason?"

This time what rushed to Raven's lips, only to be stopped yet again, was "Yes, *please.*" Some of the heroines in Holly's books were like Raven, glamorous and successful women who appeared confident and in control, but who in truth, in their personal lives, were tormented by deep and seemingly unhealable wounds. Holly found happy endings for those heroines. No, Raven amended silently. Holly created heroines who found happy endings for themselves, who bravely overcame even the most immense obstacles to heal and rescue themselves.

Raven had tried to rescue herself. She had loved with every ounce of her soul. And she had failed.

And even the master dream-weaver could not craft a happy ending for her.

It might help simply to talk to Holly, to share the sadness; but not now, not when Holly so obviously needed to see Jason.

"Thank you, Holly, but it's all too new, too fresh for me to talk about yet. I haven't really slept for days, and I think that's what I need most of all right now."

"Are you sure?"

"Yes. Very sure." Raven forced a smile into her voice. "I'll be okay. But I would love to see you, meet you, sometime."

"I'd love that too. I'm not sure how long I'll be in Los Angeles."

"Well, if not now, next time, okay?"

"Yes . . . okay."

She's not sure there will even be a next time, Raven thought after they had said goodbye. But there will be, Holly. There has to be a lifetime of next times for you and Jason.

Raven stared at the silent phone and thought about the calls she should make to Dr. Rockwell and to Nick. Sara Rockwell had told her to call if she passed tissue, and she had explained why: the passage of tissue meant that the miscarriage had happened, but it might not be "complete." If not, if remnants remained in the womb, the dead tissue could trigger serious complications— bleeding and sepsis—for the mother. That was why she needed to be seen and examined, and why, if the miscarriage had not been complete, she needed to have a D and C.

Raven did not really care about the sometimes lethal dangers to the mother. And as she made the decision not to call now, but to simply go to Dr. Rockwell's office in the morning as already scheduled, she thought grimly, I'm probably not at any lethal risk anyway . . . because I'm not really a mother.

She did need to call Nick, though. She needed to tell him that the cramping pain had stopped and that she was going to try to sleep for the eighteen hours between now and morning. That would forestall his calling tonight, and forestall as well any possibility of his coming over. She needed to be very much stronger before she saw him again.

The pregnancy was over, but Raven still felt its earliest symptom: the shaky emotion that lurked just beneath the surface, ready to burst into a torrent of hot tears without any warning whatsoever. That symptom had been perplexing at first, and had then become quite wonderful, proof of a miracle. And now Raven wanted to cling to it, to make it stay with her forever, as if in so doing her baby of love would be alive still.

No, she commanded her foolish heart. *Face the truth.* The tears are all still pooled deep within, that's all. After I call Nick, I'll allow them to flow . . . until I've emptied myself entirely of the symbol of the tiny life that once was alive but is no more.

Nick was out riding with the girls when she called, so it was Nick's mother, her baby's grandmother, to whom Raven gave the cheerful message that she was much better, would be fine after a long sleep, and would talk to Nick sometime tomorrow.

## ❀ 30 ❀

Holly could not arrive unannounced at Jason's front door. The famous actor-director lived in the penthouse of a high-security condominium building. The closest she could get without his express permission was the uniformed doorman in the jade and white marble lobby.

Which was fine, she decided. It gave her a place to leave her luggage and the doorman assured her that he could get a cab for her the instant she was ready to leave.

The doorman placed a call directly to Jason, and in moments Holly was ascending to the top floor in the penthouse's private elevator.

When the gleaming brass doors opened, Jason was there, waiting for her, his blue eyes darkly circled, his voice very gentle. "Holly."

Holly forced herself to ignore the gentleness. "I need to talk to you."

"Please come in."

Jason led the way to the living room, where Holly silently rejected his suggestion that she be seated on a comfortable overstuffed couch. She didn't reject the couch altogether, however. She used its massive bulk as a shield, standing behind it and bracing herself against it as she confronted him.

"There are things I need to know, Jason."

"Okay."

Holly took a steadying breath and then spoke the words she had so carefully rehearsed. "I want to know if we might have spent the entire weekend at the lodge, just a few miles from my father's home, without your ever mentioning that you knew he was alive."

"Yes," Jason answered softly. "We might have."

The quietly solemn confirmation of what she feared suddenly released the anger that had been building inside her. The anger was at what Jason had done, *what he might have done,* and although some of the outrage she felt was for herself, most of it was for her father.

For Holly, the discovery that her father was alive had been an extraordinary—and never anticipated—gift of joy. She hadn't been searching for him and in all likelihood would have never known to search. But for her father, *every day* of the past seventeen years had been fueled by sadness, torment, and the relentlessly haunting fear that he wasn't doing enough to find his lost daughter.

Would Jason really have been so cruel? Would he have actually destined Lawrence to an entire lifetime of such anguish? *Yes.* He had just admitted it. Now she had her answer. Now she could leave. Except that her rage—and her heart—wanted to know why.

"You would have done that to my father? If I had told you that I barely remembered him, or that sometimes he got cross with me because he was tired from working so hard, would we have spent the weekend exploring Seattle and never seen him at all?"

Jason saw her immense hurt, her abiding belief that he had betrayed her after all, and knew that he was fighting for his heart, his love, his very life. He had only one weapon in his arsenal: the truth. And that's what he told her. "If I believed that it would have been painful for you to see him again, more painful than happy, yes, that's what would have happened."

"If *you* believed? If the Academy Award–winning

director didn't think the scene would be enacted precisely the way he wanted it, there would have been no scene at all? Is that what you're telling me?"

"Yes, Holly, that's exactly what I'm telling you."

"I owe you so much, Jason. But right now I hate—"

"Will you give me a chance to explain?" he asked softly. It seemed a futile request. Her angry eyes seemed incapable of seeing any explanation that would excuse his presumptuous manipulation of her life. "Holly? Will you let me at least try?"

Her answer was a faint nod of her golden head. She didn't want to speak because her rage had suddenly been undermined by the gentle sadness—it was almost despair—that she heard in his voice. She needed another surge of anger, a river of rage on which she could flow away from him forever. Surely his arrogant explanation would evoke that necessary surge.

"Pretend for a moment that we're characters in one of your books," Jason began. "You're the heroine, of course, and, as difficult as this may be, pretend that I'm the hero."

Her reply came, hot, swift, and sure. "None of my heroes would *ever* do what you did, what you might have done. None of them would *ever* have been so cruel."

"You're wrong, Holly. I've read all of your books, and believe that given the same circumstances your heroes would have done exactly what I did, and for the same reason." The magnificent blue-green eyes which had flashed with defiant anger blazed still; but as he paused, waiting for her to truly hear his words, Jason saw shadows of confusion as well. When he believed that she was listening, really listening, he continued very gently, "Your father might have been a monster. He might have done monstrous things to you as a little girl. I didn't want you to be hurt. I wouldn't let you be. I don't pretend to be a hero, Holly, but can't you imagine one of the men in your books behaving the same way?"

Yes, of course she could, but only if, only because
. . .

Jason watched the shadows of confusion give way to
bright shimmering hope. "I love you, Holly. That's why
I did what I did. Because I love you."

"Jason."

He moved to her then, around the couch that had been
a barrier between them, and when he stood before her
she raised her face to his and he saw what he had seen
yesterday morning above the thundering falls: the
unshadowed belief in the wondrous magic of their
wondrous love.

Yesterday Jason had felt an urgency about the
wondrous moment, a desperate need to seize it before it
was washed away by crashing waves. But now he felt no
such urgency. Now, he knew, was the glorious beginning
of a lifetime of such moments.

For a very long time, they simply looked at each other,
treasuring the wonder, marveling at its boundless joy.
But finally, for both of them, the need to touch became
overpowering.

With exquisite tenderness, Jason caressed her lips, first
with his gently trembling fingers and then with his gently
loving mouth. And even though Holly had never been
kissed before, she knew how to welcome the kisses of the
man she loved.

It wasn't a single kiss, but a thousand different kisses,
flowing from gentle hello to ravenous hunger, from
tender warmth to passionate fire, from the most delicate
whisper to the most demanding desire.

It was a kiss that began with lips caressing lips. But
eventually it wandered, wanting more, needing more,
needing all there was to share.

"Oh, Holly," Jason whispered, stopping for a
moment, needing to.

They were on the couch. What had once been a barrier

between them had now become a welcoming haven for their love.

"Jason?" she asked, surprised. Then, with a glowing look of exhilarating confidence, she whispered, "Make love to me."

Jason drew a steadying breath. "Don't you want to wait?"

"Wait?"

"Until our wedding night." Jason had believed her lovely eyes could not glow any brighter. But he was wrong. And when he saw her radiant happiness, he discovered something else. Holly's joy at the thought of their marriage caused a rush of desire within him that was far more powerful than even the most passionate of kisses. It was several moments before he could speak again, but finally, softly, he clarified, "It might not actually be a wedding *night.*"

"No?"

"No. I've been thinking about our wedding for a while. And what I thought, if it's what you want too, is that we could get married in Barrow in June. We could exchange our vows just as the setting sun pirouettes off the horizon."

"Oh," she whispered. And then, her eyes glowing still and her kiss-dampened lips smiling with pure joy, she gave a slow gentle shake of love-tangled golden curls.

"No? You don't want to marry me?"

"Oh, yes. I want to marry you."

"But not in Barrow?"

"Yes, in Barrow. But Jason, I don't want to wait to make love until then. There's no reason to wait. We're married already, aren't we? Our hearts are already married . . . aren't they?"

"Oh yes, my love. Yes." Their hearts were already married, and very soon their bodies would wed, and as his hands tenderly framed her lovely face, he marveled at how lovely she was, how hopeful, how trusting . . . and despite the passion of her kisses, how very innocent.

Holly saw his sudden frown and guessed quietly, "You're worried that I might get pregnant?"

"No," he answered swiftly. "I think that would be wonderful."

"But something is worrying you."

"I don't want to hurt you, Holly," he confessed softly. "Not even for an instant."

The look of exhilarating confidence with which she had asked him to make love to her returned now. "Our loving couldn't possibly hurt me, Jason, not even for an instant."

Together, with wondrous joy, Holly and Jason celebrated their love, wrapping that magnificent gift with the tender union of their loving bodies. It was the beribboned adornment about which Lauren Sinclair had written, the elaborate embellishment which came only after the gift itself had been chosen with reverent care.

There was reverence in their loving, and wonder and joy. And afterward, as she lay in his arms, encircled with tenderness, Holly's eyes glowed still with the astonishment she felt.

"I never knew," she whispered. "I wrote about making love but . . ."

"But you did know, Holly," Jason countered softly. "You knew that its greatest meaning, its greatest wonder, was when there was already a committed love."

"Yes, but still I never knew . . . never imagined . . . that it would be like this."

Jason kissed the corners of her glowing eyes, gentle, reverent kisses, and as his fingers caressed the golden curls that framed her face, he confessed, "I never knew either, Holly. I never knew about love until now. Until you."

* * *

They could have spent all evening lost in their enchanted world of love. All evening, all night, forever.

But there was a father who had searched for seventeen years for his daughter, and who had so generously let her go even though she had just been found, and neither of them forgot about him.

Jason left, to retrieve her luggage from the lobby, and to get something for dinner, but mostly to give her privacy to make her call to Issaquah. Lawrence answered the phone on the first ring, and even before Holly shared her joyous news, his heart pulsed with relief at the happiness he heard in her voice.

Holly told him first of their love, and then of their plans to marry and their hope that Caroline and Lawrence would travel to Barrow to witness that event. "We will be there," Lawrence promised, and Holly heard his smile as he added, "I'm sure Katie's owner will be happy to puppy-sit Juliet."

Then, as Holly shared with her father the other plans that she and Jason had made, she heard his quiet joy. While Jason was filming in Dallas, she would return to Issaquah. That would give them more time together, and it would also enable her to help Lawrence with something that was very important to him: thanking all the people who had helped during the long years of searching, who had offered their expertise, their access to the media, or simply their sympathy and their concern.

Before saying goodbye, Holly said quietly, "There's something I need to ask you about yesterday morning."

"Okay."

"Why did you think that Jason came to see you first? Did you think that I had sent him?"

"I honestly hadn't thought about it," Lawrence admitted. He hadn't spent one second questioning the miracle that had reunited him with his daughter. But now, as he heard the worry in Holly's voice, he instantly understood what had happened. "You didn't send him, did you? You didn't know either."

"No, I didn't know." Holly wanted her father to know that, no matter what he had become, she would have wanted to see him. But . . . "Please don't be upset with Jason."

"Upset?" Lawrence echoed softly. "How could I be? He did what he did because he loves you so much. I might have changed, Holly. It might have been very disturbing for you to see me again. Jason didn't want that for you." Lawrence paused, needed to, because even though the next words were honest ones, the realization of all that he might have lost caused a flood of emotion. Finally, steadily, he said, "And I wouldn't have wanted it either, Holly. If it had been better—best—for you never to see me again, that's what I would have wanted too."

"Raven."

*"Raven?"*

They had made love again, and as they held each other in the aftermath, they had marveled in soft whispers that it had been even more wondrous this time, and then there had been a few beats of silence, filled with the most gentle of kisses, and then, quite suddenly, Holly had spoken Raven's name.

Now she clarified to her husband-to-be, "I think we should invite her to our wedding."

"Okay," Jason agreed without hesitation. "Why?"

"Well, if it weren't for Raven, if she hadn't suggested that I come to Los Angeles to talk to you about *Gifts of Love,* we would never have met. And besides, I think she would like to see the sun dance off the horizon. I think that it would mean something to her."

"I think so too," he concurred as he silently reflected

that there probably weren't many people in Los Angeles who would imagine that the splendor of the summer sun twirling off the horizon would move the ice queen at all. But Holly believed that it would, and so did he. "I didn't realize that you knew her so well."

"I don't, not really, but I would like to get to know her. When I called her this afternoon to get your address, she was very sad."

"She admitted that?"

"Yes, but she said that whatever it was, it was too fresh for her to talk about. Maybe tomorrow, while you're solving all the problems that need to be solved before Dallas, I'll call to invite her to the wedding and see if she wants to get together to talk."

Twice since she had known him, Raven wondered if she would see fury on Nick's face. The first time had been when they'd met, when he had rushed to her just moments after his lightning-quick reflexes had averted the almost lethal calamity caused by her. But there had been no fury then. There had been only gentle concern. And the second time, when he'd discovered her sipping lemonade with Sam on the rose-fragrant verandah of his magnificent estate, she had expected fury and had been prepared to match it with her own. But that day there had been only apology, and tenderness, and love.

Raven knew that Nicholas Gault was quite capable of fury. Melody had described his anger when a woman named Jeannette had tried to insinuate herself in their lives and tarnish their young minds with archaic notions about the role of women. And she herself had seen glimpses of what his fury could be when he had told her about his discovery that Deandra had decided that his youngest daughter should never be born.

But even that fury paled in comparison to what greeted her when she walked into her house early Monday evening. She had known that he would be there, although they hadn't actually spoken. Raven had a full day of meetings, as did he, so after several rounds of telephone tag, Nick finally just left the message with her secretary that he would see her at her house after work.

Nick wasn't the only one with whom, despite several attempts, Raven had never connected. Holly, too, had finally simply left a message, an invitation to a wedding, and an invitation as well for Raven to call, if she had time, a telephone number in Issaquah.

Raven and Dr. Sara Rockwell had also failed to connect, both in person and by phone. Raven had kept her early morning appointment as scheduled; but Dr. Rockwell had not been there, having been called away to perform an emergency Caesarean section on a woman with placenta previa. As a result, the pelvic exam that was to have determined the patency of Raven's cervical os, and therefore the "completeness" of the miscarriage, had not been done. Dr. Rockwell's nurse checked her vital signs, which were stable; drew blood samples for hematocrit, a coagulation screen, and a repeat serum pregnancy test; and after scheduling a return office visit for eleven the following morning, placed Raven's name on Tuesday's OR schedule for a D and C at noon.

Raven hadn't been aggressive in returning Sara Rockwell calls. She knew that the serum pregnancy test would confirm fetal demise and that, even if on pelvic exam the miscarriage seemed to be complete, a D and C would be recommended to be absolutely safe. Raven knew what Dr. Rockwell's message would be, even though, because of confidentiality, the doctor had left no message with Raven's secretary beyond the request that Raven return her call.

She must have called here, Raven thought as she walked into her house and met furious gray eyes. When a man answered, as if he lived here too, Dr. Rockwell must have felt comfortable giving him the message.

Why is he so angry? Raven wondered as she met eyes

the color of molten steel and ablaze with messages of pure danger. The answer came swiftly, powerfully, and her heart, which she had believed could feel no further pain, screamed as if the molten steel had been poured onto its raw and weeping wounds.

Nick is furious because you lost his baby of love, because you were unforgivably careless with that innocent life. Nick blames you, Raven, birth of death, just as you blame yourself.

Nicholas Gault's perfect vision was blurred with rage. He saw Raven through a smoky mist that enabled him to see only the monstrous truth which he now believed and which obscured entirely everything else.

What Nick saw was a ravishingly beautiful woman to whom appearance was everything. Her perfect body was impeccably adorned by the designer clothes she loved, and she had made unspeakable plans to make quite certain that her perfect figure would be preserved. Nick saw that self-absorbed woman, and more. He saw a woman who had betrayed him after all, a calculating seductress who had deceived not only him but his daughters and who would have gone right on deceiving them until she had everything she wanted . . . including their hearts.

In short, what Nicholas Gault saw was the Snow White Shark.

What he did not see, what the smoky veil of his immense rage obscured entirely, was what had truly happened to his lovely Snow White. His own anger did not permit him to see that the once sparkling sapphire was cloudy now, empty of all hope; nor did his fury permit him to see the truth about her once rich snow-white skin. It was translucent now, the bluish white of ice stretched too thinly over treacherous waters; and like that thinnest of all ice, it was fragile, precarious, destined to shatter.

"I walked in just as you were getting a message on your machine. I think we should listen to it together."

The rage in Nick's eyes was hot, molten, fiery; but the sound of fury in his voice was even more terrifying. It was ice cold and very still, dangerously, deceptively calm.

"Nick . . ."

Blood pumped powerfully from his powerfully enraged heart, causing angry thunder in his ears; but nonetheless amid the thunder he heard the soft despair in her voice—and its falseness merely fueled his fury.

"I mean it, Raven."

The answering machine in the living room was on a low table in front of a window. Raven walked to it and pressed the replay button. She couldn't face Nick while she listened to the message, nor could she gaze outside at the garden of roses he had planted for her, so she simply stared down at the machine.

"Raven, it's Sara Rockwell. I'm very sorry that I missed you in the office this morning and that we haven't connected this afternoon. Unfortunately, I don't have the results of today's serum pregnancy test. The tube was dropped while the test was being set up in the lab. Which means I need to ask you to come by to have another sample drawn at eight tomorrow morning. The lab promises a fast turnaround time, so we should have the result when I see you at eleven. The D and C is still on the OR schedule for noon, so please don't eat or drink anything after midnight tonight. I'm sorry about today's test. I know that this is difficult for you, but hang in there. It should be resolved definitively tomorrow. Please call if you have questions, or if you develop bleeding, fever, or any other of the symptoms that we've discussed."

Raven stared at the machine after the message was over and as it made the whirring sound that signaled the message was being rewound and saved. Finally, still staring at the machine, she said quietly, "I didn't want you to know."

"I'm not surprised." His voice was ice still, but now

there was contempt amid the chilling fury. "My finding out what you were planning for my baby—or is it even mine?—would pose a very serious threat to our relationship, wouldn't it? You undoubtedly remember what happened to my feelings for Deandra following a similar discovery."

Nick was still glaring at her through the smoky veil of rage, but even through that angry mist he saw what happened next. The perfectly dressed perfect body that had been so straight and stiff, almost courageously so, now began to crumble. It was as if his words had caused an immense invisible hand to come down from the sky to crush her, as if the heavy weight of the unspeakable truth, now exposed, had come to destroy.

As he watched, Nick's anger waged a violent battle with a rogue part of his heart that was seduced by her still, ensnared still in her silken web of deceit. That defiant part wanted him to rush to her, to hold her and comfort her and forgive her . . . and love her still.

Raven had almost died yesterday, when she had lost her baby, and now she *was* going to die, her heart was, and she greeted the revelation with relief. All the places that could still be hurt would hurt no more. They would cease to exist, leaving as gravestones for hope and love only thick bloodless scars. Nick's words were the final death blows to those fragile places in her heart, and as Raven felt her frail body yield to the immense weight of hopelessness, she welcomed her own death.

Weep, Willow, weep! Die, death bird, die! Nevermore, acid baby, nevermore.

Her heart was dying, and her mind, deprived of oxygen by the crushing weight that allowed no breaths, began to float . . . and Raven realized vaguely that far more than just the fragile places in her heart were going to die. *She* was going to die, really die.

You're going to die, her floating mind promised. It will

all be over soon. There will be peace, and the pain will be nevermore.

But, a gasping voice defiantly reminded, the man you love is going to believe forever that you planned to kill his baby.

So? I *did* kill his baby. The acid baby killed the baby of love.

But he still needs to know the truth! He still needs to know that you neither deceived nor betrayed him. Nick needs to know, and before they die, the much-maligned Raven and the ever-proud Willow and even the scarred little acid baby need a chance to speak their own truths: they weren't worthy, they knew that, but they tried, *oh how they tried,* to love.

Raven felt her body begin to straighten, pushing against the immense weight and miraculously conquering it. As her gasping lungs drew a deep breath of air, she turned to face him.

He was surprisingly close, rushing toward her, as if despite everything he believed about her, he could not bear to watch her die.

"It was your baby, Nick, our baby, and I lost it. I tried so hard to save it, so very hard, but I couldn't."

"Raven?" The mist of rage was clearing now, and he saw with excruciating clarity the eyes that matched the despair in her soft voice.

"I miscarried this weekend. Yesterday. The cramps and bleeding started Thursday evening. The purpose of the pregnancy test drawn today was to confirm that the baby had died, and the D and C that is scheduled for tomorrow is . . ."

Raven faltered then, and very softly, Nick asked, "Is what, Raven?"

"Is for me," she confessed with quiet apology. "In case there are remnants of tissue that could cause infection or bleeding."

Nick heard the apology and saw on her lovely anguished face that she truly believed that nothing should be done for her, for her safety, because she was somehow undeserving of such care.

"Oh, my darling," he whispered. He pulled her to him then, cradling her tenderly in his loving arms. He felt her trembling frailty, and her trembling courage, and something else that terrified him. Raven was in his arms, a trembling island in the sea of his love, but like that island, she was quite separate from him, quite contained within herself. "Why didn't you tell me? I should have been with you this weekend."

"I didn't want you to know."

Her voice was flat, and she was close but terribly far away, and even though the hazy smoke of rage had cleared from his steel gray eyes, Nick felt a molten remnant course through him. "But you were going to tell me about the baby . . . our baby . . . weren't you?"

"Yes. When it was safe to tell you, when the pregnancy seemed safe. I knew you would want it, and love it, and welcome it into your family."

"What about you, Raven?"

His question seemed to confuse her, or perhaps it was the tenderness with which it had been asked that was confusing. After a moment she shrugged softly. "It seemed most important for the baby to be with its father and sisters and grandparents."

A shiver passed through her then, forcing Nick to focus intently on her cold translucent skin and exhausted ashen face.

"We need to get you tucked into a warm cozy bed." Her eyes flickered surprise at his concern for her. "I even brought something for you to wear."

Despite the fact that her baby was gone, and yesterday she had cried until she believed there were no more tears, Raven still had no control over her emotions. At his words, they raced from heart to her eyes: sadness, betrayal, and finally, worst of all, resignation.

Nick had been battling his own emotions, hiding his own sadness, his own grief, for her, because of her. But now it was he who felt betrayed, and when he spoke, his voice held a sharp edge of pure steel.

"Oh, Raven," he whispered harshly. "Do you honestly think that I'm talking about a sexy negligee? Do you really believe that on this evening when we—*we,* Raven—are grieving the loss of our unborn baby I would do such a thing?"

"I . . . don't know."

"Well, you *should* know." What Nick meant was that she should know about him, the kind of man he was. She should know that his feelings about her went far beyond sex. But even as he spoke, Nick realized that it wasn't him that she was questioning, but herself. What Raven Willow Winter didn't seem to know was that she was worthy of being given a gift to wear to bed that was anything other than a celebration of her sexuality, the pleasure she could provide. All harshness, all knife-sharp steel left his voice as he repeated softly, "Well, you should know."

With that, Nick removed a small purple velvet box from his jacket pocket and handed it to her.

"I hope you'll wear it all the time, Raven. In bed, out of bed, everywhere."

Raven's pale fingers trembled as she opened the box. Inside, on its own luxuriant bed of velvet, was a diamond, glittering fire in flawless ice, a brilliant-cut solitaire set in the most traditional way of all, the elegant six-pronged Tiffany setting.

"Nick . . ."

"Will you marry me, Raven?" Nick watched her emotions then, each with its own shade of blue, each shimmering through the tears that filled her eyes. What he witnessed was a battle between what she had always believed about herself and what she could come to believe with their love. Just when it seemed that love was winning, conquering even the most defiant of doubts, he saw worry. "Raven?"

"What about the girls?"

Nick smiled. "I admit that I wasn't sure how to go about this. I decided it seemed that you should be the first one to be asked, though, and that's what I had planned. Even though the ring wasn't ready until today, I thought I would ask you over the weekend in Santa Barbara, and if you said yes, we'd figure out together how to tell the girls. That was my plan, but it turns out that the girls were plotting as well. When we returned last night, they called a father-daughter conference in which they demanded to know if I was in love with you and what I was going to do about it." Nick paused to kiss a tear that spilled onto a pale white cheek. "I think they were very bothered that we weren't all together for the weekend. When a family member is sick, the rest of the family should be with her, loving her, helping her. They love you, Raven, and so do I. I love you."

Raven believed that she had cried away all the tears yesterday, and with them the shaky emotions that had been with her since the beginning of her pregnancy. But both the tears and the emotions were there still, trembling, spilling, bursting. And they felt so hopeful . . . as hopeful as the tiny brave life who had died.

Nick saw her thought, her sadness, and whispered gently, "Let me grieve with you, Raven. It was my baby too. Let me stay with you tonight, all night, and we'll talk about the baby we lost, and we'll make plans for our love, and in the morning I'll go with you to see the doctor. Okay?"

She nodded, and she was about to say "Thank you" but stopped. That was what the old Raven would have said, the one for whom any gestures of kindness, much less of love, were greeted with disbelieving gratitude. Now, instead, she was going to say something else, words from the place in her heart that had always held the defiant belief that the acid baby had gifts to give after all.

Looking up to the man who had given her so much, and who had made no demands, and who now deserved to know, Raven Willow Winter proclaimed with quiet joy, "I love you, Nick. *I love you.*"

## ❊ *32* ❊

"This is Nicholas Gault," Raven said when Dr. Rockwell entered the examining room. She added softly, "The baby's father."

"Hello," Sara Rockwell greeted with a smile.

"Hello," Nick echoed. "I'd like to be with Raven throughout everything that's planned for today—your exam, the D and C . . . everything." Seeing what looked like hesitation on the doctor's face, he added, "I promised her that I was going to hold her hand all day, and not let go, so the truth is you're stuck with me."

"It's fine," Sara assured. "Why don't we go ahead and do the exam right now, then?"

A pelvic exam was something that Nick had never before witnessed, and he really saw very little now. He knew that Sara Rockwell was causing Raven no pain, however, because the pale hand entwined with his didn't clutch more tightly than it already had been.

The entire exam only took a few moments, after which Raven sat up and they both awaited the doctor's assessment of what needed to come next.

"How do you feel, Raven?" Dr. Rockwell asked.

"I feel all right. I was able to rest last night and there has been no bleeding or cramping since Sunday."

"Do you still feel pregnant?"

A frown touched Raven's face, but she answered

truthfully, "Yes, I do. I guess the hormones are still affecting me."

Sara Rockwell smiled then. "They should be, Raven. The serum pregnancy test from this morning showed markedly higher levels than the two from last week. As far as I can tell, from both the laboratory data and my exam, you are still very much pregnant."

"I am? But . . ." She stopped the soft protest, because she had no wish to protest at all, and no reason whatsoever to question the valiant triumph of the baby of love after all.

"What you thought looked like tissue was probably clotted blood. You told me that your periods have always been remarkably light, so it was probably something you'd never seen before."

"What does this mean, Doctor?"

The question was Nick's, quiet and laced with hope, to which Sara Rockwell offered a hopeful reply. "What it means is that Raven has had what's called a threatened miscarriage. The fact that the bleeding and cramping have stopped entirely means that the threat has passed. Bleeding during the first trimester is quite common. If it doesn't result in a miscarriage, then it's usually of no-long term significance, just minor adjustments made between the uterus and placenta. There's no doubt that the crisis is passed, and the pregnancy now seems quite normal. It's very likely that it will progress without problems." She smiled, glanced at the hands that were entwined, and added lightly, "Why don't we talk about future visits, in my office, as soon as the two of you get Raven dressed?"

Nick simply held her, embracing her, embracing the miracle, his own emotions far too near the surface to speak.

It was Raven who finally pulled away, just a little, just enough to see his eyes as she spoke.

"The baby's going to be fine, Nick," she assured softly. "From the very beginning I've felt its strength, its will to live, its eagerness to meet its daddy and sisters and grandparents."

"I wonder, though," he countered tenderly, "if we should just wait a little while before telling the girls."

"All right," Raven agreed, even though she knew that such caution was no longer necessary. The baby of love was fine, flourishing. "I guess the news that there's going to be a wedding and that they're going to have a new mother is enough of an adjustment for a while."

"They'll adjust instantly, happily. But Raven, you won't be their new mother. You'll be the only mother they've ever had."

"I hope I can do it, Nick."

"You already have, my darling. You already have."

He curled her back close against him, and she could hear the powerful beating of his heart. Then there were gentle words, whispered over and over, a chorus of love and joy.

"I love you, Raven," Nick whispered as he held her. "Love you, love you . . ."

She heard his gentle words, and for an astonished moment she remembered that she had heard the same words before, spoken so differently, with contempt not love, a mocking question, not an answer of joy. *Love* you, Raven? Love *you?*

There was pure love in the words that serenaded her now, and it enveloped her in wondrous warmth, melting the ice, vanquishing it forever, and cloaking with cherishing tenderness both the acid baby and the baby of love.

Love you, Raven. Love *you.*